THE COMMUNIST'S SECRET

THE COMMUNIST'S SECRET

A Novel

Suzanne Parry

Book 2 *of* The Leningrad Trilogy

SHE WRITES PRESS

Copyright © 2025, Suzanne Parry

All rights reserved. No part of this publication may be reproduced, distributed, or transmitted in any form or by any means, including photocopying, recording, digital scanning, or other electronic or mechanical methods, without the prior written permission of the publisher, except in the case of brief quotations embodied in critical reviews and certain other noncommercial uses permitted by copyright law. For permission requests, please address She Writes Press.

Published 2025
Printed in the United States of America
Print ISBN: 978-1-64742-934-8
E-ISBN: 978-1-64742-935-5
Library of Congress Control Number: 2025905819

For information, address:
She Writes Press
1569 Solano Ave #546
Berkeley, CA 94707

Interior Design by Kiran Spees

She Writes Press is a division of SparkPoint Studio, LLC.

Company and/or product names that are trade names, logos, trademarks, and/or registered trademarks of third parties are the property of their respective owners and are used in this book for purposes of identification and information only under the Fair Use Doctrine.

This is a work of fiction. Names, characters, places, and incidents either are the product of the author's imagination or are used fictitiously. With the exception of historical figures, any resemblance to actual persons, living or dead, is entirely coincidental.

NO AI TRAINING: Without in any way limiting the author's [and publisher's] exclusive rights under copyright, any use of this publication to "train" generative artificial intelligence (AI) technologies to generate text is expressly prohibited. The author reserves all rights to license uses of this work for generative AI training and development of machine learning language models.

For Lindsey, Brad, Stephen, and Julia

AUTHOR'S NOTE

I hope this novel strengthens the case against dictatorship. After a brief flirtation with democracy, Russia has become a place where the leadership does not value freedom of thought or expression or even human life, except perhaps its own.

Someone once said, "Democracy is a slow process of stumbling to the right decision instead of going straight to the wrong one." Often characterized by complexity, inefficiency, and difficult consensus-building, democracy doesn't always get it right, but it adjusts and evolves and inches closer. Dictatorship, on the other hand, makes no mistakes. There is ever only one path and the people have no say. If they fight or contradict or oppose, they end up like Russian opposition leaders Alexei Navalny and Boris Nemtsov. Or perhaps like Vladimir Kara-Murza and Ilya Yashin—now free to live their lives, but never in their homeland.

The main characters in this novel are entirely fictitious. Staraya Russa however, is a real town that was occupied by Nazi Germany during much of World War II. The slaughter of thousands of mostly young volunteers near the town of Luga early in the war actually happened. Russian partisans were active in much of Nazi-occupied Soviet territory, particularly in the second half of the war. This story includes both actual historical events and things that could have happened during that terrible time. While it is no more violent than many World War II novels, it contains several scenes of extreme brutality, including a rape.

Any inaccuracies are my own.

vii

MIDSUMMER IN LENINGRAD
July 1941

The clock tower appeared first, rising just high enough to be seen from a distance. Next came the arches of the false arcade that stretched a full city block. Katya Karavayeva and her daughter hesitated in tandem, taking the measure of it. She had to admit it was elegant for a train station, but the strong resemblance to European buildings irritated her. After all, Soviet architectural styles were plenty good enough.

The station thrummed as Katya and Yelena elbowed their way through the crowd and down the correct platform where an engine belched a near continuous cloud of steam. They were early, but it didn't seem so, and they passed the time chatting about unimportant things in the way people do when anxious. Neither of them spoke of the war, of German divisions hurtling toward Leningrad.

When the conductor called out the train's imminent departure, a chorus of farewells rose in response.

"Take care of yourself, Lenochka," Katya's throat tightened. "I'll be back before you know it." No matter her unease, Katya was determined to appear confident. She had joined the volunteer militia thinking it might be a path to restoring her good name and assumed she would be among the thousands of citizens already laboring on a network of trenches around the city. Instead, her unit was headed south, toward the fighting.

"Of course, Mama. We'll be fine." Self-assurance ran in the family.

"And listen to your grandmother." Katya trusted her mother-in-law even if they weren't close. "She knows her way around. She'll keep you safe."

People scrambled to board and Katya pulled Yelena close, breathing in the distinctive smell of her shampoo, a piney scent that edged toward medicinal. A flash of her daughter as a bright-eyed toddler jabbed Katya with regret. She'd spent those years focused on herself and her career, every morning anxious to leave the house and most of the parenting to someone else.

Before loosening her embrace entirely, Katya gazed at her daughter's face, flawless despite the tears threatening to spill. At fifteen, Yelena was as tall as Katya, with the same long flaxen hair. Everyone said they looked alike and Katya saw herself in the elegant arch of her daughter's brows and her wide sensual mouth. When the massive metal beast shuddered to life and lurched forward, Katya pecked Yelena's soft cheek, grabbed her duffel, and dashed up the steps before the train gathered speed. The last thing she heard before entering the carriage was her daughter calling out, "Take care of yourself, Mama. I love you. I'll write."

The conductor scowled as she edged past. Instead of looking chastened, Katya glared back with her best "there's a war on" look. Even though she'd been a dutiful rule follower as long as she could remember, conformity had not served her well. And now, headed away from the protections a city like Leningrad offered, trivial regulations seemed entirely out of place.

Years of obedience to the powerful and the ordinary had not protected her. Instead, some senior Party official had taken the word of an envious liar and sacrificed the Karavayevs on the flimsy altar of state security. Of course, she shouldn't have been surprised when Aleksandr was taken. Yet she was. She had closed her ears to the rumors of arrests and worse, maintaining a powerful loyalty to the leadership because it seemed the only way. But, when they also took

The Communist's Secret 3

her Party card and the job she loved, the first doubts about Stalin latched on like a leech—imperceptible and painless, but nevertheless sucking the devotion right out of her.

Losing her job had felt like a death. She missed the status and authority that accompanied her as she went door-to-door installing receivers for Radio Leningrad. On the rare occasion when she found an illegal private radio in someone's apartment, the person's eyes would go wide, begging her not to report them. Even for a clear violation, Katya didn't automatically turn people in. She wielded a serious bit of power and liked to think that along with her mother's hard-nosed devotion to the Party, she also possessed her father's discerning and generous spirit.

Katya edged her way through several cars as the train rumbled across Leningrad's industrial district. The corridors were jammed with teens calling to each other and finding friends and every compartment she passed was more than full. The Volunteer Corps drew heavily on those too young for military service, sixteen- and seventeen-year-olds, as well as university students. Katya was relieved there were few middle-aged folks on the train who might know of her husband's sentence. To have a chance at restoring her respectability she had to avoid those who had heard of her family's fall. If she could do that, and also contribute to the nation's defense, surely the doors to the Communist Party would once again swing open.

Unable to find a real seat, she picked a compartment that looked like her least bad option and squeezed onto the end of a bench after a young woman grudgingly scooted over. Half a seat was her punishment for boarding late.

Almost immediately, she regretted the choice. The teens talked loudly, teasing and laughing with no regard for those who might want peace and quiet. The train jerked, and several girls squealed as one boy lost his balance and fell on top of them. Katya glowered at the culprits. They reminded her of why she found most teens tiresome

4 Suzanne Parry

and annoying. Thank goodness her daughter was nothing like these hooligans.

It was too late to find another seat and she didn't want to stand all the way to Luga. Resigned to her temporary misfortune like a good Soviet citizen, Katya tried to ignore the pointless chatter.

"Did you see who's in the next cabin?" The boy's suggestive tone was meant to draw attention.

"You think I care?" A female voice replied with mock indifference.

"Everybody knows you're sweet on him," the boy continued.

"Everybody but him," said another.

"Yeah, his dick must be asleep," said the first, and the boys laughed.

Katya waited a second or two for the embarrassed girl to defend herself. Instead, the teen stared at the floor like she wanted to disappear.

"*Eto nuzhno*? Is that necessary?" Katya glared at another boy who seemed about to say something equally vulgar. "We're at war. The most serious endeavor imaginable, and you're talking about trivial and inappropriate things." The boys snickered and elbowed each other.

There was one girl sitting in a corner, away from the larger group. Her eyes narrowed and her lips were pressed together in a tight line that Katya took to mean she too was annoyed by their rude behavior.

Determined to put an end to the conversation, Katya continued. "Steadiness and focus are needed to support the Red Army. Our soldiers are battling the invaders, some paying the ultimate price." She lifted her chin in case her words weren't sufficient. "You shouldn't be wasting energy telling jokes and exchanging insults. Did you not hear Comrade Stalin?"

When the Great Leader addressed the nation, his voice had quavered with emotion. The country's very existence was at risk, he said. Freedom in victory or slavery under the Fascists.

"All the more reason," said another teen, self-assured in the way of one with little life experience. "If we're going to die, we'd best have fun while we can."

"We're not going to die." Katya snapped, trying to strike the right combination of boldness and backbone. "We're going to help stop the Nazis." She wanted to talk about duty, patriotism, and fidelity to Soviet socialism, but held her tongue. Speaking when she shouldn't had gotten her into this mess.

The boy sat back, contemplating his next retort and the cabin went quiet. A moment later, he and another smart aleck leaned together. "Political officer," one whispered.

Katya wished it was true. She would enjoy the chance to lecture them. But she could never become a political officer now that she was a persona non grata, the wife of an "enemy of the people." Still, these delinquents didn't know that. She could have some fun.

"Are you Komsomol members?" Katya knew that most of the teens in the initial wave of recruitment would be from the Communist Party's youth wing. "You aren't acting like the Party is important. You never know when you may encounter a political officer. Or when someone might report your behavior. And you should save your energy for the real work."

One of the boys turned white; another focused on his feet. The solitary girl had been watching and a smile crept over her face.

"All right, all right, *Matushka*," said the offender, calling her a nickname for mother. "No need to get all huffy."

As the conversations became whispers, the unfairness of her predicament ate at her. In the months since her husband's arrest, she had kept her head down. After the disgrace she was lucky to have any job—even her miserable factory assignment. For that matter, she was lucky to have avoided prison herself. But she didn't feel lucky. She hated that word. Lucky. No doubt some would say that Aleksandr was fortunate when he received a sentence of ten years instead of twenty-five. But to Katya, good luck was when something positive happened, not when one simply escaped a worse fate.

Startled when the brakes squealed like a high-pitched distress signal, she stood and opened the compartment door, claiming a spot at the window as the train rattled slowly across a bridge. The water below was dark and wide, but in other places the Luga River was nothing more than a brown ribbon meandering half-heartedly to the Gulf of Finland. The Luga Line they were calling it.

THE VOLUNTEER CORPS
July 1941

The train rocked to a stop and Katya stood to one side while the unruly crowd rushed for the exits. The silent, stern-faced girl hung back as well, waiting for the mad scramble of bodies and bags to ease before reaching for her short-handled shovel and rucksack.

"Look at them," the girl said when it was just the two of them left in the compartment.

"As if they might miss the war," said Katya. "They have no idea what's coming."

"Do you?" The girl challenged.

Katya liked her spunk. "More than most. I've lived in Leningrad since the Revolution." Even though that was before this girl's time, everyone knew the city had suffered and struggled. Katya's experience went further, having married into a military family. But she wasn't going to reveal that.

The two women followed the stragglers along the corridor and out to the packed platform where groups of teens gathered, laughing and gossiping, gravity still in short supply. Katya spotted a woman with a clipboard.

"Over there." She nudged the girl.

They elbowed through the throng until reaching the official. Sweat trickled down the woman's temples and her shirt clung in all the wrong places.

"Karavayeva, Ekaterina Ivanova," Katya said, her height and clear voice commanding attention.

Her young friend sidled up. "Grigorova, Svet Andreevna."

"Grigorova, Svetlana Andreevna," the woman repeated as she searched the list.

"It's Svet, not Svetlana," said the teen.

The woman raised an eyebrow of disapproval, but checked off both their names. "Follow that group there. Bus number eight will take you to your duty station."

Svet. Light. A simple word, but unusual for a name. Katya looked at the sturdy teen. Pale skin and dark hair. Her gray eyes added to her ethereal look. At the same time, she was robust. A real Russian. Her parents must be romantics, giving her such a name. Katya recalled a girl at university named Luna. Another strange, symbolic name. That poor girl once confided that she was often singled out, and not in a good way, by teachers and classmates. Which reinforced what Katya's mother had always said about attention—it was good when it drew neither too much envy nor too much ridicule.

As if reading Katya's thoughts, Svet explained. "I was born on the twenty-first of June. In Murmansk. I guess my parents thought that was important."

The longest day of the year. Above the Arctic Circle the sun didn't set at all in late June.

"Everyone assumes I'm Svetlana," she continued. "I get called everything you can imagine: Sveta, Svetka, Svetik, Svetlanka, Svetinka. But it's just Svet. Except my mother and *babushka* call me Svetochka." A hint of a smile appeared.

Katya nodded. She called her own daughter Lenochka. Mothers and grandmothers, friends and family all over the Soviet Union called loved ones by such nicknames. It conveyed affection. Russians weren't much for expressing intimacy with words, but this was one way they did. How often did she actually tell Lenochka that she loved her? Had she even said "I love you," at the train station? Her throat tightened. She always let a look, a brief touch, or an affectionate form of address carry that message. She should have said it.

The Communist's Secret 9

Bus number eight rumbled north out of Luga several kilometers. Although Katya had been raised in this part of the country, the dusty, flat landscape was unfamiliar. The town of Luga itself was an unremarkable pause on the way to more important places. You could continue southwest to Pskov or connect to a train for Novgorod. Now that was a beautiful city. Perched on the Volkhov River just north of Lake Ilmen, its stunning ancient fortress made Katya think of it as a miniature Moscow.

No city, not even Moscow, could compare to Leningrad of course. It was the beating heart of the nation, even if Moscow was the capital. Soviet socialism had germinated in Leningrad. Katya's parents brought her there during the maelstrom of the Revolution. It was no small feat, and the older she got the more she realized how capable her parents had been. Her father smuggled food into the city where violence, chaos, and starvation prowled like a hellish troika. He embraced danger, but could be practical—traits that helped him succeed. Despite his heroics, he was more anti-starvation than pro-communist. "Mark my words," he said. "The Bolsheviks won't be any better than the Tsar."

Her mama disagreed. She threw the force of her personality behind the Reds, claiming squeaky-clean credentials as the daughter of peasants and wife of a worker. Quick to accept that some people would suffer in the creation of the new Soviet state, her mother earned a reputation for getting things done and became a hard-nosed Communist with a capital C. She worked in housing and every day made decisions about which bourgeois families would get turned out of their residences or forced to share with some of the impoverished thousands flooding the city. Late at night her mama would be hunched over papers with columns of names and addresses. Katya felt a shiver of guilt. Her family never had to share their living space. From its revolutionary beginnings, the Soviet state was built on who and what one knew.

The volunteers disembarked and stood in the hot midday sun waiting for instructions. Someone blew a whistle to get the crowd's attention. Katya's stomach lurched when she saw the Party official's familiar face. She ducked down a bit, trying to make herself less visible.

If he recognized her, all hope of making a name for herself would be lost. He knew what had happened to her family. She looked around the large crowd, watching and wondering if she could escape the notice of this soft and sunburned *apparatchik*. The creases between his eyes gave him a permanent frown. Shirt-sleeves rolled up above his elbows, he tapped a pencil against the clipboard in undisguised irritation. The tilt of his head and his tight jaw emphasized his annoyance and made it clear this wasn't exactly a plum assignment.

"You may call me Comrade Director Sokolovsky," he said to the restless crowd. His voice dripped with self-importance.

Not very Soviet of him. He should embrace the simple address all citizens use: Comrade. Or Comrade Sokolovsky, or even Comrade Director without his surname. But not all three. Stalin himself discouraged elaborate forms of address. He preferred Comrade or Comrade Stalin. She glanced at Sokolovsky. His loud sigh told Katya he thought he was above all this.

"First things first," he continued. "My assistants are collecting your documents." The low rumble of an approaching storm of complaint began. "Quiet down," Sokolovsky said. And then, in an effort to tamp down the crowd's unease he added, "You'll get them back before you return to Leningrad. It's just to keep things secure." Like everyone else, Katya hated giving up her papers, although they might well be safer with those in charge and she certainly wouldn't need them in the middle of nowhere.

Next, he informed them that work began every day at half-past six, after breakfast. He pointed toward the makeshift canteen nestled in some trees where they would have meals. There were rows of wooden tables and an outdoor kitchen where the cooks busied themselves. To the left of that, a scattering of rough tents spread across a field—little more than tarpaulins on sticks. Katya swallowed her surprise at sleeping in the open. She'd expected barracks, or perhaps a local school converted with cots. As the director droned on—too long given the heat—the crowd grew restless. Katya felt sweat gathering under her arms.

When Sokolovsky walked several meters away and began an agitated exchange with another official, she slunk to the back of the group. Svet followed. Low conversations rose in the crowd and the two women took advantage of the momentary pause to toss their rucksacks onto a couple of unclaimed sleeping pallets. They were gone less than a minute, but when they rejoined the group he spotted them.

"Comrades, come forward. You two," he said, pointing directly at them. There was nothing they could do but shuffle to the front of the crowd. "Your names," he demanded.

"Karavayeva, Ekaterina Ivanova." Katya's face burned. The busloads of volunteers had gone quiet, watching the unfolding drama.

"Grigorova, Svet Andreevna." Svet appeared unruffled, her face blank.

"So my instructions aren't interesting enough for you?" His disdain was crystal clear.

Neither of them said anything.

"You have quite the reputation, Comrade Karavayeva. You recently had your Party membership revoked, isn't that correct?"

Katya stared at the ground, wishing she could disappear.

"As the wife of an 'enemy of the people,' I'd have expected you to be especially focused on supporting Comrade Stalin and our great nation."

Katya glanced up, realizing he was enjoying himself. The look of superiority on his face was unmistakable. He continued. "Is paying attention difficult? Do we ask too much of you?"

Katya froze, worried about much worse things than embarrassment. She stared back at him because it was all she could do. In the next instant she felt Svet move.

"We heard every word, Comrade Director," the teen said. Her voice was loud and her enunciation crisp. "We took advantage of the momentary interruption in your orientation to stow our rucksacks. We thought it a judicious use of time. Now we are ready to begin work the moment you conclude your instructions."

Katya heard a bit of shuffling from somewhere in the crowd, but nearly everyone was silent, rapt at the spectacle in front of them. Svet had made her little speech entirely straight-faced and without a hint of irony. She was as convincing as any loyalist. The director examined them, puzzlement and confusion obvious in his hesitation. His eyebrows shot up and his face was a question mark. He didn't seem to know what to think of Svet's rather articulate explanation.

After a long, awkward pause, he said, "Well, Comrades, we shall soon see whether you know how to work or not." He returned to his orientation.

"Drinking water is here," he pointed at the first of two open-topped barrels. "That other one is for washing up. And the toilet is there," he said, pointing in the general direction of the woods that stretched past the cook's domain. Katya could just barely make out several partitions that would give a bit of privacy for those who needed more than a few seconds to do their business. An open trench. She hated using the toilet in front of strangers.

When he finished, giving them five minutes to stow their things or relieve themselves, Katya filled her water canteen. It was her husband's old military one, dented and worn, the little chain that attached the cap long broken. She looped it across her body and lined up behind Svet while the others scrambled about.

The entire group of volunteers, well over a hundred by Katya's estimate, was assigned to build a row of anti-tank trenches—large,

The Communist's Secret 13

deep ditches. Four stakes marked the corners of the enormous, narrow rectangles they were to dig. As they started, Katya deftly braided her hair, knotting the end and tucking the tail into her shirt collar. Her lips pursed as she pulled a headscarf from her pocket, unconvinced she should use it. Soviet women everywhere wore them—peasants and workers, teachers and store clerks. But to Katya the head covering meant peasantry, old age, or a lack of education. Sometimes all three. This was another lesson she learned from her mother who said it detracted from her looks and was incompatible with her senior position. When circumstances absolutely demanded a headscarf, her mama's reluctance bloomed like a lily: big and attention-getting.

Still, these were unusual circumstances, and the more Katya blended in, the better. Plus, it would keep some of the dirt out of her hair. She pushed her mother's voice aside and tied the scarf. This was not a time to focus on appearances.

While Svet dug, Katya hauled the dirt and rocks in a wheelbarrow down the length of the slowly deepening pit. Each load was wheeled up and out of the trench and then deposited along the southwestern side of the ditch—the direction from which the Nazis would attack if they got that far. Eventually the dirt would form a small rise that would make the trap invisible from a distance. The enemy's tanks would be slowed, maybe even stopped by the trenches.

At the end of that first day, stinking with sweat and body aching, Katya waited in line to rinse off the worst of the filth. She wiped her face with her headscarf and spat to get the grit out of her mouth. She glimpsed Svet's hands. The girl didn't have gloves and her palms were a mass of oozing blisters. Katya made a note to wrap them the next morning with clean cloths.

At the barrel, she splashed her face and mouth several times, then scooped water over her neck, relishing the coolness. There was a long line behind her.

"Hurry up! It's no beauty contest," a haughty voice complained.

Katya bristled. She wasn't preening. All she wanted was to rinse the dirt. Instead of hurrying, she splashed her face and neck one more time just to aggravate the annoying woman down the line.

The cooks served up bowls of *shchi*, cabbage soup, from enormous pots hung over open fires. Not Katya's favorite, but even so the smell made her mouth water. She grabbed two pieces of bread from the huge pile and found a spot away from the canteen. Svet joined her on the ground. They leaned against a tree trunk and devoured their food.

"Thank you for what you did back there," Katya said.

"*Nichevo.* It's nothing. He's arrogant and self-centered. Like most men."

"Well, I appreciate the way you stepped in." Between bites, Katya laughed. "He didn't know if he was coming or going. Probably still doesn't realize you were making fun of him."

"That's what happens when people focus on themselves," Svet said. "Their noses are so high in the air that they can't see what they're stepping in."

Still smiling, Katya returned to her food. Svet was a quick thinker with an independent streak. She didn't seem to be a Komsomol member, unconcerned as she was with fitting in. It also seemed unlikely that she was gathering evidence against Katya. The Party didn't have the time to care about one disgraced former member in the craziness of war. Whatever her motives, Katya was grateful the girl had diverted some of the negative attention now headed Katya's way.

Svet didn't seem the type to pry either. She'd hardly spoken the entire afternoon as they labored in the sun. Her reserve suited Katya. Thanks to the director, everyone knew she'd been kicked out of the Party. But they didn't know why and Katya wanted to keep it that way. No one needed to know that in a moment of exasperation or annoyance or pique she'd said something about her husband's apparent

The Communist's Secret 15

lack of devotion in front of someone who'd twisted the meaning and then reported it to the authorities. Katya still didn't understand why she had opened her mouth. Had she been so unhappy that the risks didn't matter? But the "why" wasn't important. The fact remained that she'd broken the cardinal rule of life in Leningrad—never say something that can be used against you.

She wiped her empty bowl with the last bit of bread. So much for getting back in the Party's good graces. Katya wished she'd listened to her daughter. Yelena urged her to stay in Leningrad. "You could join the war effort here. The Kirov factory needs more workers." But Katya rarely listened to advice that contradicted her own views.

This time she regretted it.

THE FIRST ATTACK
August 1941

The two women inhaled their dinner and hurried toward the Luga River. Once a week—women and men on different evenings—everyone had the chance to bathe and wash their clothes.

The dusty earth was an insidious enemy. It found its way inside everything, collecting in the creases of Katya's skin where it chaffed and irritated. Every day she buttoned her shirt to the neck and tucked her pants into her boots, but still the dirt worked to make her miserable. Her scalp itched constantly, a particular torment since she couldn't very well scratch it while wearing gloves.

Despite the futility, bathing in the river was the one thing about the situation that Katya enjoyed. She and Svet settled on a couple of large stone slabs at the river's edge and stripped off their grimy garments. The paper in Katya's pocket rustled. She'd finally received a letter from her daughter and was waiting for a moment of privacy to open it.

The first few steps into the river were a shock as always. It wasn't cold like the Gulf of Finland, but Katya still inhaled sharply and walked on tiptoe until she adjusted, holding her soap in the air. Few volunteers had brought any. It would have been so simple to put soap on the short list of things they should bring. As much as Katya revered the Party, this was the kind of incompetence that drove her wild. Those in charge handed down all sorts of important sounding regulations, but forgot to tell the volunteers to bring soap.

Katya wouldn't have brought any herself if it weren't for her mother-in-law. "You'll need this," Sofya said as she handed Katya a new bar. Her expression was warm and non-judgmental and her eyes didn't harbor the enmity Katya deserved after Aleksandr's arrest. Katya nodded and wordlessly accepted the gift. Her mother-in-law had good instincts about such things and, after all, they hadn't been told to bring paper for the toilet either, but Katya had already tucked a stack of newspaper squares among her spare clothes. Best to be prepared.

Katya washed herself and her dirty clothes, then passed the soap to Svet. The contrast between the teen's sunburn and her normal alabaster skin was vivid. Her forearms, face, and the back of her neck were pink and peeling. The rest of her body was the white of a marble statue in the Hermitage. Katya's long-sleeved shirt provided more protection and her skin just took the sun better. She spread her wet garments on the rocks and sat on the huge stone to pick at the dirt under her toenails. Dozens of women were bathing now, their splashing and laughter a pleasant background noise. While she relaxed, Katya remembered the letter from Yelena and pulled it out.

Dearest Mama,

No doubt you will be home soon. Nevertheless, I had to write because the best thing happened. Papa called. He's in the Red Army as a captain. He sounded wonderful, although sad that he could not see us. You can write him with the 16th Army.

Other than that, there is not much to report. Grandma is busy with rehearsals and performances. I'm working hard with my brigade. Although we hope the war will not last long, we will be prepared if it does.

I hope you are well and taking care of yourself.

Your loving daughter,

Yelena

Such news! Shura was getting the second chance he deserved—out of prison and fighting the Nazis. Her mind spun to the best possible outcome. Perhaps his remaining sentence would be commuted after the war. There hadn't been anything to smile about for a long while, but she was smiling now. Her stupidity hadn't killed her husband.

She lay there, propped up on her elbows, happy but uneasy too. Releasing prisoners to fight—even falsely accused ones—seemed an extreme step. Perhaps the war was not going well. Perhaps the enemy had the upper hand. A new kind of fear, an existential dread, chilled her.

She dressed, put the letter in her pocket and collected her wet things. Off to the side, Svet held her own clean, soggy garments in a ball, ready to hang on tree branches back in the camp.

They fell into step along the path and almost collided with a woman barreling toward them.

"Have you h-heard?" The wide-eyed woman stammered. "They've taken Pskov."

Katya glared. Pskov was hardly two hours by train. Could the Nazis be that close? And where was the Red Army?

"That's not possible," Katya said. "We've stopped them just inside the border. They couldn't have gotten that far."

The woman gave a little snort and shrugged her shoulders. Katya knew what she meant. The government was afraid of telling the truth. No one seemed to know where the front was or how far the Germans had penetrated into Soviet territory. Or, if they did know, they weren't telling the citizens of Leningrad or the volunteers on the Luga Line.

"I overheard a peasant pleading at the canteen for food and water just now," the woman continued. "She had a babe in arms and another child. Walking for two weeks, she said. Dragging a few belongings, trying to stay ahead of the Fascists." Katya had also seen locals moving north the last few days—disorganized rag-tag groups streaming away from the western border.

Katya looked at Svet for a reaction as the woman continued toward the river. The teen never voiced opinions about controversial topics and this was no exception. Her silence helped Katya believe it wasn't true. The woman was a rumormonger. A political officer warned them of this before they left Leningrad. German sympathizers and spies would try to infiltrate, sow fear, and weaken the population's resolve.

The next day began like all the others. Katya took a few great gulps of cool morning air as she waited for her scoop of kasha and piece of bread. She ate hurriedly and wrapped Svet's hands with clean foot cloths. They joined the others headed to the worksite, barely noticing how the butter yellow sun generated just enough warmth to take away the early chill.

Hours later, as time for the midday meal approached, Katya pushed a last load of dirt out of the ditch and around to the far side of the nearly completed tank trap. From her vantage point she couldn't see much besides the dust rising from the other trenches, a brown haze covering everything. Her stomach rumbled. She'd never worked so hard in her life and there never seemed to be quite enough food. She turned toward the town of Luga, appreciating the wide-open landscape when a distant glint caught her eye. At first the dots in the sky registered in her brain as birds, but very quickly Katya understood they were something else. It took some seconds for her to accept the reality. The shiny specks grew larger and soon filled the sky like a plague of metal insects. She heard the growing hum of their engines over the noise of her comrades working. Transfixed as the first planes dipped toward Luga, Katya saw another formation headed their way. She raced into the trench as the aircraft began to roar.

Katya grabbed Svet and pressed her against an earthen wall, trying to make both of them disappear. The ground shook from explosions and they crouched in the ditch, pelted by earth and stones.

For a minute or two, there was nothing but the buzz and rumble of attacking planes, the *rat-a-tat* of their guns, the concussions of bombs, and the steady assault of dirt. As those sounds faded, screams and plaintive cries for help took their place. Katya shook off the grit. Svet's curly hair was dusted with soil and her eyes were large and wild. They clambered out of the trap, the small shovel in the girl's belt clunking awkwardly with every step. Katya turned to watch the air squadron bank and wheel, headed back the way it had come. But for how long? A well of panic opened and the catch in her chest confirmed her fear. The Germans could have only one objective in this part of the Soviet Union—Leningrad.

THE LUGA LINE DISINTEGRATES

August 1941

Breathless, Katya watched other volunteers rush to help their comrades as the director rattled off instructions. "Gather the wheelbarrows. Help the wounded. Anyone with medical training?"

Two women came forward. "We completed our nursing program in June," one said.

The director pointed to a grassy area near the canteen. "Let's get the seriously injured over there. You two do what you can. We'll use the wheelbarrows to take the survivors to Luga."

A grim-faced teenager pulled off his shirt and ripped it into strips. Katya recognized him as one of the delinquents in the train car. She turned to Svet and without a word they ran in different directions. Svet rushed down the trench line while Katya hurried back to where she'd been working.

The wheelbarrow was still at the top of the rise and from there Katya could see the extent of the destruction. Not far, a girl sobbed next to a body. The bare-chested boy and another teen were bandaging someone's wounds. Farther down the work site, a huge crater had swallowed one of the ditches and volunteers were digging and calling for help in a frantic race against time. Katya shivered at the thought of someone buried alive and then turned toward Luga. Black pillars of smoke rose from the town.

Her husband had shared many things about war. A ground attack would follow the planes. You stun and demoralize from the air, but you need soldiers to seize and subdue. She scanned the distant landscape and stopped, transfixed as it came alive. A roiling cloud of dirt and dust churned like an approaching sandstorm. Only one thing could turn the horizon into a billowing, thundering reddish-brown sea.

She raced back and found Svet. "Tanks are coming." She nodded toward the advancing tempest. "We have to get out of here." She glanced around and pointed at the forest. "There. Hard for tanks to maneuver. But first, I need to warn the others." She ran to the director.

"That's it," he said. "One or two injured to each group of volunteers." He glanced repeatedly at the sky, as if waiting for the planes to return.

Katya stood at his elbow. There were a dozen names on his clipboard. The dead. She took a deep breath. "Comrade Director, there's going to be another attack."

"Of course there's going to be another attack," he said.

Was he mocking her?

"That's why we have to get to Luga as quickly as possible." He barked and pointed. "Get over there and help."

She stepped in front of him, trying to remain calm. "Comrade. We don't have time to reach Luga. We must run. To the woods. Tanks are on the way." She pointed toward the oncoming threat, only from where they stood the view was obscured by the hills of dirt alongside the tank traps.

"Compose yourself!" he snapped and turned away.

Had he heard her? She grabbed his arm, panic rising. "There's no time." Her voice became high-pitched and shrill. "They're coming!" she screamed.

He pushed her to the ground, eyes blazing. "Comrade Karavayeva, I will be reporting this. Interfering with a superior." He sneered. "You're the type that never learns. Get out of my way." He spat at the ground next to her.

Svet stepped forward and offered her hand to Katya. "Ignore him," the teen hissed.

There was nothing Katya could say to convince him. Instead, she yelled at his retreating back. "You're going to get them all killed." Then she and Svet ran, pointing out the distant boiling earth visible in the gaps between trenches, and urging other volunteers to take cover. "Run to the woods!"

Just as she and Svet ducked out of sight, gasping for air, the ground began to tremble and the murmur of the leaves became a fearsome rattle. They crouched behind a dense stand of trees. Visible now, the tanks were moving faster than Katya had ever imagined possible, faster than her husband's descriptions. The air was full of their grinding and clanking and like huge plows they seemed to lift the earth around them, dust rising in their thundering wake.

Frozen by the terrifying vision, the two women watched the steel beasts fire over and again as people ran. Katya gasped as a girl fell under the metal tread of one tank. Most of the mechanical monsters swerved to avoid the anti-tank trenches, perhaps warned by the Luftwaffe. But one launched through the dirt and plunged, gun barrel first, into the trench that Katya and Svet had dug. The rest of the roaring Panzers took their storm toward the Luga bridge and a strange quiet descended amidst the cries of the injured and dying.

Katya stood, trying to see what was left of the encampment. She opened her mouth, but nothing came out. Although shocked into silence like everyone else, an intense focus possessed her as she and Svet made for the worksite.

Diesel exhaust and dust hung in the air, a cloying, poisonous cloud as the volunteers emerged from the woods. Katya went straight to the open-air kitchen. The main table was on the ground, riddled with bullets. Both cooks were crumpled, their once gray aprons already dark, a puddle of viscous crimson spreading under them.

Katya fought a wave of nausea and pressed two fingers to each of their necks in turn, but there was nothing.

The nurses had fled at the last moment, but one had been hit. Svet unwound the cloths on her hands and used one as a tourniquet. Someone else called, "Help! Over here," from a small birch grove where the director and other survivors huddled. His once white shirt was scarlet. A volunteer pressed on his wounds in a futile attempt to stop his life from leaking into the ground.

Katya stood at his feet, silent, dizzy at the sight and holding a tree trunk to steady herself. She felt something ugly, satisfaction at having been right about the tanks perhaps, but the reality was anything but satisfying. The director wheezed, unable to speak, his face contorted with pain. It wasn't much good being right when this was the result. She bit her lip to keep from speaking. He knew she'd tried to warn him. He'd enjoyed humiliating her. She stepped closer. A corner of his mouth flickered and his chest rattled. He struggled for a few seconds and was gone.

The girl stopped pressing and held her bloody hands out, as if not knowing where to put them. "I heard you," she said. "He should have listened." Her eyes were bright with tears.

The words helped but Katya felt responsible. If she had tried harder, or been calmer, or taken a moment to explain what was about to happen, he might have listened. Or perhaps not. He'd had it in for her from the beginning, looking for reasons to make an example of her, always criticizing, singling her out, sometimes even demanding she stay at the worksite after the others had gone to the canteen. And now his pride and arrogance had made a terrible situation worse.

Svet stood close, supporting Katya, telling her without words that she'd done the best she could. One of the other volunteers touched Katya on the back. "You tried to warn him. At least you saved us. I wouldn't have run if it hadn't been for you. It was brave, going against him."

She looked at the supportive young woman, glad the teen couldn't read her thoughts. "Thank you." Katya glanced at the torn landscape, the dead and wounded scattered as far as she could see along the length of the work site. No wonder Stalin had sounded so grave in his speech. Fear turned her thoughts toward Leningrad and Yelena. She had to get home.

What else had Shura told her over the years? Infantry usually accompanied mechanized units. The fearful reality caught in her throat. Tanks wouldn't be the last of it. The remaining survivors needed to make some quick decisions. She spoke with authority, addressing the several dozen volunteers now gathered in twos and threes. "They aren't done. It's not safe to stay here. Soldiers will come. Infantry."

"How do you know?" A voice challenged.

"She's right," a young man spoke up. "My uncle is in the army and he's talked about the same thing."

Katya nodded at the teen. She thought again of the frightened woman at the river. A city wasn't occupied by bombs or even by tanks. That took soldiers.

"My husband is an officer in a tank division. Infantry comes with mechanized. German troops are coming," she continued. "That's a fact. So let's talk about our options. Going to Luga is one. Although we don't know the extent of the damage there, the injured should be able to get medical attention." She exhaled and raised her voice. "Another option would be to try to outrun and outwit the Nazis. Hide in the forests and swamps. Difficult without food and supplies. There are no major towns close by. And the injured . . ." She stopped. Transporting the wounded would put them all at risk, but she couldn't suggest they abandon them. Or could she? Heartless, but practical. A terrible thought rose from her communist core. It made sense to sacrifice the wounded to give the living a chance.

A woman stepped forward. "I'm from Gatchina. We could go in

the direction of Kingisepp, then move through Volosovo to avoid the forces that just went north." Several others murmured their approval and stepped forward to join that effort. "We'll get the injured to Luga, and if our soldiers there have a better plan, we'll adjust."

"We're going to Luga too," said the bare-chested young man, pointing to a group standing behind him. "At least we can get supplies there, which we need to continue on foot." The surviving volunteers all seemed to favor Luga as a destination.

Katya understood. Luga was a known quantity. She nodded her approval, even though she didn't really approve.

"You should do what you think is right. The Nazi infantry might not arrive for a few hours, but I don't think they'll be far behind the Panzers. As long as you beat them to Luga, you can probably find help. But it's risky. The Wehrmacht could be close. I don't want to end up in a German labor camp. Or worse."

"So, what are you going to do?" someone asked.

They looked so young. They needed help considering the options. Katya drew herself up.

"Novgorod is east of here," she said. "Probably eighty kilometers. It will take the better part of a week—a lot of slow-going, forests, bogs, and swamps—but once there I'll make my way up the Volkhov River to Lake Ladoga and Leningrad."

"That's assuming there are no Nazis that direction," one scoffed.

She spoke with an authoritative edge. "True. All our options carry risk. But the swamps and forests make it especially difficult for an army." She paused. "Listen, it's up to you."

"What about them?" The bare-chested boy pointed at the injured. "We can't leave them."

"I'm not proposing that," Katya said, hearing the undercurrent of defensiveness in her words. "If no one else wants to go to Luga, I will take as many injured as I can there. But, if you've decided on Luga, then I'll go east. Best if we split up. Increases the chance . . ."

The Communist's Secret 27

She stopped as the others closed ranks. The still stunned volunteers began moving away, muttering in skeptical voices. "Eighty kilometers of rough terrain? That's impossible."

It didn't surprise her. After all, she and Svet had been outcasts since the first day. And did any of them understand what would happen when the enemy came? The Nazis had already killed dozens of their comrades. Didn't they realize they would be next?

Everyone focused on readying the injured, while Katya turned to Svet. "You haven't said anything," she said.

"What is there to say? It's obvious you know more about this than anyone else. Besides," Svet's eyes narrowed. "Being in a crowd is a bad idea. You and I, we have a chance."

Katya squeezed her arm and nodded. "What do we do about the bodies?" They walked the site, counting as they went. Halfway down the long line of trenches, they stopped and looked at each other. They'd already reached thirty.

As if reading Katya's mind, the girl from Gatchina approached, shaking her head.

"What a slaughter. There are too many bodies to do anything. More important to get to Luga quickly and try to save the living."

"I hate to leave them," Katya said. "To animals and such."

The girl nodded thoughtfully. "We'll tell the authorities. They can send a team. Save yourselves. And good luck," she said.

"You too," Katya replied, even though she didn't believe in luck. It was about making the right decisions.

All around, the others bandaged wounds and organized for the trek to Luga. They had over a dozen wheelbarrows, into which they loaded the most critically wounded. Katya watched for a moment. The girl from Gatchina wasn't wasting time. Maybe they would make it.

Doubts crept in about her own plan for going the other direction. A flurry of thoughts about the attack and what they should do kept her mind jumping. There were thousands of volunteers in the area. She'd seen other worksites from the train. It seemed impossible that they had no warning. Her stomach churned with the reality that they'd been abandoned.

She refocused and turned to Svet. "The tank that fell into the trap. Nazi soldiers inside."

She hurried back to where the director lay. Avoiding the gore, she slid the pistol out of his holster. She and Svet went to the edge of the trench. The tank had gone in turret first, like a failed acrobatic stunt. Katya crouched on all fours and Svet knelt alongside.

"Do you know how to use that?" Svet nodded at the gun.

"My father taught me how to shoot," Katya said. "And my husband had one like this."

As was Katya's habit, she hinted at more expertise than she really possessed. She checked the magazine and released the safety. On her belly, she inched toward the edge of the ditch, pushing aside her muddled thoughts about the correct course of action.

She propped her elbows on the edge just in time to see a Nazi soldier struggling out of the tank. He strained to hold the hatch open, finally squirting out, landing arms and head first on the ground with a thump and a groan. He clambered to his feet and yelled something toward the hatch, which had already clanged shut. His back was toward Katya, and it was as big a target as she would get. Without really thinking, she aimed and exhaled. Her first shot pinged off the tank, but she kept her cool and when the soldier pivoted, reaching for his gun, she squeezed the trigger a second time and hit him square in the chest. She looked at the gun as if surprised.

"Give me that," Svet said and yanked the gun away. "Stop wasting bullets."

Katya eyed her. "And you're a better shot?"

Svet flashed her a withering look. "I grew up with guns. Two shots is one too many."

They lay there, waiting what seemed like an eternity but was probably two minutes. A second soldier's head and shoulders appeared and Svet fired. Katya saw the head snap. She was a good shot. The soldier slumped in the tank opening while the hatch pressed on his lifeless body.

"There's at least one more inside," Katya whispered.

Svet raised her eyebrows in a question.

"My husband is a tank man, remember?"

"How do we get him to come out?"

"Unless you have a Molotov cocktail, he will sit tight until his friends show up."

They stood, but Katya turned. "We should get his gun." She pointed at the motionless soldier in the trench. "I'll go. You make sure no more come out."

Svet crouched again while Katya nimbly descended the rocky ramp. She hurried to the first soldier, sprawled on his back, the blood from his chest wound a nearly invisible wet patch on the black uniform. Eyes closed, his face unblemished, he could have been asleep. Someone's son. Maybe someone's husband or even a father. She imagined a little tow-headed toddler giving the Nazi salute.

She took his gun and found a spare magazine, then unbuttoned his black uniform jacket while avoiding the blood. On his collar points were two gold death head symbols. The horrible insignia made her hesitate. Svet hissed at her to hurry. In his jacket she found personal things, a photograph and letter, which she ignored. Then her fingers struck gold: a small brass-edged compass. She stood, jamming gun, magazine, and compass into her pockets when something grabbed her ankle. She screamed at the soldier's vise-like grip and fell, yanking her leg and kicking at him. She scrambled away as Svet fired, killing him a second time.

The work site had taken on an eerie quiet with the band of volunteers already turning for the road to Luga. It was a strange caravan.

The less-severely injured hobbled along, supported by healthy volunteers while the wheelbarrows held those with more serious wounds. Uncertainty roared back. Rescuing the injured might gain her recognition by the Party. But getting to Yelena was the most important thing. This was no time to think about her career. She brushed aside the remaining flecks of indecision and followed Svet to the outdoor kitchen. They drank, and Katya refilled her canteen when Svet poked her and pointed. Again, something rose in the distance.

They grabbed what they could in the way of supplies. Svet brushed off a couple of loaves of bread laying on the ground and found a cook's knife. Katya picked up a dirt-covered slab of pork belly that had been meant for soup. She wrapped it in a dish towel hanging from a tree branch. Together they made for their tent and grabbed their things. Katya saw trucks and infantry closing the gap. Hearts pumping with adrenalin and fear, the two women raced for the forest as the first shots sounded. Katya felt a sharp sting in her left arm as she took cover in the woods. Glancing back, she saw Nazi soldiers headed their way.

ESCAPE FROM LUGA

August 1941

The undergrowth grabbed at her legs as she followed Svet, the two of them dodging branches and trees, crashing through shrubs and zigzagging more than running in a straight line. Katya felt fit from the weeks of hard work, but running was something else. She soon struggled to keep up, sucking in air and exhaling hard. No doubt Svet heard her falling behind but instead of slowing, the teen continued to push the pace. And Katya refused to ask her to slow, knowing their lives depended upon getting some distance between themselves and the enemy. Just as Katya lost sight of Svet the teen paused. They rested a few moments, letting their breathing calm. The leaves swished in the summer breeze, a bird called to its mate, a ground squirrel rustled. Perhaps they had lost the soldiers. Katya clutched at her upper arm and Svet turned her attention to the trickle of blood.

"You were lucky," Svet whispered, taking a close look.

"Lucky would have been not getting shot at all," said Katya. "Or the Nazis choosing a different place to attack."

"Still, it could have hit you in the back," the teen continued.

"Or the head," Katya said, giving in to the girl's line of reasoning.

Svet pressed on the small wound and wrapped it with the last strip of cloth from her hands. She frowned at the dirty rag. "Wish it was clean."

"Can't think about that," Katya said.

"Let's slow a bit. It'll help stop the bleeding." Svet tightened the makeshift bandage.

Katya checked the compass and led the way at a brisk walk. Just as her heart and lungs settled into a comfortable rhythm and she felt confident the soldiers weren't following, a distant male voice filled her with adrenalin. Katya turned to see the teen's wide eyes and the two broke into a run. After another six or seven minutes of crashing through the brush and dodging trees, they came upon an oak grove. Svet stopped at the first magisterial tree, looking up, examining its large limbs and canopy of leaves extending far above. The branches were high—above their heads by at least a meter. Suddenly, the girl turned to Katya, her fingers interlaced, ready to boost her into the tree. "We can't outrun them," she said. "But they'll never look up."

Katya nodded and stepped into her hands. Svet lifted while Katya grabbed the first branch. She hung there for a heartbeat, then swung a leg up and over and pulled herself onto the huge limb. Katya lay face down on the branch, one long arm extended toward Svet. The teen ran at the tree and jumped, but missed Katya's hand. The second time, they grasped wrists and Katya pulled. Svet's upward momentum helped her scramble into the crook of the massive oak. Without a word, they climbed higher.

They lay there, perhaps a dozen meters above the ground, each stretched along different branches. Katya tried to slow her breathing. A tiny noise, a "*psst*," came from Svet and she waved her pistol. Katya withdrew her own, checking that it was loaded, and released the safety. The tree's rough bark pushed into her body and she adjusted herself on the limb so she could view the forest floor. The wound throbbed, and she was glad it was her left arm that had been hit. Seconds ticked past. Katya strained to hear anything beyond the rustling of the leaves and the occasional bird chirp-chirping.

She stared at Svet's motionless form, when suddenly a single finger pointed. Through the leaves, Katya saw two, then three, then four soldiers, rifles at the ready, moving methodically. They turned from side to side as they came, separate, but advancing together as they swept through the forest—a strange kind of ballet. One paused directly beneath them and rested his rifle against the tree trunk. Katya's heart pounded so hard she was certain he would hear it. The soldier whistled to the others and they gathered, speaking German which Katya couldn't understand. She saw the one in charge examine something. They were fit, enthusiastic-looking, and young. Not a single grizzled veteran among them. They looked like boys playing dress-up in their fathers' uniforms.

Controlling her breathing required so much concentration that at first Katya didn't feel the trickle of blood. The bandage had shifted when she climbed. Now gravity pulled at the line of red inching down the back of her arm to her elbow where it gathered. Katya couldn't wipe it away without shifting and making noise. She tried to pull her left arm in against her body, thinking to tug her rolled-up sleeve down to catch the blood. The scarlet drop fell just as she began to move. It somehow missed all the branches and leaves and landed exactly below her on the map the soldier was holding. The little splat was like a bomb.

The soldiers' heads snapped up. Katya saw confusion in their frantic faces. A loud bang startled her. One soldier fell to the ground. The others raised their weapons and began firing wildly. Svet hit a second soldier and he also went down.

The remaining two scrambled for cover. Katya concentrated on one. She missed twice but finally found her mark. He fell, twisting, one arm flying out to the side. The shooting stopped and Katya glimpsed a soldier crawling away into the undergrowth. Svet dropped to the forest floor and disappeared after him. Katya herself shimmied to the main crook and swung down. She edged toward each of the three soldiers in turn. One was still alive. He stared back at her, eyes pleading, saying *"bitte, bitte, nicht schiessen."* Looking into his young face, she thought about waiting for Svet to do the dirty work. Shooting someone from a distance was one thing. Killing someone face-to-face was another. Still, she couldn't leave him alive. She had to pull her weight and didn't want Svet to think her cowardly. Her stomach turned as she gathered her nerve. It was war. And that's what she said to him before she pulled the trigger. "It's war."

She stepped away, feeling nauseous, and took several deep breaths. Then she turned to where Svet had gone after the last Nazi, walking with care, watching the signs—the earth ever so slightly pressed down, bushes broken here and there, and then the blood. She placed her feet lightly, listening, afraid she might startle her friend and get shot herself.

Just as she was beginning to panic, wondering who was hunting whom, she heard the *pop* of a single shot. Katya recognized the sound of Svet's gun and followed it. The teen was already going through the soldier's pockets.

"The rest dead?" Svet asked, glancing up but finishing her task.

Katya nodded and they returned to the others, taking the time to search each body in its identical grey uniform. They took a service rifle each, plus several semi-automatic pistols and cartridges. They had food from the worksite, the compass from the Nazi in the tank trap, and now more weapons and ammunition than Katya could ever imagine using. The wound on her arm came back to her, throbbing and aching. It seemed so small, hardly more than a scrape, but it hurt like hell. She readjusted the bandage. "Do you think they'll come after us? After whoever did this?"

Svet put a hand out for the canteen and drank deeply. "Hard to say," she paused. "By the time they start tracking us, if they do, we'll be long gone. And they won't know what they're looking for."

Katya double-checked the compass for an easterly heading and swung the canteen back across her body. "I like our chances," she said. "The tree was quick thinking. And where did you learn to shoot like that?"

One corner of Svet's mouth twitched. "My father wanted a son. No time for a daughter, or a wife for that matter. And not much to do living in Murmansk. I learned to hunt and shoot. Took a while, but I figured out how to protect myself." Her nostrils flared and her eyes burned bright. "Only good thing about my childhood."

In the weeks with the volunteers, Katya had grown used to Svet's short answers. She chose her words with care. The opposite of impulsive. It wasn't just that more than one bullet was too much, but more than one word was too many as well. It was almost as if she hadn't spent much time around people, or didn't like them. But now, talking about her childhood, Katya could see Svet burying the urge to say more. It seemed they both had secrets.

THE VILLAGE

August 1941

That first half-day they walked six hours, urgently putting distance between themselves and the dead soldiers. They slept in the open, huddled against a downed tree on a mattress of decaying leaves. Summer was losing its heat and when the sun dipped toward the horizon a chill seeped through their lightweight clothes. Katya shivered, ears alert, and passed a few fitful hours.

The next day they began again but with a bit less fear driving them. They battled bogs with clouds of midges for company as they headed away from the soldiers and they hoped toward Novgorod. That night they rewarded themselves by cooking the pork belly and keeping the fire fed for two hours before extinguishing it for the night.

On the third day, they rose at first light and managed a full twelve hours. There were rest breaks, of course, but still they must have added twenty-five kilometers or more to their total. Now, on the fourth day, Katya could no longer keep up. Fatigue pulled at her legs. The forest grew sparse and they stopped to rest, placing their rucksacks and weapons down. Before Katya could even tell Svet how poorly she felt, a familiar fearful rumble sent them scrambling. They crept along the ground until they saw the steady line of trucks and other vehicles out in the open beyond the thinning trees. Many were marked with the grotesque white and black crosses Katya had seen on the planes that attacked the Luga Line. How dare they? Katya was an atheist, but her dear grandmother had been a devout Russian Orthodox. And the kind of slaughter the Nazis engaged in was far from what those crosses and her grandmother stood for.

She lay on the ground, transfixed by the long convoy rumbling north. Ten minutes passed, then twenty. More than thirty minutes before the last vehicle disappeared.

"*Kakoy koshmar.* What a nightmare." Another German army streaming north. This one toward Novgorod and the Volkhov River. And probably Leningrad beyond that.

They lay there for some time, afraid to move, afraid they weren't alone. Disheartened, Katya wondered how the volunteers could have been left exposed to the German attack. Thousands of them, unprepared and unarmed. There was no way to make sense of it. Stalin gave an inspiring, emotional speech rousing the citizens to the nation's defense but he didn't protect those who had answered that call. She stewed, angry and fearful.

"What do you think?" Svet finally spoke.

"Maybe south around Lake Ilmen, then north on the other side?" Katya hung her head. "I have to try to get home."

"*Vozmozhno?* Is that possible?" Svet said.

Katya felt her eyes welling. They could never get ahead of the Germans now.

"Leningrad will be heavily defended," Svet reasoned. "The Red Army will protect the citizens. And you said yourself that your daughter is capable."

Katya wiped her eyes. "True. She and her grandmother are resourceful." She sat up. "It's just . . . I should be there."

"We'll think of something," said Svet. "But, we cannot go the same way as the Germans."

Katya nodded a reluctant agreement. Every direction was risky. She struggled to stand.

"Are you all right?" Svet said. "You don't look well."

Katya cradled her left arm. "My arm is worse. And my entire body aches."

At the end of the first day Svet had washed the wound hard, making it bleed again, trying to keep infection at bay. It wasn't deep. Probably didn't even need sutures. And with the Germans close behind it had been low on their list of worries.

Svet touched Katya's forehead. "You're warm. Sit." She pointed at a moss-covered log, then pulled up Katya's sleeve and removed the bandage to reveal a raging infection—her arm was red, swollen, and angry. "We may need medical help for this," the teen said. "Let's go southeast. Toward that town you mentioned."

Katya had told Svet about Staraya Russa, the sizable town not far from Lake Ilmen where she'd grown up. But it was still some distance. They hadn't even caught a glimpse of the lake. She didn't say what she was thinking. That there was no way she could walk that far now.

Within an hour, her legs were like iron, every step demanding focus and will. They both glanced around, fearful the enemy might materialize out of the trees. They intersected a well-worn cart path. Ahead they could see where the forest ended and a bog took its place. Rectangles of freshly-cut peat lay scattered, as if something had interrupted the task. This was the time of year peat was collected. The bog would supply a nearby town or village. Katya had seen this in her childhood: rectangles of peat, stacked to dry and cut into brick-sized pieces for fuel in winter.

"I can't go much farther," Katya said. "And the peat means a village is close."

"Let me," Svet took Katya's rucksack. "We'll go as slow as you need."

The cart path ran alongside a field and then disappeared into a heavy stand of forest where the yellow and gold leaves of the birches shimmered in the sun. The warmest season was past its peak but it was

The Communist's Secret   39

a beautiful late summer day. Blue sky and a slight breeze. Warm enough that a jacket wasn't necessary. They walked far slower than the previous day's steady pace and stopped to rest every few minutes. Katya listened for the comforting normal sounds of the forest, the gentle rustles of wind and animals. There was nothing out of the ordinary—no fearful thrum of engines or thud of boots crashing through the undergrowth.

The woods ended abruptly, pulling back to reveal a prosperous-looking village. Katya leaned on a tree for support and eyed the harmless *izbas*—small wooden homes dotting the dirt streets, each one surrounded by a metal fence, a gate in front and a garden plot in back. Katya had grown up in the same kind of simple dwelling made of rough-hewn logs. The memory used to embarrass her, but now it embraced her. All she wanted was a place to lie down. A huge stove like the one her father built with a snug sleeping shelf and a simple quilted mattress. The warmest spot in winter.

Beyond the homes and gardens were planted fields—ripe barley from the looks of it. A wagon sat idle with no horse attached. A few smaller dirt streets intersected the main one, and at the far end Katya glimpsed some businesses. And, of course, a church.

They moved along the forest edge until certain the village was deserted. No sign of anyone. Livestock gone. Laundry hung behind several of the log homes. How long had it been there?

"This gives me a bad feeling," Katya said.

"Perhaps the people had only a few minutes to flee," said Svet.

Katya nodded. But it was equally likely the Germans had taken everyone prisoner. What happened to them? Families with small children and old folks.

They crept along, peeking in open doors. Scattered belongings told the frightening tale of a quick exodus. The garden plots were lush with green beans and cucumbers and onions. Katya bent down, snapping off a handful of fresh long beans, crunching them with delight and nodding to Svet who followed her example.

They made their way from cottage to cottage until they came upon one nicer and larger than the others, with glass-paned windows. A scratching, rustling noise came from inside—a sound that didn't belong. Svet pulled her pistol, pushed the door and tiptoed in.

She lunged for the startled chicken, which had been contentedly scratching for seeds. It hopped and squawked and flew about the room, landing on the table and sending a couple of metal dishes clattering. So much for being quiet.

The teen subdued the noisy bird and broke its neck before Katya could react. She used the large cook's knife to cut off its head on a tree stump in the backyard. "A while since I had chicken," she said, and strung the bird so that the blood would drain.

Katya sat in the open door and watched. "We'll have to wait until dark to cook. The smoke." As the blood dripped, she went back inside and crawled onto the first soft thing she saw—a straw mattress in a corner of the living area.

Svet pulled off Katya's boots and covered her with a quilt. "I'm going to get some things. I saw marigolds. A paste will help fight the infection."

Later, kitchen noises woke Katya. A fiery light from the low sun streamed through two windows.

"Look what I found," Svet said. She shook a glass jar filled with small white crystals. "I'll make a hot salt bath for your arm. It'll draw the infection out." Svet's voice sparkled with excitement and relief.

Katya closed her eyes, remembering a time her papa soaked his foot in a hot salt bath.

The teen started a fire and when the water boiled, she poured most of it into a shallow pan. She sprinkled salt heavily, stirred it and set it on the table. "I know you're exhausted but you must soak your arm. Be careful. You don't want to burn yourself. As soon as you can tolerate the heat, make sure the entire wound is under."

The Communist's Secret   41

Katya edged her arm into the hot water while Svet fried the chicken and sliced a tomato and a cucumber. The crispy cucumber gave off a delightful fresh scent and the tomato was exactly, perfectly ripe—firm with no bruises or soft spots.

"Were there lots of overripe tomatoes?" Katya asked.

Svet shook her head. "I thought of that too. Not many. They've been gone less than a week, I think."

After dinner, Svet ground some of the marigolds into a paste. She coated Katya's arm with the remedy and rewrapped it with a clean foot cloth. "Take the bedroom. I want to be near the door. All you need is sleep. In the morning we'll do the salt again and more poultice."

The next day was uneventful. Katya's fever diminished. She drank lots of weak tea and they ate cold chicken. She soaked her arm again while Svet ground more marigolds.

"How do you know these remedies?"

"My grandmother," Svet said. "We lived a long way from anything, and it wasn't easy to get medicine. I wish I'd paid more attention, but at least I remembered that field marigolds fight infection." She flashed a rare smile.

That afternoon, Katya felt well enough to help gather supplies. Cold weather was on the way and they found heavier shirts and work trousers, foot cloths and underthings, a pair of work shoes, and padded cotton winter coats. In one hut they found a small basket of cotton rectangles cut and pined together. Dealing with their monthlies had been bad enough on the Luga Line, and Katya had been thinking how they had to find something in this village that would work. Svet rolled everything into two tight packages and they returned to the cottage.

The next morning Katya wanted to leave. She tried to convince Svet when the teen came back from the stream. "There's something not right about this place. So many supplies."

Svet's eyes were drawn together and her lips pursed. Katya felt the wave of her irritation. The girl was used to making her own decisions.

"You're still too weak to travel. One more day of rest. I'll hide some supplies in the forest while I search for another of my grandmother's remedies." She handed Katya a loaded gun. "Keep this close while I'm gone if you're feeling nervous."

Katya narrowed her eyes but took the gun.

"I haven't seen anything," said the teen. "But I don't like leaving you alone. Be sure to sleep with one eye open."

Katya smiled. "I have a mother's sixth sense. I'll hear if something is amiss."

Svet nodded, with the same slightly annoyed look she often wore.

Katya woke to a rough hand over her mouth. She tried to sit up but the hand pushed her back onto the mattress. There were several of them. Laughing. The one pressing on her mouth smiled and signaled with a finger to his lips that she should be quiet. It suggested that she should comply with what was about to happen, but fear coursed through her and she knew her only hope was Svet. The moment he took his hand away she sat up, screamed and called out. He struck her across the face. There were flashes in her vision and she fell backward on the bed. When she struggled again, the soldier pressed a knife to her throat.

She stopped fighting and the powerful hand on her shoulder relaxed. He yanked hard at the collar of her shirt and ripped it open, buttons popping off. She wondered if they'd let her go if she cooperated, but the moment the thought came to her, she realized how wrong it was. She fought again, kicking and thrashing until he knelt on her legs, pinning her to the bed. She tried to claw his face and her nails made two little red lines on his cheek. He punched her, then placed the point of his knife against one breast, hard enough to break the skin and focus her attention. She yelped with pain and stopped

The Communist's Secret 43

struggling. He continued to cut her, drawing the blade in a small arc on one side of the breast. She whimpered, clenched her teeth and froze, staring at the beads of blood rising along the red line.

"You have beautiful breasts," he said. "It would be a shame if something were to happen." Her eyes flicked up to meet his and she saw he knew he had won.

He tore off the rest of her clothes and unbuckled his uniform trousers. Her mind raced, searching for a path forward, a way beyond the attack, a way to survive. He forced her legs apart, and Katya told herself she could not die, brutalized by these monsters. She glanced at the other two, entertained as if at a carnival sideshow. One was enjoying a cigarette while he waited his turn. She wished he'd drop a live ash and the house would catch fire.

Her eyes fixed on the ceiling. She tried to will one of the beams to fall and crush her attacker. Where was Svet? If only she would walk in now. Then Katya remembered the gun under her quilted straw pillow, loaded and waiting. Maybe she couldn't kill them all, but she could kill at least one. As the first soldier focused on his pleasure, Katya slid her hand under the pillow and gripped the weapon. Her finger found the trigger and she pulled it out in a single motion and shot him in the chest. He fell backward and Katya turned to the other two stunned soldiers. She fired wildly, shooting one before he could draw his weapon. She heard herself screaming and cursing and vowing to kill them. And just as the third soldier started to raise his weapon, she saw Svet enter the room, gun in hand, and in an instant his head snapped and his brains painted the wall.

Svet came close and stood over the rapist. Katya realized he was still alive. Svet aimed her weapon and he began to plead. She lowered her gun a bit, pointing at his groin and let him realize what she intended to do before pulling the trigger. Svet watched him, while Katya watched Svet. The girl's face twitched, in disgust or delight Katya did not know, and she fired again, staying beyond his reach but not far. He continued to scream and cry out, begging, but there could be no mercy for such a creature.

"Having fun, were you?" Svet said. "Well, how's this for fun?" She shot him again, also a non-fatal bullet. Katya wanted him to suffer too, to glimpse his friends crumpled on the floor and know he was also going to die.

With an especially serene look on her face, the teen let the filthy pig whimper and writhe for another number of seconds and then put a last bullet into his forehead.

ON THE RUN

August 1941

Katya struggled into her torn clothes as Svet pressed her to hurry, her voice full of urgency and fear. "No time to waste. There must be others."

For Katya, the small, normal task of dressing felt foreign, like she didn't know herself. Yet it was her body she was covering. Her feet that she put into shoes. She hardly paused to examine her cuts and bruises, just pressed a cloth to the small half-moon cut on one side of her breast. There was no time to cry about being pawed and beaten. No time to think about the filth who'd been between her legs. Much worse would happen if they were caught.

She stood and stepped around the dead soldiers, pausing to glance at her attacker: the neat black hole in his forehead and lifeless eyes, his pants still around his ankles and the slick, spreading pool between his legs.

As if reading her mind, Svet said, "He deserved worse." She handed Katya her rucksack. "Quickly now!"

In a few minutes the village was behind them.

At first, Katya struggled to keep up. Svet paused and turned. "*Ladno*? All right?" Katya nodded and followed. Fear and adrenalin gave her strength. It helped that the teen carried everything except Katya's rucksack which was filled with clothing and weighed little.

When they stopped for water, Svet asked her again if she could continue. Katya grunted in reply and returned her hard-to-read young friend's gaze.

"What about you? What happened to two bullets is one too many?"

"He needed to suffer," Svet said. Her eyes were dark and intense and seemed to contain terrible things.

"If you hadn't come," Katya said, letting the conclusion hang in the air. When they first met, Katya thought she was the experienced one. The one in charge. The one to establish them with the volunteers and, if need be, to save them from the Nazis. But with her remedies and her gun, Svet was doing most of the saving.

"Your scream warned me," Svet said. "And you really didn't need much help."

Katya shook her head. "I'd be dead if it weren't for you."

Svet shrugged and they walked on until she stopped to check the compass.

"I was asleep," Katya whispered. "I didn't wake until he had his hand over my mouth."

"You fought back," Svet said.

Katya touched her face where she'd been struck. "Instinct."

"And they got what was coming to them." The teen paused and then said with a bit of a sneer, "My father always said I had it coming."

Katya had gotten used to Svet's lack of emotion and guarded speech. But now a chasm opened between the words she'd spoken and their meaning. A giant wave of nausea dizzied her. She gripped a tree branch and doubled-over, vomiting and crying at the same time. Her body heaved, trying to rid itself of everything that had happened. Of the Nazis and of Svet's history too. The teen held her hair back until Katya's legs gave way and she sat on the ground in front of the puddle of vomit.

She swallowed a last sob. "Your father. How awful." What Svet had done was starting to make sense.

"I used to think my father was right," Svet sat next to her. "That I was responsible for what he did. But inside I knew that couldn't be."

She paused. "I've been on my own since I was thirteen. With some help from my grandmother."

"So the Volunteers was an escape?" Katya said.

The girl shrugged. "I'm a patriot too."

"You're more than that. You've already killed a half-dozen Nazis. You're a hero." Katya took a few sips of water while Svet looked down, uncomfortable with praise.

They sat for a few more minutes. Katya waited for her churning stomach to settle. As soon as it did, she turned and stood.

"*Davai.* Let's go. I can walk."

They gathered the supplies and weapons Svet had hidden and then decided to cross the main road they'd avoided several days earlier after seeing the German army moving north. Once in the open, they looked in both directions, not quite believing it was deserted. They scurried across and into a ditch on the opposite side. After a few moments, Svet stuck her head up to check that it was still clear. They continued southeast to the safety of the trees. The teen was surprisingly nimble, loaded as she was like a pack animal. Katya carried only her rucksack and a pistol. She concentrated on putting one foot ahead of the other, pushing aside thoughts of the attack, refusing to replay the tape of what had happened. Every now and then, Svet would turn and look at her, not saying anything but staring until Katya returned her gaze and gave a slight nod to let her know she had the strength to keep walking.

They stopped to sip from the canteen and nibble the fresh vegetables Svet had picked. A couple of times they rested longer—maybe fifteen or twenty minutes—taking off their packs, stepping behind a bush to relieve themselves, or sitting on a downed tree to rest. Once Svet lay flat on her back on the ground. Katya did it too, to relax the muscles that were working hard. The daylight went on forever and Katya lost track of time. She had no thought but to get as far away from the village as possible.

Finally, the angle of the sun shifted. The shadows began to slant and there was more color in the sky. Had it been only hours since that repulsive Nazi had pushed inside her? She touched her bruised face, her fingertips hesitant on the swollen, torn spots. She held her breast for a moment. How long would it take to heal? And it burned when she peed. Maybe the soreness between her legs would never go away. Maybe he'd infected her with something awful. Syphilis. She pushed aside the fear.

"We'll sleep here," Svet said.

Katya unpacked a meager dinner. The teen took the shovel and began to dig a long, shallow hole next to a large, decaying downed tree. Katya had seen plenty of *zemlyankas*, earthen dugouts, before her family moved to Petrograd. This was the start of one of those underground homes.

They washed in a stream after they ate. Svet rebandaged the old wound and Katya put some poultice on her breast. Then she pulled on a coat and lay face up in the shallow hole.

"I'm going to hide everything," Svet said. "Won't be long."

Katya breathed in the rich, pungent earth and the smells of the forest: the musty odor of decay and the slight sharp, almost chemical scent from the pines. She stared at the bits of sky through the trees, watching the pinks and reds deepen as the sun moved toward the horizon. She emptied her mind as best she could, pushing away thoughts of the Nazis, refusing to think of the soldiers headed toward Leningrad, headed for Yelena and Sofya. The army of trees around her seemed to grow taller. She noticed their bark was like scales: a deep reddish brown in the center and almost black at the edges. Armor of a sort.

Her body began to relax as she focused on the feeling of safety. She patted her pocket for the familiar crinkle of Yelena's letter. She'd already read it several times and its creases and stains made it seem months old. When Svet returned and began arranging branches over them—propped against the tree with only her head and shoulders uncovered—Katya relaxed even more. Svet crawled in next to her, feet to her head, and Katya whispered, "*Vse khorosho*? Everything good?"

"Yes," Svet said. "And I have a gun. Now, sleep."

Katya imagined Leningrad—the heightened energy and fear as people prepared for war. Had the Germans been stopped? She saw a single star wink through the branches. Her mind turned to Aleksandr. The wonderful but fearful news that he'd been released to fight. A strange freedom, but a second chance of a sort.

Everyone deserved that.

MOTHER NATURE STRIKES
September 1941

The morning after that dreadful day, Katya woke when the world around her came alive in the early light—birds chirping, forest denizens rustling, the day's first breath of wind. She caught sight of a noisy ground squirrel. It scratched through the leaves and underbrush with quick deliberate movements, then sat on its haunches clutching something between its delicate and dexterous fingers. The creature was no more than a meter away when suddenly, its eyes caught her own. She held her breath and stared into the tiny, bright black orbs no bigger than peppercorns until the unsuspecting creature dashed away for home and safety.

After a few more minutes of listening, watching, and admiring the legion of trees standing guard, Katya pulled herself out of the earthen cocoon, trying not to wake Svet. She looked at the teen, peaceful, curled on her side. What was it about adolescents that allowed them to sleep so deeply? Her Lenochka was the same.

She, on the other hand, had not slept well. Her legs were stiff and sore. Whether from the attack or the long hours of walking she didn't know. But sleeping on the ground was hardly comfortable in any circumstance. She hobbled a short distance and squatted. Already it burned less than yesterday.

The welcome earthiness of the forest filled her lungs. High, wispy clouds crowned the trees. Standing in the cathedral of pines, she saw his face and felt his hands on her. Her breath came quick and shallow at what was to come.

The Communist's Secret 51

It wouldn't always be the first thing that came into her mind. One day, hours would pass before she recalled the horror of those minutes. She had survived worse things. The fear that terrorized her hour by hour as little Sasha drifted away, then breathed no more. Nothing could be as awful as that. She had wanted to die with her baby boy, to hold him close in whatever lay beyond death. Afterwards, Shura appeared. But so briefly she could barely recollect his presence, holding her upright in the cemetery and no doubt dealing with his own grief and guilt.

Then her husband was gone again, and an iron fist through her heart pinned her to the bed. Her mother-in-law brought Lenochka for comfort. Her little daughter would talk about what she'd learned at school, and how she couldn't wait until Mama was stronger so they could go ice skating. Slowly, slowly her darling daughter had pulled her from that deep well of grief.

The pain had been a hundred, no, a thousand times worse than what she felt now. Rage was different than sorrow. Sorrow incapacitated. But the rage she now felt gave her purpose and a strange sense of satisfaction. She was alive and they were dead. To live would be her revenge.

Svet had rolled out of the shallow dugout when Katya returned.

"You're up," the teen said. "How do you feel?"

"Bruised and sore." Katya watched her pull down a bag of supplies from a nearby tree. "And hungry."

The girl placed the back of her hand against Katya's forehead and nodded her approval. She examined the shrunken scab on Katya's arm. "Better." Svet's assessment was understated as always, but Katya had turned a corner. Even her split lip was closing. She took what was left of the poultice and rubbed a bit along the cut on her breast.

They gathered rocks to encircle a fire and Svet balanced the small skillet on top. She rubbed the visible dirt from two potatoes and sliced them into the pan along with an onion. Everything about the place made Katya feel safe. The canopy of green, the nearby creek, the natural depression for a *zemlyanka*. They could make it deep enough to sit and sleep.

"What do you think?" Katya said, gesturing at their surroundings.

The teen pursed her lips and Katya thought she was going to press to go farther. Instead the girl said, "It's a nice spot and you need to recover. Besides, we don't really know where would be safer, do we?"

Ten days later, they were still there. Katya expanded the dugout and wove pine branches to protect them from the occasional rain. Svet explored their surroundings and set spring snares for small game. They ate well enough thanks to those traps and the supplies from the village.

Then, one afternoon the teen returned to camp with an armload of bark.

"What's that?" said Katya.

"The inner bark makes a reasonable flour," said Svet. "You have to use recently downed pine or yellow birch because it deteriorates quickly. And you can't use live trees because that would signal our presence."

Kneeling over the strips, Svet began scraping the fleshy inner layer. "With birch, you just scrape it off. With pine" she said, picking up a different piece, "you make a cut like this." She drew her knife width-wise across the inner bark and pulled pieces away. A mound of pale bark shavings quickly formed, almost white in color. "It'll dry overnight. Then we'll grind it and make flat cakes. A woodsman's blini."

"Too bad we don't have any sour cream or jam." Katya flashed a quick grin. They weren't starving, but her stomach was often an empty weight. The idea of the thin pancakes brought it back to life. She could almost taste one with a bit of butter. "Show me what to do."

"I was hoping you'd say that," said Svet. "I don't mind gathering the bark. But scraping is tedious."

The Communist's Secret

"I can do tedious," said Katya, squatting next to her friend. Simple repetitive work like digging their *zemlyanka* soothed her. "Your grandmother taught you this too?"

Svet nodded. "And tomorrow we'll make tea from pine needles."

Katya grew anxious as the days passed. She had recovered and thought less of her comfort and more of returning to Leningrad. Although they couldn't go to Novgorod as originally planned, they could go around Lake Ilmen and head north up the other side. And they could get shelter and information in Staraya Russa—if they could find it. While Svet explored, ranging farther and farther from their campsite, this plan grew more detailed in Katya's mind.

One late morning, Svet returned from one of her forays, worry lines on her face.

"Bad news," she said, ever to the point. "A large dirt road, filled with tracks and footprints. Surrounding vegetation crushed by heavy vehicles."

"You're sure?" Katya said. "Boot prints aren't ours?"

Svet shook her head. "I found this." She held up an empty magazine. "It fits." She waved her Luger. "They're headed north, but close enough that we should move."

Katya exhaled as if trying to expel the anxiety bubbling in her chest. There could be Nazis just beyond the next bog or forest. Where was the Red Army in all this?

"Time to find Staraya Russa," she said. It seemed the only reasonable option. But every time Katya mentioned the town as a place they might shelter, the teen responded negatively or didn't say anything at all.

Some hours after setting off, Katya glimpsed a strip of blue on the horizon to the north. She poked Svet and examined the compass. "That's Lake Ilmen. Means Staraya Russa isn't far. That way," she pointed southeast. Fearful of being out in the open, Svet pushed to go toward the nearest tree line. But as they approached, Katya recognized marshland. "Swamp. My uncle used to scare us with tales of children wandering into swamps and disappearing. It actually happened to a local child."

Intent on pushing forward, Svet ignored Katya's gentle warning. "A good way to stay hidden. And it'll take too long to go around. We'll lose daylight."

"Look. The trees are shorter and broader," said Katya. "We need to go around."

They skirted the marshy area for twenty minutes, tiptoeing along the edge like shy debutantes. Finally, exasperated and insistent, Svet turned directly into the murky depths.

"Come on," she said. "This looks like a good path."

Katya was too tired to argue. Although there was plenty of daylight, the moment they entered the dense vegetation, everything dimmed. Grays and browns and greens pushed all else aside. The air grew thick and heavy. Katya pointed out the safe sections as the light closed about them, reminding her friend to stay where bushes and shrubs indicated firm ground.

"Rooted vegetation," Katya said. "And watch for wet spots. One step might be just forty or fifty centimeters of water, but the next might be a meter. There's muck beneath the water. It's like tar. If that stuff grabs you, it can pull you right under."

They moved slowly, each step a calculus of what lay underneath. Katya's anxiety grew and she felt a fragile hollowness inside. Svet was capable, but she didn't have any experience with the deadly whims of Russian swamps. Murmansk was too far north for anything like this.

A moment later, Svet stepped before Katya could stop her. The swamp swallowed her lower leg. Instead of pulling back, she took two more quick steps in an attempt to reach the solid ground opposite. The water rose to her armpits.

"Stop!" Katya yelled. "If you move, it will pull you under."

The Communist's Secret 55

Time stood still. Katya inched toward a tree and steadied herself there. Svet wasn't far, but it was a deadly chasm. Katya hooked her rucksack onto the tree and pulled out several foot cloths and a shirt. She tied them together to make a crude rope. Svet was sinking, her head already tilted back as the water crept up her neck.

"Listen carefully, but don't move. I'm tossing this to you. Wrap it around your wrist and hold it with both hands. When I start to pull, you need to yank your legs out of the mud. You'll go under before you come out but don't panic. When you break free, float on your back while I pull. Now take a deep breath, one, two, three." She tossed one end of the cloth rope and both of Svet's arms lifted to grab it. At the same time the teen's head disappeared under the murky surface. As soon as Katya could see Svet holding tight to the makeshift rope, she began to pull. With one leg anchored around the tree and the other dug into the small patch of soil in front of her, she focused every muscle on the task.

At first, nothing happened. Katya counted the seconds silently to herself. When she reached thirty with no result, she forced herself to pull harder, refusing to let the swamp claim her friend. She channeled her strength into her arms and shoulders.

Suddenly, there was a jerk and the surface boiled. Svet must have freed a leg. The dark water churned and Katya knew the teen was fighting. Forty-five seconds. The boiling increased.

Svet thrashed. Then she broke the surface and gasped for air. She sputtered, coughed, and tried to breathe all at the same time.

"Stay calm," Katya ordered. Her heart thundered, her entire body rigid with effort, as if she stood on the precipice of a cliff straining to keep from plunging over the edge. "I've got you." She tugged as Svet rolled over and floated face up, her heavy pack a lead weight trying to drag her back under. Both Svet's hands were above her head clutching the fragile lifeline. Katya pulled her within reach and grabbed her outstretched arms. "Careful now, don't struggle."

Still holding the cloth rope, Katya reached under Svet's armpits and pulled her out of the brown, stinking water. Huddled on the small spit of ground, Katya propped her against the tree. She pulled off her monstrous duffel. Then she clutched her in a fierce grasp until the teen stopped trembling. She opened the canteen and rinsed the girl's face.

"Can you walk?" Katya said, taking charge. "We need to get to the lake." She wasn't sure how far it was, but her confidence would help Svet and they had glimpsed it after all. She tried to switch rucksacks, thinking she should carry Svet's leaden one.

"No," said Svet. "I can carry it. You already did enough."

Katya consulted the compass to lead them out.

At the swamp's edge, Svet set down her pack and exhaled. "My boots," she said, looking at her bare feet. They'd been sucked off in the swamp.

Katya heard her friend's dismay. More than anything else they couldn't manage without footwear. "Not a huge price to pay for your life," Katya said. She rummaged through Svet's waterlogged rucksack and found the extra pair of work shoes from the village. She tied them to Svet's small feet and gazed kindly at the teen. "They'll do until we find a replacement."

"Thank you," Svet whispered. "I'm sorry."

Katya put her palm gently on Svet's cheek. "We all make mistakes."

The words hung heavy, reminding Katya of her own failings but also carrying the promise of forgiveness.

LAKE ILMEN

September 1941

Without a word, they hunched in the low vegetation as the lake shimmered and beckoned. Fear coated Svet like the stinking, tar-like mud of the swamp. She trembled from her fearsome escape, but also from the danger of discovery should they venture across the wide expanse to the water.

Katya, on the other hand, felt her confidence grow. For the first time since they'd fled the Luga Line, she knew precisely where they were. And she also knew the Germans would be equally exposed on the approach to Lake Ilmen.

"We can see them too," she said.

Svet nodded and her mouth relaxed a little. Her weapons were coated with muck so Katya gave the teen her own rifle and then pulled out the handgun in her waistband. They picked their way toward the slash of blue where the sun had already begun stitching a blanket of reds and pinks as it dropped in the sky. Comforted by the beauty, Katya recollected nights in Leningrad when the sun painted the Gulf of Finland as it disappeared below the horizon. Perhaps Yelena was seeing the same explosion of color.

A gentle breeze brushed them as they neared a steep bluff above the water. Almost gleeful, Katya said, "This is the Ilmensky Glint. We can stay here while you get cleaned up. And then find Staraya Russa in a day or two." The lake was too exposed for them to remain any length of time. And they needed supplies, especially boots for Svet.

"Staraya Russa is too big," said the teen. She had been opposed to anywhere larger than a hamlet from the start. "Someplace small and out of the way," she added. She'd said this before.

"Why do you think smaller is better?" Katya snapped back. "The village was small."

Svet shrugged, as close to admitting Katya might be right as she would get. The girl's idea was to hide in the wild. How long could they do that? Winter was coming. Finding a town where they could shelter seemed a far sight better than wandering aimlessly.

Katya tried to win the argument. "We're more likely to get what we need in a larger town—food, protection, and maybe even anonymity. Wandering the countryside won't result in anything reliable or permanent." Why was Svet so stubborn? Katya was already distressed about not being able to get to Leningrad. And it was clear they needed shelter and supplies.

They walked down to the wide pebbly beach that spread both directions. The cliffs rose on their right with several rocky promontories jutting toward the water. They picked their way around the formations to a sheltered, private spot. Svet set her pack on the ground and began to strip. Katya, too, set her things down and walked toward the water. Dozens of small rivers fed this lake and the Volkhov River drained it north to Lake Ladoga near Leningrad. At this time of year, the lake was low.

Still annoyed with the teen for her constant opposition to civilization, Katya unloaded Svet's mud-filled pack as the girl ventured into the shallow water. The rank smell of decomposed plant matter seemed lodged in Katya's nostrils and made her queasy. She dropped everything that could be washed into the water. Their food had been in Svet's pack—the extra bark flour, the last servings of kasha, and some left-over flat cakes. There was nothing to do about the flour, but she rinsed the handfuls of ruined kasha and set it to dry. She took the best of the flat cakes, too, and tried to remove the muck. A few

The Communist's Secret   59

pieces might serve as fish bait. The potatoes could be salvaged, and she scrubbed them until only a faint hint of swamp remained.

Svet emerged from the water looking clean, although Katya knew the stench would take a long time to fade from the girl's skin. The teen dipped and rubbed her clothes, over and over.

When she finished, Katya handed her a spare shirt and pants from her own dry pack.

"Potatoes, but that's it," said Katya. "I may be able to fish with the kasha and blini. I fished here as a girl. The water's shallow and warm and there should be plenty."

Svet eyed the ruined food. "We'll figure something. Right now we need a fire." She was shivering in a bone deep sort of way.

Katya emptied her rucksack and took it along the shore to gather driftwood. The cliff hid her unless the Nazis came by water, which seemed unlikely. And the Germans wouldn't know the lake. It was very shallow in places. Like here. A boat would need a dock.

The water glowed with optimism. The multicolored sky guided Katya as she filled her pack with scraps of wood. She slung it over her shoulders and picked up three larger pieces on the way back, one eye still on the huge, calm lake shimmering with pinks and reds.

In the shelter of the cliffs, they cooked the potatoes and boiled water for drinking as night fell and the moon rose. It was quiet in the way of vast, deserted spaces, and the familiar, bright orb lent a measure of calm as well as light. Sitting across the fire, Katya watched her silent friend, wondering if she was all right. As if on cue, Svet exhaled.

"There was a moment back there." The teen stared at the embers. "I was trying to remain still. Every twitch made me sink a little more." She stirred the fire. "I'm not afraid of dying. I've imagined breaking a leg outside in winter, or being charged by a bull elk while hunting—which actually happened once. I'm not afraid of being shot or stabbed. But to die in that swamp? Horrible muck gripping my feet and legs, pulling me under." She shivered.

Katya also thought a lot about death. Ever since little Sasha it had never been far from her mind. Her baby son was just starting to walk, toddling about on unsteady legs like an old man or a drunk. She would sweep him into her arms and he would erupt with glee. His happy shrieks made her laugh and then he would giggle even more. When he first fell ill, she thought nothing of it. A runny nose. A cold. Shura was away on a training exercise or some kind of deployment. She didn't remember. All she knew was that as her baby got sicker and sicker, she was alone with her growing fear. After one terrible night she took him to the hospital where he died three days later, struggling for every breath while she watched, helpless, begging a God she didn't believe in to save her baby and take her instead.

Svet was still talking. "Thank you. I'm lucky you knew what to do."

"We're both lucky." That ridiculous word popped out of her mouth. But maybe she was lucky to have met Svet. The girl had already saved her twice from the Nazis. It was difficult for Katya to deny there was some element of good fortune in their partnership.

"I almost killed us both," Svet said. "I'm sorry."

"You don't need to apologize. It could have happened to either of us." She felt a lump in her throat but if Svet wasn't going to cry, she wasn't either.

It had been a while since Katya had done any fishing, but when she woke the next morning, dawn spreading over the calm lake, she thought of Aleksandr. He loved mornings like this. In a small boat with his rods and fresh bait. She learned a lot about fishing from him and preferred local rivers to the Gulf of Finland. Whenever she went out into the dark waters of the Gulf, even with Aleksandr, she had to work hard to keep her fear at bay. The vast expanse of water and speed with which it could change made her feel helpless.

The Communist's Secret 61

But she knew her way around rods and lures. She gathered the spoiled kasha, a few scraps of leftover flat cake, her rifle, and a pin. She found the twine from the village in her rucksack. Svet snored softly, and Katya imagined her surprise at having fish for breakfast.

She climbed to the top of the bluff, looking for the enemy. Behind was flat shrubby vegetation, spotted with marshy areas. In front, stretching all the way to the horizon was the silent lake. It was almost as if the war had vanished. Katya walked back down to the beach. She took off her boots and pants and wadded in. When she got thigh deep, she tossed the spoiled kasha into the water. It floated on the surface. She stood still, waiting, watching the sky lighten. Before long, something nibbled. She'd baited her pin with the best of the rotten flat cake and tossed the twine out. It wasn't long before she got a bite and pulled gently until she could grab the fish with her hands. Bream. Tasty, but small. She carried it to shore and repeated the process. Exhilarated, she hurried back as a bank of high clouds moved overhead, already dulling the daylight.

"Are you awake? Look!" Katya dangled the fish. A rare smile lit the teen's face. Svet got her cook's knife and walked a short distance away to clean them.

Katya called out as she went. "Save the bellies, will you. Good bait." She could catch anything with fish belly on the hook. Svet turned, one eyebrow raised. Katya enjoyed being able to surprise her.

They stayed a second night, and then several more. The weather was changing, the temperature dropping. Katya fished each morning while Svet fidgeted, rinsing her clothes and cleaning their weapons multiple times. Katya tried to coax her into fishing, but she didn't want to stand in the water.

"What if a fish bites me?" the teen said in complete seriousness.

Katya swallowed her instinct to laugh. "These fish are too small for that. One might brush your leg, but lake fish don't bite humans."

They couldn't explore for fear of being seen, so instead paced the beach in front of the cliffs or huddled against the rocks when the sky started to spit. They spent hours staring at the lake, waiting for the Germans to appear. For long stretches, one or sometimes both of them took a position at the top of the rocky bluff where they could see all directions.

Katya swam every afternoon. She'd played here as a child and didn't mind the vegetation on the bottom. She could go a long way out before she couldn't touch and remembered her papa once standing far from shore, surrounded by water in what seemed like the middle of the lake, a small figure waving and laughing. As she shivered on the rough beach afterward, her coat loose on her shoulders, she thought of other water. The dark, deep Gulf of Finland near her family's *dacha*, their tiny summer house. On rare, warm summer days the local children would gather at the town pier to jump into the cold water. She'd stand on the very end, balancing on the balls of her feet, then spring off, diving elegantly into the depths. She liked to show off.

One afternoon the two women sat together in the shelter of the cliffs, comfortable with their own thoughts until the teen started to shift about like a five-year-old that had to use the toilet.

"What happened to your husband?" said Svet.

Katya exhaled and gazed at the water. Svet had hinted at the past before, but this time Katya wanted to tell her.

"A few of us were gossiping at a Party function. I'd had an argument with my husband. I was exasperated and annoyed and muttered something about his apparent lack of devotion. Which I meant in a private way. He was arrested less than a week later. My mother-in-law was demoted from her position with the Leningrad Philharmonic and I lost my job and Party card." She clenched her teeth against the rising emotion. "I didn't expect my words to be used against me, but I should have known better."

The Communist's Secret   63

"What a country," said Svet and then went silent, a faraway look on her face. "You can trust me, you know."

Katya nodded. "And likewise."

They sat, staring at the muddy blue expanse. Katya clutched her guilt like a life preserver. What she hadn't told Svet was that after her husband was arrested, she'd never tried to visit. She was too worried what might happen if she was seen in line at the prison. And she never wrote him either. Once he left for the camp, she just stopped talking about him, hoping to wake up one day to a new reality.

On their way back to the cove, a tiny speck appeared on the horizon. Katya had been waiting for this moment, and she suspected Svet had too. The afternoon had turned gray, the sky hung low, the way it did before it rained. They hurried to gather their things as the boat grew larger. They both knew there was no choice but to flee. They'd discussed the fact that it would be impossible to tell if a boat held a fisherman or the Nazis until it was close enough to make escape difficult. In less than five minutes they had scrambled from the shore, guns in hand and rucksacks on their backs, and were hurrying across the scrubland toward the distant woods.

Katya hoped she was leading them to Staraya Russa, the large town on the River Polist, which emptied into Lake Ilmen. They could reach it that day if they moved quickly. Civilization was their only choice. They needed a place to hide and warmer clothes and boots for Svet. Katya wanted information about Leningrad and the rest of the war. Staraya Russa might provide those things. Svet wore a look of grim acceptance. They were out of options, plain and simple.

A light rain began, and the temperature dropped. Katya hoped the drizzle hid them from view. Before entering some trees, they took a long last look behind them. Lake Ilmen was a band of gray and the boat had disappeared. Together they turned toward the trees and soon entered a dense forest. Katya was confident they were close to

Staraya Russa one minute, but then unsure and confused the next. "I thought it wasn't far, but now I don't know."

She watched Svet eye a downed pine that created a somewhat enclosed space with several other trees. The earth was flat and welcoming.

"I'm going to scout before dark," said Svet.

They'd stay the night if necessary. Katya should have been relieved. Staraya Russa wasn't far, yet her spirit felt flat, her energy gone. She closed her eyes and woke to Svet standing over her.

"Found something better than a town." The teen's eyes glowed. "A farm. Looks abandoned."

Svet had a way of forcing her views and preferences on Katya. The teen didn't try to argue her case, she'd just move in the direction she wanted to go. She'd lived alone a lot and Katya could see she was used to having her way and making decisions. The girl didn't want to be in a town and she'd found an alternative. But the last time Svet had bulldozed her way to a decision and Katya had gone along with it, Svet had nearly died. And she was doing it again. Still, Katya didn't argue. She was worn down, exhausted, and didn't have the energy to push back even though she still believed the town was their best bet.

"You know," Katya began. "A long time ago there was a government project to supply Staraya Russa with meat." Svet turned toward Katya just a fraction, which indicated she was listening. "Someone in the Party decided to build a rabbit farm. Everything started out well enough until one night some local teens opened all the hutches. Been good hunting ever since."

The girl was quiet, mulling it over silently, as was her habit.

"What would you do in Staraya Russa?" Svet said as they walked, the closest she'd ever come to admitting it might be an option.

"A job," said Katya. "Maybe a factory. My papa managed a textile factory. Maybe it's still there. It doesn't really matter. I need to get

The Communist's Secret

news of Leningrad. I need to figure out how to get back." Her fingers touched the pocket with her daughter's letter.

Svet nodded. "I know you're worried. But what would I do?"

"You would trap rabbits. Set up a stall in the local market. I bet you could do very well. The meat, the fur." If Svet could hunt for a living, it just might work. They both fell quiet again, their footfalls crunch-crunching through the leaves.

"Don't you want to know what's happening?" Katya continued. "Figure out where we can go without encountering the Wehrmacht? Even if I can't reach Leningrad, I need to join the war effort." She looked down. "A big plan from someone who doesn't even know what day it is."

"It's the twenty-fifth of September," Svet said. "And I don't want to tangle with the Wehrmacht either."

"You against a couple hundred Nazis?" Katya teased. "Sounds like a fair fight to me."

MASHA AND THE COLLECTIVE
October 1941

They were not lost, not entirely anyway, but after an hour tramping through the woods it seemed quite possible that Svet could not reconstruct the path to the farm. The maze of trees and her obvious confusion bore down on Katya's fragile spirit. All they had was the compass, their own guesswork about distances, and the teen's possibly unreliable memory.

They stopped to rest and drank from the canteen. The birches had lost their leaves, their stick arms barren and unwelcoming. The rain became a thin, fine snow. Without a word, they consulted the compass and began again. Soon the trees thinned and they were at the edge of the forest, staring into a flat nothingness. Fields. A stubble of crops poked through the dusting of winter like a five o'clock shadow and a distant apparition beckoned beneath the darkening sky. A long, low structure for grain, a barn, outbuildings. A collective farm.

Bone-weary, Katya sat. She felt no spark, no optimism. They'd had much harder days than this, but she'd already lost her momentum and desperately wanted to lie down, to sleep and wake to a different reality. Just as she moved to take off her pack, Svet grabbed her arm.

"We need to get there before dark." She dug a shallow hiding place for their weapons.

Katya understood they shouldn't arrive armed to the teeth, looking like partisans. She pulled out her Tokarev. "This?"

The Communist's Secret   67

Svet nodded. "One each."

They buried the rest wrapped in their blanket and then moved toward the *kolkhoz*. The buildings grew. On their left a road appeared that led to the farm. Pausing in a shallow ditch, they crouched in the damp undergrowth. Katya listened for animals, vehicles, people.

"Looks abandoned." Katya's eyes were fixed on their goal. "And the Nazis can't be everywhere," she said, giving voice to their hope.

Svet raised an eyebrow. "Not just the Nazis I'm worried about."

Katya knew that in the nearby Baltics, so recently taken over by the Soviets, there were people who hated the Red Army even more than they did Hitler.

"The citizens will defend Mother Russia," Katya said with conviction.

Svet's nod was half-hearted. "Many will. But people fight for what they love. And they may serve the Nazis to save their families. That will be more important than Stalin or the Motherland." She turned to Katya. "My father used to work in a fish cannery. Lots of workers were forced out and forgotten when the Soviets nationalized. Probably not the only reason he became a miserable angry man, but Stalin hasn't taken care of the workers. My mother used to say that they were slaves to the cannery before the Revolution and afterward they were slaves to the State. Always in bondage to someone." Svet's eyes flashed about, taking in everything.

"Just because I support Stalin doesn't mean I'm not sympathetic to those who've suffered," Katya said, an edge to her words. "I know a lot of people lost their livelihoods." Like her uncle, who once had a productive farm not far from where they sat. When Stalin forced individual farms into large, state-controlled collectives, her uncle refused to join. Stalin seized his farm and exiled his family. Katya remembered this so clearly because her parents argued about it. Her father thought the policy unfair while her mother had invoked one of Stalin's favorite sayings: "*Les rubyat, shcheptki letyat.* If you chop wood, chips will fly." Her papa never liked the way Stalin seemed to justify his harsh policies in a folksy way. He'd rebuked Mama. "Easy to say when you're the one doing the chopping."

He'd also pointed out that destroying the wealthy peasant class was a terrible idea. They were the smartest, hardest-working farmers. How would the collectives manage without them? Her uncle's fate niggled at her like a scab demanding to be picked. Neither she nor her parents had raised a finger to help their relatives, afraid of getting on the wrong side of history.

Svet continued. "My father trapped and hunted and drank to escape. And when he was drunk, he took out his anger on my mother and me." Svet was flushed and breathing hard. "I'm not making an excuse for him. Men often lose their jobs or fight in wars or do other difficult things and don't end up like my father. But as far as Stalin goes? He does not care about the people. Simple as that. We're all just chips of wood spinning off his chopping block."

Svet was right. But it wasn't just not compensating people when their businesses were taken that nagged at Katya. It was the way distrust and lies had come to drive society. Aleksandr's arrest was an example. There was something wrong with a system where people's livelihoods were taken without any provision for their future. Even more so where a casual comment could be reason for arrest.

Neither woman spoke, a kind of a truce settling between them. Svet stood. "No sign of anything or anyone. Let's take a look."

They crept from building to building. Katya stared at the blackened remains of a row of peasant dwellings across the road. They stopped alongside a silent barn. "No livestock," Katya whispered. It had been ages since she had fresh milk and for a moment the creaminess slipped across her tongue. She missed simple things the most. Milk, eggs and real tea.

The world had gone silent, their steps soft on the snow. Katya sniffed. The smells of manure and hay were absent, but she caught a

The Communist's Secret   69

faint scent of smoke. She sniffed again—peat smoke. As they came around the barn, a largish cabin appeared where rutted tracks ended in a tight circle. A wispy, black curlicue strung upward out of the chimney.

There were no recent tire tracks and few footprints around the buildings. Just a well-worn walkway from the front door to a cement cistern and a lesser-used path to the barn. They glanced around, seeing no obvious signs of partisan fighters or Nazis. Still, Katya was suspicious of her own desperation. And someone was there. Katya sniffed at the aromatic smoke. Only a local would burn peat.

"Make sure you can reach your pistol," she said, patting her own pocket as she stepped to the door. "And look friendly."

Svet exhaled, irritation evident. But Katya had seen her in action with the volunteers. She was prickly and pointed with those she didn't like or didn't want to know.

"You know what I mean," Katya added. "We don't want them ratting on us to the Nazis before we can win them over."

"Win them over?" Svet scoffed. "With what? Our charm? One look at us and . . ." The teen shrugged.

Katya examined Svet, taking in what a stranger would see: dirty, torn clothes, shoes tied on her feet, a workman's *shapka* on her tangled hair. Katya fingered her own disheveled braid, trying to tuck away the stray bits. She brushed the front of her coat, although it did nothing to make her more presentable. The teen was right. At this moment, in this situation, any concern about appearances was ridiculous. Nothing could mask their shabbiness or cover the misery that clung to them like manure to a pig. They needed help. It was as simple as that. Katya ignored Svet's annoyance and pushed down her own fear. "Maybe they'll take pity on us," she said.

She stood on the uneven planks of the single-step porch, comforted by the familiar heavy aroma of burning peat. She rapped on the door as the earthy smell settled into her, resurrecting her youth and the years before Leningrad—of cutting peat bogs and stacking the rectangles of decaying dirt. When she was a child, peasants could not afford to burn coal, and wood wasn't always available, but peat was free. She recalled how the pungent scent would remain on her skin and clothes all through the cold months, soaking into her very cells. She sniffed again and smelled her long-dead grandmother.

Unbidden, the past embraced her, squeezing her chest and making it hard to breathe. Instead of awakening disdain for the poverty of her youth, the heavy odor filled her with an overwhelming nostalgia for home, safety and loved ones. The surge of emotion broke the composure she'd worn as a badge of honor these weeks. It shattered her resistance into tiny pieces and she began to weep.

Svet put an arm around her and Katya neither accepted nor rejected her touch. She trembled from recent memories—the experiences of war and living off the land. The peat smoke became the dust of the grinding and clanking tanks, speeding toward the volunteers. In it she smelled tobacco on the Nazi's breath as he violated her. Then the bewitching aroma became the scent of fish grilling over their small fire, casting an invisible net of safety during those uncertain nights in the wild. In the smoke she even found the musky scent of her husband. Her dear Shura, fighting somewhere, struggling to defeat the Germans. With the familiar odor came the desire to apologize, to beg his forgiveness, to tell him she loved him.

Katya was still crying, wiping her face and nose with a sleeve, when the door creaked open. A wrinkled face with jet-black eyes poked through the crack. The door swung a bit further to reveal an ageless *babushka*. A woman that could be found anywhere and everywhere in the Soviet Union. A woman that was Mother Russia herself—short and sturdy, wearing a shapeless brown canvas dress and a dark kerchief over her hair. She pulled the door wide and a gnarled hand motioned them inside.

Katya continued to sniff while Svet introduced them. "I'm Svet

Andreevna. This is Katya Ivanova." She held Katya tight around the shoulders, nudging her to stop crying—to no avail. "Sorry to disturb. We were near Luga when the Germans attacked. Been running ever since."

"*Vy bednyye dorogiye.* You poor dears. Come in. I'm Mariya Borisovna, Masha to my friends." She eyed them. "Put your things there," she pointed at several hooks by the door. When they removed their coats, she clucked. "My, oh my. Look at you. Nothing more than skeletons. A difficult journey, I'm sure. Of course, it's a terrible time for everyone." She shook her head. "No better here than anywhere else, except perhaps Leningrad."

"Leningrad? Do you have news?" Katya sputtered through her tears and then froze, afraid of a final judgment on Yelena.

"We get our information from the Nazis you understand, but they say the city is surrounded. Cut off." Her voice dropped, as if her words were too terrible to hear. "The citizens are starving. Filthy fascists. Hardly human. To starve innocent women and children."

Katya went limp, her legs crumpling at the old woman's words. Svet broke her fall, and then knelt, patting her cheeks, trying to revive her. "Maybe if we warm her up," the girl said, lifting Katya by her armpits and dragging her to a spot in front of the stove.

"She needs sugar," said Masha who deftly poured some tea and scrabbled around in the kitchen. She found an ancient hard candy and dropped it into the cup.

Katya's eyes fluttered open, and Svet helped her sit up and drink.

Masha faced them. "Sorry for the news of Leningrad. Been under a rock, haven't you?"

Svet nodded. "In the forests mostly, avoiding German patrols. Katya's daughter and mother-in-law are in Leningrad."

"Oh, my. How terrible. What about your family?"

"I'm from Murmansk." She nodded at Katya. "We were in the same volunteer brigade."

They moved Katya to a small cot which doubled as a sofa and propped her against a straw pillow. Katya said nothing, but pressed a hand against her heart.

"Don't assume the worst," Svet encouraged. She looked at Masha for support.

"Absolutely right." Masha nodded, eyes wide for emphasis. "For all we know the Germans are just bragging." She looked at them conspiratorially. "You know how men are."

Katya smiled weakly. Men were difficult. Full of themselves one moment and needing lots of attention the next. She'd worked with men like that. The director of their volunteer brigade was a perfect example of a man who always needed to feel superior. The Nazis bragging made sense. It made them feel powerful. It wasn't much different from the way her own government handled the early days of the war. Telling the people that they'd roll right over the Nazis. That they'd send them scurrying for Berlin with their tails between their legs. The Party wanted to project power and keep the population calm, but at what price? Now, the Nazis had blockaded Leningrad and the citizens were trapped.

"Any other news?" She glanced at a dirty pile of newspaper next to a stack of kindling.

Masha lifted her chin toward the pile. "That's months old. But Staraya Russa isn't far. A few kilometers. I have an old friend at the textile factory. He knows everything. An interesting character. Romashkin, Arkady Petrovich. Trustworthy." She stopped, looking at the two younger women. "But you can't go to Staraya Russa. The place reeks of Nazis. They've taken the entire region, and Staraya Russa is their headquarters."

Katya and Svet looked at each other, digesting the news that they were now under Nazi jurisdiction. News that they perhaps suspected, but feared nevertheless.

"Besides," Masha added, "you need rest. From the looks of you it's been a tough time." She began pattering about. "Nazis never come out here. First thing they did was disband the collective and take what was left of the livestock. Can't work the land without animals to pull the plows. No petrol for our little tractor either. Most of the *kolkhozniks* had left before the Germans even got here. All I've got are a few chickens for company. Miss my cow. The milk, you know. But I'm lucky to have eggs. Before the cold set in, my hens were laying well and my granddaughter came every week for the extra eggs. Now she comes less often, to see how I'm getting along and bring my rations. She was here just a few days ago, so she won't come out again for some time. Told me herself it was getting too dangerous to leave town." Masha paused, examining her hands, looking a bit embarrassed. "Listen to me going on."

Katya wiped her tear-streaked face. "Please. We know nothing about the war."

Unable to resist the invitation, Masha continued. "All sorts of difficulty. Some people taken to work camps. Most Communists left ahead of the Germans and the Nazis have found those that didn't. They are good at getting informers. Plenty of mean-spirited locals, even some Red Army deserters all too willing to cooperate. Germans want to know which families have soldiers in the Red Army. Of course, that's nearly everyone. And even the Politsai know you cannot rat out the entire town. So, they pick and choose, informing on those they don't like. All personal grudges and such." Masha shook her head. "You don't want any part of that. You should think long and hard about going into town. Once there, it's living by your wits again. Now," she said, standing and resting her hands on generous hips. "I'm sure you're hungry. And I'll start some water so you can bathe." She nodded at the high-sided tin washtub near the stove.

Katya ran a fingertip across one cheek feeling dirt and grunge mixed with her tears. She hadn't looked at her reflection in weeks. In the warm cabin she smelled the sourness of her body and the strong scent of swamp decay rising from Svet and her rucksack. They'd never get rid of it without lots of soap.

"We're grateful," she said, regaining a steadiness, but her mind swirled with everything Masha had said. "Been a long time since we were warm or clean. The fire is wonderful." Katya looked at Masha. "The peat smoke is what started me crying. Reminds me of my childhood."

"The past can do that," Masha said. "Sneak up on you. Sometimes I get teary thinking of my husband and our early years." She grabbed a bucket and then headed for the door, turning her back on the emotional past like a typical stoic Russian.

Svet followed Masha outside and took charge of heating the water, carrying it from the cistern and filling the large pot over the fire. The old *babushka* moved the cheap tin samovar from the stove and put a skillet in its place. She dropped a generous dollop of lard from an ancient looking tin can. When it began to sizzle, she sliced several potatoes into the pan.

Katya sniffed at the delicious savory aroma of potatoes frying in grease. The simplest of meals, but it smelled like a banquet. Masha hovered over the stove like a worn, wrinkled gnome. Her eyes nearly disappeared when she smiled. The ancient woman pushed the crispy potatoes to one side, cut three slices of dense, dark bread and proceeded to fry those too. She pulled clay plates off an open shelf above the sink, and slid equal portions of potatoes and bread onto two, placing them on the table and nodding to Katya and Svet. A third, smaller serving she took for herself, waddling to a stool. She pulled up her skirt when she sat, scratching and adjusting her wool underwear.

"Delicious." Katya smiled. "Thank you."

"We must look out for each other," Masha replied. "Life's too hard alone."

Svet was devouring the plate of delicious, greasy potatoes with her fingers, using the bread to wipe up any bits of fat that might

The Communist's Secret 75

otherwise escape. Katya ate slower. She let each piece sit on her tongue for a moment before biting through the crispy edges into the softer potato centers. They hadn't had butter or lard since they'd been on the run, and she made each mouthful last. She held the fork Masha offered—the first time she'd used a utensil since the slaughter at Luga. She appreciated the feel of it in her hand, the way the tines speared each morsel of food and the way her hands didn't get greasy. Eating with her fingers was part of living in the wild that Katya had not gotten used to.

"So, Comrade, you aren't afraid, alone out here?" Katya asked as she ate.

Masha smirked. "Comrade? Ha! Masha will do. Been afraid since my husband died in the last war. After that came the Revolution and the Reds and Whites fighting. Years of being afraid." She shook her head. "Then Stalin took our farm. Nothing but struggle. And now it's even worse. Scared for my sons. Scared when the Nazis burned the *izbas*—a warning not to aid the partisans even though there aren't any around here. So, now I'm alone and still scared. Fear is just part of life. You have to learn to live with it."

She gathered their plates. Svet heated more water, filling the tub one kettleful at a time.

"But it's different now," Masha began again. "There's something evil. To put them off the scent, I complained about Stalin: shutting the churches, arresting the priests and murdering the *kulaks*. And told them that the Communists—with all their high-minded, meaningless gibberish about the proletariat—forced us to turn everything over to the State. This *kolkhoz* still doesn't produce like our little farms did. Slaves in our own country." She snorted and mumbled.

"Mind you, I didn't tell them plenty of Russians think life under the Germans would be better. And didn't admit my sons were Red Army. Also forgot to mention that I detest Hitler." Her eyes twinkled, and Katya smiled in return. "That weasel with the silly mustache.

Trying to conquer the world." She shook her head in disgust. "Does that answer your question? Yes, I'm afraid. Of the Nazis and the Politsai and the partisans and Stalin. None of them care about me. Only an idiot wouldn't be afraid."

Katya nodded. She shared the same fears of the enemy and of her own government. You either went along or it was prison, the camps, execution. And maybe for your loved ones too. People began disappearing in earnest after Kirov was murdered. Loyal revolutionaries, military officers, even original Bolsheviks like Bukharin. She'd met him once. Hard to believe he'd committed treason. She'd accepted Bukharin's guilt because she didn't want to believe the Party would turn on its own. Now she wondered about him and the others. What if Bukharin was the true Bolshevik and not Stalin?

"Anyway, I don't think too far ahead," said Masha. "War makes it impossible. It's just survival—one day at a time. Right now my biggest concern is the chickens. With the cold weather, they aren't laying well. I might kill the worst layers, freeze the meat and hide it. That way, if the Nazis come for the chickens, I'll at least have the ones I froze."

Katya stared at Masha. Life was a balancing act and had been for a long time. Masha was still talking.

"The Nazis think they're so smart." Her eyes flashed and she leaned forward. "Just between us girls, I let two young pigs loose in the forest when the Germans arrived, hoping they would survive. One managed to escape. I can see that feisty thing, squealing and slipping away, the Nazis falling over themselves trying to catch it. Eventually they gave up. Then I put food out and built a little burrow under a tree log. I didn't figure it would make it, but just before you arrived, I trapped it. Hate to slaughter the spunky thing, but that pork will feed me all winter." A flush rose on her face, visible even on her leathery skin.

Katya reached over and patted the woman's arm. "We won't

share what you've told us." What choice did she have but to let the Nazis take what they wanted? Stalin probably thought she should put a bullet in her head rather than cooperate.

Masha dropped the subject and poured more hot water into the tub. "Sorry I don't have a curtain or anything. It's just me out here, and I don't worry about anyone seeing." She chuckled and grabbed a handful of her ample middle. "Let them look if they want." She set a couple of rough but clean-looking pieces of cloth on the chair and then disappeared into the bedroom.

"She's a character," Katya whispered. She stripped off her clothes and looked at her own stomach—as flat as a young girl's—then clambered into the warm water and scrubbed off layers of dirt and dead skin. Svet set more water to heat and helped rinse the soap from Katya's hair.

When Katya swung a leg out and reached for a makeshift towel, the teen added more hot water and stepped in. Her legs and arms were sinewy, but her ribs and hipbones also betrayed their limited diet. After sponging herself pink, the teen leaned her head back against the edge of the tub and closed her eyes.

When Svet stood, Katya threw their filthy clothes into the water. "Here. Before you climb out, kick these around a bit. It'll make it easier." Katya had wrapped herself in one of the threadbare towels and tucked it into place under an armpit. She sat in front of the stove trying to comb through her hair with a clean fork while the clothes soaked.

"Maybe Masha has a comb," Svet said. Her curly locks were a gnarly, knotted mess. "Or a pair of scissors." Despite Svet's sardonic tone, Katya thought cutting their hair might be a reasonable thing to do.

The door to Masha's bedroom cracked open and she called out. "Getting along?"

"A luxury," said Katya. "Thank you."

Masha came out with a huge gap-toothed grin. "Need anything?"

Svet returned the old woman's genuine smile, her teeth flashing and her eyes filled with warmth. "Scissors?"

Masha looked at their matted locks. "Normally I'd suggest rubbing a bit of grease into it and then working a comb through, but there isn't enough soap to get the grease out."

"We can cut the worst of the tangles," said Katya.

Masha nodded and found a pair of shears and pulled a chair in front of the fire.

Katya sat. "I don't want my hair too short. At my shoulder blades. I'll manage the rest of the tangles." Her blond hair was almost to her waist.

"Hold still," Svet commanded and in four swift strokes the bottom of Katya's hair fell to the ground. She ran her fingers through the remaining locks. "Just a couple of spots you need to work at," Svet said. "Now me." She handed the shears to Katya. "Make it short," she said as they traded places. Her hair was shoulder-length.

"At your chin?"

"I said short. Above my ears," said Svet. "Easier to take care of."

"*Nu tak.* Well, then. A revolutionary haircut." Many young women wore their hair short during and after the Revolution. A sign of their devotion to the no-nonsense lifestyle of the Bolsheviks. "Just sit still. It'll take me a while to get it even."

Katya set to work, cutting it short in back and on the sides, but leaving some length on top. When finished, she said, "Don't be too shocked." Katya carefully removed the towel on Svet's shoulders, trying to collect the hair. Masha reached for a broom and spoke first.

"*Prekrasniye.* Beautiful. You look like someone in a fashion magazine."

And she did. A few curls fell strategically on her forehead. The height on top set off her angular features and with her white skin she looked, if not beautiful, then exotic. Her eyes seemed larger with her hair short, and their pale gray hue was a striking contrast to her dark waves. Even her cheekbones stood out more, which helped diminish her largish nose.

Mute, Svet stared at her reflection.

"Like it?" Katya asked. "It's very flattering. Sets off your eyes. You're very beautiful."

Svet began to cry silent tears.

"Oh, I'm so sorry," said Katya. "You don't like it." She put an arm around her young friend and tried to console her. "It'll grow out."

"No, no," Svet sputtered. "It's not that. It's . . . my whole life I was told I wasn't worth looking at. *Gadkiy utenok.* An ugly duckling."

Katya squeezed her shoulders. "Well, that was a lie. You look like a beautiful swan to me." She pointed at the mirror. "The truth is right there."

THE GERMANS PAY A VISIT
October 1941

The next morning, gray and cold with enough fresh snow on the ground to obscure the previous night's footprints, Masha prepared breakfast and insisted they make themselves at home. "You'll stay as long as you like," she said, placing a plate of kasha with homemade jam in front of Katya. A moment later the old woman slid a perfectly cooked fried egg alongside. Katya could not remember the last time she'd had an egg. They were scarce even before the war. One of those impossible to find items unless you had *kontakty*, contacts.

Katya was not sure if the old woman meant they could stay for a week or a month or until the war was over, but it didn't matter. She and Svet needed to escape the grinding fear, violence, and aimlessness that had brought them to Masha's door.

All through their odyssey, Katya clutched the belief that she would aid her loved ones and fight the Germans. But Masha's news of the blockade sent the grains of that plan slipping through her fingers like so much sand. And already she recognized the tremendous comfort and safety she felt with the old woman. Last night, a deep sleep had welcomed her for the first time since Luga.

Masha set two more plates and Svet joined them. Katya watched the old woman shyly across the table as she ate. The *babushka* approached the day with a steady, warm demeanor, something that must have helped her conquer a lifetime of troubles. Katya aspired to do the same. Her final moment of conviction that they were fated to

The Communist's Secret 81

be on the farm came to her that afternoon when Svet came bouncing back from the forest with a half-smile on her lips and talking about all the rabbit tracks she'd seen.

They found plenty of ways to make Masha's life easier even though the old woman never made them feel as if they owed her anything. Katya repaired a broken latch here and replaced a board there. One sunny day when the snow melted off the roof, she and Svet got a rickety ladder and fixed a leak. In her previous life, she'd never have climbed the roof of a *dacha*.

The top edge of the door stuck every time it was opened or closed. It grated on the frame, requiring a strong shoulder or two-handed pull. She and Svet took it off its hinges, set it on the table, and in ninety minutes had smoothed both top and bottom edges while a heavy blanket nailed over the opening kept the worst of winter at bay. Katya glowed when Masha called her *master na vse ruki*, a jack of all trades. Her work colleagues would have described her as hard-nosed or driven rather than skilled or helpful.

She managed the peat piled in the loft of the barn. Hay also filled the space. Masha explained that after the men went to war, the collective's women and teens cut and brought in what they could. The animals were gone by mid-August, so the hay continued to take up space, losing nutrients with every passing week. Soon it wouldn't be good for anything but bedding.

Katya climbed the unstable fortress of dried earthen rectangles like she'd grown up in the mountains of Georgia—where Stalin himself was from. She unstacked the mosaic bit by bit, dropping pieces from the top, watching each hit the floor with an explosive *thunk*, dust rising and filling the barn with tiny particles of dirt and decaying vegetative matter that made her sneeze.

While Katya worked, Svet hunted and hauled water. The cement and stone cistern at one end of the house filled when it rained, or when the sun melted the snow on the roof. Masha explained that the reservoir would soon freeze, and they'd have to draw water from the deepest of the property's wells, making the chore far more time-consuming. No matter what was broken or what was in short supply, Masha never complained.

"We're in the middle of a war and that woman never gets up on the wrong side of the bed," Svet said, her eyes bright with admiration.

"It's a special person who is both capable and content," said Katya. She shut her mouth before she gave voice to the thought that she should be more like Masha.

When she wasn't managing the peat supply or fixing things, Katya cooked with the old woman. Masha's stories and good humor set her apart from others of her generation. She didn't complain the way Katya remembered her own grandmother. And she wasn't like her mother-in-law either—a perpetual motion machine, always doing, always organizing. Sofya was genuine, but exhausting.

And then there was her own mother who was happiest when the center of attention. Katya had parented Yelena in the same self-centered way. When her daughter was little, Katya had wanted her focus and affection. But after baby Sasha died, she found the cost of love too high. She expected less and less from her daughter but gave less as well. No wonder Yelena was close to her papa. Aleksandr always found time for his beloved Lenochka. He did not hesitate to cut work short or skip a Party meeting just to play chess or go for a walk with his darling daughter. Yelena was never an inconvenience to him.

Well, you reap what you sow.

The first time Svet walked in with two furry bundles hanging off her belt, Masha squealed with delight. Katya took a deep breath and followed Masha's instructions. She cut the rabbit's feet off with a cleaver and working from the incision that Svet had used to gut the animal in the woods, pulled the skin away and off each leg. "Now just pull

The Communist's Secret 83

it up over the rabbit's head." Masha was so excited that when Katya hesitated, she grabbed the animal and the cleaver and did it herself.

They cooked a rabbit stew with one and put the other one in the barn to freeze. Katya used some bark flour and made small gamey dumplings that they tossed into the stew. They ate like royalty.

It wasn't possible for Katya to feel fortunate in wartime—there were too many difficulties and horrible experiences, and besides, it wasn't her nature to feel content—but with food, shelter, and safety at hand, the thundering in Katya's chest was no longer a constant companion. Of all the terrible possibilities, they'd stumbled upon this generous *babushka* with few failings. The idea of returning to Leningrad had faded under the reality of the city surrounded, and Katya sometimes thought about waiting out the war with Masha. But the gnawing ache about her daughter did not disappear.

For weeks, the collective was quiet. Masha's granddaughter came once but she was in a hurry and stayed only long enough for a cup of tea. Katya and Svet had been in the forest. But a week later, the Nazis appeared.

The morning had started like any other. The three women ate their bowls of kasha and sipped their cups of weak tea by the light of a single candle. Katya did the breakfast dishes right away as always. They hid the extra bedding so nothing would indicate there was more than one person living there. They knew the necessary precautions.

Days were short by late October and when dawn finally lit the landscape past eight o'clock, Svet went out to check her traps. She often disappeared for hours at a time. Katya and Masha sometimes talked about how comfortable the teen was in nature. "It seems a bit unusual, don't you think?" said Masha. "She has no interests other than being outdoors or killing things." Katya had never thought of it that way. The killing things part. But it was true that Svet feared almost nothing. And she did seem to enjoy killing when it involved Nazis or rabbits.

Katya had just unloaded rectangles of peat from her wheelbarrow and was stacking them along the back wall of the kitchen when the foreign sound of tires crunching on snow made her heart jump. She ran to the small window and pulled a corner of the curtain aside. A black car was coming up the rough, snow-covered road.

Masha was in the privy just behind the house. Katya stepped out the back door and bounced a stone off the outhouse. "They're here," she hissed and raced back inside as the sound of the car slowed. They'd made a plan for this situation, although the plan didn't include Svet being in the forest. What if she came striding out into the open, a string of rabbits on her belt? Katya lifted two floorboards in a corner of the bedroom. A couple of wooden steps led to the storage pit Masha's sons had built ten years earlier to hide food from the Communists. Katya pulled the boards back into place as the car doors slammed. In a moment, she heard Masha rustling above her, replacing the rug, and then a sharp knock rattled through the house. Masha called out, her voice cheery. "*Moment*. Just a moment." Then, the gentle thuds of her feet and the opening of the front door.

"*Dobroye utro*, Good morning." The man's voice was pleasant, respectful even. Not at all what Katya expected. "How are you getting along?" His Russian was poor, but at least he tried.

She heard boots on the floor. How many were there? Two? Three?

"*Vse khorosho.* Everything's good," said Masha. "A bitter start to winter, but I have plenty of peat. I haven't been to town in ages. Five kilometers seems longer every day."

Masha was allowed to get four weeks of flour at a time because the Nazis had taken the last of her transportation. The Red Army had requisitioned her truck and the horses, and a short time later the Nazis had come through and taken everything else—even the little donkey that pulled her cart to town. Not that Masha was at any risk of starvation. She'd secreted away bags of grain from the last

The Communist's Secret 85

harvest—some of which Katya was leaning against—and her garden produced more potatoes and beets than she could eat.

Katya's ears perked up. What did they want? Why the polite small talk? What if Svet appeared, strolling toward the cabin, rifle over her shoulder? Her stomach tightened. She hoped they wouldn't stay long.

The officer continued. "There's been some unlawful activity in the area."

Katya stifled a laugh. Wasn't starting a war and invading another country unlawful?

"This *kolkhoz* could easily be used by the partisan criminals—as a meeting place, or a spot from which to launch attacks."

"Partisans? I don't think so," said Masha. "With so many German soldiers around and the Red Army close, it seems unlikely." Masha had told Katya and Svet that the front was only a handful of kilometers the other side of town. The Red Army hadn't been able to hold Staraya Russa, but they'd dug in just east. The result was a huge concentration of Nazi soldiers in town. "And anyway," continued Masha, "I may be alone, but I know everything that happens out here. I'd know if there were any visitors."

"Perhaps," said the officer. "But small numbers of partisans can maneuver anywhere."

"I've seen nothing," said Masha.

"Still, they could shelter here. And in winter, shelter is something. You'll let us know if you see anything."

"Of course. I have no interest in helping those bandits."

Katya wondered what the Nazis looked like. She imagined them stern, with little reaction when Masha said negative things about the partisans.

"And remember, we protect you," came the man's voice.

It was true that the Politsai stayed away.

"I'm grateful," she said. "Take a look around. The keys are right there." Masha always hung them on a hook by the door.

The jingling of the keys and the sounds of the door opening and closing drifted down to Katya. She remained silent, wondering if one of them was still in the cabin with Masha.

"They're outside." Masha's voice startled her, hissing from above. "No sign of Svet."

"Nothing we can do," Katya said. "Just hope she sees them before they see her."

The minutes ticked past. Katya sat still, trying not to fidget. She listened to Masha moving in the cabin, straightening things, cleaning up. It seemed to take forever for the Nazis to finish looking around.

The sudden sound of the door made her jump. Boots thudded on the wood floor. She heard them hang the keys and exchange a few words with Masha. Then the door slammed again, followed by the car starting and tires crackling on the snow.

Masha moved the rug and floorboards. Her figure was a squat black outline in the sudden light. "Any sign of Svet?" Katya said. "I was sure she'd walk right into them, come strolling up the way she does."

"Thank goodness, no," Masha said, pressing a hand to her ample bosom. She smiled. "And they left my chickens."

The Nazis were treating Masha well because they saw her as a source of information. They'd be back. Katya realized that as long as she and Svet were on the collective, someone might notice something. It was clear. The longer they stayed, the more dangerous it was for Masha.

LEAVING THE COLLECTIVE
November 1941

Over the next days, the three women circled each other in an awkward dance of avoidance. Each waited for the other to begin the necessary conversation about the Germans. Like an unpleasant chore that one put off as long as possible, it colored every task and every conversation with a dull gray patina.

When Katya finally broke the stalemate, she did so impulsively, as was her nature. The main point was simple and straightforward. Staying on the collective put Masha at risk. As much as they loved her soothing company, it was not a long-term solution. And although she didn't voice her fears about Yelena much, that ache and the disturbing feeling that she wasn't doing enough for her nation nagged at her like an annoying relative who doesn't know when to leave.

"It's not safe for you if we're here. Besides, I should be part of the war effort. Fighting the Nazis instead of hiding. I'm going to Staraya Russa."

She hadn't spoken to Svet first, knowing that the teen might refuse to go along. Katya hoped presenting Svet with a *fait accompli* would make her more likely to comply, which would save Katya from breaking up an arrangement that was working so well. She blurted out her plan before she could change her mind.

Masha grumbled, but didn't seem surprised. And neither did Svet.

The teen looked at her feet, but spoke clearly. "Masha and I have a plan of our own. I told her you would want to go to Staraya Russa— it's what you've wanted all along. But I can't."

This was what Katya struggled with most but knew in her heart. Svet could not live in a town full of Nazis with their rules and regulations, with their cruelty and brutality.

"Svet's going to stay," Masha exclaimed in a too loud voice. "If the Nazis come again, I'll say she's a cousin from Leningrad. Her family tried to evacuate but she's the only one that made it. It'll be clear why she doesn't have papers."

Katya looked from Masha to Svet. The old woman was right—such things happened everywhere in wartime. And perhaps she'd be able to get Svet documents after she herself was settled in Staraya Russa. She began to pace. Back and forth over the small distance between the stove and the door. There was logic in Svet staying on the *kolkhoz*. If she was careful, she could remain hidden. And it would be better for Katya too. One stranger in Staraya Russa might go undetected, while two would draw attention.

"They will come again you know," she said.

Svet nodded. "I'll be prepared. Extra precautions whenever I'm in the forest. And if I'm here when they come, I can hide just like you did. And if that doesn't work, we can use Masha's story of being a refugee from Leningrad."

"What if none of those work?" Katya glared at the teen.

Svet looked at her clear-eyed. "I know how to protect us."

The girl wouldn't hesitate to kill several more German soldiers. That frightened Katya as much as the idea of her being caught. "Please don't be rash. Even if you were able to flee, killing Nazis here would have terrible consequences."

"Don't worry. I won't go off half-cocked," Svet said. "I promise."

A few days later, Katya's departure was upon them. All three women had been forestalling the inevitable. Katya had just finished a batch of bark flour. The bright, white shavings filled a flat pan that she set on the stove to dry. Masha fiddled with a needle and thread, pretending to sew.

The Communist's Secret   89

Svet stood just inside the door, examining nothing. She would accompany Katya partway to say goodbye in private. Katya put on her coat and gathered her things. Masha followed, hunched over, suddenly looking her years. They hugged and the old woman clutched her.

"Do you remember how I arrived here?" said Katya. "A blubbering puddle. My nerves shot. You fed me and told me stories and helped me sleep. You brought me back to myself. I can never repay that. Thank you."

"You're like a daughter to me," said the old *babushka*. The two women held onto each other until matter-of-fact Svet stepped in, moving the departure along.

"I'll be back in an hour. Two at the most," Svet said to Masha.

The old woman sniffed and nodded and wiped her eyes.

They left her on the porch and walked in silence. Big, fluffy snowflakes drifted down. It was the kind of snow that reminded one of childhood. Of sledding and skating and laughter. An auspicious kind of snow that would cover their footprints in no time.

They trudged along the rear of the outbuildings toward the forest. Svet slid a bag off her shoulder as they walked. She pulled out a small bundle wrapped in newspaper. "This is fresh, from this morning. Cleaned, skinned, ready for the pot."

Katya resisted. "You should keep it."

"I caught two. Besides, it'll help you make friends. You might need a favor."

Katya nodded and put it in her rucksack.

As they made for the forest, every step was a miniature explosion. Under the fresh flakes a hard layer of icy snow cracked and popped as their boots went through. One of the first things Masha had done after they arrived was spirit away the teen's floppy, ill-fitting shoes and give her a worn but reliable pair of boots in their place. Masha had quite a collection of such things. She was used to trading and bartering, and helping people was in her nature.

Svet gazed at the endless white of the fields. Katya tried to see what the teen saw: the way the horizon disappeared, nothing more than a dirty smudge where the earth became the sky. The absence of birds. The occasional animal track.

To calm her nerves, Katya reviewed her arrival plan. Find Arkady Romashkin, get a job and a place to stay. Katya tried to recollect the textile factory. It had been over twenty years and she did not want to ask for directions. As a backup, Masha had given her a scrap of paper with her daughter's address.

Wherever she ended up, she could not reveal who she was or where she'd come from. The people of Staraya Russa would be wary, fearful, and protective of their food and their secrets. Even if she presented herself as a harmless woman displaced by the war, they might not welcome her. She knew she maintained a polished veneer that suggested an easier life but hoped her clothes and family history would convince both the locals and the Nazis that she belonged in Staraya Russa.

Svet broke the silence as they entered the cover of the forest. "I hope I'm doing the right thing. Masha didn't push me to stay. She didn't want to come between us but knew it would be better for me. But I've also been feeling that I need to be with you," she began to sniff, holding back uncommon tears.

"Makes sense to stay," said Katya. "And Masha needs the help." She cast the teen a sideways glance. "I just hope I can manage without you." At those words, Svet cracked a rare smile and Katya continued. "You'll be happier with Masha. Besides, you can always change your mind and come into Staraya Russa. After I establish contacts and get papers and such."

They stopped where they'd hidden the extra weapons. Katya dug a shallow hole nearby—a quick four shovelfuls of earth—and handed Svet her beat-up tool that had been with them since the beginning. She buried her Tokarev—the first gun she'd used to kill a Nazi and

The Communist's Secret   91

the one that suited her—wrapped in a sturdy piece of cloth. Maybe there'd come a time she could use it again, but that time wasn't now. A weapon could be a dangerous complication.

When they reached the river and there was no chance she'd lose her way, Katya stopped.

"I know where I am." Her emotions were rising inside her like a cyclone. "I want to tell you how much you mean to me. How much I admire you. And I haven't thanked you enough."

Svet kicked the snow, refusing to look Katya in the eye. "We helped each other."

"We will again," said Katya. "Maybe join the partisans."

"I've been thinking about that. Not sure I can be in close quarters with a bunch of men, although I would like to kill more Nazis."

"Me too." Katya smiled.

"Don't trust anyone," said Svet. "Don't tell anyone about the Luga Line."

The teen's instincts always veered to the distrustful side. With such a suspicious nature, she would have made a good Communist. She was right about holding everything close. The fact that they had survived when so many others had been slaughtered might be seen in a negative light by their own government. And what if an anti-Stalinist found out that she'd worked for the nation's defense? All it would take was one jealous person to turn her over to the Germans.

"And remember, you don't owe anyone anything," Svet continued. "Not the Party, not Stalin. Do things for yourself and those you love. And keep your head down."

Katya smirked. "I know we joined the Volunteers for different reasons. But, there's just one enemy now." Defeating the Nazis was all that mattered. "Don't worry," she continued. "I'll steer clear of the Politsai and the Germans." From everything Masha had said, Katya felt certain she could trust Romaskin. She pulled the shorter, sturdier woman close and did not let her go until she felt the teen squeeze her in response.

"Go on now," Katya said. "*Uvidimsya*. We'll see each other." She watched Svet vanish in the heavy, fresh snow, wiping her eyes as she went.

INTO STARAYA RUSSA

November 1941

Katya rehearsed the story as she walked. She'd use her maiden name—Belikova. If pressed to elaborate, she'd claim to be a schoolteacher from a small town near Novgorod. Not that she wanted a teaching job in Staraya Russa should the schools even be functioning. Small children tried her patience and older ones, well, what could she teach them? Other than taboo subjects like Party doctrine and political philosophy, she didn't know much.

She'd say she fled when the Nazis attacked. That part was true. If the townspeople got nosy, she'd explain how she used an abandoned *dacha* for a while. With winter coming, she made her way to Staraya Russa. It was her childhood home, after all.

As the woods thinned, the snow thickened, collecting on her coat. She reached the main road where there was little traffic. The closer she drew, the more the town opened to her. The first homes on the outskirts looked peaceful—snow clinging to them like icing sugar. She recalled different neighborhoods, landmarks, and something of the physical surroundings—memories of the river and the ravine north of town swept in.

But under the quiet surface, the shadows of war were everywhere. Ruins had taken the place of once prosperous buildings. Planks of wood covered windows. The closer she got to the center of town, the greater the destruction. Entire blocks contained nothing but shattered buildings and broken weapons of war. She passed several crippled trucks and saw the red star of the Soviet army on one door, faded as if from loss of blood.

Only the river was untouched. It snuck in from the right, gaining in size and momentum as she moved closer to the town center. She and her papa used to fish on the Polist. Their favorite spot couldn't be far from where she was now.

Katya's plan was to stay along the left bank of the river which split the town in two. Both her childhood home and her father's textile factory were on the left side. She knew from Masha that the factory had survived the initial Nazi onslaught although it didn't seem that much else had. It would be her first stop. She had to make contact with this Romashkin fellow. Masha had gone on and on about the man, so much so that Katya felt she knew him. Which was altogether possible since according to Masha, he'd lived in Staraya Russa his entire life. When she plumbed her memory she recollected a friend of her papa's—a handyman that worked on the looms. He called her Katyusha. It could be the same man.

According to Masha's granddaughter, the textile factory was operational, and he was in charge. Masha had described how the Nazis were setting up a Reichskommissariat in Staraya Russa to oversee everything. There were varying degrees of collaboration and according to Masha, although Arkady ran a factory for the Nazis, his loyalty was to Russia. Katya hoped he also had some communist sympathies.

Head down, scarf around the earflaps of the *ushanka* Masha had given her, Katya made her way along the river. She worked to cultivate a manner that would convey innocence rather than generate suspicion. A look that wouldn't attract attention—not beleaguered, but not overly confident either. Just a look that said she belonged, on this street, on this afternoon.

The first Germans she saw were nothing more than boys—like the ones she and Svet had killed that first day in the forest. A

The Communist's Secret   95

pressure grew in her chest. She had no papers. She took deliberate but unhurried steps, pushing the fear down and staring at the ground ahead, trying to look purposeful. Everyone walked with intent in a snowstorm.

She glanced at them as they approached. Their rosy cheeks glowed with youthful vigor but the set of their jaws betrayed a harshness and their serious expressions told her they meant business despite their youth—or perhaps because of it. What did they know of life? They hadn't lived enough to understand much of anything.

They passed by with hardly a glance.

Katya's heart was still pounding, and although she had planned to go straight to the factory, she turned at the next side street and walked all the way to the end, perhaps three hundred meters. Only two fully intact homes remained. She was certain her family's cottage had been here. She stood in the center of the street, counting, and realized the burned remains in front of her was her childhood home. The massive stove her papa had built was all that remained—a hulking piece of metal.

Katya returned to the main street, pushing aside the nostalgia rising from the pile of ashes. She examined the graceful sweep of the river as it curved. Across the water the domes of the Monastery of the Transfiguration were barely visible behind the thick veil of white. She passed several sad, small businesses that were open but speckled with bullet holes. When she caught the eye of an old *babushka* in a doorway the woman turned away.

She continued into a section of town less heavily damaged. Thinking it a hopeful sign, Katya quickened her pace. In the next moment she spied another patrol several blocks distant. The snow lightened and she felt their gazes. She tried to remain calm, but the powerful undertow of fear threatened to carry her off. They were going to stop her. Her panic rose, her heart thudding until the only choice was to flee. They were still more than a block away when she reached a familiar intersection and took her chance. She turned sharply and disappeared around the corner. She heard them call out, but once beyond their sight she sprinted down the side street. Instinct took over, and she knew precisely where she was. She glanced over her shoulder as she turned into an entryway. They hadn't yet reached the corner. She raced through the empty courtyard and out the back entrance. The factory was just a few buildings away and the snow was a mass of hard-to-follow footprints.

Again, they yelled for her to stop. "*Devushka! Ostanovis!*" She was still out of sight and slipped around the factory to the loading dock. There was a maze of tire tracks. She pulled the door and slipped inside, catching her breath. Perhaps she could crawl into the piles of drab-colored wool blankets stacked halfway to the ceiling. As she looked in the adjacent storage room filled with huge spools of thread, she realized they might search the factory.

Instead of hiding, she went into the women's toilet where she took off her rucksack, coat, hat, and gloves. She brushed the snow off her face and work pants, and adjusted her scarf to cover her hair. She knocked the remaining slush off her boots and hid everything behind the toilet in a stall marked "*Zakryto*. Closed." Thank goodness for things in disrepair.

She crept onto the factory floor. One end was mechanized. When did that happen? She stared at the metal looms and the giant spools that fed them. Stalin had promised industrialization and here it was. In little Staraya Russa they were producing fabric by machine. Several workers operated the mechanical looms. A quick glance and she saw the manager's office upstairs on a small, open second story, with a clear view of both sections of the factory.

Katya's gaze returned to the factory floor, landing on the far side where two rows of wooden looms were as she remembered. Ever focused, the weavers sent the shuttles through the threads at a steady pace. She glanced at them, all women, searching for a compliant type who wouldn't question her. She walked silently behind the looms—pedals thumping, treadles clacking, and the rhythmic bumps of the beams—until she reached the last one. She tapped the youngish woman on the shoulder.

"Romashkin wants to see you," she lied, hoping the weaver would go to the manager without question. The woman relaxed her feet on the pedals and held the shuttle in one hand.

"What does he want? It's not time."

Katya shrugged. "He told me to finish up for you," she said, hoping, praying, not wanting to get into an involved conversation. The Nazis could come in at any moment. She pressed down the fear, trying not to give herself away.

The woman placed the shuttle on the edge of the loom and rose nimbly as if to confirm Katya's suspicion about her youth. Despite the dull cloth covering her head, she was pretty, with a smooth complexion and even features. Brown, wavy hair peeked out from under the scarf and cascaded down her back. The yellow armband almost escaped Katya's notice because she was focused on the woman's face. A face she thought she knew. Katya's mind started to jump down a rabbit hole of possibilities when she snapped back to the urgent present.

She could imagine the Nazis searching the courtyard across the street, entering the apartments one-by-one, looking for the woman who had disappeared. Soon they'd be at the factory. First, there was Romashkin. How would he react when this woman asked him what he wanted? Would he draw attention to her, bellowing for whoever had just entered his factory?

No one seemed to notice her brief interaction with the young woman, but Katya's fear fed her still powerful panic. She swiped at the beads of sweat on her face. The longer this took, the more likely others would notice. She was grateful weaving required a lot of concentration and the other women were intent on their looms. The shuttles were still moving back and forth and no one looked up. The noise was loud enough to cover a multitude of sins.

Katya watched the young woman climb the stairs to the open office. She gesticulated in Katya's direction, and the manager stood, leaning forward toward the floor, his eyes finding Katya, who gazed at him, her expression pleading. He nodded, maybe said something about how yes, he needed another weaver, and this woman was a friend of a friend. His hand gestures seemed to indicate there was nothing out of order when the Germans burst through the main entrance. He moved assuredly down the stairs to greet his unwelcome guests.

"Good afternoon, Herr Kommandant. Gentlemen. To what do I owe this visit?"

The three Nazis stepped toward him, one holding a rifle at the ready and pointing it indiscriminately—at Romashkin, around the factory floor, and up toward the office at the woman with the yellow armband. Katya picked up the shuttle and her feet found their place. She focused on the loom as the clack-clacks of the other treadles slowed. The weavers noticed something was going on. She strained to hear the conversation.

"A woman . . . this neighborhood . . . search the premises."

The manager replied, but she couldn't hear him. He waved an arm across the room.

With a quick sideways glance, Katya saw a soldier step toward him. He leered at the pretty woman standing rigid at the top of the stairs. The weavers had halted their work now, frightened and frozen at their looms. The soldier spoke in German, but Katya could tell by the way he licked his lips that he was making an insulting comment. The silent young woman focused on the floor and Romashkin ignored the soldier.

"Just organizing your order," said Romashkin, addressing the

The Communist's Secret 99

Kommandant. "We try to be precise." The Germans could relate to that. Precision, double-checking orders.

The man Romashkin addressed as Herr Kommandant said a few sharp words to the soldier who'd spoken out of turn, then walked up and down the factory floor with the grace of someone who belonged. He glanced at the mechanized section and sent his men into the back. The women at the wooden looms sat, heads down, hands folded in their laps. He ordered them back to their work. No one met his eye.

Katya started weaving in earnest, finding the shuttle fit comfortably in her hand and that her feet remembered the pedals. But as the Kommandant started down the row of looms, a thread broke. She knew what to do, how to fix it. She relaxed the beam so there was some give to the threads. His boots stopped behind her. Feeling his eyes, she tied a precise knot, so small it would disappear into the fabric, cut the ends and expertly returned to her pedals and shuttle.

"Excellent work, *Fraulein*," he said.

She knew she should acknowledge his compliment so lifted her eyes slightly and glanced over one shoulder but quickly turned back, afraid he had somehow recognized her. What if he had caught sight of her hair as she raced away? He came around the loom and she glanced up to meet his eyes. They were warm. His face was, of all things, kind. His hat caught her attention. The same fearful death heads she'd seen on the tank officer's collar points were on his visor cap. Such a strange contrast to his demeanor. She turned back to her work but he didn't move. She felt him watching her, wanting something. Finally, his boots click-clicked again along the cement floor.

After he finished inspecting the production areas and his colleagues returned from the loading dock and storage room, he addressed the foreman. Once again it was impossible to hear their conversation over the noise of the looms, but she could imagine he was telling Romashkin to keep an eye out for the woman they'd chased. Whatever the Kommandant said, she saw Romashkin nod in assent.

The Nazi turned on his heel and his junior colleagues followed.

From the way he moved and spoke, Katya could tell he was an important man, this Kommandant. Yet he didn't flaunt his superiority. The youngish woman remained frozen at the top of the stairs, gripping the rail. Romashkin waved her down, spoke gently and leaned close. She got her coat and left. The clacks of the treadles, the thuds of the pedals, and the slight whooshing of the shuttles again filled the space.

An hour and forty-five minutes later, the shift ended and the weavers readied their looms for the next day. With a wave or kind word to Romashkin or each other, they disappeared into the evening. The whirs and clicks from the mechanized looms stopped and that section emptied as well. Katya deliberately took her time, tidying her workspace and the loom until she was alone in the factory with Romashkin.

His dark hair stuck out from under his flat cloth cap. The gray stubble on his face didn't hide the wrinkles and folds of skin under his eyes and along his mouth. Grizzled but calm. There was a spark in his eyes, but his voice betrayed nothing.

"Tell me I won't regret that," he said.

ARKADY ROMASHKIN

November 1941

Katya liked him instantly. She sensed an undercurrent of empathy in his otherwise unemotional and straightforward manner. "I am sorry," she spluttered. "I have no papers and when they saw me on the street I panicked. I'm Belikova, Ekaterina Ivanova. Katya to my friends." She didn't offer her married name, Karavayeva, or that she had been a Communist Party official until several months ago.

"Belikova you say." His eyes glowed. "Are you from here? Your father isn't Ivan Borisovich?"

Katya nodded and stood a bit straighter. "Yes to both. I grew up here. My father worked in this factory until we left for Petrograd during the Revolution."

"Of course. I remember you spending time here with your papa. A good man, your father. He taught me everything, the entire business. Had a way of spotting those with a talent for weaving. Something about their hands, he said, although I've found it's an ability to concentrate that's most important. He brought me in because I could fix things." The wrinkles around his eyes deepened. "How is he? And your mother?"

"I remember you too. You always had a kind word for me." She looked down. "My parents both passed years ago."

"Accept my condolences." He didn't move, but his words and tone were so genuine that Katya felt almost as if he were embracing her. "Why are you here?" he continued.

Katya shifted about. Despite Svet's warnings, she was certain he

101

could be trusted. He hadn't exposed her, and he had spoken warmly of her parents. He handled the situation as if neither her appearance nor the Nazis barging in and demanding answers was reason for alarm.

"The Volunteer Corps on the Luga Line." The words popped out. After the attack, she and Svet never talked about it. Shattering that tacit agreement to silence felt courageous. "Built anti-tank trenches to slow the Nazis," she added. "When they attacked, I fled on foot." She stopped short of mentioning Svet.

"I heard it was a bloodbath. Filthy Germans. But you escaped."

"Yes. Lived off the land for a couple of months. Made my way here." She paused again, still unsure how much to say. "I thought to return to Leningrad, but it became clear that wasn't possible. With winter, I needed shelter. I stumbled upon the *kolkhoz*, nearly dead on my feet. Masha told me to come to you. Said you could be trusted. And goodness knows I need that." She fidgeted. "I almost stayed out there, but it's risky for Masha. I need papers, a job, a place to live. All I can offer is this." She pulled the bundle out of her rucksack. "Fresh rabbit."

A flicker of appreciation crossed his face. "Meat is hard to come by. The Nazis don't let us go far enough beyond the town to hunt." He took the bundle. "But you have more than this to offer." He nodded at the looms. "You know how to weave."

She shrugged. "I'm rusty." She tried not to sound too eager.

"You underestimate yourself. You fooled the Kommandant and he's no fool. Now that he's noticed you, I'll have to find a way to get you assigned. He won't forget you."

She could see his mind working.

"Good thing you didn't stay with Masha," Romashkin said. "Sooner or later the Nazis would've found out. You'd be in a labor camp. And Masha, well, they don't trust her even though she's harmless. They don't trust anyone," he grumbled. "Of course, we're used to that. Our own leaders don't trust us. They see treachery in every home."

His subversive statement shocked her into silence, and she struggled to hide her reaction.

"The Germans represent violent subjugation," he went on. "Terrible, yes. But not so different from what we're used to." The bluntness of his words increased their effect. He stared, waiting for her to say something.

"Our leadership has made some mistakes," she said, thinking especially of the last five years. The trials of old Bolsheviks. The culture of informants that permeated Leningrad. And probably everywhere else too. "But the Nazis want to destroy our nation, our way of life. It's not the same thing."

"True. It's not the same thing. But what excuse does Stalin have?" He smiled a tiny, sad smile. "According to him, people are nothing more than a simple commodity, some worth more than others. His five-year plans destroyed people and their livelihoods. Out here, things were simple. Family, church, a bit of land, a place to live. You need to understand what he stole from us—religion, resources, an entire way of life as you say. It's a wonder people are loyal at all."

She felt uncomfortable, queasy almost. But before she considered the truth in his words, the Party line jumped out of her mouth. "To move forward, sacrifices had to be made."

"That's all well and good until you're the one making all the sacrifices. People out here tolerate the Party. They accept Stalin because they have no choice. But they are loyal to their families, to their neighbors, to their heritage, to Russia."

"I am Russian too," Katya said with a sharp edge.

"I am not suggesting otherwise. You are loyal to the Motherland. But you're also loyal to the Soviet state—something not as widely shared as you might think. You need to be careful what you say. There are those who wouldn't hesitate to turn you in to feed their children."

She nodded. "Masha warned me. The Politsai."

"A strange mix of Russians and Estonians."

"And those people hate us," she said, recollecting how the Baltic countries came under Soviet rule only two years ago. Their citizens detested the Soviet Union.

"Understandable, isn't it? We take over their country, persecute them. If I were Estonian, I'd hate us too. And now they are happy to do the Nazis' dirty work, enforcing the occupation. And as for the Russians who've joined the Politsai, Stalin laid the groundwork by weakening our compassion and encouraging distrust. Rewarding it even. Instead of appreciating our neighbors, we turn them in. The Politsai grew out of that."

She felt sick to her stomach. He was right. People didn't trust each other. Stalin and the Party didn't care about the old *babushki* sweeping the streets, or the scientists in the laboratory, or the soldiers in the field.

"I guess it's good that I'm no longer a Party member," she said.

"Best you pretend you've never been one."

So far, she hadn't worried about her opinions. Neither Svet nor Masha discussed political matters. Like most Russians, they accepted things as they were. She hesitated. "Is that how you got this job? Denouncing Stalin?"

Arkady shrugged. "Didn't have to go that far. Lack of Party affiliation helped. And telling the Kommandant what he wanted to hear—that Stalin undermined loyalty when he took our farms and nationalized our businesses. But I also criticized the Politsai. Told him they couldn't be trusted." He reached inside his jacket for a cigarette. It had been rolled in a square of newspaper. They used newspaper for everything—the toilet, cigarettes, wrapping meat. He lit it, pulled deeply and offered it to her.

"I don't smoke," she said.

"That's good. The fewer vices the better. Tobacco is scarce. If you

The Communist's Secret   105

have the opportunity to get some, or vodka either, don't pass it up. You never know when you might need a bribe."

Katya thought of the bribes she'd often seen in a box in her mama's office—bottles of alcohol, packets of Stalin's favorite *Herzegovina Flor* cigarettes, imported sweets instead of ordinary Russian chocolate.

"After the dust settled in September, the Kommandant left me in charge here and ordered that we convert to blankets. I swallowed my disgust. Sometimes you have to dance with the devil. I helped your papa build this place, saw it taken by Stalin, and now by the Nazis." He shrugged. "After we defeat them, I'll be demoted again. Maybe the ultimate demotion."

Katya pursed her lips, and nodded her head ever so slightly. She knew if he refused to run the factory, the Nazis would get someone less devoted to Russia and more focused on saving their own skin.

"I support the war effort my own way," he said. "I am not an informer, a traitor, or a Nazi sympathizer. I'm a Russian patriot through and through and I'm going to help us win this war." He looked at his watch. "Curfew begins in an hour. Tomorrow I'll start on your documents and find you a place to stay." He moved toward the factory rear. "In the meantime, this way."

His honesty was powerful. And anyway, what choice did she have alone at night in a town full of Nazis? She dashed into the bathroom to use the toilet and grab her things. When she came out, Romashkin was carrying a cup of water. She drank half of it and followed him to the storage area. Folded and stacked blankets filled the space.

"You can sleep here tonight. But during the workday tomorrow you will have to use this." He pushed a strategic stack from along the back wall and popped open a panel revealing a space large enough for a couple of people. Katya wondered who else had been hidden there. "There's a torch," he reached inside for the flashlight, "but emergencies only. Batteries are impossible to find." He pointed at a bucket in the far corner. "You can't be seen, and there are too many people around during the day. Your presence has already raised questions. My girls are good people. They won't say anything. But we need to let today's incident fade."

He pulled a can out of his pocket. "You must be hungry."

She whispered her thanks.

"Absolute silence," he continued. "They patrol night and day. If you're discovered, it won't be just your life. I'll come first thing in the morning. Early. Before my workers arrive."

His eyes widened and mellowed, the bit of wonder in them warming her.

"Welcome home, Katya Ivanova. Who would have thought? Our Katyusha, back at her papa's factory."

THE TEXTILE FACTORY
November 1941

The blankets smelled like Aleksandr's heavy military greatcoat when he got caught in the rain. A familiar, musty combination of animal and earth. Nothing like the rotten swamp stench they'd been unable to remove from Svet's clothes despite the scrubbings and soakings. When she hugged the teen goodbye, the scent of decay was still there.

Before he left her alone in the storage room, Arkady shifted a gray and brown pile to reveal a space the size of a coffin. There was some comfort in realizing she wasn't the first person he'd hidden. Katya ate, and then shimmied into the claustrophobic space feet first. She'd be invisible unless someone was directly in front of the exact spot. If she had just a few seconds warning she could scoot deeper into the wool mountain and put a blanket in the opening.

Instead of exhaustion claiming her, Katya's mind churned as she waited for her anxiety to fade. Romashkin had quite a balancing act. He spoke to the Nazis as if he had nothing to hide, using openness to avoid suspicion. The invaders probably thought he was compliant and subservient, and that kept them from suspecting him. He reminded her of her father, another temperate man. Taciturn by nature, her papa always chose his words carefully, and he urged her to do the same. "Think before you speak," he would say, especially when he overheard her gossiping or complaining.

Despite her admiration for her father, most of the time she didn't follow his advice. Responding to others with reserve went against her instincts. In the moment—and there had been plenty of regrettably outspoken moments in her life—she had difficulty keeping her mouth shut.

Such were the thoughts buzzing in her mind as she breathed the thick smell of wool.

She startled awake to the sound of a dog barking. Nearly blind in the dark, she scooted out of the cocoon and spotted a faint light from one window. There were male voices now too. The light she'd seen disappeared and reappeared—a torch. The voices grew louder, as did the dog barking and its chain rattling. Could the dog smell her? Through the windows and door? She froze and remembered the empty tin of beef. She felt for the wall, and in the darkness ran her hands down to the floor where her fingers found the tin and the cup. With one hand on the wall, she made her way to the far side of the room and set them in a corner.

They were almost at the door when she crawled back into her hiding spot. The dog barked and pawed. Katya felt him straining to get to her. Guttural voices snapped in German. She pulled two folded blankets in behind her to fill the hole. Then, a loud crash and they were inside. She shrank into herself, remaining perfectly still as the dog bounded about the room, sniffing and barking. She held her breath.

A strident voice yelled and the dog squealed. The metal can and cup bounced. Another voice joined, sharp as glass. There were more reprimands and the sound of something being hit, followed by the dog yelping and whining. She imagined the torch playing around the room, over the blankets. There were more harsh words punctuated by the dog's squeals. They moved away, into the factory proper, and Katya breathed. But minutes later they returned, exchanged a few words and then the outer door slammed shut and they were gone.

Katya trembled. She loosened the blankets so air could get in, but otherwise remained in place, her arms drawn tight to her chest, her shoulders hunched up around her neck. She lay there, hoping for morning and for Romashkin. She dozed, but even the slight sound of a rodent scurrying along the floor kept her on the edge of wakefulness.

The next thing she knew, there were footsteps and a low mutter.

"Stupid bastards!" the voice said. "Katya. Are you all right? What happened?"

She pulled herself out and felt the catch in her throat but held back her tears.

"They came. With a dog. I left the empty beef tin right here. I'm sorry. I didn't even think about a dog smelling it through the door. I had just enough time to move it, to try to throw the dog off my scent." Blankets lay scattered about the room.

"Unfortunate," he said. "They've come before, never for any real reason it seems. To keep us on edge. But no matter, I already have a place for you. We'll go at the end of the day."

Katya exhaled her relief and nodded her thanks.

"Some food," he held up a bag. "And I'll get tea."

Katya washed her face and did her business. When she returned, Romashkin was restacking the blankets. He handed her a different cup. She sniffed at the steam. A hint of tea.

"We're short of everything," he said. "I have to reuse my tea."

"I went weeks without until Masha's." Katya said. "Before that it was boiled pine needles." She wrinkled her nose. "This is heavenly by comparison." One side of his mouth curled up in understanding, and she smiled and raised her cup.

They leaned against the blankets. Katya had taken off her gloves to enjoy the cup's warmth. The storage area was unheated and puffs of condensation formed as they talked. She had thought she'd try to hold back, but it wasn't possible.

"Can you tell me anything about Leningrad?" She did not mention Yelena.

His face darkened. "It's difficult. The city is cut off. Surrounded."
So, what Masha had said was true.

"There's no food. The bread ration has fallen to 125 grams for children and dependents. Higher for workers, but still grim." He paused as they both tried to imagine a city without food. "Frequent bombings since September. They destroyed the Badayev food warehouses and some power stations." His voice faded. "You have family there?"

Katya swallowed hard against the tears and nodded. Her darling Lenochka. Thank goodness Sofya had hoarded food as the war began. That smart old woman. The cupboards were bulging when Katya left. Still, how long would it last if the city's supplies had been destroyed?

"My daughter," she blurted out. "Sixteen next week. And her grandmother, my mother-in-law." She looked away, letting the bleak news sit. She saw Yelena and Sofya in her mind, huddled together in the apartment, perhaps reading by candlelight—they both loved books.

"Maybe they evacuated. There were trains all summer. Lots of children. Some factories and workers relocated too."

She breathed in the glimmer of hope. Yelena evacuated. Sofya could have seen to that.

Arkady reached over and rested a hand on her arm. They sat like that for some minutes until Katya changed the subject.

"So, these," she waved an arm over the muddy-colored stacks. "For the Germans?" She tried to wipe her face free of judgment. What choice did Arkady or any of them have?

He slurped his tea. "I don't like it, but by being on decent terms with the Nazis, I can do a lot of good. A different way to fight the war."

"But when it's over you'll probably be shot as a traitor." Katya closed her mouth so hard her teeth clacked. Why did she say such a thing? Arkady knew all that.

Romashkin drained his cup and set it on the floor. "Another example of our leadership's misguided policies." He spoke without rancor, then pulled his tobacco pouch from an interior pocket and pinched a few fingers full, sprinkling the precious, sweet-smelling tobacco onto a square of newspaper before rolling it tight and licking the edge so it would stick. He lit the homemade cigarette and inhaled. "So, you don't believe in fighting the Nazis from within. You think we all should have shot ourselves when they marched into Staraya Russa?"

Stalin demanded that of soldiers. Suicide rather than be taken prisoner. Did he expect the same of civilians too?

"I hope that doesn't mean you won't work in the factory?" Arkady said. "The Germans have seen you. There's really no choice now. Even if you disappeared from Staraya Russa, they would know I had covered for you. They would hold the entire factory accountable."

Katya understood what would happen to him, the young woman, the other weavers.

A wry smile momentarily lightened his otherwise grim countenance. "Perhaps in six months you can disappear, might be a partisan unit in the region by then, or another way to rebuild your good Soviet reputation. But for now, you've already joined the ranks of collaborators." The corner of his mouth twitched as he teased her.

"I'd never put you in danger," she glared. "I know right from wrong."

"And our own leadership doesn't. When the war is over, if Stalin chooses to punish those from the occupied territories, it'll be just another reason to hate him." His cigarette glowed in the dim light. "Unlike Stalin, I do not have the luxury of worrying about after the war. I have to face the present. I think eventually I'll join the partisans, but right now I'm valuable here. And I'm not going to live my life motivated by fear of my own government."

He took one last pull from his cigarette, ground the minuscule stub under his heel and picked it up. "Leave no trace."

Katya nodded. She and Svet had lived that way while on the run.

Arkady glanced at his watch. "It's time. Remember, silence. We need their memories to fade. If anyone asks, I'll say I was trying you out."

As Romashkin went to the factory floor, Katya used the toilet a second time, still processing everything. Arkady hadn't hesitated when she appeared, the enemy hot on her heels. He'd covered for her, distracting and soothing the Nazis with his unflappable demeanor. And even though his views about Stalin were decidedly unpatriotic, much of what he said made sense. She stretched for another minute or two and then pressed on the wall as she'd seen him do. The panel popped open. She grabbed the supplies he'd brought and crawled inside just as she heard other voices.

The building came to life with the taps and thumps of the looms and the distant thunder of the mechanized section. Whirs and clicks created a storm of vibration. The rumble echoed in her tiny chamber. She pressed a hand to her chest, feeling it even there.

She turned on the torch for a few seconds. The space wasn't very deep, perhaps four or five feet, but plenty long enough for her to lay down. The ceiling was too low to stand, but she could sit. She opened the bag and pulled out bread and cheese, then turned off the torch and ate. She lay on one blanket, covered herself with the other, and used her rucksack as a pillow.

Although exhausted from the previous night, her mind refused to quiet. Yelena and Sofya were trapped in Leningrad. They were both capable, but Yelena was light-hearted and happy too. She didn't have an iron shell like Svet. What would the war do to her daughter?

And her own fate? She, Katya Karavayeva, daughter of former senior Party official Marina Belikova, would now be cooperating with the Nazis. "Forgive me, Mama," she whispered, hoping Romashkin was right and there was more than one way to serve Mother Russia.

SETTLING IN
November–December 1941

She woke to a light knock and tapped back. The panel popped open. "Katyusha. *Ladno*? Good?"

"Fine." She offered a half-smile and clambered out. "Except I didn't want to use the bucket." She rushed down the hall.

When she returned, Arkady was leaning on a pile of blankets. She stretched. "I've arranged for you to stay with my sister. She lives on the edge of town, twenty minutes from here. And your papers will be ready soon."

Katya felt her anxiety fade.

He continued. "You'll work here, but that may take a while to arrange."

Despite what might happen after the Soviets won the war, she'd already started to make a sort of peace with fighting Arkady's way. Sometimes things were decided for you. She felt surprisingly content with the lack of choice.

Olya lived alone on the western edge of town. The simple home sat back from the street and was separated by a healthy stand of birches on one side and a small creek on the other, keeping it largely free from the unwelcome surveillance of nosy neighbors. A spacious garden sprawled behind the house, with woods beyond. The home's unique seclusion was obvious.

The wooden exterior was traditional, but it was a bigger version of the typical peasant izba. A heavy stove with a sleeping pallet on top dominated the main room—the exact space Katya had claimed as a child. But the similarities ended there. Numerous glass-paned windows lent light even when the days were short. A table with chairs and a small cot that doubled as a sofa filled the living area. A long window seat provided storage. An alcove to the right had become a semi-private bedroom. She noted a sink with running water.

Katya felt humbled by the woman's generosity. This was the second *babushka* who'd taken her in. She whispered her thanks as the woman gestured toward the curtained corner.

"Is it Olya? Or Olga?" Katya asked.

The older woman smiled. "Olga was my mother. She passed only a handful of years ago. I've always been Olya."

That first evening, Katya learned Olya's children had lived in Staraya Russa until the war scattered them. Both sons and son-in-law had enlisted: one in the south, two on the Moscow Front. One daughter-in-law had fled to Moscow where she had family, taking two of Olya's beloved grandchildren, but taking them to safety. It was unthinkable that Moscow should fall, but the fighting there was so intense that Olya's family had already evacuated to Kuibyshev on the Volga. The Germans would never get that far. The rest of her family—daughter, daughter-in-law, and their children—lived across town.

Katya waited for the Germans to forget about the woman they'd chased near the textile factory. Arkady didn't think the Kommandant would return anytime soon. The bigger risk was that she'd be noticed by a busybody, or worse, an informer. Until she had papers, she stayed close, going no further than the land behind Olya's to gather firewood.

One day, when Katya noticed Olya had only a few hundred grams of flour remaining, she gathered pine bark. She found a downed tree, then cut and stripped the bark and piled the wheelbarrow full.

"Bark flour?" the older woman asked as Katya dropped an armload of long bark strips.

"We can mix it with regular flour so the taste isn't so strong," Katya said.

"So clever," Olya smiled. "For a city girl. We did the same years ago, when the Party took most of our food during collectivization."

Katya held back, not wanting to get into another conversation about Stalin's policies. What she wanted to talk about was what was happening in the war. Before she began to probe, Romashkin arrived. The dismal look on his face made it clear that things weren't going well.

"*Privyet*, welcome, dear brother," Olya fussed over him, taking his coat and hat and gloves, and giving him the best seat by the fire.

He smiled and patted her cheek. "I wanted to come earlier, so I could visit and still get home before curfew," he said.

"Don't worry," Olya nodded at the sofa he often used.

"More troops are arriving in Staraya Russa. More demands and less food. I'm concerned people will be displaced from their homes." His mouth was pinched in a hard line. "Families might have to double up. And not everyone who has space will be generous." He stared at the floor, rubbing warmth from the stove into his hands. "I'm worried the last of the livestock will be taken. Right now, families with children get three eggs a week, but what if the Nazis requisition the chickens? And the cows. Less than twenty milk cows left. I don't like to think about what will happen if they take those." He sighed, a deep, weary sound.

Almost as an afterthought, Arkady turned to her, speaking softly out of habit. "But one bit of good news," he reached into a pocket. "This is yours." He held out her new documents. "And I have a spot for you at the factory. Sadly, one of my weavers cannot continue. You'll start tomorrow. Seven in the morning until six in the evening. Just report to the front door like everyone else. A short break for lunch. Olya will get your rations. It sounds demanding, but as long as we stay on schedule with our orders, there's flexibility."

Katya made a point of dressing like a local, but her striking looks were no help. In wartime, beauty was not a good thing. Despite her shabby coat and simple cloth *ushanka*, the Politsai always spotted her. Even from a distance, something gave her away—her height, the way she held her head. They tried to shake her down for food, money, or nice clothes, but she had nothing and the encounters never went well. Finally, she complained to Arkady. "I'll take care of it," he said. The Politsai steered clear after that.

The truth was, despite having been born and raised in Staraya Russa, she was an outsider. Her family had left more than two decades ago, and it was a strike against her. The locals had long memories. On the town's streets, people avoided her gaze and almost never offered a greeting. In the market, at one end of the expansive arcade in the town square, Katya was pushed out of line on numerous occasions, usually by a short, sturdy old woman who would hip-check her like a ruffian playing ice hockey on Leningrad's frozen canals.

Although she wanted to be accepted, she knew their coolness probably had little to do with her. After the terrible weeks of street fighting in August—and the Red Army leaving Staraya Russa to the Germans—it was no wonder people were wary. Perhaps they thought she was a Nazi informer or, closer to the truth, a rabid Communist, identifying those she could report as collaborators when the Soviets won the war. Katya realized it didn't matter why she was slighted or even whether the offenses were intentional. War was reason enough.

Olya and Arkady worked to melt the icy armor of the townsfolk. "Remember the Belikovs?" Arkady would say. "I worked for Ivan'ich until he left for Petrograd. A bit of a hero. Smuggled food when the Whites had the city surrounded." At the beginning anyway, the Revolution was for all of them and the common people sympathized with the Reds. Katya's own well-placed remarks also helped gain acceptance. "Nice potatoes," she said to the old *babushka* whose

The Communist's Secret 117

vegetables always had the dirt rubbed off and were arranged in neat rows or little pyramids that demanded admiration. "My uncle grew potatoes here. I used to help with the harvest. My cousins and I would race to see who could dig the most," she said. "Like searching for treasure." The corners of the woman's mouth turned up. This particular *babushka* was someone Katya wanted on her side. Not just because she was friendlier than most, but also because she was a good source of information.

Katya suspected the woman had a radio and that was why she knew things no one else did. Private radios were illegal everywhere, not just in cities like Leningrad. But they were easier to hide in the countryside. So this woman had hidden hers first from the Communists and now from the Nazis. Katya understood why she took the risk in order to get war news. It was deeply disturbing not to know what was happening. Katya befriended her, learned the names of her grandchildren, and frequently stopped at her stall. "*Novosti?* News?" was all Katya had to say, and the woman would pull her a few steps away to tell her the latest from the front.

It was strange, starting with a clean slate. No one in town knew how she'd betrayed her husband or that she'd been disgraced and expelled by the Party. Or how, before that, she'd led a charmed existence in a private apartment in a lovely part of Leningrad. Just a year or so ago, a colleague suggested her living arrangements weren't Soviet enough. In response, Katya let drop the fact that her husband's uncle had been Lenin's comrade—hinting their apartment came from that relationship. It thrilled her that her living situation was something that set her apart.

There was, of course, a price to be paid for Party status—a slavish devotion to Stalin, endless meetings and other activities that perpetuated the myth that the Communist Party served the people. When Katya was young, those functions made her feel part of something. As she got older, the Party filled a different hole in her life—the growing gap between her and Shura. Although it was crystal clear that the Party had become little more than a form of self-congratulations and a mechanism to exert control, more and more Katya felt it was all she had.

It began after baby Sasha died. She'd swallowed her grief and the chasm between her and Shura deepened. It became harder and harder to love. To make matters worse, they never talked about what happened. Keeping their pain to themselves was just what they did.

So, perhaps that moment not quite a year ago made sense. She had complained about her husband openly. Shura had not been at her side when she needed him most. He left her alone to watch Sasha die. He *should* have been more devoted.

She hadn't been surprised by the consequences. Not really. Envy was a staple in the Leningrad diet. When the secret police came a week after her misstep, pounding on the door and demanding Aleksandr, Katya knew she was paying the price for breaking the cardinal rule of life in the Soviet Union—never say anything that can be used against you.

She tried to cling to the lifeline of her Party connections by refusing to visit Aleksandr in prison, but the dominoes quickly fell and she was expelled from the Party—just one of the numerous consequences of her near fatal error. Her new reality was so bleak that she tried to block out what she'd done and went to bed every night hoping it would all go away.

Now here she was, in a bombed-out town under Nazi occupation where no one knew her past. Somehow, war had become the great equalizer.

ANNA WEISSMAN

December 1941

One thing that was entirely unexpected was her aptitude for weaving. Katya had been a novice weaver—a teenager—when her family left Staraya Russa. It was true that the single-color wool blankets they made at the textile factory had a straightforward pattern, but it had been more than twenty years since she'd sat at a loom. Yet it came back to her. Most days there would be a moment, sometimes several, when she sensed her father standing at her shoulder, instructing and encouraging. Those were minutes when the war disappeared and it felt like a simpler time.

And then there was the brunette who hadn't ratted her out. Anna welcomed her with a smile and some encouragement.

"*Kak dela*? How are things?" the dark-eyed beauty said.

It was a simple phrase that meant nothing and everything. It could be casual, focused on the everyday, or laden with meaning. "*Kak dela*?" to a coworker was a common enough greeting. To a friend who had a tyrant for a mother-in-law, it was "How are you surviving? What can I do to help?" To a woman recently chased by the Nazis, it was more. It meant be strong. Don't let them wear you down or weaken your resolve. It meant, this is our country and we'll find a way.

Katya could open up or brush her off. Anna's simple question did not oblige her to answer. But kindness did. And of the many things she owed this woman, kindness was the easiest to repay.

"I'm Anna," the woman continued. "Weissman." Her eyes flickered to the band of yellow fabric on her arm.

Katya ignored the woman's self-conscious glance. "Belikova, Katya Ivanovna. Nice to meet you." She dropped her voice. "I'm grateful."

"*Eto bylo nichevo.* It was nothing," Anna said. She had the warmest eyes. Pools of chocolate. "Would you like to walk a few minutes? Weather's nice."

Katya hesitated. There could be trouble: random stops by Nazi soldiers, arrogant Politsai, and the faint but frightening possibility that someone from Leningrad might recognize her.

"I love being outdoors," Anna continued. "But it's risky alone."

Katya nodded and took her arm. As a Jew, Anna had a lot to fear. And Katya already knew she was trustworthy. Before she even started at the textile factory, Arkady told her about the Jewish woman she'd tapped on the shoulder that day. Her father was a respected doctor who'd lived in Staraya Russa his entire career. Katya realized Anna's father was the one who had set her family's broken bones, reduced their fevers, and operated on her papa when his appendix burst. The Weissmans were good people.

The two women began spending most midday meals together. In all but the harshest weather they would bundle up and walk a few blocks to the river, chatting amicably. They both enjoyed the fresh air, and their meager lunches tasted better outside. Sometimes their walks transported Katya to Leningrad, to Aleksandr and Yelena. As a family they often strolled the city. On a free day, they might make an excursion to the countryside. They fished in the warmer months and ice skated on the city's waterways in the winter.

Katya had only ever had two kinds of friends: school chums and Party comrades. In all those relationships there had been below the surface pretenses and calculations of what could be gained or lost from the friendship. Her secret thoughts and desires remained

The Communist's Secret   121

hidden—not even Shura knew her doubts when Bukharin was found guilty a few years back. Similarly, she hid her distaste for the way the Party encouraged people to report on others. Her dutiful facade was always shiny and polished. She'd thought of her parents many times during the difficult years of arrests and trials. Her mother would have jumped on the purge bandwagon, pointing a finger at Bukharin and anyone else Stalin accused. But her papa would have been sickened by it all. He would never have supported what went on.

Katya's path was neither of the strong choices of her parents. She always dealt with her doubts and confusion by playing it safe. And safe meant revealing herself to no one.

It was different with Anna. Perhaps because she was Jewish and under terrible scrutiny. Or perhaps because in war they had a common enemy. Maybe it was just that Katya enjoyed having a friend. Whatever it was, she didn't keep things as close. She was herself and relished their little confidences and snippets of humor. Most of all, having a friend gave Katya strength.

Supplies were unpredictable in Staraya Russa. The town had been half destroyed in the August fighting. There were several residential districts which escaped somewhat unscathed—Arkady said that was one thing the Red Army did right, fighting primarily from the central arteries and business district to spare the citizens. The Germans had moved block-by-block, west to east, and south to north, capturing the town methodically. Finally, the two forces had dug in east of town on a line that ran up to Lake Ilmen, then followed the Volkhov River north to Lake Ladoga.

The townsfolk had hidden food and themselves in their cellars, and many garden plots had survived the persistent summer skirmishes. Now, some of that bounty—beets, turnips, cabbages—appeared in the market. Not today though. Only six kiosks were open and Katya saw nothing useful on offer: no food but potatoes, and nothing exciting like matches or shoes or coats. Katya always kept an eye out for a new coat for Svet.

Looking down the short row of stalls, Katya spotted Anna. From their conversations she knew the child at her side was her daughter.

"Nice to see you, Katya," Anna said. "This is Eva."

"Hello," said Katya. "Your mama and I work together. That's a beautiful coat."

The child took a half-step, her mittened hands patting the fine wool. "Thank you."

The coat was a gorgeous thing—scarlet, with a black velvet collar and cuffs—quite out of place in wartime. Out of place on the streets of a provincial town like Staraya Russa as well. More a thing you'd see in Moscow. Or Paris. Such elegant attire was hard to find in the Soviet Union. And bright colors were considered un-Soviet.

"Such an extravagance," Anna said, her voice soft. "But my mother bought it when Eva was a baby. First granddaughter. My sister has two boys, and my mother had been waiting for a little girl to spoil." She sighed. "She passed two years ago, before Eva could wear it."

"Oh," said Katya, glancing down, her mind spinning back through the years. "You must be very attached to it." She knew exactly what the coat meant to Anna. "I'm sorry about your mother. I lost my parents some years ago and I still feel their absence."

"Thank you. I'm sorry for your loss too. Such a struggle. My poor papa misses her so."

"How is your father?" Katya asked. They moved to the fringes of the market.

"Well enough," Anna shrugged and lowered her voice. "The Nazis have called him in on a difficult case. One of their generals has a strange malady. They're forcing Papa to treat him." She flushed and spoke rapidly. "Papa says he'll be executed if the general doesn't recover. And if he does recover, what high-ranking officer would want someone around as a witness to his having received medical care from a Jew?"

There were plenty of rumors about the Nazis' treatment of the Jewish population. The majority of Staraya Russa's Jews had been shipped west when the Nazis first took control. Those that remained were the ones deemed "useful." Like Doctor Weissman. Made to wear the yellow arm band, but still allowed to work.

"Terrible," Katya said. They crossed the street before going their separate ways. "Your father had no choice. One can hope the officer he is treating will do the right thing."

The warmth in Anna's eyes faded. She turned toward Katya and away from her daughter so the child couldn't hear. "Hope is about all we have left."

"Hope and friendship." Katya took her arm. "Do you think . . .? I'd like to visit your father sometime. Perhaps a short hello after work one day?"

Anna's eyes glistened. "You are a true friend. I don't know. It's dangerous for you to be seen with us."

"You shouldn't worry about me. A consultation with the town's doctor? Surely that's nothing out of the ordinary. Even the Nazis themselves seek him out for treatment."

Anna smiled. "True. I know Papa would love to see you. Someone from the old days. Let me ask what he thinks."

Katya nodded. "In the meantime, I'll see you at work." She waved to Eva. The little girl raised a tentative hand and cocked her head in a way that made her appear much older.

THE KOMMANDANT
December 1941

Katya was under her loom trying to fix a sticky treadle when the workday ended. She wore a workman's jacket over a thick wool shirt and a cotton layer. On the coldest days she pinned a wool blanket around her shoulders as a cloak and never took off her *ushanka*. A few of her fellow weavers wore heavy winter coats over work pants or long skirts with woolen undergarments. The factory had electricity, but heat was provided by two large wood-burning stoves. A couple of young boys, eight or nine perhaps, earned a few kopecks by bringing firewood to the factory. It was never quite enough.

The other weavers scurried to check their spindles and examine the fabric to ensure it was taken up cleanly, without wrinkles. The woolen cloth they produced was on the bulky side and didn't always roll smoothly. They ran their fingertips over the weft, checked the alignment, and saw to it that spare thread was within easy reach. After sitting so many hours, they rose carefully, their first steps halting, making them appear older than they were.

Before the war, this was the moment they would relax and exchange compliments or other remarks, inquiring about family. But there was little small talk now. If they dawdled, it might mean less food for their families, so they hung their aprons and hurried out. Several called farewell to Arkady, who grunted or waved from his office above the factory floor.

Anna stuck her head under Katya's loom. "Everything all right?"

The Communist's Secret   125

"An uncooperative treadle." Katya flashed a smile and sat back on her heels.

"I'd wait but I really need to collect Eva." Anna said.

Katya nodded her understanding. "You go ahead. I'll be fine. Perhaps Arkady can walk with me. But you should go before the streets empty."

After work the two women sometimes walked as far as the bridge together. Katya believed her presence protected Anna from serious harm. For all Katya's prejudices—toward the devoutly religious, intellectuals, and non-Party types—she didn't care that Anna was a Jew. She should dislike the Weissmans. They were not Party people. They weren't pursuing Soviet socialism. But they were hard-working, kind, and devoted to the community. Dr. Weissman served anyone in Staraya Russa. In Katya's view, his and Anna's actions were in accord with building a socialist state. Even though Katya was an atheist and saw religion as a weakness, she had a hard time believing it was such a terrible thing. At least not when compared to Hitler.

The door to the factory bumped shut behind Anna while Katya focused on the remaining sticky spot. She oiled it carefully, and then worked the treadle with her hands until it glided as it should. She turned to the pedals and placed scant drops where they attached, pressing on them several times, forcing the oil through the joints. She squatted on her haunches and removed the communal work gloves used for such purposes, then stood, a satisfied smile on her lips.

The factory was quiet and she called up to Arkady. "Ready to leave soon?"

He grunted. "Two minutes."

She disappeared down the hall to the toilet when the front door rattled open. The unmistakable sound of hard-heeled German boots clicking against the concrete floor echoed in the high-ceilinged building. Arkady greeted the visitors in his flawlessly neutral voice. They thudded up the stairs to the office. She couldn't stop herself from creeping closer. One voice possessed Arkady's authoritative calm, but demanded information about the partisans.

"You do realize there are no fighters within a day's walk," Arkady said. "And even if there were, they wouldn't think I'm on their side. I manage this factory. You purchase my blankets. Why would any partisans trust me? They think you're protecting me."

"And we are," said the clear, smooth voice. A voice neither angry nor disappointed.

"Yes, but as I've explained," she heard Arkady lie, "there are no partisan groups in the vicinity. The front line is close. Anyone wanting to fight would just join the Red Army. Second, even if there were partisans nearby, they wouldn't trust me. I work for you. Now, if you want information on the Politsai, I can probably help." The Politsai worked with the Nazis to control the local population. They'd turn in a neighbor for the smallest bribe.

"Still," the calm, accented voice continued in passable Russian. "I have no doubt you can make our lives easier. The partisans may be few, but this war will not be short. As it progresses, there will be pockets of opposition."

Pockets? Katya stifled a laugh. More like the entire nation.

The Kommandant continued. "You hear things, learn things. You will know when they gather and what they plan. And we'd like to know what you know. We will talk on a regular basis. An opportunity for both of us."

Poor Arkady. He had lost the argument. Dealing with the occupiers must be a huge weight. Katya retreated from her spot near the stairs and went to the toilet. She rinsed her hands and face after finishing and stepped back into the hallway where a mirror hung, convenient for everyone. As she ran her fingers through her hair, taming the strands, a figure appeared behind her in the glass. She inhaled sharply and turned. The Kommandant stood close, his wide-eyed puzzlement reflecting Katya's own reaction.

The Communist's Secret 127

"Pardon me," he said. He seemed comfortable speaking Russian. "I didn't know anyone else was still in the factory."

"I stayed late to repair a loom," said Katya.

His gaze was that of a man, not a soldier. Appraising, but also warm. "Kommandant Gerhardt Mueller. At your service."

Katya knew she should contain herself, smile demurely at his gallant attitude and kind words, but everything in her rebelled at the idea. She stared at him. At his epaulettes, at the iron cross at his throat, the leather gloves hanging from his belt, and the gun strapped on his hip. Everything about him conveyed a message of strength and superiority. In fact, it was true of all the Nazis. Did such things matter to them, or were they just weapons of intimidation?

"*Pravilno*? Really?" she said. "At my service? What exactly does that mean?"

Unfazed by her lack of courtesy, he explained. "It means that I will help you with any reasonable request."

She was breathing hard, angry at his calm. What right had he to be so cool and composed? "Will you leave our town?"

A smile played at his mouth. He seemed to find her insolence entertaining. "*Fraulein* . . .?" He reverted to German.

She responded in kind. "*Nicht Fraulein. Frau.*"

"*Izvinite, pozhaluysta.* Excuse me, please," he said. "I didn't mean to insult you. I wasn't presuming anything." He flushed, but then flashed a smile, revealing perfectly even, strong white teeth. The kind of teeth built upon good food and good medical and dental care. Unlike what she had grown up with. A sense of inferiority—her own and her nation's—enveloped her. She checked the hole in the back of her mouth with her tongue, glad it wasn't visible, and then regained her poise and returned his intent stare with an enigmatic one of her own.

"I apologize for my limited Russian," he continued.

How did he do that? Maintain a casual but authoritative air. The demeanor of someone who knows their position but feels no need to flaunt their superiority. "No apology necessary. Your Russian is excellent. But if you wish to be of service, you could start by getting your soldiers to pay the going rate at the market. Whenever they don't like the price, they threaten us or steal the items they want. It's miserable. People are frightened. If you plan to win the war and then govern fairly, you really should start now." Katya felt herself flush, her anger rising. "But perhaps I'm mistaken in my assumption—that you might want to govern fairly. Maybe you will simply rely on force. Seems to be a German habit."

His attention was complete. But the silence that followed her outburst, her insult, was too long. Why couldn't she keep her mouth shut? Restrain herself? It was coming. A labor camp—if she was lucky. Perhaps he would just shoot her. She dared to look him in the eye. But he didn't look like he was going to shoot her. He looked entertained by her.

"You have strong opinions. Outspokenness can be an interesting quality, but also a dangerous one. You're lucky to have chosen the right German to insult. I suppose that speaks well of you. You correctly judged my character. I am not easily offended. Especially in wartime." His eyes did not leave hers the entire time he spoke. They were a blue similar to her husband's. The same deep set. "Now, back to your point about my men's behavior, or misbehavior as the case may be. Tell me, what do you know of governance?"

She paused, trying to look thoughtful. She didn't want to overreact a second time. "Well, I know a thing or two about governments that don't value and care for their citizens. Russia has a long history of such neglect. The nobility treated everyone with disdain and condescension." She paused, trying to collect her thoughts for a balanced answer, an answer that wouldn't betray her personal perspective. "The Soviet state is also dispassionate toward its people. A devotion to Mother Russia is born in us. But loyalty has to be earned."

She didn't say that the Soviet state had long ago earned her loyalty. Her parents had thrived under communism and she had too, until her fateful error. She looked down, afraid he might see she was lying. When she raised her head, he was gazing at her in a way that made her uncomfortable. Listening carefully, and also assessing her somehow. Unruffled, he radiated energy, authority, and something else too. He looked like he wanted to reach out and touch her. He had perfect lips. For an instant she imagined those lips on her own. After a fraction of a moment she stopped, horrified. The Kommandant might be handsome, cultured even, but inside, he was no different from the pigs who had attacked her. Again, she raised her eyes in anger, only to find he was smiling at her in amusement. How dare he flirt with her.

"*Gospazha* . . . Mrs.?"

She still hadn't told him her name. She didn't want to tell him. Or rather, she wanted to tell him her real name. She wanted to say that she was Katya Karavayeva. And her husband, Aleksandr Karavayev, was one of the best tank commanders in the Red Army, and even now he was busy slaughtering the Kommandant's colleagues outside Moscow. She was breathing rapidly again, feeling light-headed, and then told him what he already knew, or could easily discover from any number of people in Staraya Russa.

"Belikova, Ekaterina Ivanova."

"Thank you. And please call me Gerhardt."

Katya shook her head. "You are Herr Kommandant. I cannot be on a first-name basis with you. People would make false assumptions." She smiled, not really knowing why, but perhaps to keep him on his toes, to keep him from getting the upper hand, to make him think about whether those false assumptions could become a reality. And she didn't want him as more of an enemy than he was. He could make life easier—for her and for others she cared about.

He didn't use the bathroom, even though that must have been

why he came down the hall in the first place. She had unnerved him, and flustered, he touched his hat and nodded. "I hope to see you again soon, Mrs. Belikova. And I'll look into my soldiers' behavior at the market. You are correct. We need good relations with the local population. Thank you for your comments."

Arkady hustled down the stairs as the door closed. "What were you two talking about?"

"I could ask you the same question," Katya replied.

"Pressuring me for information about the partisans. I told him I don't know anything, the partisans don't trust me, and anyway they aren't within reach of Staraya Russa. My life is impossible." In a rare display of emotion he started gesticulating, his hands flying about to emphasize his words. "Maybe I can hold him off, but if the partisan movement grows, I may have to give him something." He exhaled. "We'll see. Now, what were you talking about?"

"At first not much," she said. "It was an awkward attempt at pleasantries. But then he actually asked me what he could do to make things better. I told him about his soldiers threatening people in the market, not paying. He seemed glad to know."

Arkady nodded. "Helpful. Well done, Katya. And there was nothing else?"

"Well, he flirted. In a polite way." Katya looked down, feeling color rise in her cheeks. There had been something between her and the Kommandant. Something that shamed her.

"Be careful, Katyusha. Getting close to the enemy will not end well." Arkady had that look he got when deep in thought. He turned toward the stairs. "I'll get my things."

Katya still tingled from the long-forgotten pleasure of an appreciative gaze. She hoped the spark was just the loneliness of war and the depth of her longing for Aleksandr.

THE TRUTH ABOUT SVET

January 1942

During that last quiet hour before bed, Katya and Olya often spent the time sewing—mending, darning, or in Olya's case, doing a bit of decorative needlework. A single bulb dangled from one of the beams, and Arkady had put it on an adjustable cord so Olya could lower it for close work. They were lucky to have electricity. Using local laborers, the Nazis had repaired the power station that served the main barracks not far from Olya's. Russian workers were also forced to rebuild the main bridge across the river which the Red Army had destroyed.

One evening, as the two women sat with needles and thread, Arkady swept in amidst swirls of snow. He bolted the door and pressed the dirty cloth back into the crack at the bottom, then brushed the snow off his coat and hat and hung everything on the hook reserved for that purpose. His lack of greeting was out of character, and his dark countenance meant something was amiss. He had not come to drink tea, tell stories, or discuss the war.

Olya busied herself with his dinner and gave him space. If Katya could tell he was out of sorts, certainly his sister saw it.

At first, he said nothing but glared at his food like it was responsible for his foul mood. Then he raised his eyes. "Masha's daughter and granddaughter gave me some interesting news."

Katya's head snapped up.

"Mentioned they saw rabbit bones when they took her kitchen

132 Suzanne Parry

refuse out to compost," he continued. "Now, where would Masha get rabbit?"

Katya felt a warm flush rise on her cheeks. Olya stood, took the kerosene lamp, and disappeared to the outhouse.

"When were you going to say something?" The rare edge to his voice made it clear just how upset he was. "Her granddaughter said someone was there or had been there recently. Masha denied it but there were too many tracks in the snow." He paused, pushing his food around his plate with a fork.

"I was going to tell you," Katya began. The truth would have been unremarkable if she had told Arkady right away that she'd fled from Luga with another volunteer. But Svet had insisted she not reveal anything and so Katya held back every time it popped into her mind. Arkady and Olya were good people, but by the time Katya found her footing and was no longer on edge every moment, weeks had passed and the hidden truth took on a life of its own.

"After the Nazis caught them?" he said. The sharp words stung. "After they sent Masha to a labor camp for lying? After they decided that transporting them two hundred kilometers was too much work in the dead of winter and just shot them instead? Don't you realize that I can help? That I am the best friend you have here?"

"I should have told you. I'm sorry. It's hard to know who to trust." The excuse fell from her mouth even though Katya knew it wasn't a matter of trust. She trusted Arkady.

"I would have thought you'd have figured that out by now," he said.

She stared at the table. "Silence always seems the best choice."

Arkady was waiting for more from her.

"I escaped the Luga Line with a teen," she began. "We thought it would be best if she stayed with Masha. Svet, that's her name, she's sixteen and doesn't do well with people. She urged me not to tell anyone. She grew up living in the wild half the time to escape a

The Communist's Secret 133

violent home. She couldn't manage being cooped up in a factory or something." Katya waited for him to respond. The silence grew and she felt the enormity of her misstep. Letting Svet stay with Masha had been easiest for her, but not best for Masha or the town in general. If the teen was discovered, the Germans' distrust would grow and the locals would pay for that. "She saved my life more than once. Shoots as well as any soldier. Trustworthy and capable but her difficult family life has made her antisocial." Katya stopped again.

"She needs papers," he said. "If she hasn't already been picked up by the Nazis." He shook his head, disagreeing with Katya's decision to keep such information to herself. "I still can't imagine what you were thinking, or if you were thinking at all. Keeping secrets like this is dangerous. This isn't Leningrad. People aren't looking for reasons to turn on each other or file a complaint. Without papers she could be shot. And what about Masha? Putting her at risk like that. To say nothing of how it could bring the Nazis down on all our heads." He breathed hard through his nose, something Katya had rarely seen him do.

"Masha decided she could claim Svet was a cousin."

"Is that wise? There are people in town who would know it was a lie."

"I was thinking it was safer for Svet on the collective. That's the truth. A bit riskier for Masha perhaps, but much easier for the girl to stay out of sight. If she had come to Staraya Russa, she'd be dead by now. She'd have shot a few Nazis and been killed herself. She really can't tolerate people in authority."

He shook his head. Katya was silent. What she said was true, but that didn't change the fact that she should have told him.

"Sixteen, you say?" He sighed. "I'll arrange the papers."

"Thank you." Katya mustered her nerve. "Could I take the documents to her? Supplies too. Check on both of them and stay a night?"

"You haven't been here very long to be doing such a thing. Taking rations to someone you don't even know. But perhaps Masha's granddaughter can twist her ankle or something. Slip in the snow. She's reliable and won't tell the rest of the family. I can offer you up in her place. But the Nazis don't like changes to the routine. So, we'll see."

Katya waited for him to say something else, but maybe she needed to apologize again. "I've disappointed you." Katya said. "You're right about everything. Keeping things to myself, well, it's a survival mechanism. In Leningrad you can't trust anyone. No matter who they are. You can't even trust your spouse." A little cry hiccupped out of her throat and she swallowed to fight the burning and the tears. "I guess I'm not a very good judge of character."

"It's not about me being disappointed." His voice softened. "It's about protecting Masha and the locals. And you are an excellent judge of character. You read people with just a glance—like the way you picked out Anna when you came into the factory to escape the Germans."

And the way she'd known that she could speak bluntly to the Kommandant.

Arkady continued. "The problem is that in Leningrad you were surrounded with selfish people, people of questionable character, Party people. They became the standard by which you judge things. Out here, good people are the norm. You mustn't assume those who can improve your situation are good people. Remember, even the Nazis can make things better for you."

It was just before New Year's when Arkady gave Katya a bottle of cheap Russian champagne to celebrate with Masha and Svet, along with the teen's new papers. The champagne went in her rucksack with a few gifts she'd collected. She'd traded part of her rations for a tin of fish. They ate a lot of fish—frozen, smoked, occasionally fresh— one of the advantages of being so close to Lake Ilmen. But the oily canned fish was a hard-to-find New Year's tradition. Katya couldn't wait to see Masha's face.

The Communist's Secret   135

At half-past three in the afternoon, she rose from her loom and went to the toilet. Without saying anything to her coworkers—not even Anna—she put on her coat, took her rucksack from the storage room where she'd hidden it, and slipped out the rear door. She banished the fly of guilt buzzing in her ear. It didn't matter that she missed a bit of work. She often stayed later than the others so she could walk home with Arkady.

She left town the way she'd arrived. As soon as she reached the outskirts she turned away from the main road and the river, crossed a gulley, and faded into the trees. Residents were allowed to gather wood, mushrooms, and berries within a tight perimeter of the forest, but she thought it unlikely that she would encounter friend or foe as it was nearly dark. Besides, her papers were tucked in a pocket, and she was a legitimate town resident helping Masha with supplies. The fact that she had Svet's new documents sewn into her coat was the only real concern. And although she didn't want to part with the champagne, she wasn't above using it as a bribe. Perhaps the rare and much desired gift she carried for Masha—a hot water bladder to help with her abdominal discomfort—would deflect their attention. Women's issues, she'd say.

It was overcast and threatening more snow. The *kolkhoz* looked sadder than the first time she'd arrived—layers of snow and ice gave it a dejected appearance. Even the outbuildings seemed smaller. Vigilant, Katya paused, looking into the silence for anything sinister, and then strode to the front door.

She knocked. She wanted to call out, but instead stood shivering on the porch and rapped again, a bit louder. Just as she thought she heard a noise from within, there were footsteps from behind. Svet bounded from the darkness as Masha opened the door and the three of them embraced. They hugged longer that a normal greeting would dictate, all speaking at once. Katya found the faint rancid odor of Svet's coat comforting.

"You scared the daylights out of me," she grinned.

"It's good to see you too," said Svet with a slightly goofy but genuine smile.

"My Katyusha," Masha exclaimed. "We've missed you. Come in, come in."

They hung their things, still talking over each other. Masha pulled Katya close again, pressing her soft, ample body into the much taller woman. "My dear one." Although her words were happy, Katya sensed a deep sadness.

Her chin rested on Masha's head. "Masha, my sweet Masha. I've missed you so much." She pulled back. "You were right about one thing. Everything is difficult in Staraya Russa. Damn Nazis everywhere. Living by my wits again. As you predicted."

"So, does this mean you've smartened up?" said Masha. "Are you going to stay with us?"

Katya's face fell. "I can't. Arkady needs me. Have to be back tomorrow evening." Masha looked glum. "I know, I know," Katya sympathized. "But there's nothing I can do. He has to meet his quotas or who knows what will happen. I was lucky to get away at all." Trying to distract Masha, she reached into her rucksack and pulled out the gifts. "Look what I brought."

Masha's face brightened. She took the hot water bladder from Katya and without meeting her eyes turned to put it out of sight. In a moment she returned for the champagne and opened the back door to set it in the snow against the cabin. "Now you girls don't let me go forgetting that bottle. We don't want it to explode." She laughed, her good humor returning. "And we have rabbit. Thanks to Svet, we're eating better than anyone."

As Masha turned her attention to the savory meat and vegetables bubbling on the stove, Katya undid the stitching in the lining of her coat and took Svet aside. "Memorize your name. Tell Masha too. And have you thought about selling your pelts in the market? You can

The Communist's Secret

make a tidy sum. Although some of your customers will be Nazis. And you can't refuse to sell to them."

Svet's face turned dark.

"What are you two talking about?" shouted Masha.

"Svet has papers now. She can sell pelts in the market."

"She doesn't want to go to town," Masha dismissed the idea. "Better for my daughter or granddaughter to do it. The pelts will attract a lot of attention, and so will a new face."

The old woman had it all planned.

Katya turned to Svet and shrugged. "She's right."

"She's always right," Svet said.

THE RED COAT
January–February 1942

A day or two after Katya's visit to the *kolkhoz*, old Anya, the radio *babushka*, burst through the factory door, smiling and stomping the snow off her boots.

"They've done it!" she cried. "Our boys have done it! Moscow is won."

It was the Red Army's first victory in the war against Germany, the kind of news everyone had been hoping and praying for. The weavers stopped their work and rose as one, calling out their joy, hugging one another in celebration. Arkady came down from his office with a bottle of vodka. He locked the front door and poured everyone a small bit, and they toasted to the victory, to the liberation of their country from the invaders, to those who were fighting, to their families. The only one they didn't toast was Comrade Stalin, and even Katya didn't realize the omission until later.

For weeks, the victory had the entire town talking about Napoleon and the folly of would-be conquerors who underestimated Russia and her winter. The Nazis had been stopped outside the Russian capital thanks to the bitter cold and the rallying of the Soviet army. Winter—the eternal friend of Russia and enemy to foreign invaders. Katya's spirits rose to think about German soldiers dead in snowdrifts around Moscow. Perhaps the same was happening in Leningrad too. She no longer asked about her city. She couldn't think about what it might be like with no heat and little food. With bombs and artillery attacks. She simply decided that her daughter would

The Communist's Secret

139

survive. It was the only way to put one foot ahead of the other and keep the blackness at bay.

The intense cold aided the Soviet victory but held the entire region in an iron grip. A constant fierce wind came from the north. The Germans used local labor to keep the main roads clear, several of which had snow piled high along both sides and felt like tunnels. None of the citizens had access to petrol anyway. Side streets were rarely cleared although Arkady shoveled in front of Olya's and the factory. Pathways of packed snow and ice crisscrossed the town and allowed the citizens, and their occupiers, to get around on foot.

Katya settled into the winter routine, arriving at the factory before the faintest light lit the morning sky and leaving long after the town had again been plunged into darkness. And when she was on the street, she felt very alone. Winter's ferocity pierced skin and lungs like needles and drove everyone indoors. Even the Nazis pulled their hats down and coat collars up, moving briskly to get out of the frigid air as quickly as possible.

"Would today be good to visit your papa?" Katya asked Anna as they were organizing their looms and preparing to depart. The good doctor had agreed a short visit shouldn't be too risky.

Anna raised an eyebrow and stopped what she was doing. "You're sure?" Both women looked around, eyes flitting everywhere, landing momentarily on the two weavers from the mechanized section chatting by the door. They paid no attention to Katya and Anna but seemed in no hurry to go outside.

"We don't need to go over all that again," Katya whispered. "Besides, we often walk together as far as the bridge."

Anna nodded. "Papa wants to see you. But I still worry."

Katya looked at her, eyebrows drawn together. "I have a consult with the doctor. And anyway, are they really keeping track of everyone's friendships? Even with the Politsai spying for them it doesn't seem that they have sufficient manpower to watch all of us."

"You're probably right," said Anna, "but I don't want you to take any chances."

"You're not encouraging me to do anything I don't want to do," Katya said.

Anna smiled, dark eyes flashing. She grabbed Katya's arm. "All right then, let's get going."

"So, how's Eva?" Katya asked as they walked. "Such a sweet child."

"Thank you. She is delightful. Sometimes I wish she'd stay six forever." She laughed in the way of one who knew her feelings were both universal and outlandish. "I only have one, so I don't think I know much about what makes a child charming."

"That's not so," said Katya. "I have an only child too. She's sixteen and she's the easiest, smartest young woman. Being a mother gets better every year."

"That's good to hear. I always wanted another child, but it hasn't happened. And now . . ."

War put everyone's dreams on hold.

Katya leaned into Anna. "Our husbands are doing what they need to do. Be proud. Don't let the fear take over. Besides, you're young. Might still be time for another baby."

Anna's faraway look ended the conversation. They crossed the bridge and collected Eva from a house where she spent her days in the care of a former teacher.

"Hello, Eva," said Katya. "You look as beautiful as ever in that coat."

Eva grinned and Anna pulled a brown curl off the child's cherubic face.

"Look," the little girl said, and twirled so the elegant fabric rose and spread out a bit. A scarlet fan. "Isn't it the prettiest color you've ever seen?"

"It is indeed. It is the most beautiful coat in the entire world," said Katya.

Eva smiled with pleasure and took her mama's hand.

Katya watched the two of them and a wistful sadness pressed on her spirit. What she wouldn't give to stroll arm-in-arm with her Lenochka, chatting about nothing important. Perhaps teasing her about that boy she liked.

The home was modest, but they sat at a table large enough to accommodate six adults. Something from a happier time when Anna's mother was alive and her older sister still lived at home.

Dr. Weissman insisted Katya not stay long. A ten- or fifteen-minute visit could be explained away, but a longer one might draw attention. The Politsai prowled their neighborhood.

"Anna tells me you have family in Leningrad," he said as his daughter disappeared to heat some water. "Have courage. The Road of Life is running supplies."

Katya exhaled and nodded. "My daughter and her grandmother are resourceful."

"You must have hope," Dr. Weissman looked at her intently.

Anna got her warmth from him. "Here you are comforting me, and I wanted to ask how things are for you?" said Katya.

Before Dr. Weissman's silence became awkward, Anna returned with tea on a tray. The doctor smiled at his daughter and took his cup.

"Thank you, Anna," said Katya. She set hers down and motioned for Eva to step close. When the child came forward, Katya reached into her pocket with the exaggerated motions of a magician and produced a chocolate bar.

Eva's eyes grew large. She turned to Anna. "Mama, may I?"

Anna nodded, "Just a small piece now. Perhaps another after dinner." She turned to Katya. "You shouldn't have. So extravagant."

From time to time, Katya, Arkady and Olya shared a bit of their supplies with the Weissmans, but chocolate was a treasure.

"It's from Arkady," Katya said. "He wanted Eva to have it. You know how he is."

Eva peeled back the outer paper at one end, then meticulously pulled the inner foil from the chocolate. She broke off a corner then folded both the foil and paper back into place. She set it down and began to nibble her small piece. Her smile filled the room.

Dr. Weissman's eyes crinkled at the corners as he patted his granddaughter. He turned to Katya. "Thank Arkady for us. Such kindnesses make it easier. First, most of us were sent to a work camp and the rest forced to wear armbands. Then our children couldn't attend school. After that we were limited to certain stores. Now they've restricted shopping to Saturdays, knowing we must violate our religious laws to feed our families. It feels rather hopeless."

He tapped his wrist watch. "It's time, but first I want to give my condolences about your parents." He reminisced about their early days in Staraya Russa and the first time he met them. He looked so young they thought he was a student assistant rather than the actual doctor. It made Katya homesick. Watching Anna with her daughter and papa had already pushed her to the brink of tears.

"Thank you, and for your hospitality," she said, swallowing her emotions. "And how is your patient? The important one?"

"He's making a remarkable recovery."

"It must be a relief," Katya said. "What a strain. I'm glad things have gone well."

He was standing at the door. "Now hurry along, Katya," he said. "It's late. Olya and Arkady will worry."

"They'll be glad I saw you." She smiled as she put on her coat.

"Thank you for coming," said Anna.

Katya shook the doctor's hand and kissed Anna's cheek.

"Goodbye, for now. It was lovely to see you after so many years, Doctor, and to see you again Eva," she said addressing the precocious child.

"Thank you for the chocolate," Eva piped.

The Communist's Secret 143

"Little things mean so much," Anna whispered. "Thank you for indulging her."

"It's difficult to be a child now. We must do whatever we can for them." Katya nodded toward Eva but thought of all the children suffering across her country.

Anna's eyes glistened. "*Poka*. Bye. See you at work."

THE RAVINE

March 1942

It was too early for winter to be over, but one day in March Katya noticed the springtime smell of earth and wet stone and realized the cold weather would soon be nudged aside. This brought a slight shift in her spirit, which made Anna's sudden malaise all the more apparent. The two women sat together at midday, cups of warm water and a scant bit of food between them.

"Do you want to talk about it?" Katya asked. A lifetime of holding back and pushing her feelings aside made her overture genuine.

Anna's expressive eyes showed extra concern. "Papa is acting strange. He seems more worried than usual."

Katya patted her arm, not knowing what to say. Anna and her family—all the remaining Jewish families—carried a particular burden of fear. Every few weeks there was a new regulation, a new restriction on their lives like a slow strangulation.

Anna didn't show up at work the following Monday and Katya glanced at Arkady. From his office, he motioned with a single finger. His face was dark.

"They were rounded up before dawn," he whispered. "Market Square. Rumor is they'll be marched to the train station. Nobody knows the destination." As Katya turned away, Arkady hissed, "Be careful." She grabbed a blanket from the storeroom, tucking it under her arm.

In the town center, she stood at the edge of the shifting swell of yellow armbands. Perhaps a hundred and fifty people were gathered, milling about, clutching their belongings. A few toddlers whined and one or two babies fussed, but the group was subdued. Some looked confused, but most faces were stoic. The last of Staraya Russa's Jews.

Katya weaved through the modest crowd, looking for the Weissmans. Everyone was bundled up, each carrying a suitcase or satchel of some sort. She hurried toward a flash of red.

"Where are they taking you?" Katya said, gripping Anna's hand.

"They told us to prepare for a long journey. Maybe by train to some camp or something." She whispered as she said it, knowing how the Nazis would react if they heard her saying something like that.

"Is that all you're allowed?" Katya nodded at their small bags.

"Yes. That's why we're all bundled up." She patted her middle.

Katya's heart dropped, thinking how there weren't many reasons to prevent people from bringing more than a couple of changes of clothing.

Katya moved closer and Dr. Weissman took her arm and smiled wanly.

"Did something happen to your patient?" she asked.

The doctor shook his head. "Better every day. He'll probably live a long life. I hoped he'd feel an obligation to treat my family—all of us—better than this." He paused, his heavy-lidded eyes barely slits. "The Nazis never fail to disappoint, do they?"

Katya didn't answer, her mind churning with the possibilities. There were rumors of ghettos, resettlement camps, labor camps. But also of worse things.

Suddenly, more soldiers arrived and began forcing the crowd to stand.

"You must go," Dr. Weissman urged. "Now! Before they think you're one of us."

She nodded, even though she had her papers. She wore no yellow armband. The enemy was precise about such things: lists, records, paperwork. Fear for the Weissmans settled in her stomach like a stone. If she followed, maybe she could discover where they were being taken.

Anna took the blanket and sighed, a sad, wistful look on her face. They hugged long enough for Katya to feel the warmth of her friend's cheek against her own. She patted Eva, but couldn't bring herself to smile at the little girl, to pretend that everything would work out. Then she stepped away, standing outside the perimeter of soldiers, watching as the orderly crowd moved in the direction of the train station. As she started to follow at a distance, two soldiers approached.

"*Was machst du*? What are you doing?" One raised his rifle. Katya stopped.

"I want to know where they are being taken."

"*Verboten*! Forbidden!" He stepped toward her. "Go home! This doesn't concern you."

But it did concern her. She backed away from the soldiers, to the edge of the square where a handful of other citizens bore witness. After the crowd disappeared and the last voices faded, Katya returned to safety the way she had come.

Two days after she said goodbye to the Weissmans, Katya's unease became a spreading cancer. She pestered Arkady for information, but he knew nothing. She went to the nearly deserted train station to see what she could learn.

A new Soviet offensive had begun and was bringing the fight close to the city. Artillery fell with some regularity. It was dangerous to be out and about, especially near a target like the railway station. As she drew close, Nazi soldiers were visible in all directions.

Those guarding the entrance demanded her papers. "What are you doing here?"

Katya nodded toward the stationmaster in his booth across the lobby. "His wife is not well and asked me to bring this." She held out a basket of food. She trusted both the railway worker and his wife.

One soldier lifted the cover on the basket and then waved her in. The other stood inside the door, watching and listening.

The stationmaster seemed glad for a distraction, but his eyes scanned the space. "Nothing is moving," he whispered.

"But the Jews," she said, her voice a fearful hiss.

He shrugged. "Nazis have work crews everywhere, repairing the constant damage." His voice was a bare flutter. "With the Red Army on the move, the railroads are taking a beating."

Katya knew what kind of man he was by the smile twitching at his mouth. "Thank you," she whispered and left. If the town's Jews had not gone by rail, there seemed few possibilities. Either they'd been forced into a work gang, or they'd been killed. Katya could think of nothing but the talented, kindly doctor, her dear friend, and little Eva. She tried to push the worst of it from her mind and went to Arkady for answers.

"What do you think, Arkasha?" Katya asked during dinner that evening. "No trains have departed or arrived for days. Where did they take them?"

Arkady put down his utensils and gazed at Katya, his eyes tired and sad. "Plenty of rumors. Someone stopped me on the way home. Said he saw them being marched north."

Perhaps still in denial, the next morning Katya went to the market to see what else she could discover. She didn't want to believe the rumor Arkady told her. Marched north. What reason could the Germans have to take them to Lake Ilmen? And the only thing between here and there was the ravine. Her mind jumped. A place to hide the dead. Fear began to take hold, but she didn't want to panic or come to false conclusions as was her nature. Instead she wandered among the dilapidated stalls in the old arcade, listening for useful gossip. She made her way to the used coat vendor to rummage through the suddenly plentiful pile. Many of the coats were in good enough condition to work for Svet. Katya put one on to get the size right, and then counted her Reichsmarks to pay the merchant. It galled her to have to use the currency of the German occupiers, a constant niggling reminder of who was in charge.

At first she did not notice the Nazi soldier standing on the other side of the stall. And when she realized he was there, when he spoke to the vendor, she kept her head down, not wanting to catch his eye. She folded her purchase and started to turn away when he said he had a child's coat to sell. It struck Katya as so curious, so strange, that she stopped and turned and her eyes landed on the bright red woolen coat with black velvet trim in his outstretched hand.

Katya took two steps. Her free hand reached out in disbelief to touch Eva's coat. "Where did you get that?" She aimed her words like a dagger, hoping he'd start to bleed. The coat she'd just purchased fell to the ground, and she made no move to retrieve it.

"What did you say?" he snapped, and his eyes bore into her.

She stopped herself, grasping for the self-control that was slipping away. "It looks exactly like a coat I wore as a child," Katya lied, her fear of him now stronger than her shock and mounting rage. "Of course, it couldn't be." She stepped back.

"That's a coincidence. I took this from a filthy little Jew. She didn't need it anymore."

Everything was pushed from her brain but a roar. She wanted to kill him and, as ridiculous as it seemed, checked her pocket, wishing she were carrying the gun she knew remained in the forest. Her self-control was fading and she stared down. If she looked at him again, she would launch herself at his face and use every bit of her strength to tear out his eyes and strangle him. Or so she imagined.

She stared at the bright red wool in the Nazi's hands as he haggled with the vendor. She memorized his face with the slightly too large ears and bad skin and made a silent vow.

The ravine was far enough from town that no one would see or hear the evil. It was six or seven kilometers north, halfway to Lake Ilmen and, according to Arkady, now served as the demarcation line between the Red Army and the invaders. It was entirely off-limits, and she was a fool to go there. It was quite likely she would run into the Wehrmacht, who would shoot her on sight, or Soviet soldiers, who would arrest her and shoot her later as a spy. Yet she could not stop herself. The powerful magnet of hope pulled her forward.

She remembered it as a long walk, uncomplicated until one reached the start of the small canyon which quickly became steep—thirty or forty meters deep in places. The rocky outcropping that marked the beginning was easy to find. Images terrorized Katya: the soldier yanking Eva's coat as the little girl screamed and struggled, Anna trying to defend her daughter. Perhaps Anna died first. Katya hoped she didn't see her darling daughter murdered. No one should see their child die.

Katya's hands clenched into tight balls as she walked along the ravine's edge—at first hardly more than a ditch, but deeper with every step. She drew great breaths to stop the growing pain in her gut as her body recognized what lay ahead even as she tried to deny it. The trees were thick and the ravine grew wider. In late winter, the path was slick with ice, snow, and the mud created by hundreds of feet.

Her eyes blurred as she drew close to the deepest section, tears disobeying her desire to remain calm. She wiped her face with the back of her wool mitten, leaving slimy streaks of mucous. And then she exhaled to force the tears to stop. She needed to register everything, understand everything, bear witness to what was about to reveal itself. She crept along the edge, grabbing at tree branches to keep from losing her balance.

The first splashes of blood weren't the bright red she expected, but browner and darker, marking trees and rocks and snow at random.

Still, there was no mistaking what it meant. Her mind emptied of all else save the horror of what she knew had happened.

Scattered personal items appeared—shoes and clothing and eyeglasses. Ahead and away from the edge was a large pile of belongings. Opened suitcases. She turned back to the brink and listened, wondering if anyone was still alive. A baby. A child perhaps. Eva. They might have missed a youngster. The little girl could have tumbled over the edge in the struggle over her coat. Maybe their bullets missed her and she'd fallen into the ravine with the rest of them. The thought lodged in her head. Could she reach the bodies? She walked back and forth along the precipice, calling out, "Is anyone there? Please, someone answer."

The ravine was steep—but she took a few steps down between boulders, holding onto a branch and then squatted. The sounds were ordinary. Wind through the trees. An animal moving about. The shriek of an occasional raven. She saw the birds then, at the bottom, already at work on the bodies. *Caw-cawing* as they wheeled before diving down onto a victim. Hopping from body to body. Pecking and tearing at soft exposed spots—the eyes.

Furious, hysterical, she grabbed stones and tried to pelt the birds. "Get away!" She screamed. A few flew off or hopped away, but she wasn't close enough to succeed in dispersing the scavengers. Enraged, she reached for another stone and lost her balance, sliding down, bumping against boulders until a tree stopped her fall. Her head hurt. An ankle was wedged at a strange and painful angle.

She was amongst the dead. They were everywhere and all around—lodged against trees and rocks and shrubs and each other. The three or four closest to her had been shot in the head. She tried to stand but vomited instead. She sat, waiting for the waves of nausea to pass and called for Eva and Anna and Dr. Weissman until her throat was raw. She stepped among the bodies, carefully placing each foot, her ankle painful, shooing the ravens and looking for her friend.

The Communist's Secret 151

Even the tiny children had been shot. She knew what she would find, somewhere in that ravine, but still, she could not stop herself.

She stepped over the doctor's body first. He lay face down, but she recognized his curly gray hair. She took off her mittens and put them in a pocket, then exhaled and leaned over the man who had done nothing but heal and help everyone in his path. She knew he'd been dead several days, but forced herself to touch his neck. Her hand sprang back from the unnaturally cold flesh.

A bit further on, Anna's lifeless eyes stared at the sky. Her once lovely brown curls were matted with blood and Katya rolled her over so the birds couldn't get at her beautiful face. Katya took Anna's cold hand and held it, wishing warmth into it, pressing it to her cheek as she wept with despair and rage. What fear Anna and her papa must have felt when the shooting began, when they knew beyond any doubt, beyond any hope, that they were going to die.

And where was Eva? Anna would want to be with her sweet daughter.

She was wedged against a boulder a short distance away. There was no blood on the child, but her head was twisted at a horrible angle and it was clear her neck was broken. It took all Katya's strength to lift the little girl. The weight of her, the life that had been in that body, made Katya cry again, big loud gasps of anger and pain. She stepped slowly toward Anna and lay Eva alongside her mother. She managed to tuck the once delightful little girl awkwardly under her mama's arm and turned her unmarred face toward Anna's. Her friend's words came back to her. *Now she'll always be six.*

Katya thought of her own child, also frozen in time by an early death. Little Sasha was forever a happy one-year-old and she had to live without him, without seeing him grow to adulthood with children of his own. Years had passed but the pain could still pull her under. Her mind jumped to other possible losses. Yelena. Aleksandr. She wept for all of them, sitting in the cold by Eva and Anna, broken by their senseless murders and the bleak future. She knew she should go, but wretchedness had stolen her will. And what did it matter if they came for her? She was already dead inside.

She waited in the growing dusk, then finally clambered on her hands and feet and knees out of the steep ravine. At the top, mud-covered and wet, she paused, waiting for the strength to carry on. Her eyes fell upon the gun casings then, scattered like some kind of morbid confetti. She reached for one, tucked it into a pocket and began the long trek to Olya's, hearing nothing but the rustle of the wind and the argumentative birds of prey returned to feed on the corpses.

THE ROMASHKIN HOME
April 1942

Katya stumbled through the back door hours past curfew, disoriented, barely aware of the time or where she was. Olya and Arkady sprang from their seats, faces full of fear and relief. "I'm sorry," she mumbled. But there was no scolding about the risks of violating German regulations. Hot water was already on the stove. Olya made tea and signaled to Arkady to heat more water and fill the tub. Then he disappeared into the bedroom while Katya stripped off her filthy, wet clothes. She sat in the warm water while Olya worked the soap through her hair and soothed her broken spirit with long-forgotten childhood songs.

Clean and warm, Katya curled on the sofa. When Arkady joined them, Katya stood and fumbled through her dirty clothes, pulling the single shell casing from a pocket and setting it on the table. She looked at them through eyes still clouded with images.

"The ravine. All of them," she said, the words thick and heavy in her throat.

Arkady took her hand, his expression fierce. "All is not lost, Katyusha. We cannot stop the Nazis from their butchery, but slowly, we will make them pay. Our chance will come." He patted her hand. "They have overextended themselves, of that I'm certain."

It was what she wanted and needed to believe, but his words provided no comfort.

The following week, the thud-boom of artillery began in earnest. The Red Army was attacking, and it was rumored they planned to liberate Staraya Russa. An explosion shook the house so hard the dishes rattled.

"So the Nazis' *Klein Berlin* isn't so secure?" Katya said. They all hated the nickname the Nazis had given Staraya Russa. Arkady said it was just a bit of psychological warfare. An effort to destroy the town's resolve. Staraya Russa sat in the jaws of the two armies. To make resupply difficult for the Germans, the Soviets reduced the train station to ash with an artillery barrage. Maybe it was a good thing, but Katya couldn't help but think of the stationmaster.

More and more she considered her own role in the war. The Soviets were holding their own against the modern and efficient German army. She could be part of that rising tide.

"What about the partisans?" She asked Arkady.

"Still none anywhere close to us," he said. "Might be a few small groups of boys and old men hiding in the forest, but no serious effort. Best to wait until the resistance grows."

With no possibility of joining the guerrilla fighters, Katya continued to focus on discovering useful information. The Red Army had gone quiet again, and one early morning she ventured north of Olya's, in the direction opposite the factory and near the edge of town where she came upon a swath of land under development. She hid in a stand of birches. Eyes could be following her in the pre-dawn darkness, studying her comings and goings, waiting for her to say something to the wrong someone. Russians were notorious busybodies. To say nothing of the German patrols out at all hours. But as the first hint of dawn arrived, the site was empty. The moon glinted off low-slung tin roofs. The once empty land sprouted concrete and wood. She turned and hurried to the factory, sensing an unusual buzz of activity on the streets.

Arkady was alone when she entered. "Something's up," she hissed. He put a finger to his lips and motioned her to follow him to the office.

The Communist's Secret   155

"Yes," he said. "And it's more than just some additional soldiers. We're to be a divisional headquarters. New barracks, and they've also begun confiscating homes for the officers."

"How convenient." Katya spat the words. Had the Germans slaughtered the town's Jews just for their homes? *Lebensraum*, indeed. Arkady patted her shoulder in sympathy.

"It's a good sign," he said. "The Red Army has retaken land east of Staraya Russa, and some to the south as well. A military failure for Germany, and in order to deal with the setback, they are sending more soldiers and new leadership."

"Maybe a good sign, but more misery for the town," said Katya. She stood on the stairs, still holding her coat. And what would this mean for Masha and Svet? Would the Nazis harass the two women? According to Masha's granddaughter, it had been quiet out on the *kolkhoz*.

She went to her loom as the other weavers arrived. The slap of the treadles was slow and forlorn against the news. Agitated citizens began to arrive in a steady stream. It was lunchtime when Arkady took her aside. "I'm on the list. I need your help to move out."

He spoke in low tones as they left the factory. "They told me that my home would be used for the general officers. As if I should be thankful to have high-ranking soldiers living there. As if it makes me special."

"They come in and take whatever they want," said Katya. "If they want our support, why don't they treat us better? That is the point I made to the Kommandant."

A wry grin appeared on his weathered face. "Dear Katyusha, sometimes your naïveté is startling. Stalin did the same thing in peacetime with collectivization. What explanation is there for what he did to the wealthy peasants? And why on earth should we expect the Germans to treat us any better than our own government?"

A part of Katya wanted to challenge Romashkin, but she had

watched him with admiration all morning. The way he conveyed authority without the slightest evidence of emotion. He communicated civility and empathy with a nod and a downward glance, the slight raise of one corner of his mouth, a questioning eyebrow, a warm, penetrating gaze. When he had every right to be angry or speak harshly, he was instead supportive. He was kind to his workers and attentive to the constant steam of townspeople looking for help. The effectiveness of his manner was a thing to behold. His steady words but deferential demeanor provided him much of what Katya had worked for but never achieved—the status, authority and perks of a top Party position. Romashkin commanded more respect than she could ever imagine receiving—even if she became a senior Communist official.

It was difficult to argue with him and she struggled to defend Stalin. "But in Stalin's case," she said, "he was trying to improve our lives, improve our nation. Nationalizing allowed him to determine priorities, to push industrialization. Where would we be without that? No advanced military. We'd already be part of Germany."

"Oh yes, the ends justify the means, and all that," he said. "Nevertheless, Stalin's policies came at great cost. He could have pursued nationalization without the radical and swift stealing of wealth. He could have prevented the starvation that came with collectivization."

She wasn't going to win the argument. And besides, he had a point.

As they approached the Romashkin family home, Katya worked to contain her surprise.

She'd seen grander places in Leningrad, but out here it was striking in both size and finishing detail. Arkady never spoke of his parents, but Olya had mentioned their father had been someone important before the Revolution. A landowner of some sort? A role in the community that explained this home. Along the second story,

The Communist's Secret   157

beautiful decorative carvings hung like wooden icicles. The first story windows had similar elaborately carved shutters. There was an entryway, whose very existence set the home apart. Just past that on the right, French doors led to a library. Most amazing was the telephone sitting on a mahogany hall table. Even in Leningrad, only the very well-connected had their own phones. Arkady wasn't even a Party member. The phone said a lot about his position in Staraya Russa.

Along the stairs to the second floor, the balustrade was also decorated with fine woodwork. To her left a formal parlor had uncomfortable looking chairs and a sofa flanked by dark brocade draperies. The room looked so stiff and uncomfortable that she couldn't see Arkady ever using it but imagined it would suit the Nazis just fine. A dining room was behind that. The hall went straight back to the kitchen and a toilet. To Katya, the house seemed a quaint bourgeois artifact from a lost era. Odd because its occupant, although not much of a communist, certainly wasn't a person to put himself above others.

He and Olya conversed softly, discussing the home's contents. After a quick peek around the first floor, Katya stood in the entry, trying to suppress her reaction and waiting for directions. She stepped into the library, perhaps the largest room in the house, which held a desk at one end and a large table with chairs at the other. Three walls were lined with books. Two windows facing the table interrupted the flow of the shelves, but in a way that was symmetrical and pleasing to the eye. Books always made her think of her mother-in-law, although this library was several times larger than Sofya's collection.

She walked along the shelves and looked closely at some titles, feigning interest.

"Do you enjoy books?" Arkady had sidled up.

She flushed. The topic had long been a sore spot. Katya always felt somehow inadequate among the Karavayevs. They were all bookworms. Even Yelena. Not that they ever said things to make her feel she was flawed because she avoided reading. Rather, their few comments seemed to suggest she was missing out. That books contained something special.

Examining the spines, she recognized a few Russian writers, but most of the volumes were unfamiliar. She could continue to pretend she was at home in a library, or she could tell the truth.

"I wasn't raised in that type of family, to read for pleasure I mean. My parents worked long hours. Even more so after we moved to Petrograd. Once there, reading seemed frivolous. Also, they didn't have much formal learning." She glanced down to avoid Arkady's eyes. The fact that she was embarrassed by her parent's lack of education shamed her.

"Frivolous," he repeated. The word seemed to roll around his mouth before he expelled it like a piece of grizzle too tough to chew.

"Not all books, of course. And I read plenty at university: revolutionary philosophy, social didacticism. But literature?" She shook her head.

"Yet you can learn much about human nature, about the human heart, from literature."

Katya looked down for a moment. "Yes. I remember several of Chekhov's stories."

"Did you ever read Tolstoy's *The Death of Ivan Ilyich*?" He didn't wait for her to reply. "Possessions and self-interest aren't worth much according to Tolstoy. Compassion for one's fellow man is far more important."

"I'm not sure about that," she said. "I mean, yes, self-interest must be sublimated to the needs of the community. Society is more important than the individual."

His eyes twinkled, "How else can the socialist state be built?"

He was poking fun at her again. He pulled the Tolstoy off the shelf. "Perhaps you'll want something else to read." Reticence bloomed on her cheeks. "Don't worry," he continued. "There's nothing controversial about Tolstoy."

The home was organized and uncluttered. No doubt Arkady had prepared for this day.

Important papers filled a satchel, family photographs went into a trunk with his clothes. He'd lived alone for years, widowed young, and knew where everything of import was stored or shelved. Katya thought it unusual for a man to be so attentive to detail. But then she recalled the way Aleksandr arranged things: shoes polished and in a particular spot in the armoire, uniforms always cleaned and pressed and hanging above them. He was even that way with his chessboard, securing the pieces after playing.

Arkady had already collected everything that had to do with his only child, the son who had joined the Red Army in June. The Nazis didn't know of Arkady's personal connection to the war, and he relied upon the loyalty and goodwill of the townsfolk to protect that information. Many were in the same situation, and it was as if the community had a pact not to divulge such things. Neither a slave to the Nazis nor a puppet of Stalin—his reputation as a man who put the common people first protected him.

That would never happen in Leningrad where people had nursed at the breast of the revolutionary Motherland, where they'd been nourished by the gruel of paranoia to believe serving the state meant keeping their eyes and ears on their neighbors and colleagues, senses heightened by a lack of decent food and sufficient living space. Maybe in small towns people looked out for each other. But in the cities, envy greased the machinery of the socialist state.

Arkady worked with the efficiency of someone who'd anticipated the moment, selecting the volumes he wanted for himself and those that might get him into trouble with the new occupants. "These we'll take to Olya's," he said, pointing to several stacks on the table. "And these," he motioned to a nearly full box on the floor, "we can't leave here. The Germans wouldn't approve." Katya regarded the volume in his hand: *All Quiet on the Western Front*, by Erich Maria Remarque.

"An anti-war novel of the last war," he said. "Banned under Hitler, but I'm just an ignorant peasant so how would I know?" He flashed a lopsided grin and returned it to the shelf.

After they filled the wheelbarrow and took a first load to Olya's, Katya walked with him back to his house for the questionable books.

They slipped across the river to the town center. Most days, taking a box through town by wheelbarrow would have drawn the attention of numerous locals who fashioned themselves keepers of important information. Today it was the norm. People scurried about, everyone distracted by their own urgent tasks, relocating and moving things. The Nazis barely glanced their way. At the school, Arkady carried the box down an empty hall. He led her to a supply closet and stacked the volumes—spines toward the back—on the top shelf with a few cleaning materials. He gave them a last pat, no doubt hoping they'd still be there when the war was over.

Back at their childhood home, Arkady and Olya took a final look around. Katya followed them into the library where Arkady placed a bare hand on the polished table, his eyes sad and soft, the loss inscribed in the lines of his face.

"My grandfather made this," he said. "Already survived several wars and revolutions, but maybe not this time."

Survival was indeed the question. Not of sentimental pieces of furniture, but of Russia herself. Many in Europe, when faced with the force of Nazi Germany, had chosen subservience, even enslavement, rather than risk national annihilation. The French came to mind. Katya knew that would never happen here. The Russian people would fight to the last. Pride welled in her.

Olya and Arkady leaned together. Olya patted her brother's arm and he gave her a small hug. Katya recognized in the set of his jaw a

The Communist's Secret 161

grim understanding that the Nazis would ruin what remained of his family's legacy. He would never reclaim this home.

He set the key on the hall table and pulled the unlocked front door shut behind them.

CAT AND MOUSE

Summer–Fall 1942

Although Katya looked forward to summer, in wartime it passed with an oppressive sameness. She hoped Svet would sell rabbit pelts in the market and she'd get to see her friend from time to time. Instead, just as Masha suggested, her granddaughter took on that task. Katya didn't need an explanation to understand that Svet didn't want to come to town where she might easily say or do something to draw the Nazis' ire. The *kolkhoz* was still the safe choice, but Katya missed both the teen warrior and the warm, nurturing *babushka*. Her world grew smaller and smaller.

And despite Arkady's best efforts, the Nazis refused to allow the locals to go to the collective farm and plant wheat or other staples. The German view was that everyone would have to manage with their own backyard garden plots, from which the Nazis would take what they wanted.

Like the majority of locals, Katya and Olya planted an enormous garden. Masha's granddaughter had given them seed to put in wheat which was nearing maturity. Golden stalks shimmered in the sun and rustled in the breeze. Every time she went to the privy, Katya took a moment to appreciate the view: an expansive and meticulous green and brown garden backed by a small field of wheat and the forest rising up behind.

She thought about Kommandant Mueller with a confusing mix of hatred, curiosity, and attraction. Could she learn anything useful if she spent time with him? Could she trust herself? She remembered

162

The Communist's Secret 163

how he'd looked at her with a captivating half-smile on his lips. But that was months ago. The idea that she might get close and use that proximity against him seemed increasingly outlandish until he appeared at Olya's one muggy summer evening.

Katya was kneeling in the dirt, using a finger to draw a series of short, shallow rows and drop tiny black seeds spaced exactly right so as not to waste a single life-giving speck. Radishes grew quickly and these were a second planting. The garden included potatoes and onions of course, but also green beans and cucumbers, carrots, cabbages and beets, and the perennial summertime favorite—tomatoes. While she worked, summers with her grandmother flooded back— the correct depth and spacing and how much water was necessary. The garden had become Katya's refuge, the place she went after work to do something productive, and the place she felt closest to her daughter who was at that exact moment quite possibly doing the same thing in Leningrad. According to Anya, the radio *babushka*, the citizens had turned the city's parks into vegetable gardens. From the huge Summer Garden down to the tiniest patches of green around the lampposts along the Nevsky, people were digging in the dirt.

A rustle along the side of the house alerted her that someone was approaching, and she stood, brushing the dirt off her hands. The Kommandant appeared. He removed his visor cap, smiled, and stepped toward her. In one hand he carried a beer. Drops of condensation trickled down the bottle.

At first he said nothing, clearly less self-assured than during their previous interactions. He nodded but did not move closer as his gaze roved her body. Katya knew she looked good. She hadn't yet reached the age when things started to sag and she was firm and shapely, even if thin. The old, lightweight cotton dress she'd thrown on after work showed her taut legs and nice arms, but also clung across her breasts and at her waist. Tired of wearing a kerchief, she let her blond hair hang in a loose plait. A few tendrils had escaped and framed her face.

"It's a warm evening, and I thought . . ." He held the bottle out, like an offering.

Katya smiled. "I'll get glasses." When she returned, he was still in the same spot.

Why was he so nervous? She motioned to a couple of log rounds and they sat. He filled the glasses, the golden nectar frothing to the rims. Such a rarity, but it also made sense that the Germans would have beer. They had everything. She sipped and dropped her guard. She forgot entirely about the ravine and the other horrors that bore his imprint. Instead, when he asked her about life in the Soviet Union, she talked of fishing. Of drinking *kvass* in a tiny town near the *dacha* her family used every summer. She laughed about the difficulties of daily life like waiting in lines, but made no mention of the fear or the arrests that were also part of everyday life. And she certainly didn't tell him the truth about her daughter. Or her husband.

"I wish you would have told me sooner that you like to fish. I would have been delighted to take you out on Lake Ilmen."

"There's still time. The season isn't yet over." Plenty of locals hustled for the coveted fishing jobs in the warm months. Katya remembered how far away the war felt when she and Svet hid on the lakeshore. What a gift to be on the lake, in nature and away from the occupation.

He sighed. "The next months are especially busy for me. But if I can't manage a day away, I daresay the war will still be going on next summer, so perhaps we can do it then."

"I certainly hope not." She paused, annoyed at herself for letting her first thought slip out. "I didn't mean . . ." What did she mean? "I meant I hope the war ends. But if not, then yes, I would enjoy a day of fishing."

She told herself to relax, treat him like a potential suitor rather than the enemy. She paused, and then changed the subject. "So, what about your childhood?"

He told a few stories about mountain climbing and hiking in southern Germany. He shared how he ended up as an army officer. They sat close and she found herself thinking how good he smelled. There was no sourness of an unwashed body, just the clean scent of soap. Even his hair was washed.

"But let's not talk about me. Or the war. How about books?"

Another man fond of reading. Exasperation rose in her. She wanted to say that she much preferred going to the theater or cinema or walking along the Neva River to reading a book. But she didn't want him to know her that well. She took the easy way.

"I'm reading Tolstoy, like everyone else. *War and Peace.*"

"I don't think it's his best. You should read *The Death of Ivan Ilyich.*"

The same book Arkady had suggested. The very book sitting on a shelf in the cabin. "Oh yes, Tolstoy presses his position on morality, doesn't he? Better to be a good person, than to pursue things." She stopped for a moment. "It seems strange that you would like such a book. War, domination, murder. If Tolstoy were alive today, he would not be a Fascist."

"Neither would he be a Communist," countered the Kommandant.

She pursed her lips, trying to tamp down her annoyance at his remark. She didn't want him to have time for another retort. And she was uncomfortable with the entire situation, sitting with him, sipping a delicious beer as if there were no troubles, having a charming flirtation.

Arkady chose that moment to come tramping through the back woods as if to rescue Katya from the dilemma of enjoying herself when she shouldn't. The Kommandant rose to leave.

"It's just about curfew," she said, also standing as Arkady nodded at them silently and entered the house. "Thank you for coming. For the conversation and beer." She picked up their glasses and turned to go inside.

"A most lovely evening," he said, compelling her to turn back.

She wanted to get the last word, to have the upper hand over him. Again, there was that unruffled look on his face.

"We must continue this conversation." Now he was smiling, almost poking fun at her.

"You are perplexing," she said.

"Exactly the word I would use to describe you. Goodnight, Frau Belikova." He placed his hat on his head, nodded, and went around the side of the house to the street.

Inside, Arkady sat with an expectant look on his face. Olya hurried to the privy and Katya wondered how long she had been waiting.

"How captivated is he?" Arkady asked.

"He's difficult to read. Attentive, but seems most interested in talking."

"Talking is good. Would you rather he try to bed you?"

Katya sighed. "Of course not. But I want to find a way to use his attraction against him."

"Kommandant Mueller is not the type to think with his dick, excuse my crassness. He is a calm, intelligent man. I suspect he's drawn to you not just because you're beautiful but because you say what you think. He's surrounded by sycophants, enmeshed in a culture that demands conformity and offers obedience to Hitler at all costs. He's drawn to you because you challenge him. Because you represent a different way of thinking." He rolled and lit a cigarette. "Don't worry, he'll be back."

"Do you think I can get information about the war, about German plans and operations from him? Anything that might help us?"

Arkady shrugged. "He doesn't strike me as someone who would accidently reveal secrets to either a friend or a lover. But being close may create possibilities. At the very least, it may keep you safe."

There were no guarantees that pursuing some kind of relationship with the Kommandant would result in anything, but there was the possibility. And in wartime, that was something.

THE TURNING POINT
Fall–Winter 1942–43

September had always been Katya's favorite month. As a schoolgirl, she made sure her pencils were sharpened every day. Sometimes she got paper from the stationary stall in Gostiny Dvor to cover her favorite school books and protect them from wear. In that "before" time, she loved the way everything returned to normal come September. Summer holidays meant days spent swimming and fishing, staying up late with the long light, laughing more, eating more, drinking more. But September replaced those carefree days with something even better: an atmosphere of possibilities and new beginnings. A time for work and industry and school. Even the rhythm of daylight finally felt right and Katya no longer rose in the wee hours.

She yearned for that aura of possibility. War had stolen everything except the way the brief northern summer lost its heat and the days grew short. Katya and Olya harvested. They picked berries and made jam. They pickled cucumbers and green beans. They filled baskets and barrels with potatoes and beets and loaded carrots, cabbages, and onions into the root cellar. They cut their wheat, placing a sheet on the ground and banging the wheat stalks to release the berries which they ground into flour. The work felt urgent. They hoarded what they could before another bitter winter fell on them like a wolf upon an easy meal.

As the harvest came in, there was something else in the air. Rumors spread about the war in the south. Katya saw Nazi soldiers strutting about, relatively good-humored and full of themselves. What else could it be but that the war was going well for Hitler?

The Germans and the Soviets were facing off in Stalingrad, a southern city far from Leningrad or Moscow. The entire nation held its collective breath as the titanic clash of armies raged. The Nazis had the upper hand, but according to the radio *babushka*, as October became November, the Red Army began to turn the tide, meter by bloody meter. Arkady said it was the battle that would decide if the Soviets would live free or die.

Much like a fatal illness, that single word—Stalingrad—was on everyone's lips. And while all thoughts were on the elbow of the Volga, suddenly partisan fighters began striking the Germans to the south of Staraya Russa. Those little victories made life more bearable for the war-weary civilians, but especially for Katya who had seen very little of the Kommandant and was frustrated over the lack of opportunity to help the war effort. He greeted her warmly when they saw each other, but there was nothing beyond a few friendly exchanges. Just as he'd said, his position was challenging. Occupying the Soviet Union was a demanding job, she thought bitterly. With a bit of luck, Katya would find a way to make it even more demanding.

The January news from Stalingrad was blissful, like the first soft snow of the season. The victory was won. The Red Army had Nazi General Paulus and his troops surrounded. Katya thought about how Leningrad had suffered and was elated to think of those thousands of German soldiers on the plains outside Stalingrad, freezing to death with nothing to eat. Although she didn't know where Shura was, she'd often imagined him leading a tank unit on the plains outside the city. Even before she learned of the victory, thinking about him in Stalingrad did not fill her with dread, but with pride and gratitude and love, buoying her aimless spirit in a way she hadn't felt since long before all this started. The more she imagined, the more she missed him.

On her way home one early evening after work, Katya came upon the Kommandant standing in the entry to a nearby building, alone and smoking a cigarette. He leaned against the wall, looking for all manner like he belonged. She nodded and smiled as she approached, vowing not to talk about the war and also not to insult him.

"Would you mind if I escorted you home?" he asked.

"And if I did mind, would it matter?" she said, argumentative despite her intentions.

He burst out laughing. "You are so unexpected, Katya Belikova."

"Well, it does seem a bit silly to pretend that I have much say in anything. You are the invaders. We are the conquered. Even if only for the time being." She looked directly in his eyes when she said that last sentence, so he would know she knew the Nazis' luck was running low.

"You have no reason to worry. If I wanted to force myself on you, I could have done that months ago. I think you already know I am not that type of man. I suppose what I want is some conversation, a distraction from the war. I want to think for some minutes about something other than death. And perhaps I also want for you to have a good opinion of me." He seemed untroubled by the news from Stalingrad.

She was struck by his honesty. "Why should you care what I think?"

"You are a discerning, intelligent person. I am surrounded by those who don't think or question. The occasional confused patriot like myself. But you, Katya, belong elsewhere. Refined, educated, and beautiful. I imagine you in a Paris or Berlin."

She could use this, if she could control her temper. "Leningrad— where I lived some of my life—is also such a city."

"So I've heard. Some of your country's greatest writers and scientists call it home."

That was true before the war. But what was left of Leningrad now?

Were its beautiful buildings piles of stone and dust? Its waterways clogged with the dead? She took a calming breath before responding. "An exciting and challenging place, intellectually. After moving to Shishkovo I missed it." Lying felt like a small source of power when otherwise powerless.

"I could never live in a small town," he said. "Even in Bavaria where I grew up. Small town life is filled with peculiar challenges— boredom chief among them. And I don't find the German peasantry any more appealing than the Russian."

"Rural dwellers aren't inferior. They are just less educated and less worldly. It's simply a matter of interest, education, and opportunity."

"True, but both our leaders view plenty of people as inferior. Yours murders hundreds of thousands in remote death camps."

"Yet Stalin is not responsible for this war," she said. "Hitler is entirely at fault. And any nation that goes to war must possess a moral justification for doing so. Hitler has none. Belief in Aryan superiority is not a moral position. He is crueler and more barbaric than Stalin. Perhaps two peas in a pod, but Hitler's end of the pod is rotten as well."

"I see I've lost this argument," he smiled. "And that is why I enjoy your company."

Katya ignored his compliment. She teetered close to defending Stalin further, but feared he would think her a Communist.

"And now, if you'll excuse me." More aggravated than grateful, and without waiting for a response, Katya turned on her heel as they approached Olya's. She moved swiftly away while thinking of the smile on his face—neither smug nor self-satisfied because he was not the sort of man who enjoyed the difficulties and frustrations of others.

Ten days or so passed before she saw him again and she had convinced herself that her rudeness had put him off and that it was

The Communist's Secret 171

simply too difficult to get close to him. When the opportunity presented itself, she couldn't control her tongue. But then she saw him in a dark corner of the market, partially hidden from view. He seemed to be waiting as she approached.

"Shall we walk?" he said.

"It will give everyone the wrong idea." Anything more than a brusque exchange in public risked undoing all the goodwill she had built with the locals.

"Meet me on the other side of the water tower." He nodded toward the stone structure rising at the far end of Market Square, the main public square in town, and turned away. She continued through the long building of the arcade with its graceful arches—where the actual market operated safe from the elements.

When they were beyond prying eyes, she spoke with her usual hint of exasperation. "I don't know what you want, but I cannot help you. And this is dangerous for me."

He chuckled softly. "You wonder why I enjoy your company? It is this boldness, this rashness in your speech. Laced with humor. I find it both entertaining and charming." To provide her a cover he snapped loudly in German and grabbed her arm. When they were out of sight, he relaxed his grip. "Come, let's sit a moment in this alleyway." It was a deserted spot. "No one will see us here. And I promise not to put your virtue in question." His eyes sparkled. He motioned her to sit on a step.

He aggravated her. Charming and interesting and handsome as well. There was no way for Katya to reconcile those contradictions with his role in subduing the Soviet Union. "What you have done, are doing, to my country." She stopped. She wanted to confront him about the ravine, to ask if he was responsible. But she also wanted to get useful information from him.

He reached into the satchel hanging from his shoulder and withdrew a thermos. He opened it and poured a brownish liquid into the cup. Steam rose and she recognized the heavenly smell of hot chocolate.

Mesmerized, she stared at the metal cup he held out to her. She could not help herself and removed a glove so that the warmth would seep into her fingers. She avoided his eyes, but felt his gaze on her, examining her face and taking in her reaction.

She raised the cup to her lips and drank. The flavor overwhelmed her in the best of ways. Rich, creamy chocolate with a hint of peppermint. Exquisite. Better than anything she'd ever tasted. Again, she sipped and then closed her eyes. She was in Petrograd, before it became Leningrad. It was the winter of 1921 when the city had just started to come alive again. There were hundreds of street urchins still, but the civil war was being won by the Bolsheviks and slowly, the old, magnificent city of Peter was coming back to life.

She was seventeen and ice-skating on the canals—she and her mama and papa. Laughing, cheeks rosy from the cold and the exertion, they unlaced their skates as the light faded. A special moment made even more so when they arrived at their apartment and her mother disappeared into the kitchen busying herself at the stove. By the time Katya changed her clothes and snuggled into her favorite corner of the sofa her mama appeared with three glasses on a tray. Glasses filled with chocolate melted into steaming milk.

Lost in the memory, she had forgotten the man sitting next to her, until his eager face turned and he said, "Do you like it?" She ignored his question, wanting to stay in the past. She sipped over and again, slowly, until the cup was empty and the memory gone. She extended it to him like a chalice, still unable to meet his eyes. What did he mean by giving her something so rare in the midst of war?

"I took the liberty of adding a bit of schnapps." He refilled the cup and drank. "I love hot chocolate with schnapps in winter and thought . . ."

He stopped and she was on her feet before he could tell her what

The Communist's Secret 173

he was thinking. She looked at him. "It is very kind of you, very generous." Her voice was unsteady. "But really, I cannot help. You must understand. The only people I can tell you about already work for you."

His expression conveyed neither surprise nor indignation. She stared at him for a long moment as the realization settled. He was simply being nice. He didn't want anything from her. In fact, she was the one that wanted something from him.

Finally, she smiled and he raised the cup to her in farewell. She hurried away casting one last glance as he sat, still sipping from the cup, perhaps trying to recall a memory of his own.

THE NOOSE TIGHTENS

February 1943

Over the next weeks, the Kommandant checked on Katya with increasing frequency. He made no advances. He didn't probe about the partisans or anything else. He made no attempt to press her for the information he hadn't been able to squeeze out of Arkady. If they were trying to use each other, neither was making any headway.

So, she waited. She believed Arkady when he encouraged her to be patient. "Remember, war is a long game," he said. "You'll recognize the opportunity when it appears."

One evening, perhaps thirty minutes before curfew, there was a knock at the door. This late, it couldn't be good. Arkady opened it.

"May I come in?" Kommandant Mueller's voice surprised Katya.

Olya and Arkady disappeared into the bedroom to save her the embarrassment of asking them for privacy. Even though they knew her motives, she was still ashamed of her relationship with the Kommandant. Whatever that relationship was.

He understood her discomfort. "Shall we take a short walk?"

She bundled up and took his arm. In his other hand, he carried a torch. There were few lights in town after curfew. He got right to the point. "The Nazis know partisans are operating in this region. Things will get worse for the townspeople if the attacks continue. We have new orders. To retaliate against those we can," he said.

Startled, she stopped. "You can't mean civilians?" His reply was silence, so she pulled away. "Please take me home." She gathered her thoughts and then faced him at the door. "What about Olya? Arkady?"

The Communist's Secret 175

"I'll do my best," he said, "but I cannot promise anything."

Would he protect any of them? Her? She disappeared into the house without saying goodbye, her thoughts now on Masha and Svet. They were in grave danger. The Nazis would accuse them of helping the partisans, of feeding and sheltering the fighters.

"What happened?" said Arkady.

"New orders. Retribution for partisan attacks. We're all in danger, but especially Masha and Svet."

Arkady agreed that Katya must warn her friends. The two women would have to come to Staraya Russa. Masha could stay with her daughter-in-law and Svet with them. They talked about the supplies on the *kolkhoz* and Katya planned that she and Svet would store some in the forest to retrieve later. Lastly, they all hoped the Kommandant would not come looking for her while she went out to the collective to warn her friends.

Katya started at first light. As she walked, she worried about Arkady, pestered for months for information about the partisans. This might be just the time to make an example of a prominent local.

"Katya!" Svet beamed from behind the door. Masha added a gap-toothed grin and Katya hugged them one after the other.

"It's good to see you," Katya said. "How are you managing? Germans pestering you? Any of our boys skulking around?"

"No Nazis. And after last winter's counterattack, I haven't seen a single partisan."

Katya hung her coat and propped her feet near the fire. She tried not to let her anxiety control her words, but her fear was right there, on the surface. "I have news." She winced. "Everything has changed. There has been some partisan activity to the south. The Nazis plan to punish locals if they can't find the guerrillas. You need to move into town. Both of you."

She was breathing hard. Masha's face fell and Svet's eyes were dark.

"This is the first place the Nazis will come," Katya continued. "You're not safe anymore. Arkady said it's imperative that you leave the *kolkhoz*. Immediately. Today."

"Oh, Katyusha, I can't leave," Masha said. Katya's eyes begged Svet for support.

The teen let out an audible sigh. "Masha, I know you don't want to go, but it sounds like there's no choice. We'd be the first the Nazis accuse."

"That's right," said Katya. "They need to show results. Sending you two to a labor camp, or worse, would be an easy way to do that."

Svet nodded at Masha. "You and I, we're easy pickings. Going to town makes sense. We won't be singled out there."

Masha sagged. Katya came and knelt by the old woman. "You'll be with family. It won't be so bad. Please, Masha. Arkady is certain that if you stay here, the Nazis will fabricate something and make an example of you."

"Damn war." Masha gave a weak nod. "Filthy Germans."

While Masha gathered her things, Katya and Svet loaded the wheelbarrow with supplies.

"Thanks for convincing Masha," Katya said. "I know this isn't easy for you, but staying at Olya's won't be bad. Her home backs up to the forest, although you won't be able to go far."

Svet shrugged in reply. "I've been expecting this. At least we will be together."

Katya gave Svet a half-hug. "I've missed you."

Svet pushed the wheelbarrow along the rough, icy path to the forest to hide the supplies and check her traps. Katya turned back to help Masha.

A strange, out of place sound caught her attention as she neared the cabin. A motor. Tires on snow. She dashed the few steps to the privy. A car door slammed. Then two more. In the still, winter morning every sound was an exclamation.

The Communist's Secret 177

In the outhouse, Katya pushed on the false ceiling and the boards popped. It was another hiding place Masha's sons had built to keep food from the Communists. She wedged herself up and slid the planks back into place, petrified for Masha facing the Nazis alone. She heard only a faint rumble of voices. Probably Masha explaining that there was nothing suspicious going on. *I don't know what you are talking about. Svet is hunting. It's what she always does.* Then came the crash of dishes. Masha would be trying to assure them that she and Svet were alone as always. The next sounds—Masha crying out, a few thuds—made her wince.

Legs folded and scrunched up on her elbows, Katya pressed close to the tiny opening at one end of the peaked-roof outhouse. It gave her a narrow view along the row of outbuildings all the way to the forest. She couldn't see the cabin at all.

Svet appeared in the distance. Nearing the barn, she stopped and set the wheelbarrow next to one of the outbuildings. She moved stealthily toward Masha's izba and crouched just shy of the end of the barn—a few steps from the open space in front of the cabin. Katya imagined the Nazis accusing Masha. *You're hiding something. We know you have sons in the Red Army.*

Masha would remain steady. She would say that having sons in the army didn't make her a communist or a fan of Stalin. It only made her Russian.

There was more yelling and Masha cried out. Would they want names? Masha had no information to give. Sure, there were partisans in the forests, but Masha didn't know who they were. *There aren't any partisans here. Look for yourselves.*

The cabin door slammed.

Two of them entered Katya's line of sight with their black jackboots, dark, heavy wool coats, and black leather gloves. One went to the barn. The other came straight her way. Katya went rigid, refusing even to blink, all the while wondering what Svet would do. She would never let them take Masha. Svet wouldn't hesitate to kill three more Nazis. She might not even think about the implications. Then the Germans would hunt them down. And they would retaliate against the locals. The possibilities grew darker as the seconds ticked past.

The outhouse door rattled open, and the entire building shook when the door banged shut. Katya heard one of them breathing and muttering something. Then she heard the stream of piss and a sharp ammonia-like smell reached her. In a few moments, the door bounced closed again and footsteps crunched in the snow. She gasped for air, then peeked through the tiny window and watched him walk toward the barn. She hoped Svet wouldn't do something foolish.

If she stayed calm, there might be no problem. The Nazis knew she lived on the farm. But if the Germans tried to take them, things wouldn't go well. It was fight or flight for Svet.

The possibilities spun round and round. Svet's pistol should be behind the peat pile, where she kept it. Together, they could kill the soldiers. And then what? They'd be on the run. Masha too. But what alternative was there?

Katya hurried out of the privy and crept to retrieve Svet's spare pistol. She shimmied along the far side of the house until the entire scene was revealed. They had tied Masha to the porch. Svet approached, no rifle, her hands in the air and the bag filled with her morning's work bouncing against one leg. The soldiers were tense, agitated, rifles raised, telling her to stop, which she did in the middle of the circular drive.

"Are you all right?" Svet asked Masha, who nodded. "Let her go," Svet continued. "She's done nothing. And neither have I." She took small steps, hands raised. She was frightening close. Just a few meters from the officer. The two soldiers were between Katya and Svet. All three Nazis had weapons drawn. The young ones might go off half-cocked and start shooting.

"Yes, yes, I know who you are," said the officer. "But you and she are in contact with the partisans, sheltering them, feeding them." Katya wanted to yell at them, the idiots. There were no more than a few handfuls of partisans around Staraya Russa. The Germans should know better. They had a divisional headquarters in town and scrutinized everything and everyone.

The officer was still talking, as if to convince himself of something that couldn't possibly be true. "She lied to me. About her sons, about everything. What a mess all these lies make. That's my first bit of advice. Stop lying. And my second is, never trust a Nazi." He lowered his pistol as he talked, then abruptly turned toward Masha. Katya saw Masha's head jerk to the side and her body crumple to the ground as the sound of the shot echoed. Katya fired from where she crouched and hit one soldier square in the back. At the same moment, Svet launched herself at the officer, who had a stunned and stricken look on his face as she leapt across the short distance between them. The blade of her knife flashed as he shot a second time and they fell together. Katya took aim at the remaining soldier who was paralyzed by the frantic scene, and he too fell. In less than five seconds, the world went quiet save for a gurgling coming from the officer.

She rushed to Svet who lay with the Nazi in a spreading pool of scarlet. Blood pulsed out of his neck. Svet had driven her blade up to the hilt and pulled it down as she fell. The Nazi's frantic eyes bulged as his life flowed into the ground. In a fury Katya shot him in the face, even though it was clear he'd be dead in another minute.

At first, she thought Svet was unhurt and knelt to touch her face, but the girl's blue-gray eyes were blank. Katya patted her cheek and spoke her name, but there was no response. And when Katya couldn't find a pulse, the roar of a wounded animal shattered the silence. A small, dark spot had started to show on Svet's coat. In disbelief, Katya watched the scarlet stain spread. It was the coat she had worn since the village. The one that almost dragged her to the bottom of the swamp. The very coat Katya had always planned to replace, but never did after that day at the coat seller's stall. Katya drew in a sharp bit of winter air and began to choke and cough. "Filthy pig!" She stood and kicked the Nazi, once, twice, a dozen times, howling with every kick, until she fell and crawled back to her friend. She lay next to Svet, her bare hand cradling the girl's cheek as she replayed the scene in her mind, trying to imagine another outcome. Together she and Svet were stronger than three Nazis. Hadn't they survived the German attack in Luga, and shot that Nazi patrol dead from the oak tree, and killed her attackers in the village too? Finally, she sat and wiped her nose on her sleeve. A growl rose.

"I will get them, Svetochka. I promise."

She moved one stubborn curl off Svet's forehead and stroked her cheek a last time. No chance to say goodbye, to thank either of them. Katya turned to Masha, sweet Masha. She'd not wanted to look closely. She knew the *babushka* was dead. She'd seen her head jerk from the bullet and her brains spatter against the front door. But Katya needed to say goodbye, so she drew near. There was a single surgical entrance wound above Masha's ear on one side. Katya thanked her silently, for her kindness, her friendship, for being the very best of Russia. She sat with the body for a moment, her hand resting on the old woman's arm. Finally, she stood, checked that the other soldiers were dead, and spat on them both.

She wiped her face on a sleeve and saw the blood then. It was everywhere. She threw her bloodstained coat and gloves in the out-house pit, wiped her boots in the snow and went into the cabin to wash her hands. Heart pumping with adrenalin, she put on the spare coat and gloves Masha kept in case of emergency. If she was caught, they'd all die. Arkady, Olya, the weavers.

How long before others would come? Tonight? Tomorrow? No amount of confusion, no absence of clarity about what had happened would change the way the Nazis would view the scene. It would be

The Communist's Secret 181

an opportunity for them to point the finger of blame at the partisans. And demand more death as payment.

A lethal stew of rage and fear filled her. She rushed to the barn for the pelts, but changed her mind when she realized they would link her to Svet. She even left the fresh rabbit on Svet's belt, hoping it would give the Nazis pause when they blamed the partisans. Her eyes rested a last time on Svet and Masha, forming a photograph in her mind the precise details of which she'd be able to recollect the rest of her life. She knew she shouldn't disturb anything, shouldn't take any weapons, but could not resist one item, lifting it from the pouch on the soldier's belt and placing it gently in her large pocket rather than her rucksack.

A sudden urge to flee, a panic really, started in her chest and spread to her limbs. She picked up the gun she'd used, glanced down the road and then toward the forest. Nothing. No one. She raced toward the cover of the trees. Her thoughts swirled, as ominous as the bank of gunmetal gray clouds which pursued her to Olya's cabin.

A NEW WAR
February 1943

Katya sucked in sharp breaths as she stumbled through the dense forest. All around the wind whistled and brought the woods to life. She sensed the enemy in every shadow, lurking, watching. Her powerful rage made it easy to imagine what she would do if she encountered a Nazi patrol. She gripped the pistol tighter. *Pop-pop.*

The blustery snow distorted the landmarks she'd come to know. Still, her mind calmed enough that she realized she could not bring the gun into Olya's. She'd long passed the spot where she'd buried her Tokarev when she first came into Staraya Russa. Now she found a distinctive tree and placed the Luger in a crook where it was nearly invisible. She collected an armload of sticks so it would appear she was gathering firewood. A corner of her mind was able to plan and make sense of things.

The kindling rattled when she dropped it on the ground by the door, shattering the quiet with a sound both discordant and commonplace. A few pieces she brought inside. The house was empty. Katya hung the strange coat from Masha's. It was longer and heavier than the one she'd been wearing all this time—the one now at the bottom of the outhouse pit covered in blood.

She checked her reflection in a mirror, certain she must look different because she'd left her heart at the *kolkhoz*. A splotch of blood lay across her cheek like a poppy blossom. She washed her face and then inspected her reflection again.

She couldn't go to work in the middle of the day. Arkady would

The Communist's Secret   183

have told the weavers she was sick. Besides, it would be difficult to concentrate on weaving. She should embrace the pretense of illness, the only reasonable excuse for missing a day's work. It wasn't entirely a lie.

She brought the dying embers in the stove back to life, and soon the fire snapped and threw some warmth. She stretched out on the sofa, pulled a thin blanket over her stunned body, and stared at the ceiling beams, afraid to close her eyes. Her heart had just begun to calm when a knock at the door made it pound again. Her first instinct was to hide, but the Nazis would not yet have discovered the bodies so she shuffled to the door and opened it a crack. The Kommandant wore a look of concern.

"Arkady told me you were ill, so I came to check. I thought you might need something. May I come in?"

Katya kept her eyes partially closed so she wouldn't look like herself, but motioned him in. The last person she wanted to see, but his presence might provide an alibi. Proximity to the Kommandant could make the impossible somewhat less so.

"I don't feel well." She coughed.

"I won't stay long," he said stepping across the threshold and closing the door. "I brought some tea. And this." He set an orange on the table.

She tamped down the thrill at such a gift and braced herself against the wall, feigning wooziness. He encircled her waist with a strong arm.

"You are unwell. Please." He guided her to the sofa. "I'll make tea and be on my way."

Continuing her act, she didn't argue but collapsed onto the cushions and pulled the threadbare blanket over her legs. She watched him glance about the room as he put water to heat. It must look shabby through his eyes, although there were several shelves of books and nice glass windows. An indoor sink but no toilet. A bit of privacy in the single bedroom. She said nothing. Illness was a good excuse for silence.

He pulled a kitchen chair next to the sofa and placed his gloves and hat on the table. He sat without talking, still wearing his coat, while the water boiled. Katya forced herself to close her eyes, to hold herself still. It annoyed her that he was comfortable with silence. A few minutes later he brought her a glass in a tin holder, precious little black leaves swirling in the steaming water. She watched the tea settle to the bottom.

"My apologies for being such poor company," she said, making her voice raspy. "But thank you for the tea, and the orange." She reminded herself she had no energy to engage in a long or detailed conversation. She picked up the glass and began to sip, then eyed the orange, unblemished, full of life.

"Let me check if you have a fever." Before he arrived, she had her face turned to the fire and now she hoped it was still warm. "You're flushed." He placed his cool bare hand against her forehead for several seconds. The intimate gesture unnerved her further. "You are warm. If you're not better tomorrow, I must insist that you see a doctor."

She wanted to spit on him. He, who allowed—perhaps even ordered—the murder of the Weissmans and dozens of other Jewish citizens. She looked in his eyes for the first time since he arrived. They revealed nothing. No indication that he understood the irony— he wants her to see a doctor yet he has murdered her doctor.

With uncharacteristic self-control, she nodded in agreement and then added, "I'm certain to be improved tomorrow. Just a cold. Thank you." The words were like sandpaper in her throat.

He tucked the blanket around her. "You must eat this," he picked up the orange. "Perfect if you are under the weather." He dug his fingernails into the thick, bumpy skin and pulled it off in several large pieces. The fresh, springlike aroma filled her nostrils, rare but familiar, a sweet and tangy scent one never forgot no matter how long it had been. He separated the orange into two halves and set one down, then pulled a single plump segment from the other half and handed it to her. Their fingers brushed, the small spark confusing her further. She held the piece of magic, its intoxicating smell reminding her how Yelena loved oranges. She put it in her mouth, crushing the segment between her teeth and swallowing the sweet juice and pulp. The Kommandant nodded and smiled approvingly. She must be appreciative. It was a special gift. She returned his smile and said how delicious it was but that she wanted to share the rest with Arkady and Olya.

Katya let her eyelids droop. He stood and moved toward the door. The fingers of one hand grazed her coat, hanging on its hook.

He turned to her. "Your coat is damp."

The accusation froze them both. Her heart slammed in her chest. Just as she saw his hand about to drift down and bump against the item she'd taken from the dead soldier, the explanation popped from her mouth. "We needed kindling." Had he noticed it was a different coat?

"You mustn't go out." His voice was filled with concern. He glanced at the wood pile.

Katya nodded as the door clicked shut, then counted to twenty before jumping up to hide the grenade.

When Olya and Arkady arrived home together, earlier than normal, Olya sniffed at the air and then eyed the nearly intact orange halves on the table. Her eyebrows popped up.

"Kommandant Mueller," Katya said before Arkady and Olya had hung their coats. Then she blurted, "Svet and Masha." And with their precious names the emotion she'd been trying to control cascaded forth. Her gasps told Olya and Arkady the horrible news. If she didn't say it out loud, maybe it wouldn't be true. In between sobs Katya finally pushed out the words. "They killed them both."

Olya inhaled sharply. "Not Masha. Not now."

She was heartbroken too. Olya and Masha were old friends, especially close when they were young women raising children and in the years before Masha was sent to the collective. Katya took Olya's hand. "I'm sorry."

Arkady stood and went to the cupboard for the vodka. He grabbed three glasses and set everything on the table, pouring them each a generous portion.

"Take a drink, Katyusha. You too." He looked at Olya so kindly it made Katya begin crying again.

"What happened? Start at the beginning, Katya. Take your time."

"We were organizing everything when they drove up. I'd only been there an hour or two. I was outside and hid in the privy. They tried to get information from Masha and then Svet came out of the forest. She must have thought she had a chance of convincing them that she and Masha were harmless." A cry hiccupped from deep in her belly. "Filthy bastards made up their minds before they even got there. The officer shot Masha in the head. I had come around the cabin and shot the other two. Svet lunged at the officer with her knife and stuck him. Right in the neck." Arkady was dry-eyed but Olya whimpered. "He managed to get a shot off." The words caught in her throat. "Gone before I got to her."

"Ah, Katyusha, don't blame yourself. You could not have protected them," Arkady said. For someone who had seen decades of cruel death, he looked unbearably sad. "And you had to kill the Nazis. They would have shot you. The Kommandant didn't give us sufficient warning."

"Last night was just a sad attempt to absolve himself of what he knew was coming. Disgusting." Her breaths were hard, hate-filled exhalations. "What happens when they find the bodies?"

"They'll convince themselves it was the partisans," Arkady said.

They sat. Each focused on their own thoughts, on their own understanding of the events, on their own loss.

The Communist's Secret   187

"I left their weapons, thinking it would confuse things. All except this." She stood and went to the window seat and opened it, lifting the grenade softly, like she would an egg. Now she could go to Nazi headquarters and blow them and herself to kingdom come. Not an entirely ridiculous idea.

Arkady's mouth turned up and he exclaimed, "Well done!"

"I could go to headquarters with the grenade."

Arkady pursed his lips. "There may be better options. We have to give it some time. You may have confused them by leaving most of the weapons untouched, but there's no protection from reprisal. Even if you martyred yourself, they would kill others too."

"What about the Kommandant? He's interested in me. Maybe I can get an invitation."

"To what?" he said. "A private dinner in his quarters? You won't be able to kill many officers from his bed." He paused, rubbing the stubble on his chin in thought. "We'll see. The front is shifting. The partisans might be a possibility for us in a few months. You and I can fight. And Olya can cook and doctor. I can see the time for us to leave is coming."

Katya said nothing. Arkady didn't know her as well as she thought. She wouldn't leave Staraya Russa until she got her particular pound of flesh.

Two days later, Katya heard the first cries, calls for help, and pleas for mercy. It was her lunch break and she grabbed her coat and went out the front door. Down the street, a military truck blocked the road. Nazi soldiers were driving through the neighborhood, collecting locals in groups of twos and threes. They were forcing them across the bridge toward Market Square.

Arkady came from behind and yanked her back inside. "What are you doing?!" He growled, eyes flashing. "Leave it alone. You knew this was coming. Just leave it."

She pulled away from him. "No," she hissed back. "The least I can do is bear witness."

She hurried from the textile factory, noticing people scurrying inside and closing doors.

The Nazis herded the civilians onto the cobblestones in front of the market. Katya drew close as the people were ordered to form a line. Mostly women, a few older children, and some old men. And then, Katya saw Olya. She ran and pulled her from behind, out of the line, and quickly took her place. But before she could hush Olya's protest, Katya crumpled from a sharp blow to the head. The soldier cursed at her, calling her vile names as she stood, a trickle of blood running down her face. He pointed his rifle at Olya and motioned her to get back in line. "Both of you." Her eyes were wide as she stumbled forward, catching herself on Katya's arm.

A Nazi officer started to speak. "Three soldiers of the Reich were murdered two days ago. Three Soviets will be executed for each." In the next instant the soldiers were counting them off by fives.

She fought her desire to scream curses at them all, those forcing the people into the line, those counting and pulling every fifth person forward, and the two soldiers who served as executioners. The first *pop* of a pistol was followed by an audible, sharp intake of air from the crowd. Incoherent cries and sobs began. Katya repeatedly glanced down the line, wiping the blood out of her eyes, and counted groups of five, trying to figure out if they would both be spared or if she needed to switch places with Olya.

In a minute the soldiers were in front of them. The person next to Olya was a three and Olya a four. The soldier counted, "Three, four, and you," he pointed at Katya. "Five. Step forward."

Time stopped for Katya. This couldn't be right. Not yet. Not before she'd fixed things with Aleksandr.

The soldiers grabbed her arms and pulled her forward when an authoritative voice rang out. "Stop! Not that one. The next one."

The Communist's Secret 189

The soldiers dropped her arms and moved to the next person. Katya turned toward the voice, but the Kommandant was already walking away. The soldiers had shot the next person in line before Katya even fully realized what had happened.

Then she glimpsed Anya toward the end of the line, her dear radio *babushka*. Oh please, not Anya. The old woman held her head high, chin out, and when her turn came and the soldier pulled her clear of the others, she shook him off like he was diseased and stepped forward to her death. In her final act of defiance, she yelled "*Za rodinu!* For the Motherland!" as the executioner raised his pistol. The soldier hesitated, his gun still pointed at her, surprised at her rebellion. Her voice rang out again, "*Za rodinu!*" and the soldier fired. There were a few gasps from the crowd as she fell, and then another solitary voice took up the cry. "*Za rodinu!*" And then another and another until the words rose above the square like a cloud of eager hope.

THE TRAP IS SPRUNG

March 1943

The two women clutched each other and stumbled away from Market Square without a word. Katya's chest was still tight when they reached the cold, empty house. She hardly thought about the fact that Kommandant Mueller had saved her. Her head throbbed from the soldier's rifle butt and she felt as if she were still holding her breath.

"You stay here," she directed Olya to the armchair then went to the mirror and wiped the blood from her face. She pressed on the cut at her hairline to make sure it stopped bleeding. "Don't worry about supper. None of us will have much appetite. I'll find Arkasha."

"Thank you," Olya squeaked.

Katya bent down and hugged her. "Will you be all right?"

"Yes. Go. He'll be worried."

By the time Katya returned to the square, the bodies hung in a single row from a beam, twisting faintly in the wind. The cobblestones underneath were speckled with blood. Small clusters of people crept forward to see who had been murdered. They held each other for support, muttering a soft rumble of pleas and prayers that sounded more like the first sign of an earthquake rather than a symbol of consolation. In a few days relatives would be allowed to cut down the bodies and bury their loved ones.

Arkady sidled up to her while she stared. She'd forgotten she'd come to find him.

"Someone told me," he said. He lifted her hair to examine the cut. "Where is Olya?"

The Communist's Secret 191

"I took her home."

He held Katya in a harsh grip, his fingers pressing into her shoulders, but his eyes were kind and full of concern. "That was foolish, Katyusha. What came over you?"

"Instinct," she shrugged. "We're both okay."

"Only because the Kommandant stepped in," he said. "It was a stupid thing to do."

They stood in the dim light far from the sacrilegious semicircle of soldiers forcing the mourners to keep their distance. The sharp, heart-rending cries of children for their mothers, the deep rhythmic keening of *babushki* for their children, and the soft weeping of friends mourning friends filled the square.

"We should go," said Arkady. "I don't want Olya to be alone."

Katya said nothing as they walked home. What was there to say? That she had tried to take Olya's place was beside the point. Nine innocent civilians were dead. Arkady didn't blame her. He'd already told her the shooting at the farm was unavoidable. She tried to save Masha and Svet and three Nazis ended up dead.

Olya had started a fire and was sitting on the sofa with her feet up. Arkady hung his things and went straight to his sister. He pulled her up and put his arms around her, holding her close in a powerful demonstration of affection, but neither shed a tear.

"I'm all right," she said. "Most of us are going to die. I'm at peace. All I need to know is that my death means something. Like dear Anya." Her voice was full of pride and fervor. She turned to Katya. "Did you tell him?"

"I heard even before I reached the square," Arkady said. "The entire town is talking about how brave and brilliant she was."

"That heroic woman," said Katya. "For months she smuggled news of the war at great risk. Now, even in her death she's helped the rest of us carry on." Katya wondered if she had that kind of bravery. Killing the soldiers on the *kolkhoz* had been a gut reaction. She would need Anya's kind of courage to do something bigger. She would need a sacrificial kind of strength.

Katya began by practicing with a grenade-sized rock in the forest, getting the feel of it by throwing it both overhand and lobbing it underhand. She continued even after she realized she could not throw a grenade with any accuracy. Still, practicing made her feel as if she was doing something rather than waiting for something to happen.

Then one evening while walking home with Arkady, he gave her an idea. "Did you know that next Sunday they will be celebrating Heroes' Memorial Day?"

She slipped her arm through his and pulled close. "What will be involved?"

"I'm not entirely sure, but remember last year there was some review of the troops and a speech or two. All the Nazis gathered in Market Square."

"And do you think I'll be able to get close?"

"I don't know. They may not announce anything since the locals will not want to attend."

"And what if they force us?" She shook her head while thinking. "Imagine the response after a grenade. Gunfire at everything in the square. They would kill all the civilians."

Arkady nodded. "You're right. But what if it's a speech at the main barracks? Might be a way to get close enough and to minimize retaliatory damage."

"If it's a big gathering of Nazis only, it might work," she said, thinking of her imprecise throwing. "I'll take a stroll in that direction soon."

"And it might help for you to have a conversation with Mueller," Arkady added.

She shrugged. "I'm not sure I see the point." Her stomach clenched at the thought of facing him. "I don't want to thank him

The Communist's Secret   193

for saving my life. He should have protected Masha and Svet. Then none of this would have happened." She was embarrassed remembering how she sometimes enjoyed their conversations, how the way he looked at her made her feel good.

"Still, you shouldn't throw away an opportunity. Many people have sacrificed much more." He nodded toward the bodies.

His words humiliated her. Masha and Svet and these civilians were dead and she was worried about facing the Kommandant. She exhaled. "As always, you are right Arkasha."

After her shift the next day, Katya passed the turn for Olya's deliberately and walked all the way around the bend in the river until she reached the barracks and parade ground. She stopped, knowing there'd be trouble if she went closer. The big open space faced the water with rows of still new-looking quarters standing smartly behind. Appearances were important to the Nazis: uniforms crisp, boots polished, barracks neat and tidy. An idea began to percolate. There was a group of trees on the left from which she might throw a grenade although an extensive patrolled perimeter meant it was unlikely she could get close enough to do anything. And how could she know where and which officers would be present.

She started to return the way she'd come, her thoughts scattering. If she was able to throw the grenade, was escape possible? And if anyone recognized her as she fled, Arkady and Olya would pay with their lives. If she made it to the bridge, its heavy stone railings would shield her some, and then across the bridge to the left through the woods. And then what? In the middle of two huge armies facing off across a no man's land. Not much of a plan.

Quick footfalls from behind startled her and she stepped out of the way.

"Frau Belikova." The Kommandant stopped alongside. "What are you doing in our neck of the woods? I can only hope you were looking for me."

"Herr Kommandant," she nodded and let a slight smile pull at the corners of her mouth. "Just walking after work, enjoying the extra daylight. Lost in my thoughts when I noticed the barracks and realized I was far past my turn. It's very nice along the river here." He had no reason to question her motives.

"I'm glad to find you. I've been hoping to see you," he said.

Had he? "You know where I live, where I work. You can find me anytime you wish." She forced a teasing tone, rather than the harsh, judgmental tenor that almost popped out.

"Yes. I admit I haven't known what to say after the recent difficult events."

All her goodwill, all her self-control fled at the thought of Masha and Svet, Anya and the others. "You mean after you executed civilians because your soldiers got in a firefight with a couple of Russian women. After you let Olya and me be part of the dragnet? Last year you killed my friend and her father and daughter and so many others. The messages you're sending are anything but subtle." The words just kept coming. She'd waited too long to say this. "Why don't you simply kill me too? In fact, just kill everyone. All the women and children. It's what your philosophy supports." She had stopped walking and glared at him. She knew he was different from the others, but she wasn't sure she wanted him to know she knew. Not yet anyway.

He took a deep breath. "War is—" he started to say, but she cut him off.

"Yes, yes. War is horrible. But your choices seem to make it worse than it needs to be. Killing innocents—in retribution or not—is hardly the act of a civilized nation."

She hated what he stood for, yet, right now, glaring at him, she felt a flash of admiration too. He didn't turn away or ignore her blunt remarks. He didn't beat her. Plenty of other Nazis would shoot her for saying such things. He stared into her eyes, taking responsibility.

"You think I enjoy killing civilians?" His voice was a bare

The Communist's Secret   195

whisper. "Nothing could be further from the truth. I wish war was easier. But it's one brutal situation after another. And uppermost for me has to be my men. I could not allow what happened to go unpunished. Those responsible, your partisans, will think twice before killing more of my soldiers. And I am sorry about you being caught up in it all."

"Your perspective is a fairytale. The partisans haven't been anywhere near us, as you know. I hear they're getting closer so perhaps they will begin to strike. When the time is right, nothing will stop the partisans from attacking you. Even if you kill us all. They will still hunt you. They are defending their homeland. They have the moral high ground. They attack you, and in turn you kill women, children, the elderly. Executing innocents is against the laws of war, against the laws of your God."

They were walking slowly, Katya still grasping for a fragment of calm. She didn't want to talk about his philosophy of war. She wanted information about their upcoming holiday. She remained silent another few minutes and then changed the subject.

"Let's talk about something less dreadful." She sighed and paused. "I hear you have a holiday coming up?"

"You mean the sixteenth of March? Our Heroes' Day?"

She nodded, glancing at him.

"It's not much of a holiday. Not for us anyway. In Berlin there'll be a parade. Here, the soldiers will march to the square and stand in the rain while our commanders bore them to death. Then they'll go back to the barracks and drink. Those who aren't on duty anyway."

She couldn't help but smile. His surprising sense of humor made her forget who he was.

"No, our next big holiday will be the twentieth of April."

"Easter?" she said.

"No, Easter's later. But there's not much planned. Most holidays don't seem worth celebrating without family."

She glanced away so she wouldn't have to say anything about her loved ones.

"I imagine you miss yours," he continued.

It annoyed her, this game of drawing him out by talking of personal things. Yet she sensed it was working.

"Sadly, I haven't family to miss." It was easy to lie to him. "My husband died several years ago. Influenza. And my parents long before that." She glanced up at him and could tell he was waiting. He wanted more. "We tried to have children, but it was difficult for me. Only one and he died as an infant." It was a partial truth anyway. Her second baby had been born after two miscarriages when Yelena was six. What a bright light little Sasha had been. Chubby, full of smiles, and just starting to walk when he died. Silent tears fell.

He took her hand and squeezed it. "My condolences. I understand your pain. My wife died in childbirth, as did our baby. In one single day, my entire life was snuffed out."

"Oh," she said. "How awful." She squeezed his hand in return and held his gaze in a moment of shared sorrow, a moment of shared humanity. He cupped her chin in his other hand, his piercing blue eyes searching for something.

Katya thought he might kiss her, but instead he dropped both hands and took a half-step back. She wondered if he saw something in her eyes.

"So, holidays," he said, suddenly anxious to change the subject. "April the twentieth. *Führergeburtstag*. Hitler's birthday. There's a celebration in the works. Special rations for the troops and an elegant cocktail party for the officers. Not a formal dinner, but fancy dress, plenty of good wine and spirits, food, cigars, and self-congratulatory chit-chat. But it will be lacking in good company. There will be no one as charming or beautiful or interesting as you."

His gaze remained on her face. She sensed he would ask her if she offered just the slightest encouragement. She gave him an equally

The Communist's Secret 197

personal look, conveying more intimacy than appropriate for two antagonistic acquaintances. She added a genuine, warm smile.

"You wouldn't like to go with me, would you?" he said.

Katya looked down, doing her best imitation of appearing demure. "I have to admit it would be very nice to have a break from all this." She paused. "Will I have to talk with others? They will look down on me. I don't think there are many officers like you." It was the only compliment she was willing to extend.

"I think I can keep you to myself." Desire was there, in the way his eyes came alive. "It will be at senior staff quarters and I will send a car for you. I'm sure I'll see you before then, but shall we say seven o'clock?" He radiated a new kind of energy.

She felt more alive than she had in many, many months. For just a few moments, she was seduced by the curious combination of his desire and the satisfaction of everything falling into place. It was a sensation she hadn't felt in a long time. Not since her early years in the Party when she'd been secure and confident, the days before all the harsh policies and the disappearances, the days before fear and secrets and whispers.

That confidence edged against the idea of her own death. She knew it unlikely that she would escape the operation. But it would be a good death. One that compensated for the bad things she'd done. For betraying her husband. For shutting her heart after little Sasha died. For building walls so high no one could reach her, no one could love her.

Still, a strong desire to live tugged. She was desperate that Aleksandr and Yelena should know she had changed, that she loved them deeply and wanted another chance. And for that to happen, they would all need to survive.

HITLER'S BIRTHDAY
April 1943

Two weeks before the celebration of Hitler's birthday, the Kommandant appeared at the factory. He and several subordinates arrived toward the end of the workday and spent longer than their usual twenty minutes with Arkady. No voices were raised, but Katya knew they were desperate for information. A German supply convoy had been attacked and numerous trucks, cargo, and German soldiers had been destroyed.

As soon as it was time, the other weavers hurried out, anxious to get away, not even bothering to straighten up. But Katya slowed her preparations for the next day, fiddling with a pedal that she knew worked fine. She wanted a chance to encourage the Kommandant.

When the stern-faced soldiers came down, Katya moved to the back hall where her coat hung, hoping the Kommandant would notice. She heard him speak to his men and in a moment he was at her side as the factory door thudded shut.

"Allow me," he said, taking her coat and holding it out.

She let a smile flicker across her face before turning to slide her arms in. After setting the coat on her shoulders, he lifted her hair and his fingers grazed the back of her neck. She shivered at the intimate gesture but was pleased that her plan was working so well.

They walked toward the rear door, moving together as two people who knew each other moved. Winter had returned and several inches of new snow coated tree branches and rooftops. On the streets and walkways, the snow was slick, a mixture of ice and slush. She took his arm.

198

The Communist's Secret 199

Katya concentrated on ways she might give him more in the way of small intimacies, which took her attention from the icy path. Suddenly, she slipped. She heard her own sharp intake of air. But the moment she started to flail, he had her from behind, both hands under her armpits. And that quickly, she was back on her feet. He steadied her gracefully, one arm tight around her waist. His face was concerned and warm.

"That was close," he said. "You must be more careful. A fall like that . . ."

She nodded her agreement. "Thank you, Gerhardt. Lucky for me you were here." She'd used his first name, wanting him to feel that she actually believed she was lucky to be with him. She hoped her intimate, breathy words would draw him to her.

He brushed a wisp of hair off her face and started to lean in. She stepped back, her eyes downcast. "We're not alone." The suggestion that under different circumstances he might have her was in her words and the way she looked at him. Her eyes twinkled. "We must be discreet."

He stepped back. "I don't care what people think. My staff doesn't care. I'm a widower. Even if I had a wife, it wouldn't matter." He paused. "But I do understand your position."

"At the party perhaps." She touched his cheek.

"Ha! You'll make me wait two more weeks to kiss you. I cannot bear it." He laughed then and took her arm, accepting her power over him.

As they reached Olya's house, he explained that the celebration was indeed going forward and that he would collect her the evening of the twentieth as planned.

"I hope to see you before that, of course, but it may not be possible," he said. "Things are difficult right now."

That was certainly true. The huge loss at Stalingrad. Increased partisan attacks. The war was no longer the story of a German juggernaut.

Katya was thinking again of kissing him. If she did, it would seal things. She would no longer need to worry about his trust. And as long as the arrangements for the party went as planned, she wouldn't have to sleep with him. Instead of turning for the door, she closed the distance between them and said, "I wish we could see more of each other." Then she leaned up, enjoying the surprise on his face. At first her lips touched his lightly, then he pulled her body tight against his. His lips were firm, the kind of lips that knew what to do. She disappeared into his embrace, the desire in his body, his delicious lips and open mouth tasting faintly of tobacco and reminding her of her husband. For an instant it was Shura's arm pulling her in, the other hand drifting down to her backside. In that moment, she remembered her husband's lips on other parts of her body, the places only he knew. She pulled away, tamping down her rising disgust at enjoying the kiss while trying to maintain a breathless façade of desire. Color rose on his face, and his eyes held hers.

"That was . . ." he said.

"A surprise?" she finished.

"Unexpected, yes, but very, very nice." He spoke softly, a seductive timbre to his voice.

"I'll see you soon," she said.

"Not soon enough," he smiled.

Continuing her performance, she returned his playful look. Then she stepped inside the cabin and after the door clicked shut, went straight to the sink and rinsed her mouth over and over again.

Arkady was already at the table. Katya didn't know how he beat her home, but by the look on his face she could tell he had seen her with the Kommandant.

"Arkasha, don't look at me that way. You know it's all part of my scheme to get him to lower his guard." Her words were light, but shame had already taken up residence.

"As long as you realize how serious this is," he said.

The Communist's Secret 201

"I understand the possible outcomes." Considering her own death did not frighten Katya. In a sad, dark way, it made sense. The longer the war continued—weeks becoming years—it was almost impossible to imagine Yelena and Shura surviving. And without them, there was nothing for her. The ache in her chest came more and more often now and she knew exactly what it was. She did not want to live without them.

"Good," Arkady said. "So let's figure out how to get the grenade inside and a way for you to survive the blast. I have an idea." He motioned for Katya to join him at the table.

"The problem is that I'll be searched," Katya said.

"Exactly." He turned to a piece of paper and began to draw the floor plan of his house. "The bathroom next to the kitchen has a window facing the garden with a large sill. I've been watching the house, and there are only a few guards on duty. Late at night they are often asleep. When the weather is bad, they go inside. I will sneak into the back garden and place the grenade on the windowsill. Behind the clematis. It will be waiting for you at the party."

A dangerous, risky idea, but perhaps the best one they had. "Sneaking around the general staff quarters?" she said. "After curfew? What if you're caught?"

"The plan fails." He didn't blink. "But I haven't been caught yet, and I've gone there twice in the dead of night to see if it's possible. This is too important. Perhaps our only chance."

She held his eyes with her own. He would die if caught. And she would be implicated. It would be the end for all of them.

"Let's review the layout of the house," he said. "You remember the kitchen and bathroom are at the back. The dining room is between the kitchen and the parlor on one side of the main hallway. Opposite, in the other front corner, is the library."

Katya could see the walls of books and his grandfather's table.

"After chatting and drinking a bit, you'll identify the best spot for the explosion. At the right moment, the moment when numerous high-ranking officers are together, you'll excuse yourself and get the grenade from the window ledge, return to where they are gathered, unscrew and pull the cap and set the grenade on a chair, a bookshelf, behind a curtain, wherever.

"The trick will be the Kommandant. If he is as attentive as I expect, he may interfere. And you may have to get creative. Send him for a glass of wine or a plate of food. This egg grenade has a yellow cap, which means it has a longer delay than most. You have six or seven seconds to escape, rather than three or four. You should head to the back of the house. The bathroom again, or the kitchen. You may escape serious injury. That is part of your plan." His eyes were dark and his voice serious.

She'd found a black dress at the market during the first winter and bought it on a whim. People had already started selling their belongings or bartering for food in earnest. It cost next to nothing and just owning something nice made her feel good. She never thought she'd use it—at least not in wartime. It was big in places, and Olya spent numerous evenings with a needle and thread until it fit perfectly: snug on her breasts, but without showing much décolletage. Katya had never been comfortable with revealing clothes—her Soviet upbringing favored modesty. The skirt was loose and moved seductively as she turned, the fabric caressing her skin. She hated that it mattered to her that all those Nazi officers see her as beautiful and desirable. That they should be a little bit jealous of the Kommandant. She came out to show Arkady and Olya.

"You need a necklace," Arkady said.

"I haven't anything," said Katya. "And besides, it may get ruined."

Olya retrieved a tin box from the bedroom and produced a silver locket with ornate filigree work around the edge.

"This should do nicely." It rested in exactly the right spot just below the hollow of her neck. "Not that you need another reason to draw attention. You're beautiful, Katya dear."

"I hope you get it back," Katya said, fingering the locket. She kissed Olya on the cheek.

Fifteen minutes before the car was due, they waited, a tense silence covering them like a fog. Katya was breathing slow and deep. Her entire body trembled with the enormity and gravity of what lay ahead. The first part of the plan had worked. Arkady had slipped through the garden undetected and placed the grenade on the bathroom sill. She stood, hugging them both.

"It'll be all right," she said. "Thank you. You've done so much for me. If you make it, please look for my daughter after the war. Tell her everything. Especially how much I love her."

"Enough of that." Arkasha dismissed her fears, though his eyes betrayed his own doubts. "You'll tell her yourself."

Katya stepped out into the cool evening. The air smelled like spring, damp but fresh and filled with promise. She stood on the porch, trying to remain calm.

The car pulled up. Gerhardt jumped out and strode over, his eyes alight. In the privacy of the back seat he sat close and slid his hand under hers, palm against palm, his thumb stroking the back of her hand. It was all she could do not to pull away. The intimate gesture made her skin crawl but she forced herself to lean into him. It was a short ride and the charade would be over soon enough.

As the vehicle approached the old, distinctive home, her heart began to pound. They stopped and a soldier opened her door. She stepped into the viper's pit. The aggressive guttural sounds of German made for a fearful accompaniment to the crush of Nazi uniforms. She had not prepared for the feeling of being surrounded by the enemy and found herself holding her breath. Young soldiers lined the porch. Soldiers just like the ones she and Svet killed in the forest.

At the door, Gerhardt apologized and signaled to a nurse who stood at the far end. "You understand. Everyone must be searched."

She nodded and offered a simple, "Of course." The Kommandant stood nearby, looking respectfully away, but shielding her from overt gazes. Katya was grateful that she didn't have to undress and took several deep breaths to expel some of the fear. The nurse was middle-aged and all business, starting with her neck and back, her hands pressing hard, fingers creeping into private areas as she moved over Katya's buttocks. The nurse motioned for her to lean over and put her hands on the table. She checked between Katya's legs, but didn't linger. In quick succession, she tapped her on the shoulder to stand and then motioned for her to turn around. The stern woman began at the top again, now rubbing her hands slowly over and between Katya's breasts and checking her armpits, abdomen, and down her thighs. Then she made Katya remove her shoes. After a brief inspection, the nurse returned them and their eyes met. Hers were dark and disdainful. As she turned away, instead of feeling violated, Katya was grateful they planned for the search. It would have been impossible to smuggle a nail file, much less a grenade.

The Kommandant apologized a second time. Katya looked at him intently, trying to unnerve him. "Well, I didn't expect to have a woman run her hands over me tonight." Her suggestion lingered in the air.

He leaned close, his lips nearly touching her ear. "Perhaps I will soon make you forget about that."

She smiled and squeezed his arm to encourage him.

The party was underway and the dining room filled with more Nazi uniforms. Many junior officers had obviously started drinking early. Gerhardt presented her with a small glass of wine. She was grateful he hadn't filled it. She'd never been much of a drinker and over the last two years had become unused to alcohol. He motioned to the food, and they filled their plates, now caught in that indelicate

The Communist's Secret   205

balancing act of having a plate of food and a wine glass and no place to set either.

She shifted about and started examining the shoulder boards all around. She hadn't yet seen the insignias she was looking for and turned to Gerhardt.

"Too crowded." He nodded toward the hallway.

The double doors to the library were open and Katya slid inside and against a wall. There were no women in the room, but several small groups of military men who seemed engaged in rather intense conversations. She spotted the red and gold shoulder straps with silver diamonds on the braided background that she'd been hoping to see.

One of the generals nodded at Gerhardt and he set both their plates on the table to make introductions. The confirmation of their rank swept away any remaining bit of doubt. She spoke a couple of sentences in German and Gerhardt looked and talked like he was proud to be with her. One Nazi general examined her appreciatively; the other did not smile, but complimented her on her German. A frosty civility.

After they were again out of earshot, Katya turned to him and whispered. "The temperature just dropped several degrees."

"Now, now, Katya, they are simply wary of all Russians."

"Are you sure it's not risky for you to be seen with me?"

"Don't be silly," he said as they ate.

Another general drifted in, followed by a much younger junior officer carrying a generous plate of food and a tumbler of whiskey. He set both in front of the general officer on the gorgeous mahogany table that had survived so much and soon would be nothing more than a pile of splinters. Katya felt a sense of loss for that table and for Arkady's home, but nothing for the lives she was about to take.

She picked at her plate and sipped her wine. She leaned into Gerhardt, smiling at him and making idle conversation. She worked hard to appear relaxed, anxious to avoid any misstep and do what she came to do. She didn't want to disappear too quickly so watched the arrogant general and his subservient handler. Twice the general sent the young officer scurrying for another drink. It sickened her. She liked to think it wasn't like that in the Red Army.

Glancing at the concentration of German brass, she decided there wouldn't be a better opportunity. Three generals and a number of other high-ranking officers clustered together. She set her empty plate and glass on a corner of the desk and whispered, "I'm going to use the toilet. Would you get me some wine? And perhaps a bit more of that caviar."

Gerhardt smiled and squeezed her around the waist.

In the bathroom, Katya set her bag on a little stool. She pulled the curtain aside and saw the grenade on the sill. She unlocked the window and pushed, then froze when it issued a shrill objection. Holding her breath, she waiting for someone to pound on the door. After several silent seconds, she reached out, took the grenade and eased the window down. How long had she been gone? Just a minute surely, although it seemed longer. She had to beat Gerhardt back to the library. She flushed the toilet and carried the grenade in the folds of her skirt.

Moving lightly down the hall, she allowed a server with a tray to pass and reentered the library. The room was even more crowded and Gerhardt hadn't returned. The generals were still there, amidst two sizable groups of officers discussing something important. They were not in a celebratory mood and didn't even glance at her. She twisted and pulled the cap without hesitation and set the grenade on a bookshelf. As she turned sharply for the door, she collided with Gerhardt as he stepped into the library, balancing two glasses of wine and a plate of caviar with triangles of toast. She touched his chest and said, "I left my bag." His head was cocked to one side and there was a questioning look on his face, but she slid past him and rushed down the hall. As she opened the bathroom she glanced back and saw he was still looking at her. With her hand on the knob, the house roared and something slammed her to the floor. She closed her eyes amidst shattering glass and flying debris. The door pinned her to the ground and there was a pulsing rush in her ears and head. After some minutes, she smelled smoke and heard a distant chaos of muffled voices. It was as if her ears were plugged with cotton. There was water. She didn't call out, but lay in the wetness, smoke gathering above her, trapped in the strange stillness that wasn't fully quiet.

Her sense of time fell away. Cries for help grew louder, as did other voices. The smoke thickened. She moved against the door, but the pain in her left arm and chest made it impossible. She tried to call for help but a squeak came out. A random soldier suddenly appeared. She cried out from the pain as he lifted the door and helped her to her feet.

"What happened?" She touched her head and her fingers were slick with blood.

"An explosion." He propelled her forward.

"Where's the Kommandant?" Her words were a bare whisper. If he had survived, it was over for her. Rushing down the hall like that, almost running. That curious look on his face was the surprise and shock of someone discovering a betrayal.

He ignored her question. "We'll get you to the hospital. You were lucky."

Lucky. She had been prepared to die, but as he half-carried her to the garden where bodies were scattered, a rush of elation and surprise settled inside. She was dizzy and still holding onto the soldier for support. Another uniformed Nazi lay nearby, his blood coating the sparse green shoots of grass, soaking into the early spring ground. As the earth began to tilt, she saw his face. Bad skin and big ears. The coat-seller's stall. Lucky indeed, she thought as the ground rose to meet her and everything went black.

When Katya regained consciousness, several white-coated medical personnel were bustling about. The smell of disinfectant meant she was in the hospital. How she wished Dr. Weissman was standing there, his soothing voice and kind eyes telling her everything would be all right. He would make the pain tolerable. A voice explained that there was insufficient anesthetic for the stitches and she wasn't in bad enough shape to require their precious morphine. She closed her eyes while they worked on her, the needle more painful than the wound itself, and the horrible pulling sensation with every stitch. Big silent tears dripped down the sides of her face and into her ears. Afterward, she stared at a spot on the ceiling where the plaster had darkened into the shape of a wolf.

When she woke the next time, her arm was in a cast and she was the sole patient in a room with four beds. Arkady was at her side. "Arkasha," she croaked.

"Sleeping beauty awakes." He stood and came close.

"What happened?" She hissed. "The Kommandant? I think he knew."

"First of all, he's dead. So are most of the senior officers. I haven't seen a casualty list, but looks like a dozen. The mortuary delivered its entire stock of coffins."

Katya felt something other than pain bubble inside. "It worked."

Arkady nodded. "I know you hate all references to luck, but so many things could have gone wrong. Instead, you're here to tell the tale." She smiled through the pain. "I wish I could get you out before they start interviewing survivors," he continued. "But the doctor says at least several days. You're pretty beat up. Arm, collarbone, ribs. And they've got soldiers inside and outside the hospital. Politsai are roaming the neighborhoods. In fact, I wouldn't be surprised if they put a soldier inside your room now that you're awake. You must be very tight-lipped. Don't speak to anyone unless you are forced. Just claim

The Communist's Secret 209

exhaustion or pain if they ask too many questions. You went to the bathroom and then the explosion. Nothing else. And grieve for the Kommandant. If you so much as look at them the wrong way they will pounce. Every day that passes they're going to be more desperate to find someone to blame."

For a while it seemed that the Nazis were in a state of shock. Then, with Katya's improvement came the interviewers. Two or three times every day. There was always at least one new officer asking the same questions but expecting different answers, expecting a breakthrough of some sort. Katya never wavered from her story, which soon felt like the truth. She'd been in the bathroom when the explosion occurred. She had no idea what happened and saw nothing suspicious. Yes, she was in attendance with the now deceased Kommandant Gerhardt Mueller. Tears sprang forth at his name. She feigned a broken heart and a broken spirit. They were to be married, she confessed. Lying was second nature for Katya.

The nurse who had searched all the women in attendance had been outside when the explosion occurred and confirmed that Katya did not have a weapon. Still, they asked the same questions over and over, growing angry and ill-tempered.

When finally released from the hospital, she thought perhaps it was over. She had killed thirteen Nazi officers and gotten away with it. But a new military delegation arrived from Berlin skilled in intimidation. Katya felt small and insignificant.

Ever since Stalingrad, failure followed the Wehrmacht like a poisonous cloud. Even at the party, she had sensed a growing gloom in their conversations. There had been nothing upbeat beyond a few obligatory toasts to Hitler. Now, day after day, peppered and pestered by Nazi officers, Katya saw their fear. Losing the war was a possibility. In their desperation, they convinced themselves that the partisans had planted a bomb.

Fear of reprisal grew in Staraya Russa, spreading from house to house faster than typhus. No one left their homes. Katya lay quietly on the sofa. Her chest hurt less when she reclined. Olya rarely left her alone, sitting nearby in the sagging armchair or bringing her tea and meals.

With broken ribs and collar bone, a fractured arm, her face swollen and discolored, and sporting a jagged line of stitches on her forehead, Katya looked ghoulish. They'd cut a bit of hair in front for the stitches, adding to her shocking appearance. A blonde Baba Yaga.

Katya and Olya began walking daily, adding a few minutes each time. The old woman's presence protected her from the harsh judgment of the locals. Injuries or no, she had been with the Kommandant. They thought her a collaborator. Or a common whore, selling herself for food and some protection. She'd never again be effective in Staraya Russa and she and Olya and Arkady huddled together, discussing the pros and cons of joining the partisans.

"The war isn't going well for Germany," said Arkady. "I smell fear and frustration. A deadly combination. As soon as you're stronger, we should go."

"It's far, isn't it?" said Katya. Walking several dozen kilometers seemed beyond her.

Arkady nodded, his brow furrowed, deep in thought. "But we can't wait. Even though there's been nothing yet, the Nazis will respond. No one is safe."

The plan had worked, yet the black dog of death remained at their heels. Katya expected to be arrested. But the Germans were a curiously precise and thorough people and they needed evidence or a witness to arrest her. Katya thought how in the Soviet Union she'd have been imprisoned immediately. Just for surviving.

REVENGE AND REGRET

May-June 1943

A German patrol took Olya without warning while Arkady was at the factory and Katya at home recuperating. According to a witness, the Nazis grabbed dozens of people from the market at random. Olya and thirty-eight other civilians—three for each of the thirteen Nazis killed in the bombing—were executed before Katya and Arkady knew it was happening.

It seemed impossible that Olya was dead. The three of them had been planning to join the partisans as soon as Katya was strong enough.

On the fifth day, Arkady and Katya approached Market Square. Neither the sling on her arm nor the pain in her chest could distract her from what she knew they would find. Death wasn't enough for the Nazis. They enjoyed the cruelty of mangled corpses, pecked at by the birds.

After she and Arkady wrapped Olya's skinny body in her favorite blanket, Katya steadied the three-wheeled cart while Arkady placed his sister, gently but awkwardly, across the old farm implement and pushed her to the monastery. The cemetery was old, even by Russian standards, with decaying, moss-covered markers from as far back as the thirteenth century. It wasn't called Staraya Russa, Old Russa, for nothing.

Hundreds of people filled the grassy, tomb-studded expanse. Never had a cemetery been so full of the living. They mourned and dug graves for their loved ones. The strong helped the frail. Olya's daughter, daughter-in-law, and grandchildren wept, but they did so quietly, keeping their grief to themselves as best they could.

The town's powerful, collective sorrow circled the crowd, bringing them close. All but Katya, whose tremendous sadness was fed by the blackness of shame. She avoided the other mourners to save them the discomfort of having to acknowledge her presence. This was different than when she killed the Nazis at the *kolkhoz* in self-defense. Then she had no choice and the reprisal was hardly her fault. But the bombing had been a calculated act of war. An act of revenge. She had known that the Nazis would lash out at the town, despite a fragment of hope they would not. Katya was tired, so very tired of all the death.

She wiped her tears, unaware she was even crying, surrounded as she was by such anguish. Perhaps she could just disappear into the ground too—crawl into one of the holes and breathe her last.

Arkady took a break from his shovel and sat on the ground with her. He pulled out his tobacco, rolled a small cigarette, and drew deeply. He patted her leg in a supportive way. She was thinking how for a brief couple of weeks she'd felt like the luckiest person in the world. Everything had come together and she had killed the enemy. She had pushed her nation a bit closer to victory. But then it turned dark. Thirty-nine people dead. And Olya, dear Olya. A cry came from her weary soul and she fought the tears. Never, ever again would she consider that God, if he existed, was on her side. Everything was a gamble; a roll of the dice. Good people, bad people, it was all the same. If you threw the dice often enough you would eventually get a good outcome. That's what had happened to her. She had killed those Nazis and survived the bombing herself, and for a brief, golden moment had been lucky. Now, she was once more mired in despair. If the bombing hadn't happened, they would all be alive.

She looked at Arkady, who had been talking the entire time. "But you mustn't let this become a burden," he said. "We made a choice.

The Communist's Secret   213

We knew there could be horrible consequences. Olya was ready to pay that price. The price of victory. Nothing more and nothing less."

Arkady understood and accepted the cost of war—had seen it first hand in the last war against Germany. Death in wartime was not personal to Arkady. But to Katya it was nothing if not personal.

Arkady patted her arm as he finished his cigarette and again took up his shovel. She coughed and closed her eyes until the daggers in her chest subsided. She shuffled over to join the old women and young children arranging wild flowers. Thirty-nine tiny bouquets.

From her perch amongst the blooms, she watched the constant parade of mourners drift to Arkady. Hundreds of people came to pay their respects, which he accepted clear-eyed. And when he took a pause from his work, Arkady too wandered through the crowd, speaking soft words of comfort, patting shoulders. Few spoke to Katya. She hadn't lost a family member and no one knew what she'd done. As far as they were concerned, she was a traitor. She'd been at the party with a Nazi. The only reason they didn't drive her from their holy work was because of Arkady.

They remained until the last body was buried, the last prayers spoken, the millionth tear shed. Katya was glad to experience the town's sorrow. She owed the people that. And she owed it to herself as well. No more whitewashing the results of her actions: not her husband's arrest nor these deaths. No more pretending Stalin wasn't culpable either. What a weakness to kill innocent citizens. That's what Stalin did with the camps. He even destroyed Bukharin and other devoted Bolsheviks just to solidify his power.

But as she and Arkady made their way home in the persistent evening light of another June—the third midsummer of the war— Katya knew she would do it again if she could. Despite the Nazis' retribution, killing the enemy was the only path to victory.

After the burial, it wasn't only the town that refused to return to normal. Mother Russia herself would not let such evil go unpunished

214   Suzanne Parry

and the Red Army began attacking the Demyansk pocket not far from Staraya Russa, squeezing the Nazis in a pincer movement.

"Now's the time, Katyusha," Arkady said. "If the Nazis don't slaughter us, the Red Army's artillery might. You and I must head south and join the partisans."

Two days later, they went to the cemetery to say goodbye to Olya a final time and when no one was looking they simply faded into the forest. Arkady guided the two of them west and south, away from the Demyansk action and toward what they hoped was one of the largest partisan detachments in the region.

Katya tucked her gun in a loop she'd fashioned in her pants at the small of her back. Arkady had hidden coats and supplies a thirty-minute walk beyond the town. They continued all day and all night, accompanied by the dusky light of a sun that barely dipped below the horizon. During one of their short breaks, Katya asked him the obvious. "How do you know the way?"

Arkady tilted his head.

"The partisans?" Katya asked. "All this time and you never told me?"

"Katyusha. How could I reveal that kind of information to anyone? I've been working with the partisans from the beginning. Leaving supplies, mostly medical, in the woods. I'm a bit embarrassed that I emptied the hospital of just about everything. I'm pretty sure Dr. Weissman knew it was me. He never reported the thefts to the Germans. Just kept on asking them for more." Arkady got a faraway look in his eyes. "He was one of the best, Dr. Weissman."

"All those interviews with the Kommandant and you just played dumb?"

"Keeping my mouth shut has been one of my most effective tools." He smiled. "Early on there was no help from the Party or the Red Army or anyone. It was all chaos. It took eighteen months before the group we're going to join got a single supply drop from the military."

The Communist's Secret 215

Katya smiled. "I didn't think you were involved."

"That was my goal. To keep it a secret. Olya didn't know either." He sighed. "It's a disappointment that she never knew. She wanted me to join the partisans from the beginning. She would be proud." He looked away.

"She knows, Arkasha." Katya touched his arm. "And she is proud."

They slept a few hours and started again, crossing into an expansive forest, an unpopulated region far from any city. It was in this dense wood that Arkady expected to find the partisan detachment.

The second day, they alternated walking for forty-five minutes and resting for fifteen and collapsed sometime after the sun fell behind the trees. How Katya had found the strength to go so far surprised them both. Arkady too was dead on his feet. They sat and sipped from the canteen and ate some stale bread. "Let's sleep," Arkady said and closed his eyes. Katya leaned against another tree trunk and fingered Aleksandr's dented and scratched canteen—sturdy and trustworthy, just like her husband. The man she hadn't loved very well when she had the chance. The man she'd betrayed, so focused on her career and connections that she'd let slip a comment that doomed him and nearly cost the entire family everything. But now, she knew what she'd lost. It wasn't just that she respected him—although she did that—it was that she loved him. Loved who and what he was. And understood even his lukewarm embrace of the Party. Because he was right about that as well.

THE PARTISANS

June 1943

Katya's eyes popped open and she jerked at the prodding of a rifle. She shrank against the tree and looked at two shabby men with guns, faces blackened with mud or soot.

One barked. "What are you doing here? Who are you?"

She looked at Arkady, his hands in the air. He nodded at her as if to say, it's all right. "Loyal Russians," he said. "We left Staraya Russa on foot day before yesterday to join the fight."

The whites of the guerrillas' eyes were bright against their darkened skin. They looked at each other. Annoyed and perhaps unsure, one spat a gob of mucous at her feet.

"You should go back to Staraya Russa. We don't take women."

Katya bristled. "Of course you do. This is the Soviet Union."

He ignored her and turned to Arkady. "And you Grandpa, go back and grow some food for us. That's how you can help."

Arkady glared at the men. "I think Colonel Baranov would see things differently."

Visibly shaken, one said, "How do you know our commander? What's your name?"

"Romashkin, Arkady Petrovich. Take us to him and you'll see that we belong."

The fighters looked at each other. "Just what we plan to do. First, your weapons."

Katya smiled. Arkady knew the partisan commander. It was so like him to keep this information to himself. She glanced his way

The Communist's Secret   217

and he nodded in that almost imperceptible way of his. No grand gestures. But substance in his subtlety. She lay the Luger at her feet.

"Where did you get that?" said the older of the two partisans.

"Where do you think?"

The fighter's eyes bulged, although Katya wasn't sure it was because her response suggested she'd killed the enemy or because he hadn't seen a woman for so long. He pursed his lips and picked up the weapons.

"Now," the older one demanded. "*Davai.* Let's go. It's a long way."

They walked single file, Arkady and Katya in between the two loutish partisans. Katya's breathing remained shallow and ragged, like that of a lifelong smoker. Every step reverberated discomfort in her not yet healed chest. The guerrilla behind her began poking her with his gun.

"Hurry up! You need to keep pace." Did he really think she was going slow on purpose? Hadn't he noticed the sling on her arm?

Arkasha looked over his shoulder repeatedly until finally turning around to growl. "Leave her alone. Can't you see she's injured?" The partisan rolled his eyes but said nothing, accepting her slower pace.

After an hour, Katya paused. "How long?"

"Three hours if we move quickly. At this pace, more like five."

She clenched her teeth and soldiered on, but after another thirty minutes, stopped again. "I have to rest." She sat on the ground and gingerly lay down. The only position that still seemed to relieve her discomfort was flat on her back. The two partisans stood a bit away, grumbling and sharing a cigarette. Arkady approached them, probably to explain what happened, her injuries and such. Ten minutes later he helped her to her feet. "Don't worry. They won't bother you anymore. I even told them you'd need to rest every hour."

Katya grunted. "What did you tell them? That I'm Comrade Stalin's long-lost daughter?"

He grinned at her. "Saving that for the next time. I just told them the truth. That if they didn't behave, you'd cut off their dicks. Or, if they were lucky, toss a grenade into their dugout."

She clutched her chest to hold the pain and laughter inside.

Katya knew they were getting close when they started passing outposts. One fighter made bird calls which were always answered from somewhere up in the trees. The other guerrilla stopped several times to rap a tree with a heavy piece of wood, signaling his comrades. Even when they arrived in the heart of the well-hidden encampment, Katya found it difficult to spot the sentries camouflaged in the tree canopies. They wouldn't be easily surprised by the enemy.

Their sour-faced escorts gave no information or explanation but took them straight to the commander. He sat in a *zemlyanka*—a larger and deeper version of the type of underground dugout she had built when she and Svet were on the run. A huge downed tree served as the roof, and the dugout was almost deep enough to stand in. Ledges had been cut into the sides for weapons and clothing. A sleeping space had been excavated to the width of a man. The *zemlyanka* must have been almost four meters long, and she guessed that the commander and his deputy slept there. Logs served as furniture. The fighters gave a rough salute, and when the commander nodded, one launched into an explanation of where they'd found Katya and Arkady. The commander cut him off and dismissed them both.

"Who are you?" He looked at Arkady.

"Romashkin, Arkady Petrovich. From Staraya Russa."

The partisan commander smiled. "Ahh, yes. Our medical supplies. Quite a tightrope in Staraya Russa." His mouth relaxed and his eyes conveyed understanding.

"The noose was too tight after the birthday bombing." Arkady nodded at Katya. "I thought we could be of some use here."

The commander turned his attention to her and she glared back.

The Communist's Secret   219

He was a short, bandy-legged man about Katya's age. She imagined him leading his men on horseback across the vast plains of Russia.

"And you?" he said.

"Karavayeva, Ekaterina Ivanova, although I've been using the surname Belikova in Staraya Russa. Originally from Leningrad." She stopped, not really knowing what she should say about herself. About Luga. About Svet and Masha.

He nodded, glaring at her hard. "Why Staraya Russa?" His face was like granite. She had no idea what he was thinking, but a kernel of fear made itself known like a blackberry seed in her teeth. Was he testing her, trying to catch her in a trap?

"I was born and raised there but moved to Leningrad during the Revolution. After the war began, I was with the People's Volunteers on the Luga Line. I escaped the Germans with a comrade. We went east. Eventually we happened upon a *kolkhoz* near Staraya Russa."

He nodded. "We?"

She didn't want to talk about Svet. The black cloud had barely begun to lift. "A young woman. A fellow volunteer."

"So, are you the one responsible for the mess at the collective?"

She nodded, head down, feeling something more like shame than pride. "I had come to warn my friends. The Nazis began to execute them and I intervened. Unsuccessfully." She stopped. She didn't need to say anything else. He knew what she'd done at the *kolkhoz*. Either he was going to allow them to stay or he wasn't.

He continued to appraise her. "At this point, we can't take just anyone. We already have a dozen green boys that we're training."

Irritation bubbled out. "I've dispatched more Nazis than most." Arkady elbowed her but she ignored him. "Nineteen to be exact. Thirteen officers. Three generals. And Arkady knows more about the Nazis than they do themselves."

The partisan commander laughed. "Well, well."

"She's not exaggerating." Arkady nodded in her direction. "The birthday bombing."

The commander was still hard to read.

"The absolute truth," she said, thinking of Svet. "I'm not the best shot, not good enough to be a sniper, but I'm capable with a rifle. Better with a pistol. Calm under fire and quick." She reached across her sore ribs to cradle her broken arm. "Or I was before this. I know how to feed myself in the wild and how to cross a swamp. A number of useful skills." A hardness coated her words. Could he see she was deadly serious?

"Your injuries are from the bombing?" He continued glaring at her.

She nodded.

"So," he said, still taking her measure. "It's not often one gets the opportunity to kill so many Nazi officers."

She looked down and exhaled. He was waiting for more information. "The Kommandant invited me to attend their celebration. The senior officers were quartered in the Romashkin home. Together," she nodded at Arkady, "we were able to get a grenade inside."

"And where did you get a grenade?" His voice grated like a rusty saw.

"I took it off one of the dead Nazis at the *kolkhoz*. Only one. I didn't take more so you wouldn't be blamed. Arkady managed to plant the grenade on a window sill the night before the party. At the gathering I got the grenade and used it."

The grizzled commander weighed her words and his face lightened. "Don't take offense. You understand, you are a stranger to us. Arkady is not. Half the brigade knows and trusts him. His endorsement, as well as"—here he smiled and his voice filled with something akin to admiration—"your *hobbies* shall we say, are enough for me. Besides, someone with nineteen kills shouldn't just serve in this unit—they should lead it." He actually laughed then, in the way of one whose secure position allows them to be generous. "We're glad to have you." He stepped forward and grasped Katya's hand, a toothy grin on his craggy face.

THE ENCAMPMENT
June 1943

Dismissed by the commander, Katya followed a fighter—flat workman's cap, rifle slung over a shoulder, age impossible to determine—whose grim attitude reflected his appearance. His cold eyes had flashed her direction ever so briefly before he set off through the camp. He was supposed to be showing her where she'd sleep, but he seemed anxious to be rid of her. Katya had to stop to catch her breath. She called out to him to slow down. He could see she was injured. And he must realize she needed to pay attention to get her bearings.

"Slow down?" He snorted. "For someone who doesn't belong here?" He turned and began walking again, but slower.

Katya seethed. What was that about? He didn't even know her and yet had a gigantic chip on his shoulder. She distracted herself from his venom by examining the dugouts, lean-tos, and underground fire pits they passed. She noted a few unique trees. A number of fighters walked about. Some glanced her way, and she nodded in return.

Word about her and Arkady would spread throughout the camp, if it hadn't already. Everyone must have heard about the bombing. She hoped she wouldn't have to prove herself. She didn't feel like much of a fighter. Her body was bruised and broken and she was beginning to think it was permanent. After seven weeks, her chest still hurt. The two-day trek was a set-back. She needed rest and recuperation.

They were many miles into a massive forest south of Staraya Russa

The Communist's Secret   223

and east of Pskov, so far from traditional roads that she imagined it was mostly safe from Nazi patrols. The enemy wouldn't be interested in sending men deep enough to get ambushed. And they would need the precise location of the camp in order to call on the Luftwaffe. The guerrillas had an impressive defensive structure. Those ringed outposts ensured they'd be warned well in advance of any German incursion.

As they walked, Katya could see that the key to survival for the partisans was invisibility. The fighters she saw weren't exactly hiding. They talked and laughed. They hadn't any fear of being discovered. She found out later that the guerrillas rarely engaged Nazi patrols. No skirmishes were allowed near the base to avoid an onslaught of Nazi firepower. And it was no small effort to move the camp, although sometimes there was no other choice.

Perhaps two hundred meters from the commander's bunker, the fighter stopped."You're free to construct whatever you want, but stay within this area." He waved his hand in a general arc, his voice still cloaked in distaste. "We recommend a dugout." He dropped a short-handled shovel on the ground. The chill in the air was hard to shake.

"Wait," she said. "Do we know each other?"

He retrieved a cigarette from an interior chest pocket and lit it. "Know each other? No. You're clearly not from around here, even though you try to pass yourself off as one of us."

"You know nothing about me," she snarled.

"I know enough," he growled back. "My family lives in Staraya Russa. I know all about your antics. Bombing German officers. Did you even think twice about what would happen? About the consequences? About the innocent civilians who would die as a result?"

His words pierced her and she stuttered, searching for a reply. "What gives you the right to accuse me?"

"I am Sergei Mikhailovich, husband of Valeria, son of Marina and Mikhail, father of Olga and Boris. Or I was until my mother and son were executed as part of the reprisal after the bombing. I don't care how many fucking Nazis you've killed, protecting our citizens is our most important job."

Katya's skin prickled, as if she'd been singed. She spoke quickly, without thinking, as she often did when cornered. "If that were the case, then the partisans wouldn't exist. Guerrilla activities have been getting innocents killed since the war began."

Katya immediately regretted pointing out the obvious. He was hurt. She shouldn't argue with him. Retribution was part of war. Someday the Red Army would march on German soil. Someday they would get their revenge. They were both breathing heavily.

"Listen, I'm sorry about your family." He turned on his heel and Katya hissed after him, "You're wrong, you know. Our most important job is to defeat the Nazis. Whatever it takes." She wiped some spittle from the corner of her mouth. Of course, he had a right to be angry. She felt her heart break a little. So many losses. So many hurts. She sat against a tree, seething and miserable. Everything she did turned to stone. All the deaths she'd caused. She thought about her choices for the hundredth time, trying to rationalize every decision from joining the Volunteers to the bombing and the thirty-nine fresh graves in Staraya Russa.

After allowing herself to feel miserable for some minutes, she picked herself up and, as she always did, put the past where it belonged. She chose a spot for her *zemlyanka* and struck at the ground mindlessly and with little effect. With only one arm, the shovel barely bit the dirt. She used the edge to scrape, making the outline of a dugout. Or a coffin.

She paused, frustrated and hungry and with a bladder demanding attention. She had no idea where the latrine was or where to get something to eat. Her escort hadn't shown her anything. She wandered back in the direction they had come and after a couple of wrong turns found the commander's bunker. The guard was the same man who'd been there when she arrived. He wore parts of a Red Army uniform. He didn't look as old as Katya, but the gray in his beard meant he could be.

"Can you give me some information?"

He raised an eyebrow.

"The other guy told me nothing. Just showed me where to dig my dugout. I'm starving," she said. "And I've really got to take a piss."

He smiled and turned to a large tree, looking up. "Ivan, piss break."

Another partisan swung down and landed a few feet away. Katya felt the tree-dweller's eyes on her in the way of so many men. "I'd be happy to show you around," he said.

"*Nu tak*, well," she hesitated.

"No, I really do need to take a piss," the guard rescued her. "I'll show her the canteen too. It's almost time." He turned to Katya. "Let's go." As they moved, he began to point out a few landmarks so she wouldn't get lost. They took a turn away from the center of things, and then he stopped, pointing out particular trees and rocks that served as markers to identify that they were approaching the edge of the camp. "We don't go beyond here, unless we're on a mission, or unless we've been assigned a specific task, like retrieving firewood."

He turned around and hurried them back toward the center of the camp. She tried to memorize things that marked the way—hard when the path itself was covered with pine needles, leaves and shrubbery. Plus, her full bladder had become a complete distraction. And just as she was about to say something, he stopped and pointed to a narrow trench. At the far end planks had been laid across to allow one to squat over the pit. One end for pissing and one end for shitting.

"The latrine moves around every few weeks, but the camp kitchen never changes."

"Would you mind?" She said, motioning for him to turn around.

He colored and moved away. She hurriedly undid her pants and squatted. The planks were disgusting—covered with shit where others had missed, and clearly not designed with female anatomy in mind. She breathed through her mouth so as not to be overwhelmed by the powerful stench. She'd used plenty of outhouses in her life, but never something as revolting as this. She'd dig her own shit hole before she used the communal latrine again. She stood and they traded places.

"Now, a quick tour." He smiled. "The younger guys tend to live together over there," he pointed at a huge birch grove. "A couple of *starikis*, old men, who fought in the last war stay with them. They teach them about life, not just about fighting. About love, women, and family. Keeps them calm, focused. Gives them some perspective which is hard for the young."

She smiled very slightly. "Is Arkady with them?"

"That would make sense, but I overheard him and the commander talking. Best if he's with the Staraya Russa guys. They're suffering the most."

She looked down, trying not to think about all those people.

They walked in silence, Katya memorizing the surroundings. Several minutes more and he stopped. She saw the canteen just ahead.

"I usually eat either at the beginning or the end," he said without explanation.

"You don't like crowds?" Katya asked.

"Something like that. And the cooks make sure there's enough for everyone."

She looked into his eyes and didn't look away.

"I escaped a Nazi prisoner of war camp," he said. "A long way west of here."

Katya could imagine food was the key to survival in such a place. And he was a big man who hadn't had enough to eat for a long time.

"I'm not much for crowds myself," Katya said. "Especially being a stranger."

The Communist's Secret   227

"You aren't a stranger." He wore a kind, relaxed expression. "You're one of us now."

"Thank you," she said, but she didn't feel that she belonged. "When will they start serving? And what do I do?"

"They're about to start. Just follow me."

"By the way, I'm Ekaterina Ivanova. Katya."

"I know who you are. Everyone in the camp knows. Your reputation and . . ." he paused and a slight flush rose on his face. When he smiled at her it was not the appraising kind of look she was used to. It was warm and respectful. "Konstantin Borisovich. Here two months."

She wanted to ask him about the camp. Where and when and how bad. But he turned toward the canteen and soon they weren't alone. Fighters hung about, some smoking, some chatting, some sitting. She noticed right away that most were clean shaven and washed. She expected they'd smell, living in the wild, but it was nothing worse than a crowded *tramvai* in Leningrad in the summer. It made sense that good hygiene was important where medical care was less than basic.

A rough line had started to form. When she joined the queue with Konstantin, there were plenty of nods in their direction. Then the whistling and humming started, a soft rumble. Konstantin leaned over. "It's their way of welcoming you and showing respect. Everyone knows about the bombing. No one has done as much for Mother Russia as you."

Her heart swelled. Not even Arkady had paid her such a compliment.

Some of the fighters stamped their feet softly, the dull thuds soon finding a rhythm—a bass line for the growing chorus of vocal effects. Katya looked at the crowd of fighters—many rough-looking but others young, baby-faced lads barely out of school. There were many nods in her direction and she felt warmth in their acknowledgment.

Someone started slapping their leg, beating out the rhythm to the song everyone in Russia knew, and a rich baritone began to sing.

> "*Rasvitali yabloni i grushi,*   Apple trees and pear trees in bloom,
> *Paplyli tumani nad rikoy.*   River mists rising all around.
> *Vykhadila na bereg Katyusha,*   Katyusha went strolling,
> *Na vysoky bereg na krutoy.*   On the steep and lofty banks."

They all joined in the other verses, and even Katya sang. If she sang, she thought it might keep her from crying. But when they came to the final verse, about Katyusha protecting the love of her soldier, she fell silent and stared at the ground. This song, the "Katyusha" song, always made her feel terrible. She was not the loyal woman of this song. She'd betrayed her dear soldier.

A few tears fell and she hoped the men would think she was touched by their welcome. She looked for Arkady but couldn't find him. She bowed her head again, trying to show humility as the sound died away. Although embarrassed by the raucous welcome, she liked the attention. She had thought she was above all that, but the same old desire for admiration remained.

Numerous men came over to greet her, and many more touched their caps in a sign of regard. She caught a glimpse of Sergei through the crowd, a sneer on his face. Her first day had become a strange mix of memorable and miserable.

The guerrillas moved on to the important business—food. The unit officers sat together in a closed circle. Arkady was with them. She followed Konstantin to a spot away from the activity. When most had finished eating, the unit leaders gave out the next day's assignments. And after that the partisans faded away, most in small groups of two or three.

"Can you find your way?" Konstantin asked. "I've got to relieve Ivan."

She nodded, trying to make her face look like she'd be fine even though she wasn't at all sure she could find her way and she definitely wasn't fine. In addition to the likelihood of getting lost, she hated being alone with her thoughts. The curse of an only child. Some only children grew up capable and independent and happy in their own company. Her husband was like that. He didn't have siblings either. But Katya disliked being by herself. She watched Konstantin disappear into the trees and thought about Sergei. What if he came back in the night to get his revenge? Ridiculous, but not impossible. She'd keep her weapons within easy reach.

KONSTANTIN

Summer 1943

As the late evening sun crept toward the horizon, Katya sat on the downed tree that eventually would be the roof of her dugout, if and when she could actually dig one. The pathetic coffin-shaped indentation forced her to accept what she didn't want to admit. With only one fully functioning arm, the task was beyond her. She could not jam the shovel into the ground, forcing it to bite, and lift scoops of dirt. She'd barely been able to find a spot soft enough to dig a very shallow toilet.

At least the weather was mild, and her winter coat would help. She walked among the long shadows, gathering leaves and fir branches for a mattress and nestled against the log. She fell asleep still feeling vulnerable and hoping Konstantin would offer his assistance. He'd seen her arm was useless and she didn't want to feed their stereotypes by asking for help.

Cornered by her limitations, she went to the mess area early the following morning. As soon as Arkady joined her, she got right to the point. "Arkasha. I need help with my dugout." She nodded at her arm.

He slapped his forehead. "Katyusha. What an idiot I am. Of course. I'll get someone."

She tilted her head until it rested on his shoulder, but left it there only a moment, not wanting anyone to misinterpret their father-daughter relationship.

He put an arm around her and squeezed her shoulder gently. "A big change, isn't it?"

The Communist's Secret   231

"I thought I'd fit right in," she said. "I kill Nazis. They kill Nazis. But I don't belong. All these men. I can't socialize with them. They play cards and chess and I'm sure they talk about . . . well, you know. That's not for me."

His warm brown eyes were full of compassion. Although she was grateful to have someone like Arkady on her side, she wasn't sure he understood what was going on with her because she was just coming to terms with it herself.

He raised an eyebrow. "I've already put an end to one source of criticism and gossip."

"Oh? Well, the fighter who first escorted me gave me an earful. But he lost his mother and son in the retribution."

"He's the one I straightened out. Don't want him spreading his bad blood."

"He's not what's bothering me." She sighed. "In Staraya Russa, I had friends: Olya, Anna, Masha and Svet, but also the women in the market and the weavers. Here, I know no one. You have friends, people from town. Me? I'm alone."

"Of course," he said while patting her knee. "An adjustment. The only woman amongst so many men. And the most capable of the lot!" He laughed and she smiled.

"If I'm so capable, why don't I have a decent place to sleep? And even if I could dig my dugout, I still don't know anyone."

"Give it time. You can't join the rotation until you're stronger. But there are other ways."

She didn't want to be relegated to domestic chores. She knew what would happen. Her arm would heal and instead of getting the good assignments—attacking supply convoys and the like—she'd be stuck cooking and collecting firewood. If she wavered on her insistence to fight with the others, the commander would give her gun and her place to someone else. It wasn't that he didn't believe she was capable, but she had to be capable right now. Past accomplishments and reputation were not enough. "If I do menial chores from the start, that's all I'll ever get."

"Baranov's fair," he countered. "He might surprise you. He's devoted to this unit above all else. I've heard he's not afraid to manipulate the central authorities for the good of the brigade. And these things take time. They're built on loyalty as well as necessity. And loyalty must be earned." He finished scraping the last bit of kasha from the sides of the bowl. "One step at a time, Katyusha." He stood. "First, I'll find someone to help with your *zemlyanka*."

When Konstantin appeared at her campsite that afternoon, his eyes downcast, looking hesitant and shy, Katya was not entirely surprised. She'd hoped Arkady would ask him.

"I've come to help." His eyes reluctantly met hers. "I feel like a moron. I saw your arm, but it didn't register. You've done so much. I should have helped you yesterday. Apologies."

She wanted to hug him. Warmth and kindness from a stranger. Her eyes filled but instead of turning away to hide her tears, she put her face in her hands and began to sob. The trauma of the bombing, her injuries and loneliness, the ever-present fears about Yelena and Aleksandr sent her into a spin.

He reached for her. Hesitantly at first, but then he pulled her close without saying anything. She cried against his chest, and the comfort of being held made her cry harder. He smelled of earth and exertion, a smell which made her think of Shura. Finally, she stepped back, sniffing and wiping her sleeve across her face. "I'm sorry."

"Nothing to be sorry about. You've been through a lot. Being alone keeps the feelings inside. I know about that. Good to let it out."

"Thank you," she said and pulled away. She knew he wouldn't tell anyone.

He took the shovel and went to work, the ground yielding. She talked while he dug, starting with the story of the magnificent *zemlyanka* she'd dug for herself and Svet, and how she hated to abandon it. Then she went back in time to the attack at Luga and how they'd fled, killing Nazis along the way. She told him about Masha, about Staraya Russa, the Weissmans, and the textile factory. She told him about her parents and how she'd become a devoted citizen of Leningrad. She told him that Yelena and Sofya were trapped there now. And finally, she told him that her husband was fighting with the Red Army but had been in a labor camp before the war. The only thing she didn't tell him was that she was responsible for that.

He dug in rhythm to her words and stories. Harder and faster during the tense parts. His face glistened and dark stains appeared under his arms and down his back. He stopped and she gave him her kerchief to wipe his face and passed him her canteen. "I don't know if my family is alive either, but I think they are," he said. "I feel it. I imagine they'll return to Moscow when it's safe."

He paused. Katya could see he was about to tell her something important.

"I was captured during the early fighting."

He leaned against a tree and took a cigarette from a pocket. He lit it and offered it to her. She smiled and declined and said nothing. She wanted to hear the story.

"The Nazis marched thousands of us west. It took weeks to get to the camp, if you could call it that. Not much more than guard towers and barbed wire. It seemed that every other man died on the way. The roadway was littered with the bodies of our soldiers, marking the way home like some morbid fairytale." His words were calm, almost emotionless, but his eyes told every bit of the gruesome tale. "The first winter we slept on the ground—in holes like this. Before the second, we built crude barracks. Escape was always on my mind.

"And one day I was on a crew cutting trees, stripping branches just out of sight when there was an accident. Someone was injured—a German guard from the sound of the yelling. I crouched amidst the chaos and after a minute or two, I took my chance and ran. Must have been close to midnight before I stopped. I was moving by the moon. That first night I nearly froze, and the next day I stole some clothing off a line and got water from a well. Then I took eggs from another farm, and so it went. After a week, I saw a woman enter a barn and followed her. I can only imagine she hated all of us—the Soviets and the Germans—but she helped me. She took one look and knew I was a prisoner. She put a finger to her lips and went into the house. I wondered if she would turn me in or come out with an old man carrying a gun. Instead she brought a coat and food. And then she drew a map in the dirt. That saved my life." He shook his head. "I don't know why I'm telling you all this. You must get that a lot. Men opening up to you."

"Less than you might think," she said. "I'm not the type of woman most men hope for, or have waiting at home. Or else they think I'm a political officer."

"Well, are you?" He smiled. "A political officer, I mean." He ground out the cigarette and started digging again.

"There was a time I wanted that." She laughed at herself. "Before the war, I was a devoted Communist. I still believe in Soviet socialism, but the truth doesn't seem to have a place here anymore and there's no way to speak out and survive. I believe in the greater good as much as the next, but the problem is, the only ones benefitting seem to be those at the top. It's all become very distorted." She sighed. "How many here are Party?"

There was a questioning look on his face and for a moment that old, hard nugget of fear settled in her gut. Had she done it again? Spoken when she should have remained silent?

"Quite a few. I'd say about half the unit. Some from Staraya Russa and other towns and villages in the region. A number from Novgorod.

The Communist's Secret   235

Demyansk. A few from Leningrad. But I wouldn't worry about them. The only one I'd steer clear of is Baranov's deputy. NKVD."

He set her at ease. "You're right to be wary, but things are different out here. Not so many rules and regulations. Still, we don't talk about such things. You're not the only one too frightened to say anything. Hard to survive when the truth has no value. I thought I'd stay here a month or two, regain my strength before trying to find the Red Army. Now . . ." He shrugged. "The rumors about returning soldiers are frightening. The camps. Or nine grams."

Nine grams was the weight of a bullet. Slang for execution. Whispers were everywhere about former prisoners of war being sentenced to Soviet labor camps when they returned home. Sometimes twenty-five years. Sometimes the ultimate sentence. Konstantin was an engineer and a committed socialist. But the first months of the war had gone terribly wrong and like many soldiers, he was taken prisoner.

"They say we've been co-opted by the Nazis and now serve Germany in some nefarious way. As fascist spies." He snorted. "Maybe a few switched sides, but most of us died. I can't make sense of it. I don't want to spend my remaining years in Kolyma. One prison camp was enough. And what about my wife and children? How will they manage? Yet the constant feeling that I belong with the army keeps me from making peace with what I'm doing here."

"I understand," she said. Her husband had that same kind of devotion. To his country, to his family, to his military comrades. Ironic that it was that single word, *devotion*, that got him imprisoned. Of all the things she could have said about him, of all the possible complaints, it was the furthest from the truth.

He leaned the shovel against a tree and nodded at his handiwork. "Will this do? I've drawn latrine duty this afternoon." The dugout was more than a meter deep.

"Of course," she said and flashed him a grateful smile. When her arm and chest healed, she could make it a bit deeper. "Latrine duty?" She raised her eyebrows. "Nice to know even the best of soldiers do menial labor. A good thing about communism, don't you think?"

"Maybe," his serious eyes met hers. "But no one in the Politburo is digging latrines."

ALONE AMONG THE PARTISANS

September 1943

Katya kept to herself much of the time, the days devolving into a weighty sameness as her strength returned. To her surprise, she found she was not anxious to start the real work of the partisans. The evening meal became the one thing she looked forward to as she and Konstantin fell into a rhythm of meeting at the canteen. They often stayed late, exchanging stories while huddled in front of the fire. Every few days Arkady would join them and sometimes a handful of other guerrillas also sat and smoked and talked after their last meal of the day. It started to feel like she belonged.

Konstantin often pressed to the front of her mind, a place that had been reserved for Yelena and Aleksandr. When he was on a mission, she felt a pang of disappointment at his absence. She knew she was developing an attachment, although nothing happened between them. Since that day he'd held her while she cried, they never touched, although sometimes she saw more in his eyes than respect. It wasn't so much that she wanted something more from their relationship as it was that she was lonely. Katya was smart enough to see how war made people need human connection and human touch. She was deeply grateful for the friendship he offered and didn't cross that line.

One morning, someone rapped on her dugout without saying anything. Even among the rough partisans, it was impolite not to identify oneself.

"Can you sew?" said a voice. No hello, no introduction.

Her skin prickled, but it wasn't Sergei, or anyone else she recognized. She stepped out to face the voice.

"Who wants to know?" She wasn't going to let anyone walk all over her.

His face softened, and he looked at his feet. "I'm the lead medic. Grigori Ivanovich."

"And I'm Ekaterina Ivanova." She paused a long time, trying to make him uncomfortable although it didn't seem he needed any help with that. He refused to look in her eyes. "Now that we've been introduced, how can I help you?"

"Well, I thought perhaps you might know how to sew," he said.

"Hmmm. And why would you think that?" Women's work. She wasn't going to step into a trap here. At least not without a fight.

The bear of a man scuffed his foot while trying to think of the correct response. He sighed. "Listen, the previous lead medic was killed on the last mission." Katya had a vague memory of the sandy-haired man with glasses that looked like he was barely out of school. "I need help and I thought you might be good with a needle and thread. All the women in my family sew."

She smiled and put him out of his misery. "Well, Grigori, I can't make clothing, but I could assist with the wounded, if that's what you need." Helping the medic might not be a bad use of her time.

He brightened. "There's a unit out right now. They should be back tomorrow. Can you stand by to help?"

"Count me in."

It turned out to be a good fit for Katya, although aiding Grigori was more complicated than she expected. She'd thought it would be nothing more than suturing a few cuts here and there and she had a steady hand and good eyesight. Instead, it was battlefield surgery of a sort, something she had absolutely no business doing. But it was war and someone had to do it. Her hands and fingers were nimble and much smaller than Grigori's. She understood why he'd asked her. And helping the injured lessened her loneliness. Others were assigned to bathe the wounded and bring meals, so she didn't feel as if she was forced to accept a menial job. And often she listened to the men she'd stitched and seen at their most vulnerable. It turned out everyone was lonely to some degree.

When she wasn't helping Grigori, she walked long distances carrying a weapon and gathering firewood, doing circuits along the perimeter of the camp to improve her physical condition. She began to sense the Katya of the Luga Line and Staraya Russa returning. The strong, capable Katya.

"Comrade, I would like to be considered for duty." She approached Baranov one morning at breakfast.

The commander squinted at her, but didn't push back as she expected. "Good to hear. We have a large engagement coming. Ten days or so from now. You'll be on the team."

In her dugout later that day she realized she didn't feel the combination of nervous excitement and anticipation she expected, the kind she felt when planning the bombing. Instead, she sensed uncertainty in her gut.

It didn't help that Sergei chose that moment to harass her. She saw feet and legs outside her dugout, but waited for whoever it was to identify himself—she wasn't going to give him the satisfaction of her speaking first.

"Something could happen to a woman out here, living by herself," he said. "No one would know."

She knew his voice. "Stop threatening. Everyone in the camp knows you have it in for me. You're not going to get away with anything."

He snorted. "I guess we'll see."

In public she never engaged with him, always walked away, but this was different.

Arkady would know what to do. His reputation had grown in

the time they'd been with the partisans. Age worked in his favor. He had all the experience of an old man but didn't look his sixty-three years. He was wiry and hard, with muscled arms. He could have been a longshoreman on the docks of Leningrad, sleeves rolled up, cigarette hanging from his lips while moving freight. Mostly it was his calm that made him a favorite. No matter what happened, whether a mission was successful or a costly failure—and the unit had plenty of both—he found value in the team's efforts. He comforted men with a sympathetic word when their comrades died or when one of them learned of bad news from home. And he encouraged everyone. She'd never forgotten the time he told her why he rarely expressed disappointment in people. "If you break someone's spirit, you lose twice; making an enemy of what could have been a friend and damaging your own reputation. Always better to encourage than to tear down."

Most important to Katya, Arkady understood her, respected and genuinely liked her. He knew she was a bit too quick in making decisions and that her emotions often pushed her one way or another. But he tolerated all that and sometimes guided her to the right choice. He was a father figure and a friend, but more the former than the latter. There were times he talked down to her and she wondered if he'd be supportive of her going on the next mission. Katya suspected that deep down, and despite the birthday bombing, he felt it was fine for women to work in the medical tent, but not for them to chase Nazis through the Russian countryside.

Perhaps she'd been rash in telling Baranov she was ready. A tendency toward trying to prove herself was part of her nature.

Katya rapped on the downed tree that formed the roof of Arkady's underground quarters. The entrance was largely hidden by pine branches that he replaced every few weeks when they dried out and the needles began to drop.

"Who's there?" He sounded grumpy, which wasn't his usual demeanor.

The Communist's Secret 241

"Arkasha. It's me," she said.

"Come on, then."

Katya stepped down, careful to avoid hitting her head on the tree trunk. "Busy?"

He motioned her to sit on a small log.

She almost asked him what was going on, why he was out of sorts, but she caught herself. "Two things. I've decided to join the rotation. And second, Sergei is at it again."

He grunted. "You're feeling better? Feeling yourself?"

She stared at her hands. "It's not so much that I'm back to the way I was in Staraya Russa, but my arm's good. I enjoy the medical tent, but I need to do the real work."

"A dangerous, difficult mission is not the time to find oneself or to try to prove anything to the likes of Sergei."

She nodded. "I know, but I'm recovered physically. It seems time," she said. "I'm a bit out of sorts, but that's all the more reason to get back at it." It was a logical argument.

"Do you want my opinion, or is your mind made up?" He muttered under his breath.

She caught his eyes. "I need to get back on course. And I want your approval."

"If you can't fire your gun in the middle of a skirmish, someone will die."

"I know that. I promise, my arm is strong and my mind is focused."

He nodded. "No heroics. Just do your job. And what about Sergei?"

"Besides the usual nasty comments? He just suggested something might happen to me."

Arkady nodded. "I'll get him under control. You focus on the mission."

THE RAILWAY ATTACK
October 1943

Katya left Arkady feeling unsure. It was not quite time to go to the canteen and she walked through the dusky light toward her site. Almost immediately, she heard what sounded like someone walking behind her. She stepped next to a tree and listened. There were low voices at some distance, but the nearby menacing sound had stopped.

As she approached her dugout she heard footsteps again, louder this time, and then a body brushed past and pushed her hard. The culprit had vanished before she got back on her feet.

Maybe it was time she confronted Sergei herself.

At the canteen she stood to the side, watching. The fighters came and ate and left in singles and small groups, and still she waited. Sergei hadn't showed. Finally, she went through the line anyway. As she took her tin bowl, he appeared and knocked it from her hand.

"What's the matter, Katyusha? Haven't figured out how to hold your own here?"

"What's the matter with you?" Her voice was filled with resignation.

He pushed her again, this time so she stumbled. "You deserve worse."

"Who made you judge?" she snapped.

Baranov's deputy stepped in, taking both Sergei and Katya aside and pressing them to stop feuding.

"I'm not feuding," Sergei said. "I just want her to take responsibility for her actions."

The Communist's Secret   243

"And what would you have her do? She risked her life to kill those German officers. It was an act of bravery, not cowardice."

"Bravery? Perhaps. But also cowardice. She sacrificed the citizens of Staraya Russa. She should be punished. Thirty-nine lives lost."

Baranov's deputy wasn't a big man, but as an NKVD officer, he commanded both respect and fear. He held Sergei by the arm. "It's not your place," he said. Many partisan units had secret police and political officers. It was Moscow's effort to maintain some control over groups that were, by their very nature, decentralized. The secret police were feared everywhere, even among the rough and tumble sometimes lawless and always independent partisan forces.

Suddenly, Baranov's voice boomed as he and Arkady stormed into the canteen. "What's going on here?" He glared at Sergei. "You. Many have died as a result of our operations—we all know this is a terrible cost of war. The civilians that died in Staraya Russa are no different than the many others executed by the Germans. I've had enough. Stop blaming her for the Nazis' brutality or leave." Sergei didn't break eye contact with Baranov. After an awkward pause, a bare nod was his agreement. "You're both on the next mission so learn how to work together."

The commander turned to the men scattered about the canteen. "Gather in. Operation Concert is well underway and we're lucky enough to have a target. The mission date has been moved up. It's a two-and-a-half-day trek. We depart at 0700 tomorrow." The days were growing shorter and they had to use every bit of daylight. The thirty or so fighters stopped talking to catch Baranov's every word. A supply train was their target. It was part of the Red Army's preparation for the planned offensive in Belorussia after winter passed. But this was no ordinary "slash and run" operation. They were tasked with inflicting German fatalities as well as derailing the train and damaging the tracks.

The fighters were divided into groups: six machine gunners who had the hardest job as they might face enemy guns from within the train. Also, the machine guns and ammunition had to be carried all the way there. Another team would build the barricade that would force the train to slow. The sappers would handle the explosion and if they timed it right, the train would jump the tracks. Other partisans would hide along the verge and shoot the Nazi soldiers who came out of the stopped train and got past the machine guns. The sharpshooters were the last line of defense. They would be in the trees along the evacuation route. It would fall to them to protect the retreating fighters.

Katya did not want to be in the trees but she suspected Baranov wanted to test her in a less physical job her first time out. She tried not to take it personally.

The day of the attack was good weather for hunting: gray and cloudy with no sun to interfere. The season's first snow would soon arrive, which was fine with them as long as it wasn't heavy enough to coat the forest floor and help the Nazis track them afterward.

The sappers set the explosion with plenty of time to spare. The machine gunners were crouched in their nests of logs and shrubs. The men along the verge—perhaps halfway between the rail tracks and the forest—were invisible. As were the sharpshooters waiting for the enemy to make the costly error of pursuit.

Katya heard the approaching train. Then the squeal of its brakes. Next came the explosion and sounds of grinding metal as the huge beast went off the tracks. But no gunfire. Not yet.

Katya could see the Nazis escaping the train in her mind. Then the bursts from the machine guns. It seemed an eternity before the fighters began to fall back, but Katya knew it wasn't more than six or seven minutes. She couldn't hear Baranov, but the fighters had begun retreating to the trees. Katya saw Sergei run past.

It was all chaos and gunfire. At one point she jumped down to defend a couple of fighters. After they disappeared toward the

The Communist's Secret 245

rendezvous spot deep in the forest, she circled back, slowly now, afraid of being hunted herself. Two Germans were creeping along a small gulley when she saw Sergei unaware of their approach. She slung her rifle over a shoulder and ran to close the distance, pulling her pistol, calling a warning to him as she shot the first Nazi. Sergei went down at the same time, hit by the second soldier who turned to find the source of the unfriendly fire. Her second shot also found its mark. Svet would be proud. No wasted bullets.

She hurried to Sergei. He'd been hit near the shoulder. She opened his jacket and saw the exit wound. That was a good thing as long as it didn't bleed too much. She knew help wasn't far, so she lifted him and he draped his good arm around her. A half-kilometer was a long way to support a man, but they stumbled together through the undergrowth. His *papusha*, the submachine gun they called "daddy," was still slung over his good shoulder and hung heavy and awkward between them. Sergei didn't speak and his breathing was a disconcerting rattle as he struggled forward. Katya staggered under the combined weight, herself grunting every few steps until they reached the others.

Two fighters took Sergei from her and carried him toward the medics. She glimpsed Arkady and started to relax. At first count they'd lost just one, and the Nazis had more than a dozen casualties in addition to the destroyed train and tracks. Arkady handed her a canteen and she drank long and deep.

Suddenly, Grigori boomed. "Where is Katya?" The urgency in his voice was explained by the blood on his hands. "There you are. Let's go!"

They rushed past the men working on Sergei to a tiny, flat clearing where a figure lay on the ground. Her heart became a vise in her chest. Konstantin.

"The leg. Bullet hit the femoral artery." Gregori explained how he'd clamped both ends. "I don't want to expand the incision. Every minute of delay increases the likelihood we'll have to amputate. And my hands are too big to maneuver. You need to do it. I'll assist."

As she washed her hands and someone tied an apron around her waist, he filled her in. "Petrov had a tourniquet on him within three minutes. Said the blood was everywhere. Kostya's lucky his comrades knew what to do and got him here quickly. He lost consciousness when I made the incision."

Sometimes they had morphine, but they'd run out of that as well as surgical gloves. A tin dish held the bullet Grigori had removed. One green-looking young fighter held a torch over the gory leg with one hand while trying to absorb the blood pooling in the wound with the other. Katya put her hand on the lower leg. It was growing cool to the touch, deprived of blood. She stared at the clamps on the damaged artery. Toward his groin the vessel pulsed strongly with every heartbeat, while the lower part was flaccid and lifeless. She took a breath and an intense focus settled over her. The artery had been partially severed by the bullet as Grigori explained, and for a moment she debated whether to close it as it was, or to cut the artery completely to be able to work with clean edges. It was like a flip of the coin. She chose to close it as it was because it would take less time.

Someone handed her a fine needle threaded with the thinnest suture they had. She didn't know where to start but did not hesitate. She used two fingers to lift the artery out of the gore and made the first stitch. It was as if someone else was working on Konstantin. One after another the tiny stitches landed. Several were perfect, and she started to believe the vessel would heal itself. But a couple of spots ended up lumpy and uneven making her entirely unsure if it would hold and heal. She finished, even managing to tie a small but perfect knot, and finally looked up.

"Three minutes," Grigori said. "Then we'll remove the clamps. They've already been on too long. I'm afraid he's going to lose his leg." While they watched the time, the small, silent crowd inched closer,

The Communist's Secret 247

Arkady and Baranov among them. Their grim faces told of their understanding that this was the type of wound most men in the field would die from. Katya stepped away. Someone brought a canteen to rinse her hands.

The three minutes were gone and Grigori motioned to her. They hunched over Konstantin and removed first the lower, then the upper clamp. Katya stared at the damaged artery, waiting for it to leak. Instead, it jumped to life along its entirety. Within another minute the color began to return to Konstantin's lower leg. After a few more, Grigori stood and patted her on the back. "Beautiful work," he said. "I'll pack it with sulfa and close. We'll give him the second unit of plasma in a few hours. It's all we've got. I expect some in the next drop but it'll be several days before we're back at camp."

Katya remembered hearing that one-third of the team would divert to the remote spot where the bulk of their supplies we're dropped by Soviet planes.

Grigori was still talking. He got like this when under pressure. "But if he doesn't do well overnight, I may have to do a live transfusion. We did it once before. There are a couple of guys who are candidates." He was getting the sulfa out of the medical kit. "He can't be moved until it's had a chance to heal. A day at least. Two would be better. The return to camp will be twice as long. We'll need two teams to carry him."

Katya was hardly listening. Her emotions were rising, and when he paused, she nodded and turned away. As she passed the group that had been watching, they murmured their praise. "Well done." "That's it, Katyusha." "Knew you could do it."

She walked as far from the fighters as was safe. Then she sat on the ground and wept.

THE END OF KATYA'S WAR
Winter 1943–44

A few weeks later Katya lay in her dugout waiting for the war to end—something she did more and more often—when someone rapped and called her name. Sergei.

She sat up and grabbed her rifle to pretend she was cleaning it. "Come in."

He stepped down and she pointed for him to sit.

"I came to thank you," he said.

She hardly knew what to say. She'd saved his life but didn't imagine his opinion of her had changed. She thought of Arkady and reached for higher ground. "*Nichevo nye bylo.* It was nothing. You would have done the same."

"I doubt that," he said, his expression contrite. "I shouldn't have said those things. I know we're on the same side."

"You had reason to be angry. Your family. I'm sorry."

He nodded. "We've all lost a lot. But victory will be ours. And you were right. That's the most important thing."

The next time her turn came up in the rotation, she feigned illness. The time after that she said two words, "women's troubles," and Baranov's deputy turned away like she had a disease. In fact, she hadn't had a regular flow for most of the war. Olya had explained that it was normal to miss your monthly when you didn't have enough food. "Same thing happened during Stalin's collectivization," she'd said.

The Communist's Secret   249

"Maybe it'll never come back," Katya replied and they both laughed. Who wanted to deal with that once you were done having children?

She avoided Baranov. Days turned into weeks, yet she remained entirely wrung out. She began helping again in the medical tent, but otherwise steered clear of everyone but Konstantin. He was moved to his dugout, and while he recovered she read to him from a couple of the worn books passed around the unit. The detachment had doubled in size from when she and Arkady arrived, making it easy to disappear in plain sight. She was no longer the only woman. Most importantly, the Red Army was amassing a steady string of victories. At the end of January came the news that the blockade of Leningrad had been broken.

The war didn't feel as it had before. On the Luga Line, when she'd killed her first Nazi soldier, she hadn't had time to think. Fear pushed aside all else. And a powerful desire for revenge propelled her through the birthday bombing. But now? She still wanted revenge, but she also wanted it all to stop. All the killing, all the brutality. She felt nothing in her chest, just emptiness where her heart should have been. And she knew if her heart wasn't in it, she wouldn't survive. Sooner or later she would make a mistake and end up rotting next to some Nazi convoy or derailed train.

After admitting the truth to herself, she went to Arkady. "I need to go home." She looked down at her boots, examining the bits of leather cracking and peeling. She'd had nothing on her feet but these work boots since she left Leningrad at the beginning of the war, not counting the night of the bombing when she'd squeezed into Olya's only pair of pumps.

"You shouldn't be embarrassed," Arkady said. "After all your contributions there's no shame in wanting to be done with it. With wanting to see your daughter."

"Leaving seems cowardly."

"No one can call you a coward, Katyusha," Arkady said. "I'll mention it to Baranov. He's already asked me what's going on with you so it won't be a huge surprise."

Although ashamed, she wanted to believe the commander would understand. Katya didn't fear Baranov, even though he was a powerful man. Rumor had it he'd once broken a man's neck with a single twist. He demanded a lot of his fighters, only a third of whom were former Red Army and understood the extreme demands, and had a way of managing the conflicts inevitable in close quarters. If soldiers depended upon their comrades for survival, it was even more so for partisans. Baranov used truth and honesty to build trust. The irony was not lost on Katya and she held him in high regard.

A few days later she summoned the nerve to disappoint him. "Comrade Commander, I would like permission to return to Leningrad."

He looked especially stern. "There are only two ways out: a German surrender, or . . ."

Was he teasing? That was military policy. Not one step back. And there were political officers in the ranks to enforce Stalin's decree, pistols at the ready. But she was a civilian. She had not enlisted in the Red Army. She never imagined the partisans had the same absolute code.

"Comrade, my family is in Leningrad," she said. "I belong there, to help them and the city recover. And you don't need me anymore. Not to chase a bunch of half-frozen Nazis."

A smile twitched at his mouth. "Yes, yes, but if everyone left because the war was going well, then soon the war wouldn't be going well. It's necessary to follow through to the end."

She looked at the ground and the truth burbled up. "I have been honored to be part of this unit. But something has changed. I don't know how to explain it, but I am reluctant." The words stuck in her throat. "Reluctant to fight. Perhaps I am simply a coward." She hung her head.

The Communist's Secret   251

"Cowardice is not driving you," he said. "There's something else."

Katya nodded, searching for the words to describe what she didn't understand. "Too much death. And my daughter. Trapped in Leningrad all this time."

He exhaled. "Under the circumstances—Leningrad, your service, and the fact that others need you even more than we do—you may go. You can serve the Motherland there. Help the brave people of Leningrad and your family. But the fighting between here and there is fierce. You can't go now. Perhaps in some weeks. A few months at the most."

"Thank you, Comrade." She again examined the ground, searching for the words to admit her failings. "I'm sorry my service to this unit hasn't been what I hoped."

"It does not matter that your best was before your time with us. Besides, on your single mission you had two kills and saved the lives of two comrades." He reached for her hand and gripped it in a powerful handshake. "After you depart, the Party will receive a letter from me. We shall miss you, Katyusha."

Konstantin left the partisans before she did. His leg had healed and he decided to rejoin the Red Army. They exchanged addresses in the faint hope of meeting after the war.

"Your husband is a lucky man."

"Kind of you to say so, but we both know that's not entirely true." She'd never told him about the betrayal, but he'd seen her for who she was all along.

He patted her cheek and stepped away, calling over his shoulder. "Perhaps you'll get another chance, sweet Katyusha."

In June of 1944, while the partisans joined the long chase into Germany, she and Arkady went north. She paused in Staraya Russa only long enough to get supplies, visit the cemetery, and extract a promise from Arkady that he would come to Leningrad to visit when the war was over. Then she followed the Volkhov River north. Just before reaching Lake Ladoga, she hopped a truck into the recently freed city of Lenin, steeling herself for what she might find.

LENINGRAD LIBERATED
Summer 1944

They swung around the southern entrances to the city, taking a circuitous route to avoid the worst of the damage. But from what Katya could see, there were few places that hadn't been struck by German bombs or artillery. Debris lined entire neighborhoods, waiting for removal. The city's *babushki* were out in force, in ones and twos and threes—an army of old women in headscarves—brooms and shovels at the ready. They worked to bring Leningrad back to life while they waited for the war to end and hoped for their sons and grandsons to return.

The truck turned toward the city center from the north, across the still intact Liteiny Bridge. As they drove above the Neva River, Katya saw the low-slung Peter and Paul Fortress resting so very close to the water as it always had, like a swimmer contemplating a plunge. The driver turned down the Neva embankment, the wide boulevard gracing the south side of the river. When they reached the former Winter Palace—damaged but not horribly so from what Katya could see—she banged on the rear of the truck's cab so the driver would let her out. The Admiralty and St. Isaac's were also standing, filling her with hope. She caught a tram up the Nevsky, Leningrad's main boulevard. Once a place for shopping and strolling, now it held more work crews than pedestrians. When the tram passed Gostiny Dvor, the city's largest shopping center, Katya noticed it was under repair.

In another minute the streetcar rumbled to a stop before the Anichkov Bridge, and Katya disembarked. The bridge looked naked without its stallions. When she was preparing to leave Leningrad at the start of the war, the authorities had arranged for the massive statues to be buried in one of the city's parks. Maybe soon they'd be unearthed and returned to their pedestals.

She stood at the bridge's center and looked down the Fontanka River, one hand on her chest. The distinctive building was there: Fontanka Embankment 54. The weight of all her fears settled, rooting her to the spot. After some length of time—a few minutes or an hour she didn't know—she forced herself to finish crossing the bridge and turn down the street. The elegant apartment building had no visible damage. If it had survived, so could have Yelena. It loomed larger with every reluctant step until she pushed open the door to the courtyard. The striking archways and angles were there. The entryway door was ajar and she entered the silent structure.

Up the stairs and along the third-floor hallway she crept, hoping beyond hope to hear her darling daughter. Let her be alive, she prayed to the God she'd never accepted. When Katya finally stood outside the correct door she stopped, unable to bring herself to knock. It was better not to know. If she left now, she could still imagine her Lenochka alive. If she knocked, the truth would bare its teeth, grab her by the neck, and shake her until her blood ran down the hallway.

She collapsed with a soft cry outside the apartment. All these months and years she'd worked hard to bury any suggestion that Yelena might be dead. Every time the serpent of death slithered in, she threw it out, insisting her daughter had survived, promising to be a better mother, vowing to never take Yelena for granted again. But now the truth was behind this simple door. She curled into herself, unable to move, unable to knock, unable to walk away and waited to be bitten.

And then, she heard voices from within. Children's voices. Confusion roused her and she covered her ears with her hands, blocking out the sounds of life. Life that wasn't her daughter's.

The Communist's Secret 255

The door opened. Someone bent over, tapping her shoulder, speaking to her.

"Are you all right? Do you need help?"

She knew the voice and raised her tear-stained face.

A shriek filled the hallway. "Mama! Mama! It's you." Arms held her, wrapped her in a strong embrace, and pulled her up. She gazed into the bright blue eyes of her daughter. "Oh, Mama. You're alive. You're home."

And still she could not speak, her heart broken open. She clung to her Lenochka and the two of them wept, her daughter's face buried against her own. Minutes passed and Katya could not let go. Almost three years she had worried and waited. She felt her daughter's thin frame through her clothes. They were both skinny, but there would be time to eat, to gain a bit of plumpness. For now, she simply wanted to hold her beloved daughter. To kiss her soft cheek and whisper the words she'd always kept to herself, "*Ya lyublyu tebya*. I love you."

The three little ones had gone quiet. They stood a few steps away, staring as the adults clutched each other. "Mama?" The little girl whispered. "Who is this? Shall I get her some tea?"

Yelena brought her mother inside with a quick explanation about the children, something Katya hadn't imagined. When she learned that the littlest one was her grandson, she cried again. And then, in a very straightforward way that reminded Katya of Aleksandr, Yelena told the children that this strange, dirty woman who carried nothing more than a rucksack was *her* mama.

Her daughter kept right on talking, answering all of Katya's questions before she asked them. "Do you remember Pavel, Grandma's violin student?"

"The tall, handsome boy from your school?"

"That's the one. He worked on the Ice Road all that first, terrible winter when the city was starving. He kept us alive. His truck went through the ice on Ladoga two Aprils ago." She held out her hand so Katya could see the ring. "My brave Pavel. We planned to marry."

Katya pulled her daughter tight. "*Dorogaya.*" The two women embraced for a few more minutes while the children remained bewildered at all the emotion.

Yelena stepped back and said, "You sit, Mama. I can imagine it's been a difficult time."

Katya sat on the threadbare sofa, drinking tea from a real glass, watching the children while Yelena puttered in the kitchen. The smells of food frying reached her and Katya realized how hungry she was.

Yelena poked her head into the living room. "Grandma Sofya will be home soon, and we'll eat." She came close to Katya and put a hand on her shoulder. "After the children are in bed, you can tell us where you've been. If you want to, that is."

Katya nodded. "But first, any news of your papa?"

Yelena's eyes began to glisten. "No news for a long while. But he survived Kursk and Stalingrad before that. He must have made it through the rest." Her wan smile showed her fear.

Still, it felt like good news to Katya. Last summer's tank victory at Kursk had come six months after the victory at Stalingrad.

"And Admiral Vasili?" She spoke softly, afraid to ask.

"He's fine. He and Grandma married right after little Sasha was born." She smiled. "She says he's too tough to die."

It seemed miraculous that they had both survived to look forward to a life together after the war. Katya felt happiness bubble inside. Sometimes the good are rewarded.

When Sofya arrived, Katya clutched the frail-looking older woman, even though they'd never been close. She murmured "thank you" and "you saved her."

Sofya took Katya's hand, patting it. "We saved each other." It was just like her mother-in-law to deflect the praise.

After dinner Katya bathed and found a spare set of her own old night clothes, musty-smelling from disuse. Sofya and Yelena sat, looking at her expectantly. There was no one else to ask after so she

The Communist's Secret   257

took a deep breath and began. Not the whole story, but the basics of her escape from Luga and her time in Staraya Russa, and the partisans. She even told them about the village, which she hadn't told anyone, not even Arkady or Olya. A wave of sadness made her pause. She should have trusted them. She should have told them.

And as she described the attack, a familiar darkness tugged her away from the truth. But this time, she didn't let it take her. Yelena and Sofya were family. And women too. They'd understand. And maybe they'd take away a bit of her shame. Katya was dry-eyed, but her daughter and mother-in-law wept at the story. She stood to get the vodka from the cupboard and they both followed, wrapping their arms around her and telling her how brave she was and repeating what she'd often told herself in consolation: living was the best revenge.

They sat again and took a few swallows of vodka and Katya finished telling them about Svet and Masha, Arkady and Olya, Anna and her family, the bombing, and the partisans. She didn't build herself up in the retelling, and ended by talking about Konstantin and the rumors about what was happening to former prisoners of war like him. It was wrong. She wanted to do something about it. At that, Yelena and Sofya looked at each other, puzzlement evident in their expressions.

"I know this all seems strange," said Katya. "I suppose it can be explained by the war. Not all our suffering has been at the hands of the Germans. Things from before the war. Certain policies." And then she whispered, "Stalin."

She fiddled with her wedding ring, the plain gold band she'd never taken off. "There's one more thing. The most important thing of all. I need to apologize to you, and eventually, to your papa." She stared at her daughter. "Sofya knows what I did, but I need to tell you. I hope you can forgive me." Katya looked at the floor. "Before the war, I caused your father's arrest. I spoke when I shouldn't have and someone twisted my words. I love your papa." She took a breath so she could finish. "But it was my fault. I knew better."

The three of them sat, silent, until finally Yelena spoke, her voice soft and tender, full of pain. "And then you never went to visit him. Did you ever write?"

Katya raised her eyes to meet her daughter's. She felt a lie stirring. She didn't want Yelena to hate her. What could she say so her daughter would forgive her? She'd been through so much, seen so much. There was nothing but the truth left.

"I was selfish and cowardly. I didn't want to risk my position." Her voice faded.

Yelena stood and went to a window. The boys were fast asleep, sharing a mattress in the corner. Katya watched her daughter, her silhouette hunched, more resigned than angry. What a disappointment she was. If Yelena could not forgive her, how could she ever think Shura might?

Sofya rose, patting Katya's arm. She went to Yelena and the two of them spoke in low tones. After a few minutes, Katya joined them. "I hope you can forgive me. I am so sorry. I was not a good person. Maybe it doesn't seem possible to you. You two were born good. You never put yourselves first." They had no idea what it was like for Katya being so attached to the Party. Surrounded by people who professed loyalty to something higher—to Stalin and the great Soviet state he was creating. It gave her something lofty to aspire after. Could her family see how that had drawn her in? And then how going along became a matter of survival?

Katya knew her values and loyalties had been rearranged, but she also knew that Yelena might not accept that. She sniffed, waiting, but her daughter said nothing. Katya took a half-step back and whispered, "Tell me and I'll be gone in the morning. I only want happiness for you."

As she shuffled to the kitchen, Yelena came after her. "I'm hurt for Papa, but you belong with us. Don't go. I love you, Mama."

A PLACE TO BELONG
Summer 1944–Spring 1945

Three youngsters under ten kept the energy level high in the Karavayev household. Yelena worked at the local school where the children attended and Sofya was performing as much as she ever had. After the Leningrad Philharmonic Orchestra returned from Kuibyshev, the Radio Committee Orchestra might not be in such demand, but all through the war—and especially now that the blockade had lifted—her mother-in-law played several times a week, devoted to the orchestra and its humble director, Karl Eliasberg.

Sofya was kinder than Katya thought she deserved. Her mother-in-law never pushed her to find work, never made unwelcome suggestions or criticized. But it turned out the older woman understood the complexities of life in ways Katya had never considered. After just a few weeks, Sofya cornered her on a Saturday afternoon.

"Come," the older woman said. "Walk with me to Gostiny Dvor."

Katya was uncomfortable being alone with Sofya. Her mother-in-law knew her flaws better than anyone, and she felt inferior in her company. Katya hoped Sofya just wanted someone to carry her packages.

The older woman took her arm as they drew close to the Anichkov Bridge, where she turned left. But instead of continuing up the Nevsky, Sofya pulled Katya into the Mikhailovsky Gardens where curved paths and abundant foliage provided privacy. Verdant waves spilt one after the other, drawing attention to themselves rather than to those who might seek the miracle of invisibility.

260 Suzanne Parry

"I hope you don't mind," Sofya said. "I've been wanting to talk with you."

"Oh, Sofya, I'm so very sorry for what happened. It haunts me every moment. As soon as Aleksandr returns, I will confess everything. I know he deserves the truth." She looked down.

"No, it's not that." Sofya shook her head. "It's something I did, years and years ago. A secret I've kept for decades but finally told Vasili and Yelena."

Katya tilted her head. What on earth was Sofya talking about?

Her mother-in-law continued. "I'm not going to beat around the bush. Aleksandr is Vasili's son."

Katya stopped and Sofya turned to look at her, grim-faced and hunched under the burden. Katya knew Vasili was Sofya's first real love, she had told her as much before the war. But Aleksandr's father? That made no sense.

"I don't understand," said Katya. "You were married to Andrei. You had a life together."

"Yes. And with time we were happy. And Andrei never knew the truth." Her mother-in-law looked down and Katya recognized the shame the older woman carried. "But the truth is complicated. Vasili and I fell in love just after I married Andrei. We ended our affair because his wife was pregnant. I didn't yet know that I was expecting too. What could I do? I never told anyone. Decades of silence and loneliness until Vasili wanted us to marry. That was around the time Yelena was expecting. Both Yelena and Vasili have forgiven me. Aleksandr is the only one I haven't told. I hope . . ." Her voice caught and Katya knew she wondered if Aleksandr would return and she'd get the chance to tell him.

She took Sofya's hand and squeezed it. "He will forgive you. He has a good heart."

No wonder Sofya had been so kind, so understanding. She knew what it was like to feel alone and unworthy. Perhaps the older woman

The Communist's Secret 261

had encouraged Yelena to forgive because she lived under her own dark cloud of betrayal.

Katya pulled Sofya into an embrace. "All those years, you must have felt very alone."

Sofya nodded. "But it's in the past. And I have my family."

Katya's eyes filled. Perhaps she and Sofya weren't so different after all. She had lived with years of loneliness too. She'd pushed away those she loved out of fear. Her baby boy. She didn't want to feel that kind of pain again. But there was no way to love without accepting the risk of being hurt. In that moment, she realized how deeply she loved them—Yelena and Shura. Without even deciding, her heart was taking the risk.

Admiral Vasili stayed at the apartment for several days every couple of months. The first time he walked through the door, Katya froze. They had met before the war, but she didn't recall such a striking resemblance. The same broad-shouldered but lean build, the same eyes, not quite the rich, bright blue of a clear summer afternoon. And the voice too. She tried to act normal, but it was difficult. It was Shura in twenty-five years.

The apartment was so full it felt like a *kommunalka,* a communal apartment. The three children slept together in the living area and the four adults in the bedrooms. For all the kindnesses, it was a difficult adjustment for Katya. The bonds between the others, forged during the dark days of the siege, were like iron. Sometimes she felt like a distant cousin who'd come to visit.

During those first months together, Katya contributed as best she could. She did some cooking and laundry and watched the children. Then she joined a street crew, moving debris into trucks that carried load after load out of the city. She didn't feel she could be in a factory, and the street work was hard, physical labor that distracted her from her heartache for Shura. Every day she checked the mail, afraid to find the official-looking envelope that would announce his death. Until one day early in the last winter of the war, an official envelope did arrive. Katya gripped it in trembling hands until she realized it was from the Party, not the military. She tore it open to find her party membership had been restored, "for her service to the Soviet Union in the war against the Fascists." She should pick up her new Communist Party card at her local District Committee.

"Well, Mama, it's what you wanted, isn't it?" Yelena said.

"It was. But now?" Katya shook her head and began to whisper. "Here we are, nearing the end of the war and still there is no rejoicing, no welcoming our soldiers home. Instead, the Party scrutinizes and accuses them of anti-Soviet activities. The same kind of suspicion and false accusations as before the war." Almost talking to herself, she continued. "A Party card will open doors. Maybe I will go to Moscow, check on Konstantin's family and find out where he is."

"Oh, Mama, you've just arrived," Yelena said, even though it had been six months. "Stay for a while longer. Don't you deserve a chance to just live? Be here with us. There will be plenty of time to help. And you're already supporting the city with your work."

Katya had told them about Konstantin and her suspicions about his fate. She feared he had been arrested as a traitor as soon as he returned to the Red Army or would be arrested upon returning home when the war ended. She looked into her daughter's eyes. "Makes me sick. Our own soldiers. It's hard to discover that something you believed is entirely wrong. I was so sure few people would suffer in a socialist state." Her eyes narrowed. "I was wrong. I can see that I just kept trying to convince myself of something that wasn't true."

More and more she worried about Shura too, anxious that he also might be arrested after the war was over. That they would send him back to the camp to finish out his sentence without so much as a thank you for his service.

The Communist's Secret   263

Despite all the risks he'd taken during the occupation, Katya never imagined Arkady would be the one the NKVD came for. The news was delivered in secret, on a piece of paper slipped under the apartment door. Winter had broken, but the partisans were still fighting so it couldn't have been someone like Sergei that brought the note, someone who might feel they owed her something. It had to be from Staraya Russa. Maybe a member of Arkady and Olya's family. The note hinted at that.

"Olya's brother arrested. Sentenced to death but reduced to twenty-five years for his work with the partisans and the birthday bombing."

No signature. Nothing that might implicate anyone.

After dinner that night, she told them about Arkady's arrest. "Now I have to go. I owe Arkady everything. I wouldn't have survived in Staraya Russa if it hadn't been for him and his sister. On top of that, I'm worried about your papa. Will he be arrested when the war ends?" She tucked a strand of Yelena's hair behind her ear. "The Nazis are done for. It won't be long. I don't want to wait until our soldiers are already in Siberia."

"Where will you stay, Mama?" asked Yelena.

"I'm not sure. Maybe Admiral Vasili can help. His daughter-in-law and grandchildren may have moved back by now. And if not, I'm resourceful. I'll find a room."

"And then?"

"Then I'll start making inquiries into Arkady's whereabouts. I'll petition the Central Committee, attend Party meetings. I'll look for former partisans and soldiers who feel the same. I'll get in touch with Konstantin's family. Find out where he is."

Yelena looked at her, beseeching. "But Mama, what will you accomplish? They won't listen to you. You'll be arrested. They'll say you're a traitor, a wrecker, a malcontent."

"Maybe so, but it's not very convincing to call someone a traitor if they've sacrificed for their country. I fought as hard as anyone. I killed twenty-one Nazis. That gives me some right to speak." Katya felt her self-assurance returning. She brushed aside Yelena's concerns, certain of her own beliefs and of the correctness of her plan. "There has to be someone in Moscow interested in the way citizens from the former occupied territories are being treated. Or the terrible injustice being done to soldiers returning from German camps. I'm certain there are others who feel as I do." She hugged her daughter. "I won't stay in Moscow long. No more than a few months. Just long enough to remind the Party of what is important."

SEARCHING FOR THE CENTRAL COMMITTEE

Summer 1945

Before she left Leningrad, Katya composed a letter, sealed it, wrote Shura's name on it, and tucked it into the drawer of the secretary. When the time came to go, she felt herself reverting to her old ways: acting self-assured and doling out quick, unemotional hugs to Yelena and the children. She knew what Yelena thought of her plans and had already decided not to listen despite what had happened the last time she'd ignored her daughter's opinion.

"First of all, I promise I'll be back. Second, I've left a letter for your father. If he returns before I do, please give it to him." She pointed at the beautiful piece of furniture, one of the things Yelena and Sofya hadn't burned during the gruesome siege.

Her daughter nodded. "We'll be here, Mama. Call or write if you need anything."

Katya squeezed her a second time, with more emotion than the first, and kissed her too. She'd been in Leningrad nearly a year and was feeling more and more at home. But she had to do this. She had to see if anything could be done for Arkady. And the pull to protect Shura and Konstantin and nameless other patriots was a powerful magnet.

It was May when she settled into a seat on the overnight train to Moscow. She hadn't been on a train since the start of the war. The shabbiness of the Moscow-Leningrad line surprised her. Such

265

an important route and the seats were stained and broken. Curtains were torn or missing altogether. Of course, the nation had been focused on the war effort—producing tanks, not fixing passenger trains. Defeating Nazi Germany had taken everything the Soviet Union had. Katya was proud to belong to a nation that wouldn't give up. The Soviets had pushed the Germans back. And she had been part of that.

She was asleep—her head leaning at an uncomfortable angle on the window where it bounced against the glass now and then—when a noise roused her. Shouting and cheering rose above the rumble of the wheels on rails. A stomping of feet rippled like a distant storm through the iron beast and Katya looked around. People were crying and yelling.

The war was over. Germany had surrendered, and General Zhukov was in Berlin. She watched the strangers pull vodka from their luggage and toast Comrade Stalin and General Zhukov. Like her, many must be thinking of their husbands and sons and fathers and fervently wishing for their return. Katya wondered if the dreams that had carried them through four horrific years would be dashed on the rocks of reality. Of course she was glad the war was over, but the chill she felt could be the disappearance of her last vestige of hope. Her task felt urgent. If Aleksandr returned, she wanted to help him and others who might face the camps—a fate most assuredly as dark and final as death.

The nation's capital crouched on seven hills surrounding the Moscow River. Loyal to Leningrad, Katya was determined not to like Moscow. The bridges were smaller and had less personality. The streets were broader, and at one time could have been grand but right now simply emphasized the emptiness of the place. When she turned into Red Square, however, she was unprepared for such a magnificent space: the Kremlin towers and crenellated walls of rich, red brick, the

The Communist's Secret   267

cobblestone expanse and St. Basil's Cathedral at one end. Lenin's mausoleum stood squat and perfectly serene against the Kremlin. Katya touched the granite wall for a few moments. The tomb itself was closed. She asked an elderly passerby why she couldn't see Lenin. "They evacuated him with everyone else. Bunch of cowards," the woman grumped. Empathy and admiration rose in Katya for the disheveled old *babushka* who hadn't fled the city.

Moscow had suffered less than Leningrad, but plenty of poor wandered the streets, homeless and begging. Katya herself could find little food, except in the thriving black market. She had thought Moscow would be an orderly, prosperous place with well-fed citizens. It had been bombed, true, but nothing like Leningrad and in any case, as the seat of the Soviet government she expected more energy, more life, just a tiny bit of swagger.

With the help of Admiral Antonov, Katya found a corner in a *kommunalka*. The old woman who was assigned the entire room—quite a luxury at the time—was more than happy to have Katya pay to sleep there. It might be illegal, but rules were easily bent, and the authorities were distracted by the war recovery. Katya made the ancient *babushka's* life a bit easier. Mornings she helped with chores; afternoons were her own and she wandered the city.

Within a few days she found the address Konstantin had given her. It was a dimly lit structure of cheap apartments, built perhaps fifteen years earlier in the constructivist style. The wealthy and well-known did not live there, which strengthened Katya's belief in her own anonymity. She knocked on the apartment door. It was early evening, dinner time, which Katya thought was the best time to find people at home. A well-built woman opened the door and replied to Katya's "*Dobryy vecher,* good evening" with "*Privyet,* welcome," but seemed not to mean it.

"I'm Karavayeva, Ekaterina Ivanova, and I'm looking for Natalya Kreshova."

"You've found her." The woman looked increasingly unhappy to have a stranger at her door.

She was nothing like what Katya expected. She'd thought Konstantin's wife would be softer, gentler perhaps. "Your husband and I served in the same partisan unit. When he left to return to the Red Army, he gave me your address."

"What good is that? You can't help us. Nobody can. That traitor. It would have been better if he had been killed. At least then the children and I would get his pension. Instead we've been branded as 'enemies of the people' too. We have this apartment only because of my parents." Her eyes flashed with anger and maybe fear too.

The sternness on her face turned to suspicion and the woman glanced down the hall. She stepped out of the apartment and closed the door most of the way. She put a finger to her lips and whispered, "Moment," then stepped partway back into the apartment. "I'm going for cigarettes," she called down the hall. "Won't be long." She pulled the door tight and led Katya out of the building, past a dilapidated playground and down a quiet street.

The news of Konstantin was a weight, silencing Katya. It was just as she feared.

"You know my husband?" Natalya's face had transformed. She was full of warmth. "I'm sorry about back there. You know. Someone is always listening."

Katya took the woman's arm so they looked like old friends or two sisters out for an evening stroll. "I met Konstantin with the partisans. He told me about being captured by the Germans early in the war. And his time in a German camp." She squeezed the woman's arm. "I'm sorry. I had hoped he might escape arrest because of his service with the guerrillas." Katya thought of all he'd sacrificed. His horrible leg injury.

"There's no escaping our future." Natalya stopped. "I'll give you the camp address." She pulled a scrap of paper and a nubby pencil out

The Communist's Secret 269

of her pocket and scrawled the address from memory. "I don't know if he gets mail, but if he does, it would be such a boost to hear from you. I can only imagine how alone he feels." She sniffed. "He was sentenced as a fifty-eight. Twenty-five years. The rest of our lives."

Fifty-eight—a political prisoner. Which meant especially harsh treatment and little possibility of release. "There was not a better man among the partisans," Katya said. "I came to Moscow to plead his case and that of another comrade. If I make any progress, I'll try to let you know."

"Since when would Stalin show mercy?" Natalya replied. "I only hope my children don't suffer under the stigma. To protect them I must hold onto my job and keep my head down."

Would Natalya be swept into a reprisal? Her children placed in an orphanage? The Weissmans popped into Katya's mind. They'd marched to their deaths with nothing but false hope. Natalya was more clear-eyed and realistic. That might help her.

"Be strong. For your children. For Konstantin." She stopped. "I'll leave you here." She glanced around, expecting to see someone in the shadows. "If he could survive a German camp, he can survive Siberia." Katya hugged the forlorn woman and hurried across the street.

Back in her corner of a room, Katya began organizing her thoughts for the Central Committee. Most of the Kremlin complex had not been damaged by German bombs, but the Grand Kremlin Palace where the Central Committee normally met had been hit and was under repair and reconstruction. Her disappointment blossomed when she learned that the Central Committee hadn't convened since before the war. The Politburo was doing everything—making all the decisions. Still, Katya held onto a sliver of belief in the system and decided to present herself to the District Committee, or the City Party Committee. She wanted to attend a meeting and speak to someone. Surely one of these lesser organizations would hear what she had to say. She clung to the idea that people in the Soviet Union had rights.

She rehearsed her speech in defense of both Arkady and returning Soviet prisoners of war, like Konstantin. *"Why should they be sentenced to prison just because they had the ill fortune to be captured? Wasn't that a result of the military situation? Of forces beyond their control?"* She wanted to point the finger of blame at the leadership but decided that was too blunt and too risky. *"These men fought valiantly for our great nation against the Fascists. Haven't they sacrificed and earned a hero's welcome? Don't they deserve to return to their families?"*

She thought of the times she and Arkady had talked about Stalin and what kind of persecution might happen after the war. Perhaps she too would be arrested. She'd also worked at the factory. Forced by the occupying Nazis or not, she knew that it didn't make any difference to Stalin. Perhaps she should use herself as an example. *"Will you imprison me as well? I had the ill fortune to be in German-occupied territory. Together with Romashkin, Arkady Petrovich, devoted patriot and hero who has been arrested, we bombed a gathering of Nazi officers in Staraya Russa on the twentieth of April 1943. No doubt you have record of this action. We killed thirteen and injured dozens more. All told, in that bombing and other operations, I killed twenty-one Nazis. Many of us in occupied towns and villages did what we could to defeat the enemy."*

She put down her pen. What was she thinking? Launching into a defense of those Stalin had already decreed guilty? Order No. 270 from early in the war made his views clear. Soviet soldiers must fight to the last. There are no Soviet prisoners of war, only traitors.

Her daughter was right. Nothing would come of her efforts. She sighed. Nothing but a clear conscience.

She started at the District Committee. There was a much longer line than she'd ever seen in Leningrad—another reason she felt somewhat smug. Leningrad was clearly the superior city. But then again, the war was ending and more and more people were returning to the capital and there were sure to be difficulties in housing and industry and everything. The District Soviet in Leningrad probably also had a monstrously long line.

But in Moscow, the line never seemed to move. So, one day the person behind her grudgingly agreed to hold her place and she went to the front of the line.

"Hey! What do you think you're doing?" said a rough-looking middle-aged woman about tenth from the front.

Others joined in, and Katya put her hand in the air. "Comrades, comrades. I'm not cutting the line. I simply have a couple of questions." She edged toward the man who stood first. Katya thought he was younger than she. The empty left sleeve of his shirt was pinned neatly to his shoulder. "I want to know how long you've been waiting."

The veteran sighed. "I started coming not long after I got out of the hospital. Maybe a month ago. My family has returned and our apartment is full of strangers. We have no place to live." He leaned toward her. "One of us keeps our place in line. Night and day. The only way."

"Do you know how many people they see every day?"

He shrugged. "Less than five." He paused and then explained further. "Sometimes only one. But the key is to stay. All night. Those who go home lose their place."

"I've slept in worst," Katya said, nodding her thanks.

She stayed on the street for the next three weeks. The old woman brought her food, and held her place in line so she could go to the toilet. The ground was hard, but the weather was warm so Katya managed a few hours of rest. Eventually she reached the front of the line.

The apparatchik did not motion her to sit, but she did anyway. When the woman looked up from her stack of papers and said, "*Slushayu.* I'm listening," Katya began.

272 Suzanne Parry

After just a few sentences, the woman raised her hand for Katya to stop. "We don't handle questions of policy here. For that you'll need the Central Committee." The woman scribbled an address on a piece of paper and handed it to her.

Katya interjected. "I thought they were closed."

"Yes," said the bureaucrat, "but a temporary office has been established."

"And why wasn't that posted at the former office of the Central Committee?"

The woman shrugged. "The temporary office was just set up a week ago."

As she made her way to this new administrative office of the Central Committee of the Communist Party, Katya considered when or if she'd be able to get off this merry-go-round. It was late July by the time she reached the front of the next line. There she encountered a dour-faced, haggard bureaucrat who told her there was no Central Committee meeting planned and why would there be? The war had just ended and there were many more important things to do.

"Well, not more important to me," Katya snapped. "And the District Committee told me to come here for matters of policy, so here I am." She paused, giving the woman time to gather additional instructions, but the woman turned back to her work.

"Listen," Katya barked, demanding the woman's attention. "I have killed more than my share of Nazis." She reached into her pocket, "I have the letter to prove it." At which point the bleak, unhelpful Party paper-pusher took the letter from her partisan commander. Even though Baranov had sent a copy to the Central Committee, Katya knew the apparatchik would pretend otherwise if Katya didn't present the letter herself.

"So, you have contributed to the defense of the Motherland," the apparatchik grumped and handed the letter back. "There are many ways to do so, and I can tell you, the Central Committee is not going to call a special meeting for you no matter how many Nazis you've killed. All you need to do is write a letter and your concerns will be taken up by the appropriate authorities at the appropriate time."

And that was that. She hadn't been able to help Konstantin or Arkady or any of the nameless patriots now languishing in prison. Yelena was right. What could she accomplish?

She composed her letter, respectful and to the point, delivered it to the same office a few days later, and went back to helping the old woman wait in line for rations.

The lack of progress weighed on her and she began to consider returning home.

When Katya thought of her years in the Leningrad Party establishment, she recollected a more responsive, nimble organization. It made sense. The capital was bogged down administratively and in every other way. She would return and seek a change from Leningrad. Someone there would be interested in the misguided treatment of loyal citizens and former soldiers.

They came for her that very night, pounding on the apartment door and scaring the old woman out of her wits. It was Aleksandr all over again. They hustled Katya into a Black Maria and took her to Lefortovo prison where she was strip-searched and put into a small cell with a tiny high window, two bunks, and a single lightbulb dangling from a ceiling wire. She soon learned the light remained on day and night.

For many weeks, nothing happened. They brought meals so ghastly Katya wondered if she would survive. Day after day, she thought of Shura in the gulag before the war and now Konstantin and Arkady. The guards told her nothing and she didn't ask. Sometimes she was alone and sometimes not. She rarely talked, assuming other prisoners were spying on her. Some were interrogated, returning to the cell silent and bruised and worse. But not Katya. She clung to a fragment of hope that she would have a trial and get the opportunity to speak.

It never happened. She was never interrogated and never beaten. She was ignored. Summer dragged into fall, until one day they took her from her cell and handed her a paper sentencing her to five years internal exile. They returned her small bundle of belongings. She was taken to the train station without any opportunity to defend herself and told to report to the District Soviet in Irkutsk.

TRAIN TO EXILE

November 1945

Katya wasn't supposed to be on this train. Her sentence of five years internal exile was more an inconvenience than a punishment when compared to the long prison terms being handed out to soldiers and civilians alike. Internal exile meant she had a ticket for a regular passenger train. Only it had been full, and when she complained to the conductor that she wasn't going to stand all the way to Irkutsk, he'd called security. She knew better than to complain, but her intolerance for authority, even for the slights and annoyances of daily life, had grown. The war reshaped her. Instead of making her more compliant, it had done the opposite. She'd given up trying to oil the squeaky wheel of her own discontent.

The men in their flat blue hats looked at her papers and marched her out of the station and into a van which took her to a village outside Moscow.

The senior NKVD officer's voice dripped with sarcasm as he handed her over to the guards on the prisoner train. "*Razve ty ne schastlivchik.* Aren't you a lucky one?" A tiny puff of both aggravation and amusement came out of her nose, soft enough that they didn't notice. They didn't know the half of it. Baranov's letter documenting her Nazi kills no doubt saved her from a fate worse than a bit of rough treatment and five years internal exile. Accused of anti-Soviet agitation after her letter reached the Central Committee, she might have been executed.

Despite the officer's annoying comment, it wasn't outlandish to say she was lucky. Just working in the textile factory during the war—working for the Germans—could have gotten her a death sentence. But somehow those records from Staraya Russa had conveniently vanished. Arkady must have seen to that before he was arrested. The fact that he hadn't also escaped didn't make sense. But did anything in the Soviet system make sense? No doubt someone with a long-held grudge turned him in. That must have happened after he'd seen to it that the stack of eye-witness reports on the birthday bombing had arrived in Moscow.

As the guards propelled her down the dimly lit corridor of one car, the catcalls began. Inmates banged and rattled the webbed steel doors with dirty, bruised fingers and said things so vile she turned away so they couldn't see her face. The guards responded with curses of their own and slammed their rubber truncheons on the doors. A few inmates yelped when their fingers were struck and the cells quieted.

Katya had heard about these train cars. *Stolypins*, they were called. Passenger wagons modified for prisoner transport. The reconfiguration did not include lights in the cells. The windows along the corridor were reinforced with metal bars further darkening the interior. The compartment door clanged shut with a harsh finality, but the woven steel meant she'd never be free from the other prisoners' noise and violence. On one wall, three identical narrow bunks hung one above the other. There was no table, no chair, no shelf. A washbasin was unthinkable. A cell on wheels. She would soon discover that prisoners were locked in without access to food or water save at the whim of the *okhranniks*. One couldn't even use the toilet except on the guards' schedule.

Once they were underway the air whistled and whispered along the corridor and through the door. Fresh air would keep the smells down. Good in the heat of summer, but it was November. She buttoned her coat to her neck and dug in her rucksack for her *ushanka*.

The Communist's Secret   277

The voices from the next compartment were clear and loud. She heard not just bits and pieces, but entire conversations. Yet even their angry rumbles were a comfort, making her feel less alone. She listened to them fight and argue, and when they played chess, they spoke their moves aloud. Sometimes she knew who was about to win before it happened.

Aleksandr loved chess. He'd taught her, but she hadn't much interest in those days. She used every spare minute to plot her rise in the Party—finagling favors and bootlicking senior Communists. Chess demanded concentration and she always found her thoughts slipping away. Now she had nothing better to do.

The food was miserable, not much better than in Lefortovo, and she ate every bit, licking the last drops of watery kasha. The guards came evening and morning to escort her to the toilet. She soon realized the twice daily trips were a kindness since the male prisoners only went once. There were a lot of them—and getting to the bathroom at the end of the car was a long, drawn-out process that always involved yelling and a certain amount of violence. Most of the time the men had to use a bucket. She could tell by the stench that seeped into her cell. She'd counted six cells in the train car: four compartments for male prisoners, one with a real door for the guards and one for females. She was alone in her cell—a tenuous position vis-à-vis the guards. She felt suddenly thankful for the open mesh doors. At least everyone would hear if she were attacked.

A few days into the trip the train rumbled to a halt at a siding not long after breakfast. Katya observed the tiny world through the corridor windows. Suddenly she spotted prisoners milling around outside. Some washed at a barrel while others wandered off to relieve themselves. After about fifteen minutes, they were lined up and marched back inside. Then another group came out. She watched the process over and over.

She'd thought she'd seen four prison cars when they forced her onto the train. Katya did the math: at fifteen minutes per compartment and five compartments per car, it would take more than five hours. Not that time mattered because they never traveled during the day. If they passed through stations during daylight hours, it would be all too easy for people waiting for a real train to notice the unmarked cars and realize it was a prisoner transport. Which would mean the rumors about the camps were true. And the truth should never be revealed.

Hours passed until she heard the steel door from down the corridor slide open and the guards yelling at the prisoners to get up. She peered out and watched as the inmates from the compartments in her carriage took their turns outside. Then the heavy door from the cell next to hers ground open. The men spilled into the outdoor space of trampled grass and shrubs. Some squatted at a distance, others lined up at the barrels. They drank from one and washed at the other. A prisoner joined the line for drinking water. His walk nudged her— something about his erect carriage. He ran a hand over his close-cropped hair in a motion that startled her. She shifted about, desperate for a better view. When he turned toward the train, Katya's heart jumped. The face was his too.

Transfixed, she watched the man wash and wander, then line up with the others. As the guards herded the prisoners, she forgot about her turn. Seeing her husband's twin pushed everything else from her mind. Then the bolt slid, the door rattled and she was out. Fifteen minutes of freedom. The brisk, cold air shocked and delighted her. She examined the tall, metal fence surrounding the small compound and glanced at the *okhranniks* with their guns.

The guards stood in two groups, smoking and staring. Even in her early forties, even after the rough war years, Katya still turned heads. She wore an ugly kerchief over her striking blond hair and never returned their overt and suggestive gazes. She knew what would come of that. She was alone in a compartment and had nothing but her silence for protection.

It was easy to tell which barrel was for drinking—the one without an oily film. She scooped up less water than she wanted. Not being able to relieve her bladder when needed was a constant and miserable battle. She hated using the bucket. At the washing barrel, she faced the train with her back to the guards. Buoyed by a ridiculous hope, she glared at the compartment with the man who looked like her husband. She removed her kerchief and shook out her hair, then dunked her head in the barrel and rubbed her scalp, trying to get rid of the accumulated dirt and sweat. She rinsed the scarf, intending to hang it on the top bunk to dry.

After washing, she stretched and walked, taking in the cold fresh air and appreciating the sky with its high clouds. In the far corner of the enclosure, she squatted behind some bushes.

"Hurry up. It's time," called one of the guards. "Or perhaps you need a hand?"

They laughed and when she came out from behind the shrubs they were still making jokes at her expense, offering help with her clothes or bodily functions. "I'll loosen you up," one said, not bothering to mask the implicit threat. She ignored them. In this situation keeping her mouth shut was the only choice.

When dusk arrived and the train started, she was still thinking about the man who looked like her husband. Could Shura be headed to Siberia a second time? In Stalin's Russia anything could happen. Look at Konstantin, arrested as a traitor when he returned to the Red Army.

Something just as soul-crushing could have happened to Shura. As much as she liked the idea of speaking to him if he were on this train, the bigger part of her wanted him free, redeemed by his victory over the Germans. Redeemed from a false accusation, a false conviction, a false wife. As soon as she had an address in Irkutsk she'd write to Yelena who would perhaps know his fate.

But the longing to see him did not vanish. It was a physical pain, a pressure in her chest that sometimes made her think she was having a heart attack. If only she could feel his arms around her again, strong and soothing. He always made her feel safe. She was desperate to tell him she was sorry and say the words, "I love you," so he would have no doubt. She needed to look him in the eye and say, "Forgive me, Shura," even if he couldn't possibly forgive her or love her in return. After all, consequences were consequences. But she wanted the chance to do the right thing.

That night, unable to get the striking resemblance out of her head, she replayed the man's walk, height, the way he touched his hair. The evening meal, such as it was, came and went. The men's voices calmed, giving off a low hum like the train itself but with a comforting undercurrent of solace.

She lay on the bottom bunk. Words, grunts, curses, even laughter floated out of the next cell and into hers. There was a boisterous group playing cards. She'd already heard a fair bit of violence and knew each compartment had its own distinct pecking order. At that moment there was no sound of conflict. She moved to the filthy floor and sat with her fingers hooked onto the steel mesh, wanting to call out, to ask for the lanky man with close-cropped blond hair and military carriage. Long after the sounds on the other side quieted, she remained wide awake, hoping for the rich baritone she knew so well. Grunts and snores were all she heard, but still she sat there, wishing for him.

Making it right with Shura was the last thing. Yelena and Sofya had forgiven her. She'd tried to help Arkady and Konstantin. Confessing to Aleksandr—whatever he might say in return—was the final piece. Then she could begin again. Serve her sentence and rejoin her family. If he was in Leningrad now, she would write. Five years wasn't so long. *Luchshe pozdno, chem nikogda.* Better late than never.

The following evening, the nagging feeling that he was in the next compartment was still with her. She summoned the courage to call out through the steel strands.

There was a bit of movement. Voices shushed, demanding quiet.

"Who's there?" The rough voice was nothing like Shura's.

"My name is Karavayeva, Ekaterina Ivanova. From Leningrad. I'm looking for my husband. Aleksandr Andreiivich, Red Army."

"Karavayev, you say. No one here by that name, but I'll ask," he said. "Maybe someone knows this Karavayev fellow."

He called out. "Lady's looking for her husband—Karavayev. Red Army."

Men grunted and shifted about. Then from deep within the overcrowded compartment came a voice. She strained to hear, but couldn't make out the exchange. There were bodies moving and a few curses. She imagined them making a space for the man next to the door.

"Hello. You're looking for Major Karavayev?" The voice was soft, perhaps so others couldn't hear, but also clear.

"Yes. Karavayev, Aleksandr Andreiivich. My husband. You fought beside him?"

"I'm Ivanov, Ivan Ivanovich. I served with Major Karavayev in Stalingrad. Although he was a captain then."

Katya squirmed. The whole nation knew about Stalingrad. The key to defeating Nazi Germany. The key to the Soviet victory. "Do you know anything?"

"After Stalingrad, I didn't see him until the war was over," said the intelligent, cultured voice, not nearly as rough as the partisans she'd lived and fought with. Not what she expected, but what she hoped for.

"After the war?" Her heart leapt. Aleksandr was alive.

"Yes. I was arrested in Leningrad. We were in the same prison cell."

Soft though it was, the voice was comforting. There was a rhythm and inflection that fed her memory. A familiar intonation and pitch. Katya's heart beat faster. Could it be? She recognized her own desperation. And with the noise from the train and other prisoners, she couldn't be sure. Besides, if it was him, he'd tell her. And why would he use a different name?

"Do you know where he is now? A camp?"

"I'm sorry," the man paused. "He didn't make it out of the *Bolshoi Dom*."

She clamped a hand over her mouth to swallow the rising cry. Her body shook as she gasped for air and began to sob. Shura gone. She loved him more completely than she ever had and he would never know.

The man with her dead husband's voice kept whispering her name, but she moved away from the door, climbed onto her bunk and curled into a ball. The promise of fixing things with Aleksandr had helped her survive the war. But her hope had been as empty as everyone else's.

The next night there were several rattles and whispers. She didn't want to talk, but this man was the last person to see her husband alive, and this was the fifth day underway. How long before they pulled into Irkutsk?

She sat by the door. "Hello."

"Ekaterina. There you are."

"Katya," she said.

"Katya, then." She could almost hear him smile. "I was worried when you didn't answer. Sorry I gave you such a shock last night."

"I shouldn't have been surprised, but I've been hoping I'd get to see my husband again." Part of her wanted to tell this stranger more. Instead, she danced around the subject. "Is there anything else you can tell me?"

The Communist's Secret 283

"He was like so many others," the voice said. "Fought like hell. All the way to Germany with Zhukov. At first he wasn't certain why he was behind bars. But then his pig of an interrogator focused on his role in liberating a German camp. He'd been responsible for the release of some Soviet prisoners. Of course, they all went home to be arrested. It wasn't like setting them free was a ticket to America or something."

Katya thought most Soviet soldiers were like that and would have refused a ticket to America even if it had been an option. And yet their country, the one they loved and almost died for, threw them into prison just because they had the misfortune to be captured by the enemy. Shameful.

How ironic that now she shared that perspective. Shura had always been reserved, skeptical even, about the nation's leadership. Now she would never be able to look him in the eye and tell him how right he'd been. The pain of his death cut deeper. First, betrayed by his wife. Now, betrayed by his country.

"Can you tell me anything else?" she whispered. "Had he seen his family?"

"Yes. He talked about them. Especially his daughter and grandson."

Katya caught her breath. "He saw his grandson, our grandson? Before he was arrested?"

"Oh, yes. He was in Leningrad a couple of months and very attached to the *malchik*. I know the idea of not seeing him or his daughter again was a crushing blow."

Katya sniffed.

The voice continued. "He was close to his mother it seemed."

Katya imagined the two war comrades lying on filthy prison cots covered with the blood, sweat, and who knew what else, of other men. Whispering so the guards couldn't hear.

"A violinist," Katya said. "One of the best in the city, although very humble."

"Yes. Near the end of her career, I think. And she had gotten married during the war."

It had been a wonderful moment when Katya returned to Leningrad to see her mother-in-law with Admiral Antonov. She deserved to be happy.

"He must have been overjoyed to discover they survived. It was the same for me. The situation in Leningrad was so terrible. I hardly dared hope they'd made it." Ivan didn't say anything and there was a long silence. She was afraid to ask, but felt she must. "And your family, Ivan?"

She heard him shifting about. "My family wasn't so lucky." His voice was the barest whisper. "Starved that first winter. All of them. My children, wife, parents."

Everyone had suffered in some way during the war. There were no untouched families. But to lose everyone you loved? There were no words for such a loss. "I am deeply sorry," was all she could murmur.

"Perhaps we can talk another time, Katya. I must go." He had nowhere to be, nothing that needed doing, but the memories were too much.

When she whispered through the door the next evening he was already there. "I'm sorry about last night," she said. "I don't want to dredge up painful memories."

"Thank you, but memories are all I have. My daughter kept a journal. I carry it even here. She marked the dates when the family died that winter: her grandparents, cousins, her aunt, her brother, finally her mama, my wife." His voice cracked. "A neighbor held onto it when my daughter also passed."

The emotion-filled silence gripped Katya and she said nothing. What could she say to someone who had lost everyone? That now

The Communist's Secret

285

their nation and people were free of the Fascists? There's little comfort in victory when you've sacrificed everything.

Ivan continued. "You can imagine what state I was in when I discovered my family gone. I lost control. Criticized the leadership. Got twenty-five years for anti-Soviet propaganda. But what do I care? I'm already dead. And someone has to speak the truth."

"It is something. To speak the truth."

There was another long pause.

"And where were you during the war?" Ivan asked.

"Killing Nazis in occupied Russia. In Staraya Russa mostly," she said.

He gave a soft, low whistle. Aleksandr did the exact same thing whenever he heard something impressive or hard to believe. Her fingers tightened on the steel mesh.

"At first, I really had no choice," Katya went on. "I was with the People's Volunteers. Sent to shore up the Luga Line. The Nazi attack came out of nowhere. Planes, then Panzers. Clanking and churning like a gathering storm. Shooting at everything. It was a horrible realization—that they were coming for us. Most of the surviving volunteers went toward Luga, but I ran east with a comrade. We hid in the forest. Eventually made it to Staraya Russa. I was able to work against the Nazis from there."

"So how did you come to be here?" the voice asked.

"How does anyone? A thousand ways, but all the same. I returned to Leningrad after the blockade was lifted, then some months later went to Moscow to check on a fellow partisan. He had done everything for me in Staraya Russa. A bit like a father. Someone must have turned him in as a collaborator. I went to Moscow to petition the Party on his behalf, which is what got me arrested. In my letter, I also spoke against Stalin's directive that Soviet soldiers once imprisoned by the Nazis should be arrested."

"Regardless of what the State says, you, my dear woman, are

a true patriot. You defended our soldiers. It takes great courage to speak the truth."

"I got off easy—five years internal exile. I might have been convicted of treason for collaborating with the Nazis."

"If someone turned you in as a Nazi sympathizer, you'd already be dead."

It was true. The selfishness of ordinary people striving to keep their neighbors down. She'd been a bit like that. Always looking for ways to move up the ladder. She'd presented the face of a devoted Party functionary because that was the way to get ahead. And she wanted to breathe that rarified air. Thinking one day she might be on the Central Committee. Power and admiration and comfort had pulled her like a gigantic magnet. She tried to believe in a society of equals, but even before Aleksandr was arrested she knew it was all a sad joke. There was no equality. Only those at the top—the small elite group running the Soviet Union—had wealth and security. She remembered how thousands of Party officials and military officers had been arrested in the years before the war.

"Are you still there?" Ivan asked.

"Yes. Just thinking about my life. Twenty-five years focused on the Party, convinced it was all that mattered. It took my husband's first arrest and then the war for me to see the lies."

"Clarity is a valuable gift. And you have time to live differently. Five years is not such a terrible fate. Not such a price to pay to shake free of the Party. Knowing the truth, just admitting it to yourself, is an important kind of freedom. And you have plenty of good years ahead. I no longer have the energy to hate the Party, to hate Stalin," he whispered. "It's difficult to find meaning without loved ones. You will see yours. They can visit."

"Yes," she said. "Something to look forward to."

Despite her words, Katya focused on her loss. Without Aleksandr, the future yawned—a dark void.

They both went quiet. The rumble of the train wheels and the creaking of the cars swaying on the tracks drowned out the snores of Ivan's fellow prisoners.

Over the following nights they whispered their histories to each other as the train chugged eastward. Katya began hoping the trip would take many weeks.

"What was he like, this man in Staraya Russa?" Ivan asked one evening.

"Arkady was the head of the factory where I worked. That was before we joined the partisans. He had known my parents and even remembered me as a young teen, so we had an immediate bond. He's one of a kind. Adept with people. Comfortable with anyone. I've never seen anything like it. He could juggle the Nazis and the Politsai and the locals. He saved me. Got me a job, papers, and a place to live. I owe him."

"Everyone needs people like that."

"Yes. And he helped me maintain perspective as we lost more and more. I didn't know if my daughter was alive. It was a black time for me. Arkady taught me to hang on to other things besides revenge."

"Revenge is tricky. Give it too much value and it replaces your soul. Did you get yours?"

"Some would say so, but the cost was very high. I killed a group of Nazi officers with a grenade. Thirteen to be exact, including three generals." She heard that low whistle again. "They executed thirty-nine civilians in retribution. That was the start of the end of the war for me. I joined the partisans, but never regained my focus." She exhaled. "You killed Germans too."

"It's different from the inside of a tank. I only killed hand-to-hand in Stalingrad."

"What was it like? Stalingrad."

"Hell on earth. A city of brick and cement skeletons. Not a single building intact. Men hiding in wreckage and basements and sewers, creeping out at night to kill a couple of Nazis and move forward a few meters.

"I'll never forget the sight. The Volga was our raw, unprotected underbelly. Soldiers on barges headed toward the nightmare. Civilians and wounded stumbling down the steep bank at the city's edge to escape across the river, dodging our arriving forces. German planes and artillery fired at anything that moved, but especially the barges filled with our men.

"Still our soldiers came. From the steppes and the Far East, Russians and Uzbeks and Kazaks, they came. All to defend the Motherland. Frightened, paralyzed, shitting their pants, still they came across that holy water. The explosions, the pitiful cries of the heroic wounded. The impossible to rescue wounded! Many of us died for every bit of that sacred ground."

Captured by his words, Katya was silent. Tears ran down her face. And his voice: Aleksandr, but not him. For a moment she was there, in eternal Stalingrad. "I'm sorry." Her words were a ragged whisper, torn by his descriptions and emotion. "And thank you. If not for you and all the others . . ."

"Do not thank me, *Dorogaya*."

Her heart jumped. Aleksandr always called her Dearest. Was it him? The way he talked, the words he used. And even though she hadn't seen him up close, what she had seen was her Shura. But it didn't make sense. He would tell her if it was him.

Ivan talked as her mind spun. She came back to his words. "It was my honor to serve, to do my part, to help defeat Nazi Germany. When winter came we had Paulus and the German 6th

The Communist's Secret

Army surrounded. They ran out of food and were forced to surrender or starve to death. That surrender made it all worthwhile. Someday, mankind shall be grateful to Stalingrad, to those who lived there, those who fought, those who died there." His voice was hoarse with the emotion of such a raw and recent time. "The thing is, in retrospect I wish we'd let Paulus and his men starve. I have wanted that particular revenge after I discovered what they did to Leningrad."

"War makes us both compassionate and cruel," she said.

"That it does. And cruelty begotten by cruelty is simply untamed anger. There are days I still want revenge. But when my anger is controlled, I am glad we treated them more humanely than they us. So much for German superiority."

His voice cast a powerful spell. The rhythm, his emphasis and emotion, all of it reminded her of her husband. It was both how he spoke and the words and phrases he chose. The way some words almost disappeared and others came sharply across the small space. All her Shura.

She cried harder then. Oh, how she missed him. Was it really to be that she'd never see him again? After all he'd suffered, and all she'd been through? After how she'd changed?

"I've upset you," he said. "I'm sorry. I shouldn't have told you."

She pulled part of her sleeve up to wipe her face. "No. I want to know what it was like. I've also seen horror at the hands of the Nazis. It's just, you sound so much like my husband. It's uncanny. And I can hardly accept that I will never see him again. I want to tell him the truth, to tell him I'm sorry I wasn't a more devoted wife, to tell him I love him very much." Her voice caught in her throat. There was a long silence while she tried to collect herself. The train rumbled and swayed. "Did he ever speak about me?"

"I don't want to hurt you."

"Please. It can't hurt as much as knowing he's gone."

"Once. He talked about how he'd loved you but you'd betrayed him. It broke him."

She buried her face in her arms, her body heaving with the pain of her betrayal, with the loss of her beloved, with all the struggles of the war years. She heard Ivan whispering, but she couldn't accept one more drop of sorrow.

IRKUTSK
November 1945

As darkness approached, the train jerked and rumbled to life. Katya listened to the men in the next compartment amusing themselves. She sat by the door and whispered. "Ivan?" He was already there.

"Katya, are you all right? I'm sorry about last night."

"It's bad enough to have done someone a grievous wrong," she said. "But when there is no chance to make it right, no chance to ask for forgiveness, well, that is a unique cruelty." She drew a deep breath. "Can I tell you what happened?"

His silence was assent.

"I loved my husband very much," she began. "But we were different. My parents were poor workers and the Communists gave us a chance for something better. The Party meant everything to them, and me. A way out of a hard life. I believed in the Party and its promises.

"My husband was born into something better. Well-educated and taught to think for himself. He could see a way in the world that would use his abilities and allow him to serve his country. He was every bit as loyal as was I, perhaps even more so because he was willing to sacrifice for his nation. He could have done many things, but chose the military."

After some silence, he said, "*Slushayu.* I'm listening."

"One evening in the winter before the war began, I was careless and made a thoughtless comment. I complained that he was not as devoted as he should be. I was speaking about our relationship with two women I considered friends. Whether they turned him in, or someone else overheard and took my words out of context, I'll never know. I meant devotion in a personal way, rather than devotion to the State, but it's a term with political connotations and I knew better. He was arrested shortly after. It was truly ironic because the arrests had finally died down. It had been so bad for military officers in the years before, but he'd made it through. Safe to the other side we thought. And then I gossiped about him." Her throat burned and she swallowed a few times, holding back the tears. "He was a good man and I destroyed him. Our daughter too. I robbed her of her father. I'd give anything to change that.

"I don't even understand why I said what I did. I felt so alone. All the way back to the death of my baby boy. Our beautiful baby." She hesitated. "Shortly before his first birthday, little Sasha fell ill. Aleksandr was on deployment. Sasha got worse and I took him to the hospital where for several days I watched him move closer and closer to death." She heard Ivan choke back a sob. "My husband wasn't there to help me or to comfort our stunned daughter or to hold little Sasha one more time. I think something died in me." She paused, fighting the still terrible grief. "Forgive me for loving my husband so little that I would betray him. I know Sasha's death wasn't his fault. It wasn't any of our faults." She'd faced it alone and a darkness set up camp in her heart, relegating her once dear husband to a distant dim corner where she couldn't find him.

After a long pause, with their own unique sorrows settling upon them, he replied. "Maybe it is not my right, but I forgive you, Katya. For Major Karavayev. He would understand. I know he loves you still. And I know he grieved for your baby too. He talked about being trapped a thousand kilometers away. He got home as soon as he could, but it was too late. He let you down. Let his family down. He should have been there."

The Communist's Secret 293

A wounded sound escaped her lips, a burble of pain and relief and compassion. Her dear Shura. They had both suffered so much. Ivan's comforting words soothed the pain in her heart. He spoke of Aleksandr like he was still alive.

"War gives men a lot of time to think. And I can tell you Major Karavayev thought about not being there when your baby died more than anything else. It plagued him."

"Thank you," she said. She wiped her tears, caught in that crushing time, but Ivan was trying to get her attention.

"Katya, listen. I really do forgive you." The voice was Shura's. "I read your letter."

She had her head down, sobbing into her knees. Her mind was playing tricks, telling her what she desperately wanted to believe.

"Did you hear me?" he said again. "I read the letter you left in Leningrad."

Suddenly unmoored, she lifted her head and everything whirled, pitching back and forth in the dark train. His words lodged there, banging around, drowning out everything. She reached for what she desired above all else. "Shura, my love."

Their words were the barest of whispers, but even so, someone in the compartment had already yelled for them to stop talking, they were trying to sleep after all.

"I have to go," he hissed. "You mustn't speak of this. I am Ivan Ivanovich now. Karavayev died in prison."

"On my life," she said.

"I love you, Katyusha."

"*Ya tozhe*, my darling. Me too."

It was hours before Katya slept. The news that Shura was here, alive if not entirely well, kept her mind and body thrumming with energy and hope. She had just begun to doze when the guards banged on the cell doors, calling out that they were arriving at a transfer point for prisoners.

The brakes squealed. She narrowed her eyes, squinting at the frail daylight through the bars. This wasn't Irkutsk. Couldn't be. The train swerved a bit as it pulled off into a siding, surrounded by nothing other than snow and trees. It might take the guards some time to get the prisoners organized. She called his name. She had pulled the little brass compass out of her rucksack and was worrying it between her fingers while she waited.

"It's your sweetheart, Ivan'ich."

The way they teased him made her smile. She really was his sweetheart.

"Katya." Shura was there. "There's a lot I wish I could say. I haven't been truthful and I regret that. I didn't tell you right away because I am a dead man. Twenty-five years is an eternity. And you can go on without me. Build a new life. I want that for you."

"Never! You are my life. I turned away once. Never again."

"I thought I was safe," Shura said with anger and sadness. "The same filth from '41 decided to make sure I wouldn't make it out a second time. Radchik." He fairly spat the name.

"Don't worry. No one will know you are anything but Ivanov. And we'll find a way to get you out. This may help." She slid the compass out and pushed it along the corridor's edge toward his cell with a pencil.

He laughed. "Oh, Darling, after all we've been through you've become an optimist."

"Not at all. Except when it comes to those I love."

"Katyusha, I'm going to hold onto that. Here's the address. Yelena and my mother don't know. They must think I'm dead."

"Don't worry, Shura. I'll find a way to tell them. A safe way."

She used the same pencil to pull the paper within reach, then pinched it with her fingers. The guards entered the carriage. Cell doors opened and closed while they barked instructions and prisoners were herded out of the train.

The Communist's Secret 295

A moment later they were at Shura's cell. A voice yelled, "Everyone out. Now!" The sickening thuds of a rubber truncheon were followed by groans and curses. She pressed her face against the mesh, watching as Shura stumbled out, fell to his knees and deftly palmed the little compass.

LAKE BAIKAL
November 1945

Not long after the prisoners got off, the train started again. Less than thirty minutes later they pulled into the Irkutsk station. People milled about along the platforms, preparing for their journeys and saying farewells. Katya had a brief flash of hope that maybe this wasn't such a backwater after all. She slipped her arms through the straps and shrugged her rucksack up onto her back. She had nothing more than a few changes of clothes and some rubles, but even so, she felt renewed. Aleksandr was alive and loved her.

She was on her own. No cell, no guards. Although not exactly free, she had her independence within the parameters of regular reporting to the Irkutsk District Soviet. The first thing she had to do was register her arrival with the authorities. Next, she would find a place to live. Third, a job. She felt confident that her experience at the textile factory meant she'd be able to find work. She'd heard there were plenty of jobs with furs and pelts—hat makers and glove makers.

Walking through the main vestibule, she glanced at the departure board. The local train to Lake Baikal left in twenty minutes. Aleksandr had been fascinated by the enormous body of water for as long as Katya could remember. He talked about making a trip someday to see the gigantic lake and its freshwater seals, the nerpas.

Why not now? Once she started working, it would be difficult to get time off. This way she'd begin her exile with something just for him. She couldn't touch him or talk to him. But she could take in the lake and write to him about it.

296

The Communist's Secret 297

It was less than an hour to the tiny settlement on the shore of the great lake where trains were put on special ferries to cross. Sometimes in winter, they actually laid tracks across the ice. She would like to see that. She had an hour to look around before catching the return train. The District Soviet in Irkutsk awaited as did the search for lodging.

When she stepped out of the station the massive body of water was close, a dark, endless expanse. She sniffed at the air. It didn't smell as briny as the Gulf of Finland. In a few short minutes she was on a gravel beach where ice gathered amongst the stones while wind-whipped waves frothed the expanse of black water. She removed a glove to feel the icy temperature, wondering when the deep lake would freeze. Regardless, the sleek-headed seals were already hidden in their winter dens.

She found a dry spot to sit and think. She had no idea why Shura had taken on a false identity. It must have been for protection. For Yelena perhaps. She reached in her pocket for the wadded scrap from Shura and smoothed the smudged, dirty edges. Scrawled at the top was the camp address. Then the words, "I love you," followed by a capital A, the way he signed his love letters when they were young. Her eyes filled and she read the simple declaration over and over, absorbing the astounding fact that her beloved husband was alive and loved her.

She would write, to Ivan Ivanovich of course. And after she settled in Irkutsk, after the harsh winter which was just beginning to bite, she would go to the camp to see him. Next summer perhaps, when the roads were passable. She would find a way. Katya read the address and her husband's beautiful words again, reciting them silently, committing everything to memory. She walked to a steel drum at the top of the beach, used by the locals to burn refuse and stay warm, and tore the message into pieces, letting each scrap float down into the fire.

Almost unbearably light, she stepped away and lifted her face to the surly sky, ignoring the icy snowflakes stinging her cheeks. It was impossible to deny the audacious good fortune of her arrest, landing on the same train, in the very compartment next to Shura. She tried to recall if she'd ever been so lucky, and her mind snapped back to her first university lecture when she glanced at the person in the next seat and her future husband shyly smiled back.

Since then, Aleksandr had always been her good luck. Now, she would be his.

ACKNOWLEDGMENTS

I am very thankful for the enthusiasm and energetic support of so many readers. Book group discussions, library and bookstore events, emails and social media comments all helped launch and celebrate my first novel. They also encouraged me to write *The Communist's Secret*.

I am lucky indeed to know Suzy Vitello and Natalie Hirt. Their skills as writers, editors, and teachers are vast and their friendships are a joy. They have been instrumental in my journey and continue to illuminate the correct path.

This story took shape during a six-month novel intensive led by the talented Karen Karbo. The K2 group as I fondly think of them, Gabrielle, Ellen, Sue, Sharon, and Stephanie, helped me understand what was working and what was not in an early draft. I so appreciate the many considerations of craft and the discipline and enthusiasm of that group.

My publishing team at She Writes Press and numerous SWP authors have provided reams of advice and help. My publicist, Ann-Marie Nieves, has molded the journey of this book in important ways. Thank you all.

The most profound gratitude to Melissa, Laura, Charmine, Joanne, Kathy, Sallie, Erin, Bonnie, Cindy, and Tim, whose friendships I cherish. Thank you for championing the creation of this novel, but especially for sharing your lives with me. You make everything better. You make me laugh more. You help me live with an open heart.

I am especially grateful for my extraordinary family. They contribute their significant insights and opinions when I ask, and their encouragement and enthusiasm even when I don't. They have made me a better writer and a better person.

ABOUT THE AUTHOR

Photo credit: Julia Eckelmann

Former Pentagon arms control negotiator Suzanne Parry is the award-winning author of *Lost Souls of Leningrad*. She holds degrees from Princeton University and Purdue University and studied Russian in Moscow. Suzanne lives on both coasts but calls Portland, Oregon home. *The Communist's Secret* is her second novel. To learn more, visit: www.suzanneparrywrites.com

Looking for your next great read?

We can help!

Visit www.shewritespress.com/next-read
or scan the QR code below for a list
of our recommended titles.

She Writes Press is an award-winning
independent publishing company founded to
serve women writers everywhere.